D0361682

"Move and you die," said Einstein, waving a sawed-off shotgun around the room.

"Easy, folks," said Ma Teresa in a calming voice. "We don't want to hurt anyone. We just want to take the money and leave."

She was smiling pleasantly as she said this, and held a revolver against the guard's head.

Little Al Schweitzer leaped over the counter and knelt at the safe. . . .

Tor books by Mike Resnick

Tor books edited by Mike Resnick

ALTERNATE OUTLAWS

Edited by
Mike Resnick

A TOM DOHERTY ASSOCIATES BOOK
NEW YORK

NOTE: If you purchased this book without a cover you should be aware that this book is stolen property. It was reported as "unsold and destroyed" to the publisher, and neither the author nor the publisher has received any payment for this "stripped book."

This is a work of fiction. All the characters and events portrayed in this book are fictitious, and any resemblance to real people or events is purely coincidental.

ALTERNATE OUTLAWS

Copyright © 1994 by Mike Resnick and Martin H. Greenberg

All rights reserved, including the right to reproduce this book, or portions thereof, in any form.

Cover art by Barclay Shaw

A Tor Book
Published by Tom Doherty Associates, Inc.
175 Fifth Avenue
New York, N.Y. 10010

Tor® is a registered trademark of Tom Doherty Associates, Inc.

ISBN: 0-812-53344-5

First edition: October 1994

Printed in the United States of America

0   9   8   7   6   5   4   3   2   1

COPYRIGHT ACKNOWLEDGMENTS

Introduction copyright © 1994 by Mike Resnick.

"Ma Teresa and the Hole-in-the-Wall Gang" copyright © 1994 by Jack C. Haldeman II.

"A Quiet Evening by Gaslight" copyright © 1994 by Geoffrey A. Landis.

"A Spark in the Darkness" copyright © 1994 by Beth Meacham.

"Common Sense" copyright © 1994 by Kristine Kathryn Rusch.

"Literary Lives" copyright © 1994 by Kathe Koja and Barry N. Malzberg.

"Saint Frankie" copyright © 1994 by Laura Resnick.

"Good Girl, Bad Dog" copyright © 1994 by Martha Soukup.

"Comrade Bill" copyright © 1994 by John E. Johnston III.

"The Ballad of Ritchie Valenzuela" copyright © 1994 by Maureen F. McHugh.

"One Month in 1907" copyright © 1994 by Frank M. Robinson.

"What Goes Around" copyright © 1994 by David Gerrold.

"Red Elvis" copyright © 1994 by Walter Jon Williams.

"Cui Bono?" copyright © 1994 by Katherine Kerr.

"Cowards Die: A Tragicomedy in Several Fits" copyright © 1994 by Judith Tarr.

"Black Betsy" copyright © 1994 by Dean Wesley Smith.

"Miranda" copyright © 1994 by Robert Sheckley.

"Riders in the Sky" copyright © 1994 by Allen Steele.

"#2, With a Bullet" copyright © 1994 by Jack Nimersheim.

"Learning Magic" copyright © 1994 by Janni Lee Simner.

"The Crimson Rose" copyright © 1994 by Tappan King.

"What She Won't Remember" copyright © 1994 by Michelle Sagara.

"My Tongue in Thy Tale" copyright © 1994 by Gregory Feeley.

"Souvenirs" copyright © 1994 by Alan Rodgers and James D. Macdonald.

"Bigger Than U.S. Steel" copyright © 1994 by Brian M. Thomsen.

"Giving Head" copyright © 1994 by Nicholas A. DiChario.

"Satan Claus" copyright © 1994 by David Gerrold.

"Shootout at Gower Gulch" copyright © 1994 by George Alec Effinger.

"Painted Bridges" copyright © 1994 by Barbara Delaplace.

To Carol, as always. . . .

And to Joan Bledig and Ed Sunden

NOTE TO THE READER

This collection of short stories is a work of fiction. Although some of the characters are real, they are used fictitiously; their thoughts, actions and words, and the events surrounding them, are entirely imaginary.

Contents

Introduction

There is something absolutely fascinating about outlaws. No matter how heinous their crimes, no matter how loathsome their personalities, no matter how warped their moral codes, we have this tendency to turn them into folk heroes.

William Bonney was a psychopath who killed his first victim at the age of twelve, murdered twenty more men before his twenty-first birthday, and if he were alive today, he would probably still be killing. But as Billy the Kid, he is celebrated in song and story, and more than a dozen Hollywood movies have tried to show the (nonexistent) human side of this inhuman fiend.

Bonnie and Clyde? Same thing. They killed people, they robbed banks, they had no respect for human life or human law—and yet they remain folk heroes to this day.

Jesse and Frank James? The Younger Brothers? Doc Holliday? John Dillinger? There has been more popular fiction making them out to be heroes than presenting them as the outlaws they really were.

Well, if historians think that *they* can skew history, let me assure you that they don't hold a candle to science fiction writers, that remarkable group of men and women who make their living by asking the question: *What if?*

For example: What if Charles Manson was an innocent victim? What if Helen Keller, with her super-sensitive fingers, was a safecracker? What if Mother Teresa led an outlaw band consisting of Albert Einstein and Albert Schweitzer, among others? What if Santa Claus was the most hideous fiend of all?

Well, you're about to find out.

But before you do, I'd like to take this opportunity to publicly thank all the contributors to the first three volumes in this series: *Alternate Presidents*, *Alternate Kennedys*, and *Alternate Warriors*. When I started editing these anthologies for Tor, I had no idea whether the project would last beyond the first volume, or receive any attention whatsoever. As it turns out, the Alternate books have exceeded all our expectations. Susan Shwartz was a Hugo and Nebula finalist for one of her stories; Pat Cadigan, Barry Malzberg, Nick DiChario and myself were also Hugo finalists. Five newcomers—Barbara Delaplace, Michelle Sagara, Jack Nimersheim, Nick DiChario and Laura Resnick—have been nominated for the Campbell (science fiction's "Rookie of the Year" award) and one of them—Laura—won it in 1993. And twenty-seven stories from the first two books—the third hasn't yet reached the stands as I write this—received Nebula recommendations from members of the Science Fiction Writers of America.

So thanks and well done, guys. I just assign and edit the stories; *you* are the stars.

—Mike Resnick

Jack Haldeman, author or co-author of a dozen novels and numerous short stories, is one of the more creative wits in science fiction. When I asked him for an Alternate Outlaw story, he started creating alternate outlaws wholesale. So come with us to a Wild West that never was and meet the Hole-in-the-Wall Gang: there's Big Al Einstein, Little Al Schweitzer, and their fearless leader, Ma Teresa herself.

Ma Teresa and the Hole-in-the-Wall Gang
by Jack C. Haldeman II

Ma Teresa hated Indians. She also hated dusty trails, bad-tempered horses, cold winters, beans, and three-legged dogs.

But she hated bankers more than anything else.

Money-grubbing bankers had taken her mama's farm and driven the poor woman to an early grave. Ma Teresa would never forget those long, hungry days after her dad died—days of sifting the weevils out of the biscuit flour and cursing the rank, rancid bacon—and how the bank foreclosed just when they were trying to get started again.

It seemed quite possible to her that the Wild West would be won not by hardworking farmers, but by greedy bank presidents with clean fingernails and fancy suits and their squinty-eyed, no-good, lowlife lawyer and accountant minions. She was doing her best to keep that from happening.

Ma Teresa and her gang were bank robbers.

They were very good at their chosen profession. The best in Idaho, bar none.

She shifted in the saddle and looked down the overgrown cowpath that served as the main street in town. Ma Teresa was not impressed.

"Don't look like there's enough money in this town to buy a lame mule," she said. "I don't know, Big Al. You sure about this one?"

Albert Einstein nodded slowly, leaned over his horse and let fly with a huge load of tobacco juice. Most of it missed his beard, which was gray where it wasn't stained yellow with tobacco, and was as unruly as his hair, which stuck out everywhere. He didn't look like much, but he was the brains of the outfit.

"Trust me," he said, biting off another chew. "The bank just sold off a large farm it stole from a widow-woman. The cash came in this morning. There's only one teller, one guard, and Little Al can get inside that safe half-asleep and mostly drunk in five seconds. It's a piece of junk."

That part about Little Al was true, thought Ma Teresa. Little Albert Schweitzer had sensitive hands, whether cracking safes or digging bullets out of his buddies.

"The sheriff?" she asked.

"Like I said, the sheriff will be busy with Dora in her room above the saloon. This is Wednesday, right?"

"Yep."

"Wednesday afternoon is his special time with Dora," said Big Al Einstein. "Everybody knows about the sheriff's Wednesday-afternoon appointment. We'll be gone before he can hitch up his britches."

"How come you're so damn sure of yourself?"

"Dora told me last night when I was scouting the town," he said with a grin. "I got two dollars coming for expenses, by the way."

Ma Teresa gathered up her reins. "I guess we might as well get to it," she said. "But it sure looks like a one-horse town."

"I count sixteen horses myself," said Big Al Einstein. "But it's all relative, you know."

Ma Teresa waved to Little Al Schweitzer and Donkey Pete, at the end of the road at the other side of town, and the four of them headed for the bank, where Spuds and the Professor were stretched out on benches, pretending it was siesta time.

Donkey Pete stayed with the horses and Spuds covered the door while the rest of them walked into the bank with enough drawn and loaded firepower to hold off a small army.

"Move and you die," said Einstein, waving a sawed-off shotgun around the room.

"Easy, folks," said Ma Teresa in a calming voice. "We don't want to hurt anyone. We just want to take the money and leave."

She was smiling pleasantly as she said this, and held a revolver against the guard's head. To her disappointment, there wasn't a lawyer or bank president in sight for her to take a shot at. The teller had fainted and was collapsed on the floor behind his cage. The two customers in the bank had their hands in the air and were looking right pale.

"Crack that can, Little Al," said Big Al. "Time is of the essence."

Little Al Schweitzer leaped over the counter and knelt at the safe. "It's only a Jensen three-tumbler model," he said with a hint of disappointment in his voice. "I was hoping for more of a challenge."

"I don't need to know its genealogy or its anatomy," snapped Einstein. "Cut the jabber and get the cash."

Schweitzer sighed. The clicks of the tumblers were as obvious as down on a duck. Five seconds later he was stuffing bills into the saddlebags draped over his shoulders.

"Hurry up," yelled Spuds from the door. "Sheriff's coming."

"Shoot him," shouted the Professor.

"I can't," said Spuds. "All he's wearing is his long johns

and he ain't armed. It's against my religion to shoot an un-armed man in his underwear in broad daylight."

"Damn your morals," muttered Big Al Einstein. "Just shoot somewhere relatively near him," he yelled. "Pin him down until we're finished."

"That I can do," said Spuds, happy with his ethics and real glad that Big Al wasn't going to make him shoot the sheriff. He fired off a quick shot that dug into the dust about four inches in front of the sheriff's right foot.

"Hold it right there," he yelled. The sheriff stood in the middle of the street in his grimy long johns with the back flap hanging loose and raised his hands over his head.

Little Al Schweitzer looked at the pile of money left in the safe and sighed. It would be a simple matter to scoop it all up, but rules were rules. Projected returns, plus eight percent for operating expenses and overhead. He'd already taken enough. Big Al and Ma Teresa would skin him alive if he took it all. Reluctantly, he put the card in the safe and latched the door closed.

The card read, "Bless you for your contribution to those less fortunate than yourself," and was personally signed by Ma Teresa. She'd had them printed up in Dodge City, and Big Al had shown her how to pen her name.

"I'm ready," said Little Al, turning from the safe.

"About time," said Ma Teresa as she finished tying the guard to a chair. "Let's move."

They headed for the street and sorted out the horses. There was a crowd of curious kids across from the bank. Spuds waved to them and shot his rifle into the air as he leaped on his horse. He liked kids, and enjoyed providing them with an entertaining show whenever possible.

They rode out of town heading north, leaving the sheriff standing in the middle of the street with all the kids capering around him and laughing.

It was hardscrabble Idaho country, and as they rode along, Ma Teresa wondered how in the world anyone could make a go of it out here even under the best of conditions. It was too hot in the summer, too cold in the winter, and the soil was mostly rocks.

Yet she admired those who tried. It was a hard life, and dangerous enough without the land-grabbers and greedy bankers poised like vultures to take advantage of any passing misfortune.

It was the same old story every time. A family would homestead a piece of near-worthless land and then improve it with a lot of backbreaking work. Sooner or later they'd need money for something—cattle, seed stock, doctor bill, vet bill—and put their land up against a bank loan. It was all downhill from there.

They crested a rise, and in the long valley below them there was a single farmhouse. A fresh-dug grave was in back of the house, surrounded by a small fence. A woman was loading a wagon.

Ma Teresa looked at Big Al. He nodded.

They rode down into the valley and approached the woman. She saw them coming from a distance and leaned against the wagon, cradling a rifle in her arms. As they got close, she raised it a little, but didn't exactly point it at them.

"Widow Parker?" asked Ma Teresa.

"That's right," she said. "But if you come to rob me, you're too late. I done sold everything I had that was worth a damn. I ain't got nothin' left worth spit."

"We ain't here to rob you," Ma Teresa said. "Little Al, toss me those saddlebags."

She caught them expertly and pulled out a pile of cash, counting it carefully. Then she leaned over and handed it to Widow Parker.

"What's this?" the widow asked, laying down the rifle and gathering the money with both hands.

"That's what the bank sold your ranch for," Ma Teresa said. Then she handed the woman some more money. "And this is what it was *really* worth."

The woman started crying.

"Now don't go bawling on us," said Donkey Pete, wip-

ing away a big old tear. "Us hardened outlaws don't like to
see no woman cry."

"You can buy your spread back, if you want," said Ma
Teresa, "but it might be best to move on and start fresh
someplace else."

"I . . . I . . ." The woman looked up. "You're Ma Teresa!"

Ma nodded.

"Then you two must the Texas Jewboys!" the widow
cried. "Big Al and Little Al. I can't believe it."

"At your service, Ma'am," said Little Al Schweitzer,
touching the brim of his hat.

"And I thought the Hole-in-the-Wall Gang was just a
story out of one of them paper novels full of words."

"Oh, we're real enough," said Big Al Einstein, spitting
discreetly away from the widow, "although reality is, to a
large degree, an illusion of perspective."

"What did he say?" asked Spuds. "I wish he'd quit using
big words when he's chewin'."

"Who's that coming hard over the ridge?"

"That's Two-Toe," said Ma Teresa.

"He's supposed to be back at the hideout watching our
stuff and fixing dinner. What's he doing here?"

"Well, he ain't stirring no beans," said Ma Teresa.

Two-Toe pulled his slavering and sweating pinto to an
abrupt halt. Both he and the horse looked about ten steps
from a shallow grave.

"Pinkerton goons hit the camp," he gasped. "That
Custer fellow was leading them."

"George Armstrong?" said Donkey Pete. "Whoa! We're
in big trouble now."

"I took the back way over, through the canyon,"
wheezed Two-Toe. "We got a lead on them, but they'll be
on our trail soon, you can bet on it."

"I hate Pinkerton goons," said Ma Teresa. "They're like
them yippy little dogs that grab your britches and won't
let go."

"We can't go back," gasped Two-Toe. "That's for sure.
We got to relocate."

"How can we be the Hole-in-the-Wall Gang if we don't live in a hole in the wall?" asked Spuds. "I ain't too comfortable leaving Idaho, to tell you the truth."

"If we go south to Kansas, we could be the High Plains Drifters," offered Donkey Pete helpfully. "That's got a right nice ring to it."

"There ain't no way I'm going to Kansas," said the Professor. "They'll hang me on sight in that sorry state, if they can find a high enough place."

"I'd sooner go to Oklahoma Territory," said Little Al. "That's fine red-dirt country, even for a bunch of outlaws on the run."

"Wait," said Big Al Einstein sharply. They stopped jabbering and looked at him.

"You got a plan?" asked Ma Teresa.

"I got a theory," he said. "There ain't no way we're gonna beat George Armstrong Custer and all those Pinkerton goons if we play him on a level, unified field. What we got to do is break the field up. Put something between him and us."

"And just what would that be?" asked Ma Teresa.

Big Al Einstein nodded east. "The Rocky Mountains," he said. "They got banks in Montana, too."

"Cross the Continental Divide at this time of year?" asked Spuds. "We're likely to hit snow."

"If we hit snow, so do they," said Little Al. "Maybe they'll turn back."

"It's settled," said Ma Teresa firmly. "We head to Montana. But first we got to get outfitted. Junction City's on the way, and they don't pester honest bank robbers. Let's move."

"I ain't going nowhere on this poor horse," said Two-Toe. "I believe it's all used up."

"You can take my horse," said the Widow Parker. "I just know Fred—bless his soul—would want you to have it."

"Much obliged," said Two-Toe, dismounting and switching saddles. "This pinto will be okay once he's rested."

The widow walked over to Ma Teresa and looked up at her with enchantment in her eyes.

"You're a saint, Ma Teresa," she said. "A real saint."

Ma Teresa pulled her hat down to hide the blush that was spreading over her face.

"You take care of yourself," she said, kicking her horse into motion. "Move out," she called.

It wasn't too far across the prairie to Junction City, which was about a dozen tumbled-down buildings snuggled up at the foot of the towering Rockies. They left the Professor on a ridge outside of town to keep an eye out for Custer and the Pinkerton goons.

"You sure this is okay?" asked Big Al Einstein as they rode into town. "If Pinkerton is after us, there must be a reward out."

"Sheriff Baxter and I go back a long way," Ma Teresa said with a sly grin and a wink. "We'll be safe here, unless Custer catches up."

They spread some money around and split up. Donkey Pete and Spuds went to get supplies. Little Al went looking for a couple of packhorses. Two-Toe, Big Al and Ma Teresa went to the saloon.

It was dark and smoky inside, and smelled of spilled beer and human sweat. A piano player was pounding out a tinny, off-key rendition of a sad song. People sat at round wooden tables, playing cards and/or drinking. The three outlaws walked to the bar.

"What'll it be?" asked the bartender, a large man with a red nose. One of his ears looked like it had been chewed on.

"Sasparilla," said Big Al. "Straight up."

"Milk," said Ma Teresa. "And leave the bottle."

"Whiskey," rasped Two-Toe. "And a glass of whiskey on the side to wash it down."

"Look over there," said Ma Teresa, knocking back her first shot of milk. "That's Doc Holliday playing cards."

"Who's that dude he's playing with?" asked Two-Toe.

"That's Doc Livingston, I presume," said Big Al. "It seems to be a table full of gambling physicians."

"I thought Doc Livingston was lost in darkest Canada," said Two-Toe, a glass in each hand.

"That newsman Stanley went in and got him out," said Ma Teresa. "I understand the Doc was not too happy about that. He had a good thing going."

Big Al snorted, and Two-Toe decided it was best not to inquire further. A one-armed man wearing a badge and an eye patch came up to the bar.

"Well, I'll be darned," said the stranger. "If it ain't the lovely Teresa come to grace my fair city with her radiant beauty."

"Hello, Baxter," said Ma Teresa. "I suppose you know my friends."

"I seen their pictures down on the post-office wall," he said. "Pleased to meet you." They shook hands all around.

"You're as lovely as ever, Teresa," said Baxter, who was missing a few important teeth. "But what have you done with your hair?"

"I've been on the road," snapped Ma Teresa. "And speaking of appearances, you seem to be missing a few more body parts since I last saw you."

Baxter looked to where his arm used to be. "It happens," he said and shrugged his shoulders. "I got to learn to be more careful."

"You ain't been careful one day in your entire life," said Ma Teresa. "That's what endears you to me."

The Professor busted through the swinging doors to the saloon. "They're coming!" he gasped. "Must be thirty of them."

"Darn," said Ma Teresa. "We best be moving."

"I'll protect you, my sweet flower," said Baxter, drawing his gun with his remaining hand. "I'll stand beside you no matter what. Our love will sustain me to the bitter end. Who are we shootin' at?"

"Pinkerton goons," said Two-Toe, draining the last of his glasses.

"No problem," said Baxter. "I eat Pinkerton goons for breakfast."

"They're riding under Custer," said Big Al, pushing his stool back.

"I—I have a pressing appointment," stammered Baxter, turning pale and putting his gun back in its holster. "I do hope you'll understand."

Ma Teresa touched Baxter's cheek, right under his eye patch. "You wouldn't be you if you weren't you," she said and kissed him lightly on the beak of his broken nose.

"Huh?" said Baxter.

"Later, Sweets," said Ma Teresa. "Let's roll!" she cried.

The rest of the Hole-in-the-Wall Gang were on horses outside the saloon. Ma Teresa leaped from the porch onto her steed. Big Al Einstein calculated vectors for a moment and did the same. Two-Toe, who had liberated an extra bottle of whiskey from the bartender, tripped and fell into the street. Spuds helped him onto his horse. They thundered out of town with the Pinkerton goons and the fair-haired George Armstrong Custer hot on their heels.

The advantage of rested horses helped. The gang pulled ahead of the goons as they headed into the mountains. Their lead was never very large, though, and no matter how hard they pushed, the Pinkertons stayed a ridge or two behind them. Hours passed. They pressed through the night and on into the next day.

"They're sticking to us like leeches," moaned the Professor, looking over his shoulder and shaking his head. "We ain't never gonna give them the slip."

"I think they're closing in," wailed Two-Toe. "This morning they were two ridges behind us and now they're only one ridge back."

"But they were short ridges this morning," said Little Al. "This is actually quite a long ridge."

"You and your constant optimism," snorted Spuds. "Your jabber could make a man look forward to falling off a train and being eaten real slowly by a hungry bear."

"That's enough bickering, boys," said Ma Teresa. "Save your energy for the big fight."

"I'd as soon pass on the big fight," said Donkey Pete, "but I don't believe we're going to be presented with that option."

"Perhaps there is a way," said Big Al Einstein. All eyes turned toward the man with the slickest brainpan west of the Mississippi.

"Spill it, Big Al," said Ma Teresa. "We are all ears."

"Actually, it's quite logical," said Big Al, biting off a huge chaw of tobacco and looking real proud of himself. "It has to do with the shortest distance between two points."

"Oh, Lord," groaned Spuds. "If this turns into another Einstein dissertation, we are as good as dead. This ain't the time for lengthy explanations."

"Consider two points," said Big Al with a dreamy look on his face. "Point one is us where we are now, and point two is us where we want to be. Consider, if you will, the most logical direction in which to proceed."

"I *knew* it," snapped Spuds. "What we need is quick, clear thinking, and what we got is a muddled orator."

"Hear him out," said the Professor. "I like puzzles."

"Well, we is standing on point one," said Two-Toe. "That part is real clear. What point two might be has me confused."

Spuds hit Two-Toe with his hat. "I can't believe we're standing here hip-deep in a metaphysical discussion while George Armstrong Custer and a whole bunch of Pinkerton goons are closing in on us with death and destruction upon their minds."

"Point two must be all those banks in Montana," said Little Al.

"An admirable long-term goal," said Big Al. "But I was thinking of something a little easier to obtain. A large and complex project can often be best accomplished by breaking it down into smaller, more accessible units."

"Make him stop, Ma Teresa," wailed Spuds.

"I think I got it," said the Professor. "We're on one side of the mountain, and we want to get to the other side of the mountain."

"Very good," said Big Al Einstein, leaning over and spitting on the ground. "Now, what would the shortest distance be?"

"There ain't but one way," said Two-Toe. "We go up this side of the mountain and when we get to the top, we go down the other side. But I do believe the Pinkerton goons have also figured that out."

"That's linear thinking, Two-Toe," said Big Al. "Try thinking another way."

"Huh?" said Two-Toe.

"I suppose it's possible we could burrow straight through this mountain to the other side," said Little Al, "but that might take a while."

"True," said Big Al Einstein. "A tunnel, under the circumstances, would be impractical. However, that's the kind of thinking I was looking for. Anyone else have an idea?"

"I have an idea I'd like to whop you upside the head," said Spuds.

"So what's the plan, Big Al?" asked Ma Teresa.

"We take a left turn here," he said.

"I believe Big Al has done wore his brain out," said Two-Toe. "There is nothing to our left but a two-thousand-foot drop straight down to a canyon floor, and a vertical rock face above it."

"It's a shortcut," said Big Al.

"Only if you want to fall off this mountain," said Spuds.

"Look again," said Big Al Einstein. "There's a ledge running around the side of the drop-off."

"You call that a ledge?" said Donkey Pete. "It don't look very wide to me."

"If we go around this mountain instead of up and over it, we gain a lot of time," said Big Al. "Probably enough to get rid of the Pinkerton goons for good."

"But what's to keep them from following us?" asked Ma Teresa.

"I'm glad you asked that," said Big Al. "There are two reasons they won't. The first is the biological truism that the prey will always try harder to get away from the hunter than the hunter will try to hunt the prey . . . unless, of course, the hunter is real hungry, but it doesn't usually happen that way."

"We ain't talking pork chops here," said Two-Toe.

"Hurry up with reason two," said Spuds. "Reason one did not do much for me."

"Reason two pertains to the weather," said Big Al. "I have been observing a very interesting phenomenon developing in the west as regards a rapidly approaching low-pressure system that is about to collide with the thermal currents over the mountain."

"A weather report!" shouted Spuds. "We are about to be overrun by Pinkerton goons and Mr. Genius here is about to give us a half-hour weather report."

"Spuds has a point, Big Al," said Ma Teresa gently. "Just what exactly is reason two?"

"It's going to snow soon," said Big Al. "If we can get around that ledge before the snow starts, they will not follow us around. Only a fool would try that narrow path in the presence of ice and snow."

"Only a fool would try that anyway," said Donkey Pete. "What if we just keep going up?"

"Then we get into the big fight within a couple of hours," said Big Al. "We will all be killed."

"And what happens if it starts snowing while we're out on that ledge?" asked the Professor.

"We will probably all be killed."

"Doesn't sound like we have too many choices," said Two-Toe. "Either we die for certain by being followed and shot down like dogs or we probably die by falling off the mountain. I vote for possible death by plummeting as opposed to certain death by Pinkertons."

"I'll go with the maybe death myself," said Donkey Pete. "But I don't have to like it."

"Are you sure about the *certain* part of the Pinkerton death?" asked Spuds doubtfully. "I got to tell you I ain't real fond of falling from high places."

"I have never in my life seen such a bunch of candy-ass dudes," said Ma Teresa, pulling her horse to the edge of the sheer face and starting out on the ledge. "You take the end, Big Al. That way, if anyone chickens out, you can toss him over and it won't slow us down much. Save the horse, though. We might need it."

The Professor and Donkey Pete followed Ma Teresa out onto the narrow ledge. Then Little Al moved out, leading the packhorses. Two-Toe shook his head and proceeded. Spuds turned to Big Al Einstein.

"You wouldn't really throw me to my certain death, would you?" he asked.

Big Al just grinned.

It was slow going. The ledge turned out to be narrower than it had looked at the beginning, when it had looked impossibly narrow. The horses knocked occasional rocks over the edge, but the bottom was so far down, the rocks disappeared without a sound.

"Just let your horse go where it feels like going," said Ma Teresa. "It don't want to fall any more than you do."

Tension was thick in the air. Two-Toe was praying that the horse the widow-woman had given him had no suicidal tendencies. Donkey Pete was humming the first four bars of "Nearer My God to Thee" over and over again.

"There's a mighty pretty river at the bottom of this canyon," said Little Al. "Of course it's so far down you can hardly see it."

"I wouldn't advise looking down," said Big Al, and as he took his own advice and looked up, he did not like what he saw. The low-pressure system was gathering steam. It would be snowing soon.

"Perhaps we should pick up the pace," he said.

"You ain't the only one who can read clouds," said Ma

Teresa a little testily. "But I, for one, am not in a hurry to take the big plunge."

They were strung out over the canyon, hugging the vertical rock wall, going single file—horse nose to horse tail—along the narrow ledge. When they were about halfway across, it started to snow.

"Mighty pretty flakes," said Little Al, catching a few on the tip of his tongue. "I hear tell that no two of these little fellows are exactly alike. Isn't that a wonder?"

"The only wonder is how you have lived so long without someone putting your Pollyanna butt in a sling," grumped the Professor.

"I don't believe I like this snow much," said Donkey Pete.

"Look on the bright side," said Little Al. "At least the Pinkerton goons will be stopped."

"I can't tell you how good that will make me feel when my horse slips and I fall to my untimely death," said Two-Toe. "This could not possibly get any worse."

But it did. The snow turned to ice, and the footing on the narrow ledge went from uncertain to treacherous to impossible. Eventually, the horses refused to go farther. The end of the ledge was within sight, but the animals would not move.

"I wish I was back in Oklahoma Territory eating my mom's rotten cooking," moaned Donkey Pete. "I should never have taken up a life of crime. If I had been a little more fond of raising chickens and pigs, I wouldn't have left the farm and ended up here fixing to die."

"For a bunch of hardened criminals, you are the most spineless whiners and complainers it has ever been my misfortune to be associated with," said Ma Teresa as she carefully slipped off her horse and gingerly crawled in front of it.

"What's up?" asked the Professor.

"I'm chipping away some of this ice," said Ma Teresa. "Then I'm going to pull this horse along behind me. Big Al will start moving from the rear. Those of you in the middle—outlaws and horses alike—have two choices: get with the program or get out of the way."

"I don't believe a horse will do that," said Spuds. "Horses are either too smart or too dumb."

"Well, I for one ain't going to stand around debating it with my nag," said the Professor. "Let's move out."

They moved out, but it was slow and dangerous going. The horses clearly did not want to proceed, but Big Al kept them moving. When they reached the end of the ledge, Spuds threw himself on the rocky, ice-covered ground, hugging and kissing it like a long-lost lover.

"That's disgusting," said the Professor, standing over Spuds. "The man has no pride."

"Judge not lest ye be judged," said Donkey Pete.

"Huh?" said the Professor.

"I had a Bible-beater for a cell mate one summer in Tucson," said Donkey Pete. "He was always saying things like that. Horse thief. Talky fellow, till they hung him."

"If we camp at the top of that rise, we'll be able to see if Custer and the Pinkerton goons try to cross," said Big Al. "I doubt they'll be that stupid, though."

It was easy going after what they had been through, but the storm was picking up as they made their way among the tall pines to a small rise overlooking the canyon and the ice-encrusted ledge. It was clearly going to be a hard night.

"Looks good, Big Al," said Ma Teresa, dismounting and looking around. "Spuds, you and Donkey Pete unpack the tent. I hear a warm, dry sleeping bag calling me."

"I hope you got a bigger tent this time," said Spuds to Donkey Pete. "I'm tired of sleeping with the Professor's feet in my face."

"Tent?" said Donkey Pete. "You got the tent, I got the food."

"No, no," said Spuds. "I was supposed to get the food. You were supposed to get the tent and sleeping bags."

"Wait a minute," said Ma Teresa. "Who got what?"

"I got beans, lots of beans," said Spuds. "A good price, too," he added proudly.

Everybody looked at Donkey Pete, standing next to his packhorse. "Well, they *did* have a good price on beans," he said sheepishly.

"Great," said Two-Toe. "We got an ice storm, two horses loaded down with beans, and no tent or sleeping bags. What a crock."

"I *like* beans," said the ever-cheerful Little Albert Schweitzer.

"Spuds, you and Donkey Pete go cut some pine boughs," said Ma Teresa wearily. "We'll have to make do with a lean-to and our bedrolls."

"I'm getting too old for this," said Big Al Einstein as he got off his horse. "Days like this make me wish I'd gone straight."

"And what would you do if you weren't robbing banks and running from the law?" asked the Professor. "It ain't like you're overflowing with in-demand talents."

"Mr. Edison would not have agreed with you," said Big Al. "He said I showed promise."

"Edison?"

"Riverboat pilot," said Big Al. "Kind of a young guy, but bright. Had a theory about capturing lightning and putting it in glass jars so you could carry them around like lanterns. He wanted me to help him work out the details."

Two-Toe snorted.

"I couldn't see spending my life in a riverboat lab," said Einstein. "I'm a man who's got to keep moving."

It took a couple of hours to fabricate the crude lean-to and find enough dry wood for a fire. It wasn't much shelter, but it was better than being out in the storm.

"More beans?" asked Spuds hesitantly, holding the ladle over Ma Teresa's plate. She nodded, and Spuds dumped some hot beans on top of her cold beans.

"I purely hate beans," she said. "But outlaws need to keep their strength up, especially when they're on the run."

"Well, there ain't nothing running out there on a night like this," said Two-Toe, helping himself to a third plate of beans.

"Think we've given Custer and the Pinkerton goons the slip?" asked Donkey Pete, breaking wind. Spuds, sitting next to him, raised one eyebrow and returned the favor.

Big Al nodded. "My guess is they'll turn back. It ain't as if we're important outlaws like Wild Bill Shatner or Buffalo Bob. They got bigger fish to fry."

"What's that?" said the Professor. "I heard something."

"It wasn't me," said Donkey Pete, blushing. "Honest. It might have been Spuds, but it wasn't me. Beans don't do that to me. Beans do that to Spuds."

"Quiet," whispered Big Al. "There's someone out there."

They all listened, and beneath the roar of the storm there was a quiet cough and a moan.

Big Al picked up his rifle, cocked it, and pointed it out into the darkness. "Come out where we can see you," he said in a loud voice. "We know you're there, you scum-sucking varmint. Identify yourself or you are dead meat."

A small figure staggered out of the stormy night into the ring of light spread by the campfire. It was covered from head to toe with a buffalo hide that was crusted with ice and covered with snow. It took two hesitant steps forward and fell to the ground.

"It's a midget," said Two-Toe. "A frozen midget."

"It's a boy," said the Professor, pulling back the buffalo hide.

"That's no boy," said Ma Teresa. "That's an Indian."

"It's a boy Indian," said Spuds. "He's just a kid."

"He's still an Indian," said Ma Teresa. "He's not moving much, though. Is he a dead Indian yet?"

"Lakota is my guess," said Little Al, bending over the boy. "Sioux. He can't be much more than ten years old."

"But is he dead?" asked Ma Teresa.

"Not quite," said Little Al. "He's all froze up, but he ain't dead yet."

"Drat," said Ma Teresa.

"What are we going to do?" asked Donkey Pete.

"I'm thinking," snapped Ma Teresa.

"We can't let him lie in the snow like that," said Spuds. "Indian or no Indian, that ain't right. I mean, he's just a kid."

Big Al sat there quietly, watching Ma Teresa. He was the only one in the gang who knew how she had lost her grandparents and all her aunts and uncles in a Cheyenne raid on their wagon train. Her hurt, and her hate, ran deep.

"I'm thinking," she said.

"I never killed a kid before," said Two-Toe. "I believe that letting this child sit out there would be just like killing him. I'm afraid my ethics won't allow me to be a party to that, even if I am a coldhearted outlaw."

"Okay," said Ma Teresa, frowning. "Bring it in. But keep it away from me."

Spuds and Little Al brought the small bundle under the feeble shelter of the lean-to. They put their bedrolls together and propped it up by the fire. Little Al started rubbing the unconscious boy's arms and legs. Eventually, the child started to stir.

"Here's some good hot beans and a cup of strong coffee," said Donkey Pete, passing a plate and a tin cup to Little Al.

The kid had taken two sips of coffee and a bite of beans before he opened his eyes. When he did, he looked around wildly and screamed. He tried to crawl back into the storm, but was too weak.

Little Al said something to the boy in a language nobody else understood. The boy stopped struggling.

"You speak Indian?" asked Donkey Pete.

"I speak some Lakota," said Little Al softly, as if not to scare the child, "but I ain't no expert."

"I learned Mexican from a woman in Laredo one night," said Spuds proudly. "Maybe the kid speaks Mexican."

"Get it fed and get it out of here," snapped Ma Teresa.

Little Al glared at Ma Teresa and offered the boy a spoonful of beans, which, after some hesitation, he took.

The gang sat around as Little Al fed the child and talked softly to him. As he filled the boy's plate again, he looked at Ma Teresa.

"The child says he lost his family," said Little Al. "Men in blue raided their winter camp and killed many people. They were led by a man with hair the color of gold."

"Pinkerton goons," said Spuds.

"George Armstrong Custer," said Donkey Pete.

Ma Teresa was silent, studying the small boy. After a few moments, she got up and wrapped her blanket around his shoulders.

"Poor kid looked cold," she said defensively. She pulled a piece of hardtack from the pouch on her belt and handed it to Little Al. "See if he wants to chew on this for a while," she said. "It ain't much, but it might help."

Big Al Einstein raised one eyebrow but didn't say anything.

Slowly the hardened criminals drifted off to sleep as the storm continued to rage around them. Ma Teresa was the only one who stayed awake. She looked at the boy shivering in his sleep by the fire. Eventually she went to him and held him to keep him warm. He did not wake. He seemed so vulnerable, so young to have lost so much.

She held him and stroked his hair until she, too, fell asleep.

The fire was out when they woke the next morning, but the storm had lessened considerably, having tapered off to a fine, light snow. They fixed coffee and got ready to leave.

"What about the Indian boy?" asked Spuds. "We can't just leave him here." He looked at Ma Teresa questioningly, with a hint of defiance.

"He comes with us until we can find some Indians to take him," said Ma Teresa. "He can ride with me."

No one dared crack a smile, but they all wanted to, all except for Donkey Pete, who was too busy finishing off the last of the cold beans to notice much of anything else.

It was slow but steady going, mostly downhill through a forest of towering pines, their branches heavily coated with snow. Ma Teresa led the way with the boy in her lap, wrapped warmly in a blanket.

There was no sign of the Pinkerton goons, and they made good time all day after it quit snowing. As it was getting on toward dusk, they saw chimney smoke from a farm and headed for it.

The man who stood by the gate was dressed in bib overalls and wore a floppy hat. He was surrounded by kids, at least twenty of them, of assorted ages. They looked at the gang with curiosity, but did not appear frightened. The man seemed hardly more than a kid himself.

"Good evening," said Big Al, touching the brim of his hat. "My name's Al Einstein and this here is Ma Teresa. We were passing through and saw your smoke. Thought you might have a barn we could sleep in tonight. Mighty cold out here."

The man eyed them carefully and seemed to come to a decision. "My name's William Bonner," he said. "Most folk call me Billy. I reckon I got some chores need doing. I can put you up if you help out."

"We can do that," said Spuds agreeably, visions of a warm barn dancing tantalizingly in his head.

"I was loading that wagon up with hay," the man said. "Snow makes it hard for our cattle to forage. Run the wagon down to the south forty. Break the ice on the lake so they can get some water." He pointed to a field south of the house. Big Al, Spuds, Donkey Pete and the Professor went off to load hay.

"All these young'uns yours?" asked Ma Teresa. There were more kids standing on the porch, and others were peeking out of windows from inside.

"In a manner of speaking, they are," Billy said. "Is that boy yours?" The boy was peeking out from Ma Teresa's blanket. His eyes were wide as he looked at the other kids.

"In a manner of speaking, he is," said Ma Teresa.

"Let's go inside," said Billy, opening the gate. Ma Teresa and Little Al followed him to the large, sprawling ranch house.

Inside, the place was chaotic. Kids were everywhere, busy doing loud, happy-kid things. The children came in all sizes and shapes, from barely toddlers to almost-teens. They came in all colors, too: white, black, red, and yellow. Ma Teresa had never seen so many kids together in her life.

Everyplace she looked there were bunks and play areas. One room off to the side had several rows of school desks and a blackboard. Banjos, guitars, mandolins, and musical instruments of all sorts hung from the walls, and there were books everywhere.

"The kitchen's this way," Billy said. "It's quieter in there."

The kitchen had a huge woodstove and a large table surrounded by mismatched chairs. Billy poured them coffee and they sat down. The boy looked at Ma Teresa and then said something to Little Al.

"Is it okay if the child goes and plays with the other kids?" asked Little Al.

"Sure," said Billy. Little Al made a gesture and the boy jumped from Ma Teresa's lap and ran into the other room.

"No offense, Billy," said Ma Teresa, "but you don't look much older than those kids."

"You got that right," laughed Billy. "Some people over in Bozeman call me Billy the Kid. They think I'm crazy for doing what I'm doing."

"And what is it you're doing?" asked Little Al.

"You might call it running an unofficial orphanage, or a foundling home," said Billy. "I take in kids who don't have no other place to go."

"Someone paying you to do this?" asked Ma Teresa.

"I wish," laughed Billy. "I do it on my own. Sometimes neighbors or townspeople will help out with food or clothes. We grow a lot of our own food, too. The kids work hard. It's good for them."

"What causes you to do this thing?" asked Ma Teresa. "You seem awful young to be so tied down."

"I don't look it, but I'm near thirty," said Billy, leaning back in his chair and sipping the strong coffee. "I was an orphan myself, grew up on the streets. I saw loads of kids like me go bad. They turned to the easy, quick money. A lot of them died young, lying in the middle of some dirt street with a gun in their hands and a bullet in their bellies. I walked a different road. It wasn't easy, but I got myself some education and saved me up some money. When I had enough, I bought this place and fixed it up. I want these kids to see that someone cares about them and to show them there are other ways to make a living than with a gun."

"You know who we are, don't you?" asked Little Al.

"I do," he said. "But I don't judge people by what I hear. Gossip don't come close to the heart of the matter. People have reasons, and until you get to know them, you don't have the right to judge good nor bad. You folks seem okay to me."

"How much we got in our operating expenses, Little Al?" asked Ma Teresa.

"Two thousand forty-seven dollars and fifty cents," said Little Al. "Roughly."

"I want you to give Billy here a thousand dollars."

"What?"

"You gone deaf? Go get this man some money."

Little Al left to get the cash out of his saddlebags. Ma Teresa turned to Billy.

"It's not a bribe, you know," she said.

"I can sure use the money," said Billy. "I thank you for it. But I would take care of the kid anyway."

"I know that," said Ma Teresa, and she knew it deep in her heart.

The men returned from the cattle, and Billy fixed up a hearty batch of stew. The outlaws ate at the big table with what seemed to be a thousand kids always coming and going. The outlaws slept in the barn, and in the morning they headed in the general direction of Billings, which was full of banks.

Ma Teresa didn't say anything about the kid, nor did Little Al, but Big Al Einstein figured it out immediately. It pleased him immensely, and the miles went by much lighter for that.

They rode for three days. At a river called Little Big Horn, they stopped to camp. It was early afternoon, but they had been making good time and thought they'd rest a bit.

"How long do you figure it will take us to get to Billings?" asked Spuds as he was unpacking the beans.

"Two days of easy riding," said Ma Teresa. "That's my guess. What do you think, Big Al?"

Big Al was standing with his back to them, looking at a small rise not fifty feet away.

"Big Al?" said Ma Teresa.

"I hear something," said Big Al. "Can't quite make it out—*Grab your guns!*"

"Pinkerton goons!" cried Donkey Pete as he dove for the rifle in his scabbard. He didn't make it. A bullet spun him around and he fell to the ground.

Things got crazy fast. Pinkerton goons were swarming over the rise as thick as buffalo. Bullets were flying everywhere. Spuds screamed and went down. Ma Teresa saw the dreaded George Armstrong Custer and tried to take him out, but she couldn't get a clear shot at him. She had a pistol in each hand and took down two goons.

"I believe we are in deep shit," said Big Al Einstein, standing beside her, firing his Remington.

Ma Teresa started to agree with him, but before she could say anything, an incredible pain exploded in her chest and everything went red. Then black. The darkness of total oblivion.

Nothing.

Nothing.

Drifting.

Drifting.

Dreams. A flicker of light. Ma Teresa found herself on a crowded street. It was loud. People were pushing her, talking in a language she did not understand. She touched her face, looked down at her body.

Her chest was an angry open wound, blood frothing and bubbling from the torn flesh. Oddly, she felt no pain. She felt nothing.

People flowed around her, too many people. The street was incredibly narrow. Ma Teresa remembered the open plains, and claustrophobia grabbed at her. A touch of panic. The smell of strange food drifted down from the open windows and mingled with the odor of too many people living too close together.

The people were dark, like Indians, but they resembled no tribe she had ever seen. They dressed oddly, the women in colorful robes, the men and young boys in loose white britches and shirts. Babies were crying, people were shouting. It all closed in.

And then she felt *everything*.

She felt the poverty, the despair, the hurt. Many were sick, nearly all were hungry. They had known nothing else all their lives. There was no hope for the future here, no expectations; only a desperate desire to get through life one day at a time.

The spirit of these people had been broken. Ma Teresa could feel that, just as she knew it was too late to change the causes of this situation. Yet . . . one at a time, they could be helped. One at a time, like widows and orphans.

Darkness closed in, the utter darkness of a deep canyon at midnight. It seemed to last forever.

She heard a sitar playing a familiar tune, though she did not know how she recognized either the instrument or the tune. The air was heavy with the smell of incense. Or was that pine smoke from a campfire?

"Calcutta," she said.

"What?" A familiar voice. Big Al. "Calcutta?"

She opened her eyes. It was painful. Her lids seemed to be glued closed.

And what she saw was a granite-faced man staring back at her. He was wearing buckskin and a feathered head-dress. His face was decorated with sharp white and red streaks of paint that contrasted with his copper-colored skin. He stared at her for a brief moment, nodded, then rose and walked away.

With difficulty, she moved her head and realized that she was in a teepee made of stitched-together animal skins, lying on a pile of buffalo robes. Big Al was sitting beside her, and he reached down to wipe her brow with his bandana, soaked in cool water. The smoke she smelled was from a smoldering fire, heavily laced with herbs, in the middle of the teepee.

"What?" she gasped in a raspy voice. "What happened? Who was that Indian?"

"That was Chief Crazy Horse, and we owe him our lives," said Big Al, wringing his bandana out in an earth-enware jug and wiping her brow again.

"They were coming," said Ma Teresa. "Custer and the goons. We were outnumbered and outgunned. I saw— Spuds! Donkey Pete!"

"Spuds is fine," said Big Al. "He just lost two fingers and part of an ear. Donkey Pete, I'm afraid, has gone to that Last Big Roundup in the Sky, relatively speaking, on account of getting gut-shot."

"And the rest?"

"All safe and sound," said Big Al. "Thanks to Crazy Horse."

"The Indian?"

"He is a great warrior and, at the same time, a compas-sionate man. His healers have great medicine. Otherwise you would be dancing in the ether with Donkey Pete and the recently departed Wu-Li gang."

"But why would he help us?" asked Ma Teresa, trying to sit up, grimacing, and falling back down.

"The boy was from his tribe," said Big Al in a quiet voice.

"Which boy? What are you talking about?"

"The boy you left at Billy the Kid's orphanage. Crazy Horse felt he owed you a gratitude. He repaid it by wiping out Custer and the Pinkerton goons at Little Big Horn. Killed every last one of those bastards. He says it gave him great pleasure."

"I had a dream," said Ma Teresa. "Is the gang around?"

"Outside," said Big Albert Einstein.

"Take me to them," she said.

"You can't . . ." began Big Al, but when he saw the determination in Ma Teresa's eyes, he shut up and helped her to her feet, supporting her as they went outside the teepee into the bright Montana sunlight.

The whole gang was there, less Donkey Pete and some assorted parts of Spuds. The hardened outlaws seemed kind of embarrassed, holding their hats and scuffing at the dirt with their feet.

"I'm glad you ain't dead," said Two-Toe. "This ground is too damn hard for digging graves."

"We're moving on," said Ma Teresa. "Soon as I'm able, we're heading east."

"East?" asked Spuds, reaching to tug at a part of his ear that was gone with fingers that had been shot off. "Why go east?"

"We're catching a boat to India," said Ma Teresa. "Calcutta."

"What for?" asked Little Al. "We've got work to do here."

"There's a lot more work to be done there," said Ma Teresa. "And we've got the crew what can do it. It's time to make a difference." She turned and went back into the teepee.

"They got banks in this Calcutta place?" asked the Professor.

"They got too much of most everything except things that can help the common folk," said Big Al Einstein with a smile. "But I do believe that is about to change."

· Given the acclaim he has received, it's hard to remember that Geoffrey A. Landis is still a relative newcomer to the field. He has already won a Nebula for "Ripples on the Dirac Sea" and a Hugo for "A Walk in the Sun."

When I invited him to write a story for this anthology, he asked if he could write about an alternate outlaw who, although fictional, has been "real" to lovers of fiction for more than a century. I said yes, and here's the startling result. . . .

A Quiet Evening by Gaslight
by Geoffrey A. Landis

In all the years that we had been friends, and often fellow lodgers, I have never known my friend to take an interest in fiction of any kind. I was quite surprised then, when on one dark, autumn evening, I arrived at Baker Street to find him deeply engrossed in Mr. Stoker's lengthy book. I was all the more surprised as it was a book of popular fiction, and supernatural fiction at that. My companion despised anyone who held any shred of belief in the supernatural; he considered such beliefs evidence of a weakness in thinking. Myself, I have always held a rather more open mind.

In the gaslight, his face was extraordinarily pale. He read with an intensity that shut out my presence—indeed, all the world—only occasionally muttering some comment in a voice almost too soft to be heard.

When he finished—he was a lightning-fast reader, but this still took several hours—he put the book down and sat silently, his eyes turned to the fire. After a while, he felt my gaze upon him and looked up. "A singularly interesting book, Watson. Have you read it?"

I admitted that I had.

He turned his gaze back to the fire.

"Doctor Van Helsing was, of course, a vampire himself," he said.

"Impossible!" I exclaimed.

"Oh, no; it is quite clear. How else is it that he could know so much about vampires, and his knowledge be so accurate, than that he was one himself? Come now, my good doctor, don't look so surprised. We two have seen enough of blood-feuds and cold-blooded murder in our time, have we not? Do you think it so outrageous that one member of that proud and sinister race might hunt another to his death?"

"Perhaps not," I admitted. "But surely you realize this book is a fiction."

"Is it?" he said musingly. "Some of it is, certainly. That mortal beings could turn into mist, or wolves, or bats—that is a fiction. But if seen by an unskilled observer, might not a clever man seem to vanish into the fog? I have even done the like myself, and only later, when I explain to you how I employ the most elementary principles of disguise, do you say it is obvious."

He did, indeed, often delight in tricks of disguise. I have myself seen him disappear when a carriage passed between us for the briefest of instants, only to find his voice laughing at me moments later, as while searching for him, I pass a wretched beggar, or the charwoman hurrying home.

"But, my dear friend," I said, "vampires? In England?"

In the gaslight, his face was abnormally pale. He has always been pallid. I have remarked on it before, attributing it to his abnormal patterns of sleeping and the way that he would often stay indoors all day, venturing out only on the foggiest of days, or long after the sun was down. Like his preternatural strength and catlike speed, his odd habits were a characteristic I had always simply accepted. I suddenly took it to mind to marvel about how very little

I knew of him, not where he was from, nor even his true age.

"Ah, but if there were indeed a race of humanity that subsisted on blood," he said, "I would think that this 'Dracula' of Mr. Stoker's could hardly have been the first of such to travel to Britain. And if one such were clever enough to live in such a manner as to avoid calling attention to himself . . ." He broke off and looked at me with a strange expression. "Ah, Watson, a superstition of ignorant peasants. Yes, yes, I am sure of it; I was merely indulging a flight of fancy."

That in itself was quite peculiar, since my companion had the most orderly thoughts imaginable, and was not in the habit of letting them wander.

The sun was long gone, and he rose from his chair to go out. It was, on occasion, his habit to dress himself in clothes more fit for a street ruffian than for a gentleman, and to vanish into the worst parts of London for the night. Often, when he returned from such a jaunt, his characteristic melancholy mood would have quite vanished, and his pallor would be livened by the briefest trace of color in his cheeks. He never told me what he did on his outings, and, for my part, I never dared ask.

I have seen his face a thousand times, but suddenly it struck me that his front teeth were singularly long, and almost cruelly sharp.

"A good night to you, my dear Watson," he said, turning to draw the door closed behind him. He paused for a moment, the door half open. "I have so few companions, Watson." His voice was quiet and gentle. "You know that you are quite dear to me, and that I would never wish you harm."

"Nor I you, my friend," I replied, but as he shut the door, I shuddered all the same.

Beth Meacham, executive editor of Tor Books, has been the science fiction field's most successful and influential book editor for the past decade. Only recently has she turned her hand to short stories, showing us just what a fine writer we lost when she decided to become a full-time editor.

I sold this book to Patrick Nielsen Hayden, another fine Tor editor, at the 1992 Worldcon (World Science Fiction Convention) in Orlando. About three hours later, I went out to dinner with Beth and invited her to write a story for it. Never one to make things easy on herself, she chose perhaps the least likely outlaw of all.

A Spark in the Darkness
by Beth Meacham

When I turned the knob left, I could feel the sharp little ticks as the pin in the lock slipped past the blocked holes. *Tick tick tick tick tick tick drop.* The pin slid into the tumbler. I stopped for a moment to catch a breath. The man standing behind me blew smoke over my shoulder and hit the back of my head. Sweat pulled him away and I started again. Turn the knob back to the right, *tick tick tick drop.* Sweat smelled stronger and I was getting hot from the fire-holder sitting on the floor beside me. I started the knob back to the left again, slowly. Smoke was shaking a little, leaning on me. It made it hard to feel the tumbler move. *Tick tick tick tick tick tick tick drop.* There. I sat back on my heels.

Smoke shoved me hard to one side; I fell, then turned to attack him. Sweat grabbed me, put his hand over my mouth and pulled me across the floor. I must have been making noise. Then he took his hand away and put one of the cool, sweet juicy things in my mouth. It tasted good.

I remember when I lived with my mother and my father and my friend in a little house with a sweet-smelling garden. I used to wander in the heat of day from plant to tree to vine, inhaling their sweet scents, touching their soft, delicate flowers and leaves. I loved the garden—there, nothing moved from its place. I think I remember the color of flowers and the brightness of the sun, my very earliest memories. But it is like a fading dream, a glimpse of lost enchantment, crimson and gold flaring in my memory.

The heavy door swung open, setting up eddies in the hot air of the room. A breath of cooler, dry air puffed out, carrying the scent of the paper that Smoke and Sweat want. There is a lot of it; they thrust packets into my pockets, down my shirt. Sweat's hand lingers on my breast for a moment, rewarding me for opening the door, promising greater pleasure soon.

I remember time from before my father died—he was so gentle with me, and he took me places that were different from the house where we lived. He took me to places that had lots of people moving quickly, and lots of new smells. He once took me on a trip in a long, narrow wagon that had many people in it, sitting in rows. There was a kind man who walked up and down the middle of the wagon and took pieces of paper from the people and made holes in the paper with a metal puncher. He let me follow him, and he let me punch the different-shaped holes in the pieces of paper, too.

Then my father took me out of the wagon to a big house. A man there touched my face and my eyes, and poked things into my ears. He made vibrations on my skin and in the air, and when I shook my head to let him know I felt the vibrations, he gave me sweets. But then he and my father moved their mouths and made vibrations, and my father cried. After that, we went home.

Sometimes my mother understood when I wanted

something or needed something, and sometimes my friend did. But sometimes no one knew and then I got so angry that I would hit and kick them, and try to breathe hard out of my mouth the way they did. After a while, my mother would carry me into a little room away from the heat of the sun and lock me in. I hated that. I cried and kicked the door and pounded with my hands, but no one came to let me out. I remember that when I was littler, I once locked my mother in a room and hid the key, and I laughed as I felt her pounding on the door as I sat out on the porch with my friend. I remembered that when she locked me in the cold room, and wondered if she was laughing at me, too.

I felt a thud when the heavy door slammed shut. Then the floor under my hand shook a little. Someone was walking very slowly—I reached out to see if Smoke and Sweat were sneaking away from me, but they were still beside me. Little puffs of breath came out of their mouths. I took Sweat's hand and put it against the floor so he could feel the steps. I tried hard not to make any sounds. At first he tried to pull away, but then he stopped when he felt the vibrations. Smoke put out the fire, and Sweat kissed my forehead. He was happy with me.

He pulled me to my feet, and they took my hands. We walked very softly away from the other person, out the two doors I had opened when we came in, and then into a street that smelled of rotten meat and rotten vegetables, rancid oil, dog shit, male cats, rats, molding leather, wet wool, and horse shit. We had walked a long way on this street before we went into the place where I opened the locks. Now Sweat and Smoke pulled on my hands and we ran back the way we had come. It was harder to run because of all the paper in my dress, but I knew that if I threw any of it away, they would beat me. After we turned a corner out of the garbage street into a street that smelled like horses and dust and baking bread, we slowed down and walked. This street was covered with big round rocks, and it would have been hard to run. Soon we went

inside and up some stairs and into the room where I had
left my cloak and hat.

I sat on the bed and took all the paper out of my
clothes. Smoke and Sweat made stacks of it and put the
stacks into a big bag made of the same kind of cloth my
mother used to have on the floor. Then I put on my cloak
and hat and we went down some different stairs. Our
horses were already hitched to our wagon and they
smelled like fresh hay. They breathed into my hands and
I hugged their necks, one after another, before Smoke
grabbed my arm and pulled me away. He always pulled
too hard. I almost fell down. He picked me up and put me
in the wagon, and then we went.

I remember when my mother locked me in the small
room after I fought with the boy who tried to tear my
dress. She was crying while she hit me—I felt her tears
when I was struggling to get away from her. I had realized
that keys pushed things inside the door locks and made
the metal pieces slide in and out of the door frames. I
thought I could push the little levers without a key if I
had something small enough to reach inside the keyhole.
My dress was already torn, so I pulled out one of the thin,
flat, hard stays that were sewn into the bodice. It was very
flexible. I broke off a short piece of it and pushed it into
the keyhole. As I moved it around, I could feel little
things poking up, and when I pushed against them, they
moved. It took me a long time, but I got that door open.
I hid my tool in the closet so I could get out again the
next time.

When my mother came home, she found me playing in
the garden. She didn't lock me up again that day.

We rode in the wagon for a long time. When night
came, we stopped and went into a place where there were
a lot of men and a lot of tables. Sweat pulled me through
the room into another room and then outside and up
some stairs. There was a room there with a straw mattress
on the floor. Someone had been sick there before we
came, and the smell made me feel a little sick, too. Sweat

and Smoke left, but they didn't lock the door; they had learned that they couldn't keep me in. I was tired, so I lay down and went to sleep.

When I woke up, they were sleeping beside me. They smelled like the fiery liquid they sometimes made me drink, so I got up and went outside. When they woke up after drinking that stuff, they might hurt me. I walked along the wall of the building toward where I could smell the horses. Our horses stamped when I came into the barn, so I could find them. I fell asleep again in the corner of the pen, on a bale of straw and wrapped in a horse blanket.

I dreamed of the day when men came and took my mother away. She had been sick for a long time; her room smelled the way the room upstairs had smelled. After they carried her away, the man who made her drink from little bottles gave me a bag and took me in his wagon to a big building that smelled like dirty people. The bag had some of my clothes in it, but not my hairbrush or my other shoes or my lock picks. The man locked me into a little close room when I tried to go home, and I didn't have anything to open the door with. When I woke up from the dream, I was scared.

Then I remembered that I wasn't there anymore.

One day when I was not locked in the little room, I was practicing opening the lock. I had found a small, flexible thing on the floor under the bed and thought it might work to open the door. A man I didn't know was suddenly behind me, and he grabbed my hand and twisted gently and then the lock was open. He breathed in my ear and laughed. And as suddenly, he went away. I was sure that the big woman who beat me would come and hurt me and lock me in again, so I hid under my bed, but no one came.

Later, the man who had helped me with the lock came again and took me away from the big building. He took me to a house, and a woman gave me a bath and put a clean dress on me. I was glad. After that, the man brought me a lot of locks. He took them apart so I could feel how they were made inside. Then he put them back together and gave me some little tools that had different-shaped hooks on the ends. I used them to open all the locks, and they were much better than anything I had ever used before. I opened the locks again and again, and the man gave me the sweet juicy things when I did it fast. I had a warm, soft bed there, and clean clothes, and the woman made me good things to eat. I missed my mother, but nobody locked me inside anything.

After a while, the man brought a different kind of lock, one that didn't have a key. He took my hands and let me feel how turning the big knob back and forth made pieces of the lock inside move until the handle would turn and the lock open.

Then he put a box in front of me with that kind of lock. It was hard to open. I sat and turned the knob for a long time, trying to guess when the little pieces moved. The man wouldn't let me have any food, even though it made the nice woman mad when he took it away from me. I had to open the lock first. At last I leaned my cheek against the box, I was so tired and hungry. And when I did, I could feel the lock pieces moving inside as I turned the knob. *Tick tick tick drop.* I had the box open.

After that, I learned to open lots of different locks that had knobs. The knobs were made differently for each kind of lock, so when I felt them, I knew to start one way or another, and how many drops before the handle would turn. It was fun.

Then Sweat and Smoke came and took me on a short trip in a wagon to a place where there was a big metal box with a knob lock. I opened it easily—it was a kind I had practiced on a lot. They took things out of the box and put them in a bag, and we hurried home after that. Another time they came and took me down into a hole in the ground and we crawled through a cool, narrow dirt passage that smelled of wet and growing things. We came out into a room where there was a box for me to open, and then we crawled back.

I realized that we were opening other people's boxes, like I had opened all my mother's boxes and doors to find out what was inside. That thought made me laugh. Like me, Smoke and Sweat wanted to know what was inside every locked place. I liked them for being like me, and finally understood why I had to keep quiet and still sometimes. They could tell when someone was coming, as I could not.

Now I lived with Smoke and Sweat all the time. The man and woman who taught me about locks had hugged me one day and put on my cloak and hat and given me a big bag to carry.

Then Sweat had led me out the front door in the heat and put me into a wagon. We went a long way that day, and the next day and the next day. After that, they took me to a door that was locked, and I opened it, and inside there was someone's box and I opened that, too. Then we ran away, but I dropped some of the paper they had given me. They beat me for that when we got into a room, and hurt me. Then they made me put on my other dress and my cloak, and we went out into the cold night and hitched up the horses and rode in the wagon until the sun came up. I was afraid that they were taking me back to the big building. But after the sun was gone again, we stopped and went into a new room, and they were kind to me and gave me good food to eat. We stayed there for a while, and then they took me to another locked room that had a locked box in it. And so I became happy, and moved to new places often and was never, ever, locked up again.

I woke up when the horses started stamping and nibbling at my hair and blanket. I was hungry. I could smell bread baking and bacon frying, so I followed the odors back to the building where Smoke and Sweat were sleeping. It was still cold. I found a door, but it was locked. It had been a long time since I had opened a door lock for myself, but it was easy. Inside, I found a hot loaf of bread.

It smelled so good and I was so hungry that I stopped to eat some of it right there. And as I was chewing, a big hand grabbed my shoulder and another grabbed my hands and pulled the bread away and shook me. I fought back, kicking and hitting and biting, and the big man choked me and picked me up and tied me into a chair.

Someone else came in the door, and then another person, and then the big man hit me hard. I don't remember anything more until I was in a closed wagon that was moving fast. I was still tied up, and I rolled around on the floor of the wagon as it moved, and my head kept hitting the walls and it hurt a lot.

Then the wagon stopped. A man opened the door and yanked me out so hard that I fell on the ground. I made noises and he slapped me hard, so I tried to be quiet. Then he carried me inside a building and gave me to a large woman, who smelled just like the woman who used to beat me in the big building. She untied my hands, and took off my clothes and shook them. When she put them back on me, all my lock picks were gone and my boots didn't have any laces.

Then she locked me in a cage.

I couldn't get out. The lock on the door didn't have a keyhole on the inside. When the woman came to bring me food, she slid it through a hole in the cage, so I couldn't run away through the open door and I couldn't reach her to fight with her.

Oh, I kicked and hit and flung myself against the bars. I threw the food on the floor and stamped on it. I fought the door, and I tore the blanket they gave me to little pieces. But no one would let me out. I fought for a long time, until I was so tired that I fell down and couldn't get up. Then I rolled up in the torn blanket and went to sleep.

I dreamed about being free. When I remembered that I was locked up, I cried and cried. The woman came with more food, but I didn't care. I could smell it, but I wasn't hungry at all. I wondered if Smoke and Sweat knew what had happened to me, or if they just woke up and couldn't find me. Maybe they ran away so they wouldn't be locked up, too. I remembered everything I could about being free, because that way I forgot that I was locked up in a cage.

Then someone touched me, and I smelled Sweat leaning over me. Smoke was there, too, and he pulled me up and hurt my arm and I was glad. The door was open and we ran down the hall. I tripped on something, and they held me up. We ran fast out the door, and our horses were right there. They tossed me into the wagon and jumped up in the seat and the horses ran and ran and ran.

The wind rushed past me and I was free. Smoke and Sweat hadn't run away, and I laughed and hugged them like I'd hugged the horses. I will open more doors and boxes for them—all the doors in the world aren't enough to give for the door they have opened for me.

Thomas Paine left England in 1774 (with a recommendation from Ben Franklin), immediately grasped the situation in the colonies, and wrote *Common Sense*, the pamphlet that convinced many Americans to join the Revolution and which is credited as a major influence upon Thomas Jefferson when he wrote the Declaration of Independence.

Using that as a point of departure, Kristine Kathryn Rusch, a frequent Hugo and Nebula nominee as a writer, and the editor of *The Magazine of Fantasy and Science Fiction*, here gives us her own history of Tom Paine.

Common Sense
by Kristine Kathryn Rusch

> . . . all men are born equal, and with equal natural right. . . .
> —Thomas Paine, *The Rights of Man*

The body twisted on the ancient oak tree, high buckled shoes pointed downward, hands clasped into tight fists. The long-boned face had turned black from lack of air, the famous blue eyes—rumored to seduce any woman who saw them—bulged from their sockets. Jailers had already taken the gold buttons and the ornate jeweled ring he always wore on his left hand. Toward evening, the shoes would disappear, as would the coat and hat, to warm lesser, more impoverished men.

Had he lived, he would have appreciated the irony. In death, at least, he had discovered true equality.

The rich in ease and affluence, may think I have drawn an unnatural portrait; but could they de-

scend to the cold regions of want, the circle of
polar poverty, they would find their opinions
changing with the climate.

—Thomas Paine, *The Case of the Officers of the
Excise*

"There he is!" Arabella grabbed Prudence's sleeve and
pulled her forward.

Prudence flicked her friend's hand away. "Go on. I will
wait here."

Arabella held up her skirts and ran across the street,
narrowly avoiding a closed carriage. A group of young
workers and townswomen had gathered on the corner,
spilling into the street itself. The air smelled of baking
bread and horse piss. Prudence stood as close to the pub
as she could, away from the puddles and the passing
horses.

Arabella had been down here every day for a week to
see the slim man standing on an overturned box. Prudence could catch half of his words.

". . . hereditary succession is a burlesque upon monarchy. . . ."

Prudence had passed here the week before, and knew
that the crowd had grown bigger. People were talking
about this man, who was speaking out against the Crown.
He had written a pamphlet that her father regarded as filth
and had thrown away before Prudence had a chance to
read it.

". . . requires some talents to be a common mechanic;
but, to be a king, requires only the animal figure of
man. . . ."

Arabella said that this man, this Thomas Paine, hated
all forms of oppression and believed that men should have
equal chances in the world. "He takes nuggets of many
philosophies, combines them and makes them his own,"
she had said breathlessly on the way across London. "He
believes that we all have the right to rule ourselves."

Prudence had said nothing. She had wanted to hear this man herself. A man who preached independence from street corners. A man whose theories attracted the children of the rich. A man who lobbied Parliament, even though to do so compromised his position as an excise man.

". . . For those of you who wish to think more on this, I have a pamphlet. . . ."

Arabella was first in line to buy a pamphlet she would have to throw away before she got home. Her new blue skirt swayed as she moved, and Prudence wondered if more than philosophy brought her friend here. Paine got off his box, handed out pamphlets with one hand and collected coins with the other. He spoke for a moment to each person who approached him.

Arabella flew across the street, cheeks shining. "Could you hear from over here?" she asked.

"Enough," Prudence said. She glanced at the pamphlet. Done on wavy paper with smeared ink, it nonetheless had a bit of charm to it. "My father considers such writings seditious."

"Of course," Arabella said. "Your father has a position with the Crown." She glanced around the street, apparently satisfied that no one else she knew was there. "I need to read this before I go home. Would you like to come to the Gardens with me?"

"I have some shopping to finish," Prudence said. She clutched her basket tighter as if for emphasis.

"You are no fun," Arabella said.

Prudence nodded, keeping a smile from her lips. "I am too serious by half."

Arabella grasped the pamphlet and hurried down the street, holding her skirts up, dodging puddles, and walking so fast she appeared to be running. If her mother saw her, she would receive a stern lecture on the deportment of ladies.

"You did not cross the street. The lecture is much more difficult to hear from this corner." The voice was low and rumbled in her ear. Prudence recognized the voice even as she turned to face its owner. Paine, commoner, rebel, and officer of the state. What an appealing combination.

"Mr. Paine," she said, and nodded toward him as any well-bred lady would do when faced by a man of lesser social standing.

His eyes were a startling blue. He had strong bones and a full mouth, and an intensity she had never encountered in anyone before. His smile lit up his face. "You have the advantage, I believe." For the second time, he used no form of respectful address. Perhaps her father was right. Perhaps Paine had been raised Quaker. He certainly adopted many of their ideas in his speeches and in his mode of address.

"Yes, I do," she said, unwilling to let this man know who she was. "You make fascinating speeches, Mr. Paine. I do not know if you are trying to receive attention for yourself or attempting to present yourself as an equal to the king."

"I am an equal to the king," he said.

She smiled. "Do not let the House of Lords hear you speak that way."

"The House of Lords believes that because I lack a Latin-school education, I have no knowledge of the world," he said. "I have more knowledge of the world than most."

Something in his self-assurance convinced her. "Now you teach people from street corners?"

"While I am in London," he said.

"You teach them to be equal to the king?"

"I teach them to believe in themselves," he said.

She liked debating him. She could remain here all day talking with him. But she dared not. She had a carriage waiting. She took her skirt in one gloved hand. "Then what, Mr. Paine? Should they try to burn down Parliament like Guy Fawkes did?"

"In a manner of speaking. They must make the laws their own."

"And you shall teach them that from a street corner?"
Her smile grew. "You are right. You are like the king. You
have no sense about what is good for the people of England."

She walked away from him, dodging puddles, ducking
beneath large, overhanging signs. An exuberance filled
her. She would like to see him again, although she knew
she shouldn't. Her father would be very angry if he found
out about even this conversation. A lord's daughter did
not speak to a common man on the street corner. A
woman did not debate philosophy as though she were as
smart as a man.

She resisted the urge to look over her shoulder as she
rounded the corner. Paine had no qualms about arguing
with a woman. Paine had no qualms about anything.

> We esteem ourselves bound by obligations of re-
> spect to the rest of the world to make known the
> justice of our cause.
>
> —John Dickinson

Benjamin Franklin rubbed his ink-stained hands on the
cloth beside his writing desk. Below, he heard dogs barking and a man shouting. A fire crackled in the grate. Even
at night, London was not quiet.

He glanced again at the letter before him. Sometimes
Samuel Adams had no sense of what was happening in
England. Adams acted as if Parliament existed to harass
the colonials. Parliament, on the other hand, was convinced that Franklin was aiding Adams in treason.

The letter Franklin had written was delicate; in terms he
knew that Adams would understand as appeasing government agents should the letter fall into the wrong hands,
Franklin argued against harsh action. He explained—
again—the political climate in London, and hoped that he
would help Adams gain an understanding.

But Franklin had come to his final paragraph, the one

in which he had to speak about his concerns for the colonies. The colonials fought for freedom against tyranny; they complained about the injustices brought to them by the king. But the colonies had no future, no vision. Although many were writing about the problems, no one was looking toward a solution beyond the immediate. The colonies needed a philosophy, a philosophy of government that would take them beyond their struggles with the king.

Franklin dipped his feather pen in the inkwell, then paused. He could not write this and maintain his position in the courts. He would have to influence the colonials in another way. But what that way was, he had no idea.

> The Almighty hath implanted in us these unextinguishable feelings for good and wise purposes. They are the guardians of his image in our hearts. They distinguish us from the herd of common animals. The social compact would dissolve, and justice be extirpated on the earth, or have only a casual existence, were we callous to the touches of affection.
>
> —Thomas Paine, *Common Sense*

"I do not like it," Paine said, taking Prudence's arm and helping her from the carriage. A thin lamp flickered over the back door to the pub. A small puddle reflected the light's thinness. Prudence's skirts rustled as she stepped onto the cobblestone. Paine waved the driver on, to wait at the nearby crossroads. "You allow your father to treat you like property."

"Under the law," she said calmly, although she was not feeling calm with his warm hand still clutching her elbow, "my father has the right to arrange my marriage. Because it has gone out of fashion does not mean that it is not done."

Paine pulled her against him in the darkness next to the

building. She liked his lean, firm frame, the familiar scent of tobacco. "I do not like it."

"Do you expect me to marry you?" Her tone had more tart in it than she would have liked. Marrying him was not a question. His background was too common, his activities too ill-bred. But exciting.

"No." He turned away from her.

She took his chin and brought his face back toward her until their lips nearly touched. "Then what distresses you, Master Paine?"

"Your husband will rule you like your father does. You will have no right to see a man such as me."

She laughed. "I have no right now. My father would kill us both if he knew. You talk treason and couch it in the voice of God."

He rubbed his thumb on the soft skin of her cheek. She leaned into it. Then he kissed her, not the gentle pecks that the men seeking her hand had given her, but a rough, all-involving meeting that left her hot and breathless.

She was not naive in the ways of men and women. Her nursemaid had made sure of that. But she had never experienced anything like this before.

"Perhaps," she said against his throat, "my future husband will not care if his wife has experienced another man."

"He will care," Paine said. He took her arm and moved her away from the wall. "But he may not be able to do anything about it."

Actually, if a center of communications existed for the proponents of radical existence at the end of the decade, it could be found not in New York where the Stamp Act Congress was held, but in London, where policy was made and colonial protests directed, where colonial agents were located and a community of Americans from the whole continent resided, and where a controversy over constitutional liberties within England had al-

ready raged. In this sense, London supplied what
was lacking in the colonies—a location where opposition to innovations in British policy could be
given continuous expression by Americans and
colonial agents, where intercolonial contacts could
be established and sustained both directly and in-
directly.

—Historian H. James Henderson

Franklin slapped the pamphlet against his hand. *The
Case of the Salary of the Officers of Excise and Thoughts on
the Corruption Arising from the Poverty of Excise Officers.* A
friend of his at the White Hart had handed him the
pamphlet and Franklin had already glanced at it enough
to know that he had something special on his hands.

The carriage wheels clacked on the cobblestones. The
driver clucked at the horses. Inside, Franklin ran his
hands along the soft cushions, thankful for their protection against the rough ride. He had heard that Paine spoke
sometimes on the corner, gathering quite a crowd. He also
was a regular at the White Hart, often winning their debating prize, the Headstrong Book, given to the most ob-
stinate haranguer. If the man spoke like he wrote, he
might be of some service to Franklin.

The pamphlet was an exercise in foolhardy courage.
Paine, an excise man, argued that the tax collectors like
himself had not received a promised pay raise because
toadies of George III had convinced Parliament to increase
the king's salary by a hundred thousand pounds a year.
The arguments about money did not interest Franklin,
but the tirades against the king did. For in his short work,
Paine had shown a view that resonated with the view held
in the colonies.

The carriage slowed near the corner, staying out of
sight. A man did stand there, on an overturned box. He
was a majestic figure in shabby clothing, an animated man
with a too-large nose and eyes that grabbed the soul. He

was debating a man in the audience about the purpose of
the monarchy, and the crowd was growing restless.

Franklin had seen enough. He had an appointment with
the Privy Council that he dare not miss.

> This is not inflaming or exaggerating matters,
> but trying them by those feelings and affections
> which nature justifies, and without which we
> should be incapable of discharging the social du-
> ties of life. . . .
>
> —Thomas Paine

Prudence ran up the steps to the great house, her hair
slipping from its pins. She almost tripped on her skirts,
but used a railing to catch herself. A footman opened the
door for her—had he left the coach ahead of her?—and
she ran the length of the hall to her father's study.

The polished oak doors were already open. Her father
stood at the window, his rotund shape looking more powerful than usual. Smoke curled off his pipe. She choked on
the scent of his tobacco.

"Your squire said you sent the men to arrest Thomas
Paine." She was breathing hard. The words came in short
gasps.

"Percival has called off the wedding," her father said,
still gazing out the large window. "He has agreed not to
shame you publicly."

Her father's voice was cool. She made herself take deep
breaths. Her heart had been pounding since one of Paine's
friends had caught her and told her the news. She hadn't
seen Paine for two days. She had been afraid for him,
afraid that the government was going to go after him. She
had never expected her father to lead the charge.

She allowed herself to walk down her father's line of
conversation. It was connected somehow, but she didn't
know quite what the connection was. "Percival has called
off the wedding? He has no right."

"He has every right." Her father turned. He had the look of King George to him: round face, overlarge, blood-shot eyes. Her father was a distant cousin to the monarch—to most of the European monarchs—but she had never seen the resemblance before. "You have shamed us all."

A flush rose in her cheeks. She knew what her father was talking about now.

"You have been seen with Paine in public houses," her father said, his speech taking on the debater's lilt it had in the House of Lords. "You have argued philosophy with him like a loose woman. You have been alone with him in his carriage. You have been seen kissing him in alleys."

Her father took a step closer to her. She had to work at not taking a step back. "Dammit, girl, even if Percival did not matter to you, didn't your reputation? Paine is a married man."

The words went through her like a knife. Paine was married? He had never told her. In all those meetings, all those debates, that last night, on his cot above the pub, he had never said a word.

She made herself swallow. "He is an interesting man, Papa."

"He is a common man and an adulterer, and he has defiled my daughter."

Odd that it mattered to her. She was going to marry someone else. They both had known that their liaison would not last. Still, her stomach was queasy, and a headache had built behind her eyes. "He has not touched me," she lied. "I merely went to hear his speeches. Arabella will testify to that."

"And the coachman will testify otherwise." Her father shook his pipe at her. "I had the traitor arrested, girl, for publishing treasonous pamphlets. I have already put in words with Pitt and the House of Lords, as well as with the king. They will make an example of him. The riots, the heresy in the streets, has to stop. And they will use him because they understand that he has defiled not just my daughter, but he has stolen my property and made my household into a laughingstock."

"He did not touch me," she said again. Her entire body felt numb. Married. Why hadn't he told her? "I am sure Percival will understand."

"Percival will understand that his future wife spent her time with rebels and anti-monarchists. His family is older than ours, girl. He will not tolerate any of this behavior." Her father waved his hand. "Go to your room. We will decide your future later. I have business to attend to."

She didn't move. She had come to defend Tom, to save him from her father's anger. But now she wasn't sure of how she felt.

"Your room, girl," her father said.

He would not listen to her. She knew that. She nodded, curtsied and walked out of the study.

Tom was married. He had made her a fool. A rich fool. The kind he despised.

How have you weathered this rigorous season,
my dear friend?

—Thomas Jefferson

The mood in London had become cold. Franklin eased closer to the fire in his grate. His meeting before the Privy Council had gone as well as could be expected. They had not charged him with any crime, and they found nothing wrong in the letters he had supplied to the colonies. Nothing illegal, in any case. He had been wrong, they assured him, to send the letters to Boston.

His hands shook as he reached for his tea. Being dismissed as postmaster general had upset him. The constant threat, the constant observation, also distressed him. He was too old to be a rebel, too old to feel more than the weight of time upon his shoulders. But he had duties to perform. His friends had assured him of that.

He glanced at the letter he had written moments before.

His position was hazardous, he had written, but the worst that could befall him was prison. He didn't like those words. They sounded too lighthearted. Prison was expensive, vexing, and dangerous to a man's health—especially a man of sixty-eight years.

He picked up the pamphlet that had sat on the table for weeks now. *The Case of the Salary.* . . . Ah, yes. Paine. He had forgotten about Paine in all the upheaval of the last month. And someone had told him something about the man—something bad.

Franklin sighed. He would find out what had happened and talk to Paine. Then he would see how the colonials could use him. Such things were part of Franklin's duties. He was the colonial envoy in London, but that meant more than working with the government. It also meant finding and importing necessary philosophy to the struggling men back home.

All hereditary government is in its nature tyranny.

—Thomas Paine, *The Rights of Man*

She escaped the house on the last day of the trial. She walked to the end of the street, where Arabella's carriage found her. Arabella wore a black dress and carried a white muff. She would not look at Prudence, nor speak to her. Apparently friendship went as far as responding to a friend's request for a ride, but not in association. All of society had snubbed Prudence since Percival canceled the wedding. He hadn't kept his promises well. It seemed that everyone knew of her disgrace.

So she held her head up when the carriage stopped a block from her destination. She walked as quickly as she could, careful not to turn an ankle on the uneven street. A crowd waited outside the court, but Prudence shoved her way through. People who recognized her moved away, and the others were too low-bred to touch her.

Inside the hall, she walked to the upper balcony, where she stood quietly near the door.

Tom had grown thin. His eyes still had fire, though. She knew they would. She had read the new pamphlet he had written from jail, the one the cook had snuck to her. Tom had argued that the hereditary monarchy was evil, that the American colonies should look to themselves and govern themselves, finding a way to embody freedom into government itself.

His words had echoed in her head ever since she learned that the trial was going badly: *"I ask, hath your house been burnt? Hath your property been destroyed before your face? Are your wife and children destitute of a bed to lie on, or bread to live on? Have you lost a parent or child by their hands, and yourself the ruined and wretched survivor? If you have not, then are you not a judge of those who have. But if you have, and still can shake hands with murderers, then are you unworthy the name of husband, father, friend or lover, and whatever may be your rank or title in life, you have the heart of a coward, and the spirit of a sycophant."*

He did not turn to look at her.

He had no reason to. For all he knew, she had turned him in to the government.

The voices droned, carrying on procedures she did not understand. She walked down the balcony, past the rows of seated people staring at her curiously. When she reached the edge of the balcony, the floor creaked. The magistrate looked up at her, as did the barristers. Finally, Tom looked.

She had forgotten the power in those eyes. He frowned, almost imperceptibly.

She opened her mouth to speak and he shook his head, at first gently, then forcefully. He did not want her to defend him. He wanted to become a martyr for some strange cause. A chill went down her back, a shock as sudden as the one she had felt when she had discovered that he was married.

He had written the pamphlet in prison and smuggled it

out, knowing that it would ruin his case, knowing that he would be found guilty of treason. He could no longer shake hands with murderers. He spoke up as he always had, and he wanted no one to make a mockery of his words . . .

. . . which she would have done had she told why her father had pushed so ardently for Tom's prosecution.

She closed her mouth and stepped away from the rail. The trial continued.

As she walked through the balcony door, she heard them sentence him to death.

> Franklin may be a good philosopher, but he is a bungling politician.
>
> —Samuel Adams

Franklin stood on the rise near the ancient oak. The body twisted from its branches, looking puny and defenseless. Somewhere Paine had lost his coat, his shoes, and his dignity.

They had needed Paine's voice. Franklin had a sense about these things. They had needed Paine's voice, and now they would not have it. Paine's arguments—the ones Franklin had heard on that afternoon not so long ago— would have made a difference in the colonials' cause.

It was truly Franklin's fault. Had he been paying more attention, he could have saved Paine from this. He could have saved them all. But he had been concerned with saving his own reputation in London and had lost his focus on the important things.

He had cost a man's life.

Who knew what other price they would pay?

> There are injuries which nature cannot forgive, she would cease to be nature if she did.
>
> —Thomas Paine, *Common Sense*

Her seasickness had eased. Prudence could walk on deck now and stare at the swirling ocean without losing the contents of her stomach. She had spent most of the trip so far in her stateroom, facing a bucket.

She wrapped her coat closer around her. Father's silver had brought a tidy price, as had her society gowns and shoes. That money, plus the trust she had cashed, would last her a long time in the colonies . . . provided she didn't squander it. Provided she found a printing press to accommodate her. She patted the pockets in her skirts. She kept the pamphlet on her. Tom's last one: *A Treatise on England, With Special Note to the American Colonies*. Sometimes the title seemed too long to her. Sometimes she wondered if a simpler title might do, one that accurately described the contents.

Common Sense.

Barry Malzberg has been the finest literary writer in the field of science fiction for the past quarter century; his output includes such classics as *Herovit's World*, *The Gamesman*, and *Galaxies*, plus more than twenty other novels and three hundred fifty short stories. His *Alternate Kennedys* novelette, "In the Stone House," was a 1993 Hugo nominee.

Over the years, Barry has from time to time collaborated with Jack Dann, Bill Pronzini, Carter Scholz, and myself—but never has he found a collaborator more attuned to his style and his perceptions than the brilliant Kathe Koja, herself the author of such major works as *The Cipher* and *Bad Brains*. During the past year, they have produced more than a dozen works of fiction together, of which this odd story of Dorothy Parker and Ernest Hemingway may well be the most powerful.

Literary Lives
by Kathe Koja
and Barry N. Malzberg

1. WRITING CALIBAN

"The truth makes me laugh but it doesn't make me happy."

The television interviewer had promised beforehand that he would stay off the subject but of course did not; why had she expected he would? *Betrayal is linked to process:*

she had written that decades ago; hadn't she? Or had she just read it somewhere, in one of *his* poems maybe, her dear dead husband; or maybe in Roethke, or Marianne Moore and what was the difference now? All of the words were the same eventually, all went into the cauldron. "You used to be a poet," the television man said, "long before you began your famous historical novels," holding up *Love's Saints*, a good long pan from the overwrought cover to her own face, composed and blameless as history itself. "Do you ever miss poetry?"

Did she ever miss poetry? Did she ever miss the sun coming through the open cracks, split like mummy's flesh in that terrible place in England, the look on his face shambling in at two, four, six A.M., claiming big business at the pub, the screams of rage that shook the baby when she would not, could not, be quieted, soothed, silenced by any means? Did she miss hitting her head on the beams in the cellar, the pain so sudden and flagrant that in the diminution of sight she could glimpse her own death like a friend on a faraway hill? Did she miss Daddy's touch in the damp night, fingers and bones, the rumor of displacement? And what else did she miss?

"Well," she said, shifting gently in the chair, in the dark silk shift tailored to conceal her body's increasing bulk, "I'm not sure how to answer that. It's as if you're asking me if I miss being twenty-one. Who could miss being twenty-one? But who would want to be sixty, given the choice? The poetry was a long time ago; then I started to write novels; I'm still writing novels," but of course this was getting her nowhere, she could see the man's long, open face shifting (as she shifted) toward a kind of studied confusion; he would ask another question soon, one she could not answer, one she did not wish to hear.

"I don't know," she said, to deflect that oncoming question, save the interview, stay on the road—Chicago next, then Detroit, hopskip to Kansas City and then she could rest, simply rest in Texas for a week before the ABA in San Francisco. Accommodate the publicists and save your life.

"I guess I miss everything," she said, smiling, remembering to smile, "but then again if you begin to think of this day by day, week by week, the extinguishing of your life by time, well then you simply can't deal with it at all, can you?" She picked up *Love's Saints* as if it was a bible, a breviary. "It's all here," she said. "Joan Garth faces that kind of dilemma, the loss of her youth, and comes through to deal with it in the way we all must. As best as I could, I made the story real." In Edwardian England, of course, but she did not add that. Everyone knew she was a novelist of that period, at least everyone who read this kind of thing, and those who didn't, who might be watching now in the torpid safety of their homes, might be more enticed *not* to think of it as a period novel. Anyway, it all came to the same thing in the end, true or false, ready or not, and the sky instead of sweeping, instead of the blue calm bowl was in fact inverted, as inverted as it had been: the window in London, her peering face: thirty years past and looking for some signal from that sky, some shaping or thrust of the heavens which would tell her, dear Lord, oh sightless God in heaven what to *do*. And of course she had seen the sign, she supposed, not at that time, in that gray place past hope or desperation but now she knew it: it was a camera, it was pointed at her.

"We'll be right back," the interviewer said, his smile embracing not only his guest but all those watching, as if on the very lip of purgatory but inclusive of heaven and hell, "to continue our conversation with the author of *Love's Saints*—" and her name, said twice, said with all the hectic charm of an incantation but she was not listening, she had closed her eyes and thought of her husband, if only he could see her now. Which in all essential senses of course he could not, the bastard having been killed with his wretched overdressed slut on a slick road in a dead night in the fall of 1963 and there was no way now to impress him with her latest and most decisive retrieval of her destiny, this hot new explosion of her success. He was gone, he could not hear, he could not see. Bastard, bastard. Dead and dead.

> The moon—the moon hard with light,
> The shuddering knife of time casting the womb—
> That broken space of storm and light
> Nestling the unborn—the unborn screams of self—
> Entering that dark and sudden chamber—
> Still poised, one blow, the speaking knife—

All that summer she had dreamed of doing it, *doing* it, put on the gas or drive the razor blade deep into her wrists to die like Marat, hiss and bubble, bubble and blood; she dreamed of her face, that stripped mask of self glinting from the open spaces of the bath or kitchen and it had been so palpable, so *close*—to die, to die—but the children had been insistent, the constant encroachment of their hungers and demands and then too what good would it have done? What good to her, to them, to him? He was home only rarely and then merely to deliver statements or demands, to shamble around in his smeared clothing complaining of publishers and colleagues and once or twice in the frantic insistence of flesh to indifferently fuck her; she would have been a whore for him, easy as a prostitute, she would have done anything but what good would it have done? She could not seize and hold his attention, and to do it in the oven, to lie back in the bath and squeeze the singing blood from her wrists seemed too dramatic a way to pull him into focus. Two young children, the weather, the flutter of the poetry like wings within her, like nesting insects, like simmering nerves and never even the time to properly plot and plan; it had been a near thing but, looking back on it so many years later, it had been a far thing too. There in the kitchen, or lying beside him as the lights went out, or out in the street with the pram and the toddler, the shops and the rain and the bitterness of the snow: her clenched face: the way others looked at her sometimes, it was all there,

she thought, she thought she knew, there for the asking
and the taking, all of her world one rebus in which one
message only could be divined and such divination possible to anyone, with eyes or without, the very blindest
could read it there. But: in the end she had never been as
serious as she had wanted to believe; she had never been
the Death Queen so much as an observer or poseur of the
situation. Blame the children; rail at the husband, her husband out at night fucking that strange and terrible woman
with her cheap sympathy and cheaper looks; think of the
gush and chill of the weather, of the lost country of her
girlhood, lost Daddy in the dirt and the regret, oh God,
the palpable regret . . . think and think of it, no point to
it, all of it one bleak dazzle to fill her with the distraction
of potential exit, but even then she had known that she
was going nowhere. Nowhere at all. Her life: milk and di-
apers and screams and the cold extracted lurch of hubby's
limbs as once or twice a week—when he could not find it
outside, when he had been driven home in failure or in
rage—he fucked her as awkwardly and distractedly as at
other times he wrote: poems, but nothing to rival hers;
even if he had lived he would have been nothing, nothing; even if he had not died, foot on the brake, brake as
useless as his bellowing, as the screams of the woman beside him; all of it as useless as her life had seemed: *that*
was her life then, ovens and the edges of knives, teasing
intimations of the forever impossible.

Well, it had been a long time ago, longer than a prison
sentence, and in that time she had read Edwardian novels
in the kitchen, stretched them over the table and read and
read her way through, trying to find an England that was
at least bearable. Certainly this London of the sixties was
not. It had been madness to come here, madness to go to
this place: *his* madness of course and his whim too but
what could she have done? In her sleep she heard their
cries after she had gone, queen of the night, riding that
farthest edge into extinction's glade and glad to be there,
glad; in the mornings she woke to slop food and wipe

noses and read books of the unraveling and genteel disaster of Empire, of Victoria's shabby legacy. The books had served her well in later times, those dull works of manners sexed up and leveled off; no one could say she had not been paying attention, no one could accuse her of that.

Of the other accusations, the other crimes, well: she had not been in the car, had she? And the police mechanics had found nothing afterwards at all. He with the bitch beside him had driven into that stone wall with jutting flowers wiping out the two of them instantaneously, broken neck, stabbed aorta, had gotten rid of all the problems with one explosion of glass in that later fall and had made her, then, necessarily focus her life into more practical channels; she got the copyrights too, for what they were worth, which in fact was not much, not so much as a reprint in thirty years, but now she dreamed of him, of seeing the bastard and saying I gave you my life but not my respiration, I gave you my self but never all my selves, and I am more famous than you, more famous than you or your little group of lunatic poets hanging out on both sides of the ocean could ever have dreamed or imagined; and rich, too, rich and on publicity tours for my Edwardian novels, rock-solid scholarship at that kitchen table, the light overhead like some dreary eye of judgment, and you were out fucking, my husband, my love, out greasing the skids, out flogging the deep and selfish humors of your desire, and what did it get you, hmm? What did it get you, or her either, that home-wrecking bitch, what in the end did it bring to you both? Why couldn't you have just paid a prostitute if you needed what I could not give? Why not make a prostitute of *me*? Whoring would be easy, she thought, far easier than the strangle her life had become: in and out, open and shut, leave the money and get out. Sometimes she walked the pram and the toddler down to where the girls worked, girls they called them though girls they were not, had not been for many years, and perhaps never: had she been a girl, too? Once? Since

Daddy died? Cheap cosmetics, purple lips like jelly and jam; tarts; it fit. Could she do that too? And what would he say if she did? *Make them pay*, that was it; or another adumbration of it, whatever it was. Sex and death: the great verities: the great building blocks of poetry, of art. And she there at the kitchen table with Edward and Victoria and the squeals and grunts of the children as outside in the big wide world he reenacted those verities, one by one, his unpaid prostitute at his side and under.

But: why now? Why think of him now? He put his car into the stone flowered wall a quarter of a century ago and there was no way, no way in which she could show him the elements of her triumph. The children, ah, the children, for whom she had hesitated, for whom she had refrained from the final leap, well: *they* knew, of course, all about her, about the books like a decorous well from which the greedy fountain of money had sprung; but if they read those books she did not know it; she never saw them anymore at all. He there in the ground and those round eyes looking at her, gazing at her from pram and nursie's arms: did you kill Daddy, Mummy? Did you tamper with the brakes, did you know they were leaking, dripping like a faucet, like a wound; did you mean for him to die? Did you kill him, Mummy? And the other lady, too?—In fact, after the funeral, she had not seen them alone for more than a day together; she had not now seen them at all for close to fifteen years.

> Here that blessed doll, pleading
> Dressed for Communion, small lips opening
> To receive the Host, the dark wafer
> And in the enfolding the big coping
> Of the immortal knife.

Dreaming of it, dreaming of the oven and the bath, that cup of dread and suffocation closing over her, the waxworks of herself slowly rising in the tinkle and scatter of light, the elevation, the dispensation. Dreaming his presence in the kitchen, to observe, to watch and smell and breathe the foul and terrible consequences of his lusts: she could see him in those moments, Daddy too, her daddy dangling in the sky: opening their mouths in warm astonishment, but somehow she could not get past that, could not move beyond their howls of grief and expiation; she could not see the children present in any of this and therefore she could not do it, did not do it, held back. The children restrained her; she hung amidst, within the little extrusions of their lives, as the flowers in that wall had waved gaily amidst the stones, as the blank and stupid wall had nonetheless made space for the flowers.

Held back, then, in that kitchen, thinking of the children, waiting for him at last to stumble in and fuck her. Scrawling her dull and desperate confessions, summer gone by and time inconstant, and then: the release, the shattering and the fire and she herself the only phoenix from that rubble, from the burned eviscerated car and oh yes, oh yes, she thought now, it had been a triumph, had it not? Had it not? Did you kill him, Mummy? Did I need to, darling?

"We're back," the interviewer said, making sure to say her name twice, identity and incantation, virgin and martyr and author of the best-selling *Love's Saints*: "Her sixth novel of Victorian England," and *Edwardian* she murmured but only to herself, what's the difference: Edward, Victoria, late century, early century, all of it coming together in a kind of surety of disaster, the same surety that drives cars into walls, that makes flowers explode in the moment of impact. Her thoughts had moved beyond this, she now supposed: under the stare of the camera she imagined herself again to be in that kitchen, looking at the skylight, thirty years younger and a hundred pounds lighter, looking for the face in the skylight which in surveyal would direct her; in this posture of attention she must at least have seen something, some indication of the future, something to gather her from there to here and keep her from a more drastic resolution, a reconstitution from which she could not, could never have recovered. The face not that of the interviewer, nor of her late husband lying in the mortuary, his restless sexuality, his cruelties stilled at last; not the face of his paramour, not the faces of his children, not even her father (although is that his eyebrow? his false Germanic pout?): no; no, it must have been her own face, her own stare and half-smile hovering in the eaves, guiding her toward this pacific and commercial destiny to which she could never on her conscious own have steered herself. "Yes," she said to the interviewer, "yes, I always wanted to be a novelist, the poetry was just a kind of girlishness, I think."

I loved him, she does not add; I loved him, but never quite enough to go into the oven, to kiss with blood the blade of the knife—and thought of the effect of these words, no real effect at all: who listens, who watches, who cares, who knows? Somewhere in the audience is a woman with a knife, a woman who at this moment is about to turn off the television and proceed to take lasting and riotous action, and if she could only reach that woman, she knew, she *knew* that she could tell her a thing or two, she could put on the brakes for good, but the images dwindled as they always did, cut by the switch, and she must sit poised now, devoid of that woman, of her own blackened resurrected history; thinking instead of the bovine, ever-pastoral features of Edward, stately step behind Victoria's casket, interment in the alley, interment of England. All life, she could have told him, all life is wrung from graves, all graves the dwindled residue of light, and she would have told him this, there in his own casket of history, would have told it to all the caskets, open and shut, ready or not, live or die, would have known it herself except that now, in the light, quite defiantly: she knows nothing that has not happened, sees nothing that cannot be seen.

After the lights had been cut, the set deserted, the good-

byes from the production assistant undergone, she refused
the offer of a limousine, said that she would walk back to
the hotel: she is not in New York that often now and it
was a pleasant day, she would get some air, some sunlight,
some sense of the day to come: but: "You've just been on
the *Morning Show*," the interviewer said, gazing at her
with genuine emotion at last, even if it was only the re-
flexive heat of narcissism. "Everyone will recognize you,
you're bound to get some attention you don't want."

His attention, now, unwanted, though she did not point
this out: that false solicitous warmth, the stupidity dis-
solving into that look, oh so blandly knowing, oh how
well did she know that look: a man's look, a husband's;
Daddy, she thought, Daddy I see it's you. But in that look
as interpreted by this interviewer there was none of the
lecherous, none of the dirt or the want, and it was that
lack which made her smile: did or could he understand
that in this America nothing, but nothing, was as invisible
as a sixty-year-old woman; if she was seen on the street by
strangers at all it would be only as a victim, and she was
not heading toward that part of town, and it was not
night. Oh, a sixty-year-old woman is a strange and queru-
lous thing, a hank of hair, a chip of bone, a swaddle of
some shape under swaddled clothes . . . but she said none
of this, no lectures from the Edwardian novelist; it had
been a long, long time since she had felt the need or reflex
to instruct the world.

She left the studio then, good-byes produced and more
firmly this time, emerged from the exit onto Fifty-second
Street into the cold indifferent blaze of the morning.
Crosstown toward the Parker-Meridian, feeling vaguely
unsteady and not at all noticeable in her heels and drying
makeup, and at Fifth Avenue, just south of Trump Tower,
saw four women, two black, one white, one vaguely Spanish: young, young and apparently soliciting the commut-
ers, in the twinkling of the morning light and rush hour,
a covey of little birds beckoning. They murmured, shook
themselves in their halter tops and wraps, shook their

tight little asses under the short skirts, and made kissing
gestures toward male pedestrians, almost all of whom ignored them, one or two of whom seemed to be genuinely
shaken. Oh those poor girls, she thought pointlessly, those
poor girls, but it was not the prostitutes she was sen-
timentalizing—if they even were hookers; maybe this was
some bizarre posturing for a photographer, a perfume ad,
cosmetics or pantyhose or shoes—but she herself the object of this inner sorrow: a thin woman in a wrap of a different kind, looking into an oven in London thirty years
ago, thinking of a vast and narrow crevice into which she
could insert herself, that Freudian insertion, that deep and
aching divide and the image of this lost self, powerfully
superimposed over the prostitutes, seized her like cramp,
like the teeth of the knife, like gas in the lungs: and: Oh
sisters, sisters, she wanted to say, your faces filled with
light, but there was no light there, no light in the oven,
darkness in and out, above and below, and surely hookers
least of all would look at a sixty-year-old woman. Maybe
that was the answer, she thought, maybe I should have
done that: taken it in and in, taken the hammering tools
of strangers into myself instead of that symbolic reverse-
fuck

—but she pushed the thought away, she did not understand prostitutes, never had; her kind had been of the
amateur and (God knows) insufficient variety, and now
she was stiff and dry, bone in a bone-season.

And hammer down that roof, tighten the nails
Bring the summer house to coffin size—
The grateful boards of wood embracing
The Dead Queen as Dead Queen always lies.

Embrace the moon; capsize the dark
And ride, ride, ride—your dull face
No wound now, nor then, but panelled, hard
As the Dead Queen's expunged and drifting lace.

I know nothing of that, she thought, turning back now, turning toward home, the hotel, the way things were and would continue to be: nothing of the hook and the stroll, in, out and gone; I know nothing of these sisters or Victoriana, of England early or late, I know nothing, nothing at all but of this: *this* I know: my face on a screen, that larger impersonal prostitution, cold light filling the air with the reconstructed face of the woman who knows nothing and cares not at all: about Edward *nor* Victoria, dead husbands and their equally dead lovers, prostitutes early or late or never at all. A hand motion to the hookers, a kiss to those other lost and expelled children, and she was gone: sixty years old, Victoria's gait, the lobby of the hotel before her as impersonal as Westminster, as anonymous as the changing face of the trick, the john, that other endless lover who comes in the dark or the daylight, who comes eternally like death between the maiden's endless thighs.

2. O TEMPORA! O WHORES!

Well, there it was: she had never been able to handle her liquor, Woollcott had been quite right, you *think* you can handle your liquor but that's just another part of being drunk, Dottie, the old twist had said, and he was right. Fooling herself, even in the old days: she had lied a lot, smiled a lot; party-girl Dottie, mouth open and the glass always close enough to smell, sniff, sniff, get hold of the booze, gin and tonic, bubble and cough. Spit on her lips, then, the smell of old cosmetics, spit on her lips now too, and she could no longer escape that knowledge, the reek of her dressing gown, the smell of semen on the bed dried to a stain like a question mark, dried in the shape of a curse: vomit behind her unreliable teeth, what remained of them, and the man there in the bathroom, crouched with pants around his knees and awkwardly wiping up, slopping the rag between his legs, and what would he say

now if he knew how many men had used that rag, how
would he act, what would he think? Yards and yards of
seed, sperm, spunk, jism, seventeen years on the stroll
(came to it pretty late in life too, thirty-nine when she
started, a beautifully preserved fifty-six now), and she still
liked to use the words, it gave her a thrill. It was a thrill
to be a bad Jewish girl, more of a thrill than to be a good
one (although she had tried that too): bad girl there in the
bed, in and out, up and down, straight and narrow, make
them shoot, and after all what fault was it of hers if times
were bad and things had gone sour? She had not caused
it, any of it, she had barely participated beyond the necessary token of friction, he crouched there above her in that
simian attitude, he had done all the hovering but there it
was anyway as Benchley would have said: the fall, the
crash, the smash of crockery all around, the spanked and
slivered explosion of a tumbling come and there at the
bottom lay Dottie, perpetrator of all this beauty, still trying
to be cute.

But enough of this self-pity or hilaria and that was all
it came to anyway, never mind that they were the same.
Weren't they? Why don't you ask that nice man there with
his wet rag and his expended load, most of it swimming
in her now, good thing she was almost a decade past the
change and had a cast-iron cunt and a womb to match,
her lone early miscarriage evidence of her unfitness. Nothing fertile about me but my imagination, kids, she liked to
say, she used to say a lot in those days to all the boys and
the few girls stupid enough to try to compete with her as
active toy, Dottie's just as fertile as Thurber's ideas and
they had laughed at that, Thurber too. They had all
laughed for quite a while until about the time Hoover
went away the laughs stopped, at least for her. Now she
did not talk at all except to herself, the witty stuff and that
only under her breath like a body under a sheet, the
sheets of this bed, in this workplace which could have
been any room in any roiling hotbed motel as was this
one, as this man could have been and was any man, every

man, all the men groaning and grunting in the bathroom, wiping himself clean of her, yanking himself shut. Paying her beforehand in *change*, for God's sake, thirty-five 1949 dollars in quarters and dimes and half-dollars, but that was the only thing that made him unusual. Otherwise he was just like the rest of them, so cheap, so dry and humorless, mean-spirited and tiny of heart, and she wanted to lie back in that bed, lie back like Cleopatra, like the Queen of the Night, and say something funny: and sharp: and cutting. And quick, oh she had always been so quick, even when she was slow: cut to the quick, Dottie, to the bone. All the way in, part the meat and slit the nerves which felt nothing anyway, how could they; how can you? How *can* you there with your miserable little quarters and your stinky little hankie and your belt closed up nice and tight like you were never going to take it out again. As someone had once taken it out for *you*, had in an act of tumble and dry horror made this man. How can you stand there now with your belt closed and your smile so silly and open, you creep, you bastard, you shitheel, you *john*?

Well, now. Listen to Little Miss Highpockets here, playmate of the gods and just as cute as a trick or at least as cute as the tricks that she had had. She just couldn't stand it anymore, that was all. Benchley's whining and Woollcott's belly and bloomers under his pants, big foul mushroom inside and out; the Marx Brothers and Kaufman with their grabass and coconuts and Crowninshield hustling her copy and her ass at the same time, humping her over the desk and then sending her out to the Algonquin to play Queen of the Night for the wits at the Round Table. She couldn't *stand* it anymore, a smart little Jewish girl with too much whiskey stranded in the Garden of Allah, oh God help her at the Garden of Allah with Alan sniffing around for boys after the lights were out and the tenth-rate copyboys over at MGM offering to take her up to the mountains, show her the heights. It had arrived with the silent thunder of true insight: *I'm a whore*, she had thought when Alan, caught once too often

in the wrong place, had said We'd better get married
again, Dottie; I know you want me and of course I love
you and she had looked at him then and thought, Well,
shit, if I'm going to be a whore, if they're going to make
a whore out of me then I'll *be* a whore, nice and honest
for the first time in my life; I'll go out there and *hook* for
God's sake and get some equity. Drunk in the Garden and
she had put the idea away, tried to smother it, but after
fleeing East again, after dumping Alan in a gritting shriek
of revulsion and anticipated collusion, after the last fuck
from some midget in a studio cap who turned out to work
in the lunchroom, after yet one more desperate fumbling
grope with hapless Benchley upstairs in the Algonquin—he couldn't take his clothes off and he couldn't take
them on, the son of a bitch simply could not move—the
idea, luminescent on five drinks in the Garden, glowing
again in the afterimage of Benchley's humping the walls
and chairs trying to find the courage to go home or kill
himself . . . the idea had assumed along with its glitter an
uncommon hilarity . . . well, then, I'll try it, she thought,
make the honest gesture for once. She knew all about it
anyway, had even written it down: Hazel Morse, Big
Blonde, that alleyway stride into parties and presents
slipped under the pillow and at last outright hooking. She
knew; she knew nothing. Trying it once as a metaphor, as
a gesture, she did it twice to punish herself for having
done it once and then again because—well, because she
liked it, it was honest, they put the money down, you
spread, they shot, you closed, they stunk, everybody
washed and they were gone. No line-of-the-day for the
boys at the table with their spilled drinks and crumbled
crackers, no tossing of tits under the cloth to keep
Crowninshield's attention, the stupid bastard, just take it
and put it out and be done with it. There was something
ridiculously clean, final, perfect about these consumma-
tions, and they fit so well into a Depression economy.
Prosperity was just around the corner, and in the meantime you sold your little apples.

No double-life for Dottie, she turned out as Woollcott had warned her way back to have talent but no scruples, a risky combination and one which had ended in her virtual undoing, at least from their viewpoint, that elegant Round Table standard. She had worked it on the streets for a little while but it was not danger she wanted, so soon she had her regulars and a list of phone numbers, soon enough there were referrals and recommendations. If she thought of them at all, Woollcott and the others, it was with a grim wonder: it had been easy, so easy to rid herself of those people and Alan too that she was stunned that they had ever had that kind of mosquito netting around her. Whim or whimsy turning out to be the guiding passion of her life; once she had promised herself that a year of this would send her back to Ohio after a stop at the clinic, but she had instead lasted seventeen.

Seventeen. And Woollcott had died, and Benchley and Crowninshield and then Mencken stunned by a stroke into long silence, Thurber furious and blind, and the Marxes out in Hollywood propagating their seed, Ross dead, Shawn in, the war come and gone and the bomb and the Berlin aircraft and here was little Dottie still on the stroll: they knew, had always known, where to find her if they had bothered to look. *Shows talent but lacks concentration,* and see how wrong *that* was, fourth-grade report card and oh, if they could just look at her now. Lacks concentration? I have nothing but concentration, she thought.

Let me tell you what I've learned in forty years, honey—
You might as well laugh because nothing is funny.

"See you later," the man said, and she rolled to her side to look at him, breasts looser and damper than the Big Blonde's had ever been in the ugly dressing gown she had slipped into, put the lid on the box while he was shaking himself off. Cheap blue imitation satin, cheap red ribbon as smarmy as a heart, and as he opened the door she opened her mouth, wanting to say something, anything, something to tell him what he was with his quarters and his dimes and his hankie but the liquor smell (hers or his? difference, please?) overwhelmed her, the subtle stench of semen and sweat and merry old booze from the bottom of a bottle, and as the door closed Dottie vomited, vomited in small bursts all over the floor and the empty bottle and the rag rug beside the bed.

Head in a lurch, oh Benchley had beseeched her *Get me out of this Dottie, get me out, make me whole*—she who could do nothing for herself was being asked to make these wretched men whole, *oh make me want you* Alan had cried to her, *make it right, make it full again,* all those pleas and screaming and for *what*? The Algonquin Round Table was the whorehouse of the world she had told them all back in 1930 before that second trip to Hollywood, that second collision with Alan and it was true, it was true but what did that make her?—oh her head was sick, *she* was sick, swimming through sickness to lean slowly back and she tried to think of something to say if only to herself, something to cheer her, something to make herself laugh in this pit of wretchedness into which—admit it, no denials you fifty-six-year-old hooker, the Berlin aircraft and the Dottie Parker downdraft in the same year—she had so evidently sunk. Where was her wit? Where was that little smile we loved so well?

> O life is joyous, life is sweet
> Life is a burst of hilaria
> It grants your wants and tender needs . . .
> And Jesus is King of Bavaria.

And here we go again, *whoops*! and into the swing shift: he smelled like all the rest of them, damp and stale only worse because it was afternoon now and afternoon had never been her time of day; past girlhood she could barely remember an afternoon when she had not been hung over except for the time in the hospital with the miscarriage, and maybe when Benchley and she had gone off for their brief, teetotaling scuttles. The thundering grumble of the trucks below, the cursing of the drivers and the scurrying of all the drunken office workers hurrying back to their enlarging stupor—oh, she should have given up the afternoon trade she supposed, she was too old for this three-a-day nonsense, iron cunt, iron womb, couldn't take it anymore . . . and for example this one here with his gritty hands and workingman's boots, he was nobody's sure thing, nobody's money down. Not even his own. She asked him to pay first, there with his hands hanging loose before him like the knot in a hangman's rope, her eyes barely open and there he was, knock-knock-knocking on her chamber door. Referral, friend of a friend's friend in from overseas, needs a quick afternooner, and all of this so fast, she without the time to brush her hair or get a drink, swab the decks before the fleet weighs in, heigh-ho and off we go: and what do *you* want she had almost asked, you silly old thing with your Santa Claus beard, but saved her mot juste because really, why ask? What did any of them want? The same thing. They were all alike really except that they were all different, something that any good hooker learned early in the game. Alan wanted this and Silly Old Bob wanted *that* and the sailors off the Bremen and the boys in their summer dresses wanted something else. Maybe at the end of it all lay the same grind and dwindle, but nonetheless—

Nonetheless she asked him to pay first, lying there on the bed with one eye open, my gal Sal in the afternoon. "Put the money on the table," she said.

"Don't you know who I am?" he said. "Don't you know my name?"

"Sure I know your name," she said, "your name is legion. Your name is john. Put the money on the table."

Some pay up, and some pay down
Some pay in flowers, or jewelry, or gown

Some pay in promise or chance of renown
But if they pay in love then you'd better leave town.

And after all it was the same thing, prepaid or not: in
and out, grunt and mumble and the scent of armpit and
something stale for breakfast, his mouth close to her
warm ear muttering staccato, baritone cheeping to remind
her of her lost canary, his cage still empty beneath its
faded carapace of elderly berets and scarves: Onan, she
had called him, because he spilled his seed upon the
ground. John here was not spilling it on the ground but it
was close; he was having real trouble down there, keeping
it out, keeping it *in*, well she knew tricks for that and she
gave him a little giveback, a few dirty words in the ear
while still thinking in absent fondness of Onan the bird:
that had been funny but it hadn't been funny for a very
long time, would not be funny again soon unless she
could do something about the weather and the nature of
the city and the political situation: forget the grunts and
mumbles, the sonority of their crooning, their hands on
her poor tired breasts in the evening and the morning and
these awful afternoons. But a girl had to do something,
had to live, didn't she? Especially when she was on the
stroll for seventeen years, was no longer a girl, especially
when the weeping walls of her limbs and her body told
her news each morning, each terrible afternoon that she
was unwilling to hear but unable to escape. She was
reaching the end of the line, end of the line for Dottie, she
had better do something different and do it soon before
her cunt turned into solid iron or one of these animate
clods of earth crushed her completely to the silence and
the unattractive consistency of dust.

There. *There.* He was finished and not a moment too
soon or late. Was it good for you too? Don't ask. She felt
the trickle, the proud evidence of his closure. Forty-five,
fifty years old, this was some ceremony to him; he probably saw the shroud in the wall as he plunged.

Well, a man had to do what a man had to do and so did

she but first she had to get rid of this one, this particular
clod, and now that his load was dumped—and how long,
really, had it taken, but then how long does it take to
die?—she shoved at him, ungentle hands on his back and
"Up," she said, "go on, get moving. You can't stay here all
day. This isn't a twenty-four-hour luncheonette, egg
creams to go."

"Wait a minute," he said. "Wait."

"Up," she said. "Get up."

So he got up, reared, looked at her on the bed then,
dense beard, narrowed slant of stare and of cocked arms.
"You don't know who I am?" he said, stabbing at his wet,
shrunken genitals with one accusing finger. "No, I guess
you don't. I'm Ernest Hemingway," he said. "Dottie, I'm Ernest Hemingway."

She stared at him. "Well so you are," she said. "How
about that? Papa himself. Isn't that surprising? What
brought you into town? How did you know where I was?"

"Word gets around," he said. Drip, drip like a runny
nose, an infected case of sinusitis; wipe that, she wanted
to say, for God's sake use the rag; she was relieved when
he reached for the sheet and began to rub it across himself. "You weren't hard to find. People thought you were
dead, you know, but I know better. There are still plenty
of people who know."

"All right," she said, "so there are plenty of people who
know. I know, for one." I know something about you now
too, Papa, it's not all toros and cojones now is it anymore?
But I'm not bringing that up; once in a day was enough.
Once in a lifetime would be enough. "It's very nice to see
you," she said, "but you're going to have to go, Ernest. I
keep a tight schedule." And a loose cunt, she thought. Go
away Ernest, she thought, it's enough. It's no shame to see
you, reminder of an old, old life, but no pleasure either,
no matter what you think. "You got what you came for,"
she said. "Now you can say you fucked Crowninshield's
favorite, the belle of the Round Table. So go."

"You don't remember," he said, "you don't understand.

I just finished this novel, it's called *Across the River and Into the Trees*. It's not good but I don't blame you for that. Don't think that's why I'm here. I don't blame you for any of this. It's something else."

Was he crazy? Sometimes they talked crazy and you could get very nervous unless you were in absolute control of the situation. "I'm sorry the novel isn't good, Ernest," she said. "My writing hasn't been so hot recently either. Not since 1929 as a matter of fact. But that's no reason to suffer. I mean, you've had a wonderful career, right?—the cover of *Life*, everybody knows you."

He kept wiping himself, would not stop, a racheting compulsive gesture like an animal grooming itself in the deep woods, cleaning out pellets of shit, maybe, from some hidden place. "We went to bed together in '22," he said. "I guess I can't expect you to remember that. You were coming back from the magazine after work and stopped in a bar and I was in New York to see O'Brien about putting 'My Old Man' into *Best American Short Stories*. It was the only story that wasn't in Hadley's trunk. She lost that trunk of stories, that bitch, to pay me back in advance."

Perhaps it was in escrow, but she didn't say that; she said nothing, but not because she had nothing to say. Ignoring her silence, he went on, talking about a bar in the Village, he picked her up or maybe she picked him up.

"I would hope so," she said. "Youth is such a gallivanting time, isn't it? But what does—"

"We went back to your apartment," Hemingway said. He dropped the sheet, some curling raft of peeled skin. She could see the stain there. "Some two-roomer in the Village with a mattress on the floor."

That had been just before Alan, she remembered, four apartments in the Village but only one with a mattress on the floor, gray-striped ticking, cockroaches as shy as virgins loosened up on cheapest gin. "Okay," she said, "so it was on the floor."

"I was drunk," he said, "I was always drunk then. Now

too, but in a different way. You were drunk, too. I wasn't so drunk that I couldn't talk but maybe it was bad enough. Do you remember?"

"No," she said. "I tell the truth always unless I can't. I cannot pretend to remember. There were a lot of men in those days," and now too, she thought, it's such a gay and merry round. "A lot of men."

"I couldn't get it up," he said. "I tried and tried but nothing happened. You offered to use your hands but that didn't work either and you wouldn't use your mouth. You said," not gazing into the distance, most true and terribly there, present, bilocated, this room and that room, "you said you used your mouth only to tell jokes."

"Oh, *that's* why I'm not funny anymore," she said.

"Shut up," but quietly. "I don't need your mouth now. After a while you stopped trying. You pointed at me and you started to laugh. Look at it, you said, it's so tiny, it's so sad. Is she not sure what she wants? you said. Would she like to see a menu? You laughed and laughed. You wouldn't stop."

"I laughed a lot then," she said. "I laughed because nothing was funny. It was nothing personal, Ernest."

"You didn't say that then," he said. Uneven on his feet, weaving on the floor and "You ruined my life, you bitch. I couldn't get it up for three years after that, one drunken mistake but you laughed and I lost it. I lost a marriage, maybe two marriages. By the time I could get it up again steady the war was coming and the booze had broken me down."

"You got it up now," she said levelly, folding her hands before her. "It worked now. So why are you complaining?"

"Sometimes it works," he said, "and sometimes it doesn't. Mostly it doesn't but I'm fifty and I've been drunk for thirty years so what is there to expect? But you ruined my life, you bitch, because you took my best years and my wives from me and you left me with nothing."

"Look," she said, seeing a pattern in the way the light struck him, the unforgiving afternoon light against his skin, his dirty beard, the iron pallor and the thready veins. He was all droop now, balance gone; there was something in his face that made her think of twilight, of the idea of survival; it was so hard to tell the difference sometimes between twilight and dawn. "Look, I'm sorry. I'm terribly sorry, really. Youthful indiscretion and all that. The twenties were a strange time, and Franklin Pierce Adams was giving me hell about them as well as various other men. If I made fun of your prick I'm truly sorry but he seems to still be around and you see what happened to *me* so by any reasonable judgment I got what I deserved too, don't you see? So we'll call it even, Ernest, and I want you to go. I'm sorry the book is a stinker but at least it's a book. I couldn't do a novel for shit, and now I don't do anything except fuck, and how long can that go on?"

"Not much longer," he said. Into the heap of discarded clothing, hand into a pocket, hey-presto and out with something shiny: a knife. "Oh come on, Ernest," she said. "This is ridiculous. This is just too silly."

Naked, he examined the knife: the hunter, Priapus wilted and enraged, turning the blade this way and that to make it glint in the exhausted midtown sun. "I dreamed of you," he said. "For years and years I dreamed of that laugh, that pointing finger. Calling it *she*. Mocking me." He showed her the knife. "The novel stinks," he said, "and that's not all. You stink too and your filthy room and your filthy underwear and your whole fucking life and my life too." He came toward her with the knife. Dust moved through the air, eddied in the light like schools of tiny fish disturbed by the passing of something deep below. "I made myself a promise," he said, "it might have been in a bullring or maybe when I was on the front in '42 again, I said if I survive this I'm going to track down that bitch, that stupid mocking bitch and kill her." He turned the knife again. "What do you think of that, Dottie?" turning the knife again, his motions slow and somehow weary, the small bag of his genitals more pathetic than ever but this was not, she thought, something she ought to mention just now.

"Ernest," she said, "Ernest, I'm frightened now, if you wanted to frighten me you have succeeded. This is the end, Ernest, please leave my room. Take back your money if you want, call it repayment of an old debt but go. Go because I'm frightened and in a minute I'm going to scream. Oh I'm going to scream and they'll all come running, I pay protection money here." I have no protection, she thought, they wouldn't protect me if I was to fall on the front desk with a heart attack, they don't even see me when I pay my bill, nobody sees women like me, fifty-six-year-old whores. Oh, she thought, as he came forward, I didn't expect this, no, I envisioned much but never this at all. Things like this just do not happen to clever little Jewish girls no matter *how* much they piss off Woollcott or Harold Ross, no matter who's using the pencil. And now—

"Is it big?" he said. Closer now, the knife at an angle so absurdly penile that she was going to have to laugh, oh please, please don't let me laugh. More dust in the air; it seemed she could taste it, a curious taste as flat as the scent of semen. "Is it big and hard? This is how you like it, isn't it?" This is not happening, she thought, and looking away from the twin grotesqueries of the knife and his slack and cunning face, looking down to see her visible heartbeat, the lolloping rhythm of terror and maybe her body knew something that she didn't but if her body was so smart then why was she here in the first place? "Is it big and hard enough for you?" he said, tilting it ever closer, his face not crazy or even angry or even it seemed much interested at all: but his eyes were not good to look at: she looked at the knife instead. "Say something, Dottie," leaning close to her now, was it her own dry perfume she smelled on his flesh? "Say something, for Christ's sake."

Say something, Dottie, Dottie make a joke, crack wise, quip and patter and it was all why she was here, wasn't it? Wasn't it? This room and this man, this hour and this knife? "Ernest," she said, closing her eyes at last, "Ernest, go away."

She felt the impact under her breastbone, rammed in like a carving knife, opening her up. She felt her blood expanding and leaping, fifty-six years of clot expunged and sizzling and "Hard enough?" Ernest said, "how hard is it *now*?" and dimly the knife slid free, went in again, in and out and "Oh yes," he said, "now you've got what you like and here and here and here" and she felt it digging in, the insistence of the blood as it laved the knife, the seas incardine reaching, the fingerings, the waxworks of blood and she felt herself receding, suddenly and absolute, felt the shiver of something inside that was not the knife—

Some give you life, and some give you breath
Some settle for candy or flowers
But the one you want most is the one you don't meet
But just once: and does *he* pass the hours!

Laura Resnick, winner of a 1989 award for her romance
novels and nominated for the 1992 and 1993 Campbell
Award for science fiction, has led the kind of life writers
are expected to lead (and so seldom do). She has been a
waitress, a kennel attendant, a teacher of foreign lan-
guages, a singer, and of course a writer, and has lived in
England, France, Sicily, and Israel, as well as the U.S.A.
As this introduction is being written, she is somewhere
between Mauritania and Cameroun, at least four weeks
from a post office or an indoor bathroom, on a seven-
month trip through Africa.

Laura has always had a uniquely skewed way of viewing the world, as the following story will demonstrate. . . .

Saint Frankie
by Laura Resnick

Hallelujah, brothers and sisters! Have you heard the righ-
teous news? Have you heard atell that that there Pope
what calls hisself Gregory IX is gonna canonize our dearly
departed friend and comrade, Brother Frankie Bernar-
done? Let the church say amen! Amen!

Brothers and sisters, it's a fine thing indeed when a dedicated Christian like our Brother Frankie is fully recognized by the powers-that-be for all his hard work. And I
do say the words "Brother Frankie" from my heart. Yes,
from my very heart. For you may not know this, my
friends, but I knew Brother Frankie from the time he was
no bigger than knee-high to a plague of locusts. Yes, indeed, Brother Frankie and me, we was raised together. We
breathed the same sweet mountain air of Assisi, we
chewed the same fat, we swapped the same bull, we shot
the same breeze. Heck, we very nearly even suckled the

same mother's milk—but then our mamas sobered up and sorted things out right quick.

And such a fine, upstanding young lad was Brother Frankie that I did not mind, no, I did not care a free Eden fig, that his daddy was so much richer than mine. For you see, Frankie's pappy was in *commerce*! Yes! He *traded* for gold! He *traded* for silver! He *traded* for dinars and shekels and ducats and other types of foreign money which a decent Christian gentleman ought not to touch unless he be collecting it on behalf of the Lord.

So believe you me, I was not jealous that Frankie's robes were made of ermine and velvet while mine were made of sackcloth. I was not jealous that Frankie's family ate meat and cheese while we ate porridge three times a day. No, indeed, I was not jealous when Frankie rode a sturdy mare to school while I walked. And why was I not jealous, my friends? *Why?* Because I knew that the Kingdom of Heaven awaited us all! And soon, my friends, soon we'll *all* wear robes of ermine and velvet! We'll *all* eat meat and cheese at every meal, and we'll *all* ride a sturdy mare, or its most appealing equivalent. For does it not say so in the Bible? Let the church say amen! Amen!

Now Frankie and me, we grew into handsome young sparks together back there in Assisi, and I do not believe I will be stricken speechless for speaking immodestly when I say those local ladies noticed us, they did notice us right well. So Frankie and me, we saw our great work in this world was beginning, and our first duty was to bring a little joy into the lives of all those poor girls and widows what was deprived of their menfolk due to civil warfare and sickness. Hard work it was, too, my friends, comforting all those sinners and leading those stray lambs straight into the fold, but we was young and virile and well-suited to the task.

Then one day we heard the Calling. I say "we," but I do not deny that it was Frankie alone who heard the Voice. There he was in the Church of San Damiano, examining that empty collection box, when an image of Christ spoke to him. Yes, my friends, spoke in a voice just like Father Martini's—who was the pastor at the time. And Christ said to Frankie, "Francis, repair my falling house."

Well, now, Frankie asked me how we could go about this because, truth to tell, we didn't know too much about carpentry and masonry and suchlike. We reckoned that someone else would have to do all the work, much as we'd surely like to do it ourselves. But where would the money come from? Sad to say, we had just lost all of ours betting on the annual horse races over in Siena; we later found out that the monk who took our money had fixed the race. There are sinners everywhere, my friends! Be warned!

So we set to cogitating on this here problem of raising money for San Damiano, who, being in a poorly way after eleven centuries of death, wasn't in no shape to take up a collection hisself. And then the answer came to us! Just as plain as day, the idea struck us like a bolt of heavenly lightning! Hallelujah! We decided to sell a bale of goods from Frankie's daddy's warehouse to pay for the repairs.

Well, grateful as I reckon Christ and San Damiano was, Frankie's father didn't see things in quite the same celestial light. In short, my friends, he disowned Frankie. Disinherited him! Threw him out into the streets and sent him away penniless. Seeing as how the old man, lacking the true Christian spirit, was also pressing charges against me, I decided to join Frankie, and we left Assisi.

That was about the time that Frankie wed Lady Poverty, as y'all may have heard recounted before. Well, brothers and sisters, truth was, she wanted to wed *me*; but I could see Frankie was plumb sick at heart over that girl, so I let him have her. We kinda intended to head straight off for Rome then, hoping to get work roping in sinners for the Big Guy, the Head Honcho, that there Pope in Vatican City. That place was a wild, wide open town in those days, full of handy poisonings and secret murders that kept everyone gossiping, and many soiled doves what surely needed comforting upon being deprived of their financial security on account of those selfsame murders and poisonings. Yes, Vatican City was a place just crying out for the strong hearts and redeeming spirits of two fine young Christian fellas.

But things didn't quite work out that way. Lady Poverty, as you might expect, commenced to having a lot of hungry little'uns all at once. So we was kinda stuck in the backwaters around Assisi for several years, until she finally took a breather.

However, Brother Frankie wasn't the type to let hisself go unnoticed, even though he was living so far out in the boondocks that even the Crusaders never came a'calling for a free meal. No indeed, my friends! It wasn't too long before that there Pope Innocent—who had some nerve calling hisself such a name, considering his lifestyle— hired us on to be roving preachers of Christ.

Truth to tell, my friends, it wasn't even Mr. Innocent's idea. No, that scoundrel ignored every one of our job applications, swearing up, down, and sideways that he'd never let two insolent young fellas like us get a foot in the door of the Kingdom of Heaven. But I say to you, my brothers and sisters, that the meek shall inherit, and they shall even earn interest on that inheritance. For lo, there came unto us, way up in our unheated home in those bitter cold mountains, a set of drawings of that Pope Innocent in very a compromising position with one of God's four-legged creatures. And funnily enough, upon being told what we intended to do with those very interesting drawings, whose veracity could be guaranteed by their creator, Mr. Innocent decided to grant us a couple of regular salaried jobs with full benefits.

And so Brother Frankie and I became Friars Minor. We founded our headquarters at Santa Maria degli Angeli— still near Assisi, since those Swiss boys guarding Vatican City had been given stab-to-kill orders regarding me and Frankie. Mr. Innocent wasn't the forgiving sort, even though he knew when his hands was tied; but, heck, those drawings made it seem like he *liked* having his hands tied. However, brothers and sisters, ours is not to snicker and judge; ours is but to get the paycheck and grub.

Well, now, our assignment as Friars Minor was to call people, high and low, rich and poor, good and evil, pretty and ugly, wise and silly as all get-out, to live a life of faith, contemplation, and penitence. We was to encourage them to renounce property, worldly learning, and job promotions.

As you might expect, no one paid us no never mind.

We wrestled with this problem for five or six days, at least, before reckoning that if God wanted folks to give up all their worldly possessions, He surely didn't expect them to do it without a little stronger encouragement than a few words preached at roadside on market day. And while we was examining our failure to enlighten all these folks sufficiently, we realized that we'd also neglected to tell them what to do with all their money and property and suchlike when they gave it up.

Well, I tell you, my friends, Brother Frankie, may his soul rest in eternal peace and harmony, was a doggone, genuine, out-and-out, ecclesiastical genius! Yes! For Brother Frankie came to me the very next morning and told me he'd had another vision! A vision from on high! Let the church say amen! Amen!

For Brother Frankie had a divine revelation! A divine message, I say, delivered from the very lips of Yahweh himself! And the Lord said unto Brother Frankie, "Yea, as thou art My servant, I command thee to *take* all the wealth that folks don't want to turn over of their own free will! I command thee to *take* their gold and jewels and riches! I command thee to *take* their fine velvet clothes and rich ermine trimmings, leaving only their linen undergarments for decency's sake! For *you* are the servant of the Lord, *you* are the head Friar Minor, and *you* are chosen to bring all of this wealth into the bosom of Mother Church." Hallelujah!

Well, Brother Frankie and me, we didn't waste no time,

but immediately commenced to doing the Lord's work on earth. We armed all the lesser Friars Minor with sturdy clubs, and that very same morning we fell upon a group of sinners who refused, upon being asked politely, to give up their gold and jewels and fine raiments to the church. Naturally, we encountered one or two problems, since those noble folks, being the ones with all the money and suchlike, also happen to travel with a plentiful supply of knives and swords and things. But there is no doubt in my mind, brothers and sisters, no, none at all, that Brother Ugolino went straight to his celestial reward on that victorious morning.

Well, after the first couple of times, during which a few other minor Friars met their Maker a trifle sooner than intended, it was almost surprising how easy it became to liberate wealth from those what wasn't willing to donate it freely. So we knew, my friends, yes, *knew* that Brother Frankie's vision was a true one and that this was indeed the Lord's work. For does it not say in the Bible, "The silver is Mine, and the gold is Mine, saith the Lord of hosts." And we knew whose Guiding Hand made us successful, for as Brother Frankie often liked to remind us, it says in Deuteronomy, "Thou shall remember the Lord thy God; for it is he that giveth thee power to get wealth."

So naturally we harkened unto these words and remembered to always give a generous cut of the takings to Yahweh—via the bank in Vatican City and the priest what called hisself "God's banker."

Then other passages from the Bible just seemed to leap right out at us, instructing us on how to continue collecting wealth for the Kingdom of Heaven without losing quite so many Friars in the process. For does it not say in the Bible, "They that will be rich fall into temptation and a snare." Following the Lord's hint, we set a snare on the highway, and pluck my eyes out if it didn't catch us a nasty old duchess lady wearing a fortune in emeralds.

Well, things was going so smoothly after a while that folks round the Appenines starting comparing us to a band of merry men what made their reputation in a similar way some years back in England. Y'all may have heard that those brothers was led by an English noble fella what named hisself after his headgear.

Indeed, Pope Innocent even decided to quit the feud he'd been carrying on with us ever since that there incident with the drawings, which took him a long and spiteful time to get over. He told the Swiss boys that we didn't need no killing on sight after all, and then he invited us to Vatican City. Mr. Innocent and Mother Church was mighty pleased with us, for Brother Frankie and I, I say with all modesty, was frankly responsible for paying for all sorts of necessary improvements to Vatican City. Using the riches we sent, they installed new ceilings on all the buildings and put some decent rushes on all the floors and painted some cheerful frescoes of dancing girls on those grim and dreary stone walls. They improved their menu quite a bit, too, since up until that time, Vatican City had been notorious for its plumb awful vittles.

Well, my friends, the pickings remained good on those mountain highways and byways for quite a few years. And Brother Frankie and Lady Poverty, they was able to fix up their home right nice on their divine share of the Lord's wealth. Me, I wound up spending most of my share on legal fees, since some ladies failed to take certain simple precautions and blamed me for the resultant blessings.

But all good things must come to an end, brothers and sisters. Brother Frankie got itchy feet, maybe afearing that middle age was approaching mighty fast by then. So one day he up and left for some foreign place, where he set to doing the Lord's work among them there Godless Moslems. Lady Poverty's little'uns got a mite bigger, and she got bored, what with Frankie being off in the desert and her kids being off in the mountains with the Friars. She started hankering after doing some of the Lord's work, too, and next thing I knowed, she opened up the Community of Poor Ladies—which, of course, has become so very famous since those days. In fact, I reckon there's hardly a fella here today what ain't helped make some of those poor ladies a mite richer.

Well, Frankie wandered back our way after a few years, but he was a changed man, brothers and sisters, a changed man, I say. I reckon those Moslems didn't take to turning over their wealth to a servant of the Lord with quite the same sense of cooperation as shown by us Christian folk. According to Brother Frankie, they was downright ugly about it, and they didn't have no respect for Mother Church's wholehearted support of his divine mission. In consequence, he'd come home a little sooner than expected, which was a darn shame, since Lady Poverty would have chased that handsome young Brother Angelo out of her house sooner if she'd been expecting Frankie.

Now, by this here time, Pope Honorius had taken over the job from Pope Innocent—don't it just beat all, the names those fellas choose for theirselves? And Pope Honorius was willing to overlook the many little'uns Lady Poverty had borne Brother Frankie and grant him an annulment, in light of Frankie's many good works.

Times surely had changed, brothers and sisters, and Brother Frankie grew melancholy. Not to mention careless. He wandered out onto Monte La Verna one day a few years back, not realizing he was being followed by one of them noble fellas whose wealth he had liberated and who was still holding a grudge. Well, that fella had got hisself a new dagger, and he used it on Frankie. I never did see such a peculiar assortment of wounds; that knife left scars on Frankie in the very selfsame place that Christ bore his own scars, and folks sure got to talking about the significance of it. I reckon that angry noble fella had a pretty sick sense of humor.

Well, what with Lady Poverty not being there to tend Frankie no more, and him being an ornery sort of person by this time anyhow, he never did get those wounds healed up good. They pained him until the very day he finally died, some two years later.

And that's the whole tale, my friends. That is the life

story, true and sincere in every respect, of my good friend, Brother Frankie. I think you can all understand, brothers and sisters, yes, I believe you can all see why that there Pope Gregory has seen fit to honor the memory of our dearly departed Brother Frankie, who gave his life for Mother Church and the divine work of our Lord.

And now, as y'all can see, there's a young lady passing around the collection box, which gives you the opportunity to show your appreciation for the moving tale I have just told. And don't pay no never mind to the way she's dressed; the cold don't bother her none. This charming lady, by the way, is our newest recruit to the Community of Poor Ladies, which, in honor of Brother Frankie's canonization, is staying open extra late tonight. Let the church say amen! Amen!

Martha Soukup is a multiple Hugo and Nebula nominee, whose worldview is just a shade warped and whose stories are never quite what one expects.

For example, one day, a few weeks after I had asked her to contribute to this book, I mentioned in passing that my wife and I had bred more than twenty collie champions during the 1970s. Three days later, this story, featuring perhaps the strangest alternate outlaw of all, arrived in the mail.

Good Girl, Bad Dog
by Martha Soukup

Not-Timmy smells bad, sticky with chocolate and anger. He does not want to be near not-Timmy, but Trainer is there making him. Not-Timmy looks furiously past the camera at the humans standing together there, then puts on a sweet smile and reaches down to pet his ears, pulling them.

"Good girl," not-Timmy says.

He is not a girl. He is not a bitch. He is a Dog.

Trainer stands away from the camera and other humans. He makes a signal with his hand.

"Woof!" says the Dog. His ears hurt. Later he will get a biscuit. He smells not-Timmy and feels the hot lights sting his eyes and wonders if it is enough.

Not-Timmy's trainer watches intently, making a signal to the boy with his eyes. "Ha ha ha!" says not-Timmy, loud like a bark. "Ha ha ha!" say the bigger humans standing on this side of the camera with not-Timmy. The humans on the other side of the camera say nothing. The human-trainer has not signaled them.

The human-trainer will give not-Timmy a biscuit, one

that smells like chocolate instead of grain and stale meat juices. The Dog does not know what the bigger humans get. There are many of them and some are stronger than the human-trainer, so it must be something very big.

"Cut!" says the human-trainer. The hot lights go off. The humans from behind the camera walk away. Not-Timmy lets go of the Dog's ears and runs off. "Timmy!" yells the human-trainer. When the human-trainer is not standing behind the camera, most people call not-Timmy by a different name, but the human-trainer always calls him Timmy.

The name they call the Dog is the same all the time, with the camera or without the camera. It is a wrong name. It is a bitch's name. It goes with saying "Good girl!" and he is not a girl. He will not use the name in his own mind.

He is a Dog. Sometimes he dreams he is Wolf.

Trainer had a wolf once.

The wolf was gray and sleek, where the Dog has ruffs of pale, soft fur. Wolf fur was thick and rough, at least to sight, for the wolf was locked in a kennel behind the Dog's, and the Dog could not get close enough even to smell him properly.

What he could smell even through bars and great distance was hatred of Trainer and kennels and commands and stale biscuits. The wolf would never let anyone call him a bitch and say "Good girl!" and pull his ears. The Dog imagined the wolf tearing Trainer's throat out. He dreamed it, and it made him whimper in his sleep, but he always hoped to dream the dream again. Sometimes he still dreams it.

Trainer did not keep the wolf for long. Maybe Trainer took him away and killed him before he could kill Trainer, with a heavy stick in his human hands; for the Dog cannot imagine Trainer's small shouting mouth at the wolf's throat.

"Come," says Trainer, using the bitch-name the Dog will not hear but must answer to.

The Dog does not want to come. The Dog puts on his alert face, the way he has been taught: head cocked, ears up, sitting straight.

"Come, damn it!" Trainer raises his hand.

The Dog decides. He makes a break for it, ducking between cables and kitchen walls that end in the middle and the shifting legs of humans. He has knocked the camera over: he can hear it landing in a noisy crash of metal and glass as Trainer shouts at him.

Trainer shouts many words the Dog has never heard before. They are very easy not to respond to. Harder is when Trainer shouts "Come!" and "Bad!" Years of hearing these words, food when he does what Trainer says, shouts when he does not, have made them very, very big. These words try to pull his shoulders down into a guilty cringe. They are harder to run past than the set walls and the humans trying to grab for him.

But the Dog does run past them. He is a Bad Dog. He is not a Good Girl.

He is like the wolf.

He is so excited, he wants to piss on the whole set, on all the human things, to mark it all as his, the Bad Dog's. But humans are still grabbing at him, and he knows he cannot stop now. To decide to be a Bad Dog is to go and keep going, all the way, like a wolf after prey.

Behind the set walls are many cables and boxes and poles and boards. It is a maze the humans are clumsy in, but a Bad Dog can run through quickly, knocking more things back in the humans' path. Soon the Dog is away from all the sounds of shouting. He keeps running. He will reach the wild. He will be a Wild Dog, a collie wolf.

He knows where the wild is. They film on it. The wild is where not-Timmy falls into a cave and the Good Girl has to stand and bark for the big humans, in front of a camera and both trainers. It is not so far from the set.

It is not so long before he is there, breathing hard but feeling alive, in the wild, not in the kennel and not on the set, no Trainer to yell at him. The wild is a small canyon,

scrub and brush, a few trees. The cameras are not there to
make it human. Wolves would live here. He throws back
his head and howls.

The wild smells tantalizingly of rabbits, but to the Dog's
chagrin, he has not been able to chase one down. It is
hard to be Wolf when you have been kept in a kennel,
trained to fetch and bark on cue instead of hunt. One rab-
bit after another, prey gets away. He smells around for another one.

There is a sour smell of chocolate and tears. He creeps
silently to find the source.

Not-Timmy is sitting on a rock crying.

Not-Timmy can tell the bigger humans where the Bad
Dog is. The Dog thinks. He thinks hard, but before he can
finish thinking, not-Timmy suddenly turns around and
looks at him.

Not-Timmy exclaims, calling him by the bitch-name.
The Dog buries a growl in the back of his throat. He has
never liked the small human, the way the boy pulls his
ears, squeezes him too hard when the human-trainer tells
him to hug, says "Good girl!" in his high, shrill voice. The
Dog takes a step back. How could he think real wild
would be so close to set and city?

"How did you find me?" not-Timmy says. These are
words he would say in front of the camera and the
human-trainer. The Dog looks around to see if all the humans are there, if he has run into a trap the humans
made. But there are no other humans, just the boy.

Trying to decide what to do, the Dog sits up and puts
on his alert face.

What not-Timmy says next is not from his trainer's
script, does not sound like the words the human-trainer
makes him say. "I hate them all," he says to the Dog. "I
hate them making me work, I hate them taking my
money, I hate them treating me like I'm just some kid
when I work as hard as any of them. If they're gonna treat

me like just some kid, they should let me act like just some kid."

The Dog does not know these words, but he knows this is not what the bigger humans make not-Timmy say for them. Not-Timmy smells different now. Through the chocolate smell, he smells a little like the wolf did. Angry. Fierce.

Maybe not-Timmy is a Bad Boy.

The Dog creeps up and licks his face. It tastes like salt, a little sour. The Dog likes salt. He licks some more.

"Oh, girl!" not-Timmy cries, wrapping his bony arms around the Dog's ruffed shoulders. "Did you run away too? We can run away from those bastards together." He sniffles into the Dog's fur. The Dog does not pull away and run off. The Dog has to think.

The Dog takes not-Timmy to a cave in which they've filmed before. Not-Timmy was in that scene, but he didn't seem to remember where the cave was. Not-Timmy is not good at being wild. When the Dog shows him the cave, not-Timmy cries "Good girl!" and the Dog tries not to snarl. He is not here to be a Good Girl. Not-Timmy should know better.

They stay in the cave while it gets dark, and gets light, and gets dark again. Not-Timmy talks a lot. The Dog tries not to listen to his piercing voice. By second dark, the Dog is getting very hungry, and not-Timmy has started to whine. The Dog knows whines. The kennel was full of them.

"They'll be missing me by now," the boy says. "They've got to be sorry by now. Serve them right if I never came back. See what happens to their show without its star. Serve them right if I never came back, but I can't stay here. They've had their scare. They'll treat me right now. I'm starving. I'm thirsty. I'm going to go home."

"Go Home" are human words the Dog understands. He has been dozing nearer the front of the cave, away from not-Timmy, but his ears prick high at the sound of the words. "Go Home" means back to the other humans. "Go Home" means be a Good Girl, not wild, not a Bad Dog. Not-Timmy wants him to Go Home. He will not do that. He buries his nose back under his leg. He will starve a Wild Dog, a Bad Dog, rather than eat another of Trainer's biscuits.

Not-Timmy has got up and grabbed his small pack. It had chocolate in it, which the boy finished eating before first dark. The pack is empty now, but humans carry their possessions everywhere instead of marking them and leaving them. Not-Timmy is going to leave the cave. He is going to Go Home. He is going to bring humans back to find the Bad Dog. Trainer will hit the Dog with a stick, and maybe tear his throat out. If he does not tear his throat out, he will make him be a Good Girl, make him Sit and Fetch and Stay and sleep in the kennel.

The Dog leaps at not-Timmy as the boy reaches the cave entrance. He knocks not-Timmy over the way he knocked the camera over, but not-Timmy sounds different from the camera as he lands on the rocky cave floor: there is a thud, a small snapping sound, and a sudden sharp cry.

"Shit!" cries the boy, clutching his leg. "It's broken!" He whimpers like a puppy. The Dog sits looking at him, not knowing what to do now.

"Get help," says not-Timmy. "Go get help. Go home. Tell the director. Tell anyone! Get help!"

The Dog knows many of these words. They do this in the scripts all the time. He runs off, he runs back with a big human, or, if a big human is the one lying on the ground saying Get Help, with not-Timmy; and when the camera stops whirring, Trainer gives him biscuits. If Trainer were here, he would be signaling the Dog when to look alert, when to touch not-Timmy with one paw, when to turn and run away from not-Timmy and the camera. This is the game the humans play.

The Dog looks at not-Timmy clutching his leg and weeping. He raises his ears and cocks his head.

"Yes, girl, that's it! Get help! Get help!"

The Dog puts his paw gently on not-Timmy's arm.

"Good girl!" says the boy. His eyes plead, full of pain and hope. The Dog can smell it on his sour human skin.

The Dog takes not-Timmy by the collar of his shirt and drags him back into the far recesses of the cave.

By next light, he is not hungry anymore.

The little girl has wandered far away from her family's picnic, and she is lost and tired from crying about it.

She hears a little sound and looks up, startled. It is a friendly collie face. She's seen it on television. It's just like television! She'll be saved now! She calls the dog by name and it comes right up to her and licks her face. Just like television.

"Good doggy, good girl, are you going to take me back to my mommy and daddy now?"

The collie pricks up its ears, cocks its head in a comical manner, and leads the little girl away from the way she came, farther into the canyon, back into a sheltered cave.

The rabbits in the wilds of Los Angeles may be difficult prey, but a Bad Dog—a Wolf—can get by.

John E. Johnston III has lived the kind of life writers are *supposed* to live, the kind that people who write dustjacket copy pray for. He's been a bounty hunter, an explorer, a professor, a diamond miner, a geologist—and, most recently, a science fiction writer.

In this story, John chooses to write about the most recent alternate outlaw of them all.

Comrade Bill
by John E. Johnston III

Maybe the satellites will be properly aligned this time, thought Bill as he jogged past the hulking Secret Service agent and into the big bathroom of his mother's house. Opportunities to isolate himself in this room were becoming scarcer and scarcer as time went by, and the Secret Service agents who made up his detail seemed to be taking their duties even more seriously than usual these days. Bill couldn't afford another missed contact: the danger of exposure was simply too great.

He opened the bathroom closet door and looked on the top shelf. There it was, nestled amid a bunch of old razors, heating pads, and hot-water bottles: the radio. It looked like an antique radio, one of those hideous box-shaped clock-radios from the fifties. Inside, though, it was anything but antique, for cleverly hidden away within it was a portable satellite transceiver of unmatchable technology. Or at least that was what the coded note that had been taped inside the unit when he had picked it up at the dead drop in Little Rock four years ago had read; Bill was no longer so sure about that. His confidence in the unit had waned, for now when he finally and desperately needed to make contact, three straight attempts to do so had resulted in nothing but bitter disappointment as the indicator LED had glowed red every time, meaning "contact impossible."

After the third straight failure, Bill had been so angry that the temptation to follow the radio's self-destruct instructions had almost overwhelmed him; he had worked too hard and come too far to put up with this kind of failure. He had to get through, but a combination of the scarcity of opportunities to use the radio and the radio's unreliability seemed to be conspiring against him. The coded note had alluded to "adverse satellite alignments" making contact difficult or impossible on occasion, but that assumed that the radio was in working condition to begin with, and of that, Bill had his doubts.

He placed the radio on the counter and turned the sink taps and showerhead on full blast. The result was a level of near-white-noise, water-derived interference that, hopefully, would make it impossible for the Secret Service agents outside the bathroom to hear Bill speaking quietly into the tiny microphone contained in the radio. He didn't have to worry about reception being overheard; the radio's miniaturized earphone was inaudible from even inches away when it was placed in a human ear.

Now was the time. Taking a deep breath, Bill pressed and twisted the buttons on the outside of the old radio in a special sequence, and the upper parts of the radio swung away, clearly revealing the false bottom and the modern miniaturized transceiver within. He inserted the earphone, took a deep breath, hit the power button, and nearly cried out in delight when the green indicator light came on: not a red for "contact impossible," not an amber for "contact possible," but a green, which meant "contact guaranteed."

Finally it was all going to pay off.

"This is Rustic Star calling Pine Island. This is Rustic Star calling Pine Island. Come in."

There was no answer. Bill tried a second time, and then a third. He checked the LED; it was still glowing bright green. This didn't make any sense at all—unless, of course, he had been duped, and the transceiver really wasn't what it had been made out to be.

His doubts quickly vanished, though, when a raspy voice in heavily accented English began coming out of the earphone. "Excuse me, please. You were calling us?"

"Yes. This is Rustic Star. Is this Pine Island? Is there a problem?"

"Oh, not really. I was in the other room, there was no one here but Misha, you were calling in English, and he only speaks Russian and Polish. Are you one of ours? Do you need help?"

"I was told to call in using English . . . and if you are really Pine Island, then we need to exchange the proper recognition sequence."

"What for? This is Yevegeny Peniakoff in Moscow. Why do I need to give you a recognition sequence? There's only this one receiver for this satellite system in the whole world. It's in the office on Dzerzhinsky Street, and I'm using it. Just who else besides us do you think that you might be talking to?"

"We're supposed to exchange recognition signals! It's the security procedure!" Bill was suddenly irate. This signal might be uninterceptible by virtue of its being compressed, coded by a special method hardwired into both transceivers, transmitted straight up to a satellite by the transceiver in microbursts, and then relayed to Moscow and similarly downloaded and processed, but the man with the raspy voice—Yevegeny? Surely he hadn't given out his real name over the radio?—was far too sloppy for Bill's properly trained tastes.

"Oh, my. Well, if it makes you happy, then I'll go get the book and look it up. What did you call us again? Fire Island?" asked the raspy voice.

"Pine Island."

"Hold on, I have to find that notebook with that name in the file cabinets, and I'm not too certain where the file-cabinet keys are. Wait a minute."

"I don't have much time."

"You're the one that wants the recognition sequence. I'll be back as soon as I find the proper notebook."

Several interminable minutes passed before the raspy voice returned. "So we are Pine Island, and you are what? Wrestling Star?"

"No, no, no! Rustic Star."

"Hold on, and I'll look you up . . . yes, here you are. You are supposed to go first, it says."

" 'I have spake'," Bill said, with a deep sense of satisfaction and belonging.

" 'Daisy, Daisy, give me your answer, do'," replied the raspy voice.

" 'Wash them all with soap'," Bill answered.

"That's it. Is that enough recognition for you?"

"Yes," answered Bill, feeling partially redeemed. "Now I am supposed to report to you. I have accomplished my mission."

"And what mission was that, Rustic Star?"

"Infiltration. Don't you have any description of my mission there in the notebook?"

"Let me look . . . yes, here it is, it was on the next page. Slava Bogu! You're one of the deep-cover people who were sent to infiltrate America years ago! No wonder you speak English and want to do all of these old code things. Amazing! Give me a minute, would you?"

The raspy voice lowered in volume and switched to Russian. "Misha, this fellow on the radio? You'll never believe it, but he's one of our old deep-cover people who's still on the job! It says here that he was substituted for a university student who was visiting Moscow decades ago and sent back to America in his place. Now he's finally calling in on the old satellite radio network. Can you imagine that!"

There was a muted sound in the background that Bill couldn't quite make out, but which sounded like a man with a deep voice and a bad cold asking a question in Russian. Then the raspy voice continued. "The university student? Always the sentimentalist, Misha. Let me look

. . . ah, here it is. Yes, they sure did. The boy probably never knew why, either."

Then the raspy voice returned to English. "Excuse me, Rustic Star, but does the name that you're using over there happen to be 'Bill'?"

Bill jerked upright and his voice climbed an octave. "How did you know that? That information is supposed to be coded and sealed!"

"Ah, no doubt it is, but someone wrote in the margin here a note next to where it says 'Rustic Star' that reads 'Comrade Bill'."

"What? That's a security violation! My identity is supposed to be secure!"

"Oh, don't worry about it, your identity is safe. There're lots of Americans named 'Bill,' no one but Misha and me ever reads these old records, and all of that coded and sealed stuff was burned a while back. This note was probably written by one of the old hardline office apparatchiks anyway, and they were all purged a couple of years ago as well. Besides, we're not allowed to call anyone 'Comrade' anymore, so I'll just call you 'Bill' . . . say, it says here that you were supposed to infiltrate the upper echelons of an American political party. So you have succeeded in your mission?"

"Well," said Bill, "you could certainly say so."

"That's great, Bill. We don't follow American political news hardly at all around here anymore, but I'm sure that the people who sent you over there would be really proud to hear that. Congratulations!" There was a pause, and the raspy voice became friendlier. "Say, do you need something? Are you in trouble? Do you want to come home? Do you need a visa or such? Is that why you're calling us? We'll do what we can for you, of course; after all, you were, er, are one of ours. Unless you want money, that is. We have a real problem with money right now. You don't want any money, do you?"

Bill's knuckles tightened on the radio. "No, I don't want any money. I don't want to go home, either. What I want to do is my job: I'm supposed to find out from your office what defense or diplomatic information you most urgently need to know and how you want me to provide it to you. I can find out almost anything that you want to know now."

"Well, Bill, we're not really into that anymore, you know. We don't get much call for that sort of thing these days; we're more of an international business research group now." There was a pause. "Say, there is one thing you could find out for us. Any information that you could get us on American soybean futures would be really handy, because we have to finish a report on world soybean markets by next Monday and we're not really sure what recommendations to make."

"I can get you all of that sort of information that you want, but we'll have to establish another secure method for me to relay it to you. But don't you want to know anything more? Anything about defense systems? Strategic plans? Secret treaties?"

"Maybe later, Bill, but first Misha and I have got to get this report done," said the raspy voice.

Bill's jaw set in a hard line. "The other thing that I was supposed to get from your office was political instructions. What do you want me to do now? What goals am I supposed to strive for? How can I best serve our country's political ends?"

"Oh, you want advice on political objectives? Well, Bill, the best political advice that I can give you from here is what they're telling us: work for democracy, openness, free markets, and an end to political corruption."

The ears of the Secret Service agent outside the bathroom door suddenly perked up. The water had stopped running, and just before it stopped, he had heard a series of odd crunching noises coming from inside the bathroom. He reacted as he had been trained to: he gave the other agents in sight the hand signal indicating potential trouble, spoke the appropriate keyword into his throat microphone, and then moved into assault position opposite the bathroom door. Before he could make his next move, though, the door opened and a grim-looking Bill walked out.

"Excuse me, sir," said the agent, looking past Bill into the bathroom, "but do you know anything about some crunching noises?"

"Yes," said Bill. "That was me. Sorry." He grinned his trademark grin at the agent. "I was reaching up into the closet when I had an attack of the clumsies, knocked my grandfather's old radio down off one of the shelves, and then managed to step on it a couple of times."

"No problem, then, sir, and I'm sorry to have bothered you. I hope it wasn't a valuable radio."

"Valuable?" An emotion that the agent couldn't place flashed across Bill's face. "Maybe it was once, but not anymore."

Maureen F. McHugh burst onto the science fiction scene with all the subtlety of a supernova. Her first novel, *China Mountain Zhang*, won the Tiptree Award, the Lambda Literary Award, and the *Locus* Award, and was nominated for the Nebula and the Hugo. At the same time, her brilliant novella, "Protection," also received a Nebula and a Hugo nomination.

For this book, Maureen has chosen a recent American icon for her outlaw, and handled the story with the excellence we have come to expect from her.

The Ballad of Ritchie Valenzuela
by Maureen F. McHugh

The two Latinos sauntered into the Mexican whorehouse. Mexican street prostitutes often wore death-face makeup, but this looked more like a fifties prom night. The girls wore wide, rustling, blue-and-pink net skirts and matching high heels, and their bare brown shoulders looked smooth. They sat along the walls of the big ballroom, knees wide, bored, watching the nearly empty dance floor. The Mexican band was in cream-colored gaucho suits, with red piping up the pants legs, ruffled shirts, and the kind of sombreros that people hung on walls in suburban tract houses in the fifties and early sixties; huge ungainly things no one would ever expect to wear.

The first young man was stocky and full of machismo. "Maria," he called a round-faced woman. He grabbed her about the waist, and she laughed a shrill, artificial laugh. "Okay," she said. *"Me llamo Maria."* Her lipstick was red, her skin wrinkled where the bare-shouldered dress clutched under her plump arms.

The second young man held back.

"Ritchie," the stocky boy said, "come on." To the woman, he said, "This is my little brother, Ritchie."

The woman said something in Spanish.

"I don't speak Spanish," Ritchie said. He was sweating in his white T-shirt. He had a cheap electric guitar slung over his shoulder and he held the neck of it as if for reassurance.

The stocky boy answered her in a rush of Spanish, and she laughed again and beckoned.

Two more women came out of the chairs in a rustle of tulle. "Ritchie," one of them said. It sounded like Reechee.

He smiled uncomfortably. "That's okay," he said and walked toward the stage. His loafers didn't make much noise on the wooden floor. He was the only man in the place not wearing boots. At the stage he stopped and watched the Mexican guitarist. The Mexican's guitar was acoustic; the wood was black and inlaid with mother-of-pearl. Ritchie's guitar was red and absurdly small. The band was playing a folk song called "La Bamba," which was usually played at weddings, but Ritchie didn't seem to notice the irony.

A girl in pale pink sauntered past him and smiled over her shoulder. She was still smiling over her shoulder when she misstepped and stumbled on her high heels, flailing for his arm, and he grabbed reflexively for her.

"Cut!" shouted the director.

"Shit," said the girl who had stumbled. "Sorry."

"It's okay," said the director. People took a couple of steps, eased themselves into movement, coughed.

"Five minutes?" asked the stocky Latino.

The director looked at his watch, shook his head. "We're already behind. We can take it from Ritchie standing at the stage. Okay, Lou?"

The actor nodded.

"It's so cliché," the Latino girl in pale pink muttered.

"What?" asked the actor playing Ritchie.

"You know—young, innocent nice boy comes to Tijuana for the weekend with his older brother, the marijuana smuggler, gets laid, gets in trouble and starts on a life of crime."

"Valenzuela really did go to Tijuana and get in trouble," the actor said.

"Right," the actress said, her voice heavy with sarcasm. "It was the turning point of his life."

"Right," said the actor, puzzled.

"I don't believe in turning points," she said. "I think Valenzuela would have been trouble no matter what happened."

"Movies need turning points."

"Yeah," she said. "They could at least be subtle."

"Real life isn't subtle," the actor said.

"Okay," said the director. "Places."

"Maybe not yours," the actress hissed, and settled herself with a rustle of crinoline.

The actor looked troubled.

"Lou," the director said, "take it from where you look up at the band."

"So you don't believe in turning points," the actor playing Ritchie said after the take. "What about when someone wins the lottery, isn't that a turning point?"

"How many turning points have you had in your life?" the girl asked. If she was aware that he was the star of this movie and that she was a nobody, an extra playing a Mexican whore, she didn't show it. Instead, she took off the pink high heels and rubbed her feet. The crew and the other extras studiously ignored the pair of them.

"This is going to be a turning point," he said, and smiled. Not exactly at her, but he was talking to her, and he did look quite nice in his peg-leg jeans and white T-shirt.

"Bet me," she said. But she smiled a little. She had a kind of hopeful look.

"Really," he said. "This picture is going to be better than *Bonnie and Clyde*. You've seen the dailies. The robbery scenes, they were so fluid, like *The Warriors*, only Valenzuela is a person you can care about, you know? This picture is going to make my career. Well, maybe not make my career, but give me exposure." He was clearly not looking at her, he was looking across the soundstage, looking at the picture he just painted.

"Yeah," she said, disappointed. "You talk like an actor."

"Obviously, it's a director's movie, but it's the kind of work I want. And nobody has ever exploited color and movement this way."

"And you studied acting in Texas," she said, bored. Or maybe frustrated.

"Right," he said, suddenly cool.

"I studied acting at NYU," she said. "Not that you care, not that anybody in this place cares. What makes you think you're going to get work after this? You're an ethnic. The part has to come along."

"Not if you're doing quality work," he said.

"You think John Lone is the only Asian actor who can really act? You think there's room in the Hollywood ecology for more than one really good Asian actor? Your niche is already filled," she said.

"Martin Sheen is a Latino," he said.

"Martin Sheen comes from Dayton, Ohio, and looks white," she said. "You and I don't."

"You've got a great attitude," he said.

"Yeah," she said. "I'm still waiting for evidence that says I should change it."

"Okay," said the director. "Walk in."

Somebody called the scene.

The Latino, Ritchie, walked into the diner. He didn't have his guitar anymore and he didn't have his brother with him, either. It was a long time after the whorehouse in Tijuana, in terms of the story. In terms of the filming, it was the next set. The camera was mounted on a boom that swam the air. Ritchie ordered bacon and eggs and toast, and the waitress, who spoke pure, broad Iowa, told him he was missing a treat if he didn't order the pancakes.

"That's okay," he said, subdued, tired. In movie time, he had been on the run for eleven days.

"Really, sweetie," she said, leaning on the counter, "you ought to try the pancakes. We make the best pancakes. It would be a waste to eat here and not try the pancakes."

"Okay," he said, dredging up a smile. He was near the end of his run, and his body seemed to know it. Or maybe it didn't know it; after all, he still wanted to eat, as if eating made any difference.

She wrote the order down on a green order pad and put it through the window for the cook.

The director said to cut, but in the video of the day's shoot that evening, the cook didn't look at the ticket, didn't look at her.

"You don't need to talk to him," said the cook, whose hair was as black as Ritchie's. He had on a white T-shirt, and the bottom part of a tattoo showed under his sleeve.

"I'm just making conversation," the waitress said.

"You need to be careful who you make conversation with," said the cook.

But she went back down the nearly empty counter. She cleaned the countertop for a bit while Ritchie stared at nothing, his heart still beating, his lungs still drawing in air, his brain still telling him he needed eggs and bacon and sleep, as if it all mattered, as if he needed to conserve his health and strength. "Where are you from?" asked the waitress.

"California," Ritchie said. "You're very nice." He wasn't flirting, he meant every word of it. "You are," he said. "You're kind. People should be more kind."

She smiled, a little embarrassed and a little confused, the way people are when someone says something that is true but maybe not appropriate.

He ate his bacon and eggs and pancakes. She slid the check next to him and smiled.

He looked at the check as if it would reach out and bite him, and the waitress looked a little concerned.

"I don't have any money," he whispered.

"Oh, come on," she said, uncertain. "You're just pulling my leg." She wanted him to smile, to laugh, to take out his money, because he seemed nice, but she knew he really wasn't. "I'll . . ." Her voice dropped. "I'll have to tell Bert."

"I'm sorry," he said, and took out a gun.

Her eyes went wide and she put her hand over her mouth in a helpless kind of way.

"I'm sorry," he said again, and his eyes filled with tears. "Everything is such a mess."

She made a funny little noise behind her hand.

"Don't look that way," he said, pleading. "I never meant things to be like this. Things just . . . happened. I'm a musician, Ritchie Valens, I wrote a song called 'Donna,' did you ever hear it?" He started to sing. "Ohh, oh Donna—"

"What's going on out here?" Bert called.

"Don't come out," Ritchie said. "Don't come out!" He got up and backed toward the door. Bert came out from the kitchen, saw the gun and stopped.

"It's just all messed up," Ritchie said, and backed out the door.

The village was sun-blasted and poor, a cliché village of chickens scratching and barefoot girl-children in faded cotton dresses. The old man was the cliché old man of villages, white-haired and wrinkled and dressed in a bleached work shirt. Soft blue against brown skin.

Films are not made in order. This was from before the diner. Ritchie was hung over from the whorehouse, and he was disoriented, and he didn't know where his brother was, and he suspected he had been abandoned and that he was alone in this village where people spoke either Spanish or some local native dialect, and all that was on his face. "Who are you?" he asked the old man.

The old man grinned and answered him with gibberish.

"My brother, uh, *mi hermano*, have you seen my brother?"

The old man beckoned and Ritchie scrambled to his feet, coltish and awkward.

The old man led him out of the village, past the shacks with corrugated tin roofs and the chickens scratching and the children standing big-eyed, out into the desert. "My brother?" Ritchie kept saying, and the old man nodded and they walked. There was a road, but after a while, they left the road and if there was a trail, it wasn't visible.

Ritchie stumbled in his loafers. After an hour, he stopped saying "My brother?" They wound through scrub and eventually started going downhill, following a wash that grew steeper until Ritchie was picking his way, holding on to the sides. It did not look like a pleasant trip with a hangover.

From a distance, the water sounded like people talking. They came around a turn and there was a crooked little river. Directly ahead of them, it was deeper, running fast. Beyond that, it narrowed and churned in sudden turbulence, barely five feet wide. The old man stopped at the edge of the calm part.

Ritchie stopped above him in the wash and looked around. Then he looked at the old man. The old man watched the water, smiling. He reached into his pocket and took out a tiny piece of wood, carved into a shape like a little boat, wide in the middle and pointed at both ends. He dropped it into the water. It flowed sideways toward where the water got rougher and then bounced through a trough and disappeared, bobbed up and down, riding the ripples.

"Oh, great," Ritchie said. "You're probably some senile old man who has just dragged me halfway to Mexico City and now can't remember how to get home." He raised his voice. "Old man!"

The old man smiled at the water.

"Old man, *mi hermano*, my brother. Is my brother here? The guy that was with me?" Ritchie sighed, exasperated, and sat down.

The old man said, without looking up, "Take a piece of wood and throw it in the river. Can you tell where it will be on the other side of the rough water?"

"You speak English?" Ritchie asked. "Why didn't you tell me you speak English?"

"Will it come out near this bank, or near the other, or in the middle? There is no man who can tell you the answer, no mathematics that can say where the wood will come out. That is turbulence." The old man looked up at Ritchie and grinned. Some of his teeth were gone.

"I'm sorry," Ritchie said. "I just don't feel good, I've got cottonmouth and my head hurts, and it's already hot out here."

The old man just grinned, looking crazy.

"So where's my brother?" Ritchie asked.

The old man's grin widened. "No speak *Inglesa*," he said. Then he started back up the wash.

For a moment, Ritchie stood there, and then he climbed after him.

"It doesn't work," said the director, watching the rough cut. "You're right, take it out."

The shoot-out was filmed in pieces over days. Even the videos at the end of the day showed only bits and pieces of guns firing and people shouting. The actor who played Ritchie wore bloodstained T-shirts for four days.

Waiting in line for saran-wrapped sandwiches and Danish, the director said, "You could turn a guy's stomach, you know?"

The actor playing Ritchie just grinned. Standing in front of him was an actor playing one of the FBI agents who finally shot Ritchie Valenzuela. "I remember that song," the actor said, "the 'Oh Donna' song. My sister really liked it."

"Yeah?" the actor playing Ritchie said.

"Yeah," the FBI agent said. "It's kind of a pity he never got a chance to see if he could make it in the music business."

"He'd probably have been a one-hit wonder," the director said. "If he hadn't gotten into trouble, today nobody would even remember him."

"How old was he when he died?" the FBI agent asked.

"Nineteen," the actor playing Ritchie said.

"Hey," the FBI agent said, "if he'd stuck to the music business, he'd probably be alive today."

Frank M. Robinson has been turning out top-notch books and stories for four decades. Although much of his output is science fiction, such as his novel *The Dark Beyond the Stars*, he is perhaps best known for the national best-sellers he wrote in collaboration with the late Tom Scortia: *The Glass Inferno* (which later became the block-buster movie, *The Towering Inferno*), and *The Prometheus Crisis*.

Frank is well acquainted with science fiction's history. He knows that despite the fact that Hugo Gernsback is considered to be our Founding Father, and despite the fact that our highest award, the Hugo, is named after him, Gernsback was a bit of a pirate who was always being sued for nonpayment by his authors. So Frank has decided to put Hugo into a situation where his worst instincts were more profitable than they were in the embryonic science fiction field. . . .

One Month in 1907
by Frank M. Robinson

Rossi's was one of the few restaurants Hugo Gernsback knew where you could buy a full-course dinner—everything from a salad through spaghetti, vegetables, and even dessert (usually little pink-iced cakes that he detested)—and still get a few pennies' change from a quarter. A huge stein of beer cost a nickle more, but money was tight and he'd decided weeks ago that he could do without the beer. It was thin American stuff anyway.

"I see you have your usual table by the window, Hugo. May I join you?"

"It's a free country, Charles."

Hugo toyed with a strand of spaghetti and watched

while his dinner companion settled into his chair and quickly ordered from the hovering waiter. Gelatin salad, a T-bone steak, baked potato, peas, white bread slathered with butter—what did Charles do for a living that he could afford a dinner like that?

He was jealous, Hugo thought with chagrin. He was heading for bankruptcy, and whatever Charles Ponzi was doing, he was doing very well at it. The dapper little man looked like a million dollars, but then, he always did. They'd come over from Europe at almost the same time— Charles in 1903 at the age of twenty-one, he in 1904, when he was not quite twenty, each of them with two hundred dollars to his name. Hugo reflected that on the whole, he'd done all right—he hadn't had to send to his father for money—but it was obvious that Charles had done much better, even though he admitted he'd lost most of his stake gambling on board ship.

"You should have gone with me to the Henry Settlement House last night, Hugo—Marie had a friend she wanted you to meet. They had a small concert and Marie played some Chopin. Not badly, either."

Hugo was naturally shy and felt uncomfortable about it. "What would we have talked about?"

Charles neatly cut off a bite of steak and pointed a full fork at him. "Certainly not business, Hugo—you talk too much about it as it is. But you wouldn't have had to say anything. With women, you never do. Be a good listener and the factory girls will love you."

Hugo found himself making a note of the comment and thinking of a funny drawing that could go with it. Mediterranean humor, but then, Charles was the quintessential Italian.

"You know, Hugo, it's not like you'd be sparking some drab sparrow—Marie and her friend work in the shirtwaist factory at Washington and Greene. They're handy with a needle, they make all their own clothes." He smiled. "Very fashionable. I didn't feel out of place at all."

Charles was a romantic, Hugo thought dourly, while he

had ... what? A more scientific attitude toward love? There were times when he thought it was all just a matter of glands, but that was probably because Charles was luckier with the ladies than he was.

"Maybe next week," he mumbled.

Charles brightened. "What about tomorrow night?" He pulled out his wallet and produced four tickets with a flourish. " 'Brewster's Millions' at the Hudson. It's a hit, in its fifth month." He rolled his eyes. "Any girl would love you if you took her."

Hugo was tempted, then felt mildly annoyed. He was twenty-three and Charles was only a year or two older, yet he always found himself letting Charles take the lead when it came to women, though he had to admit he approved of Charles' taste in the fairer sex.

"Too much money," he said flatly. "There're the tickets and dinner and flowers and someplace after the show . . ."

Charles looked sympathetic.

"Business that bad?"

It was painful to talk about it, but Charles was a close friend and had a willing ear.

"Read the papers, Charles—it's the depression of nineteen seven. Maybe not for you, but for everybody else." Hugo bit into one of the little pink-iced cakes without thinking and made a face. "The battery company's not doing well. The automobile companies aren't buying like they used to, and this morning I lost the Packard account."

Charles leaned back in his chair and patted his mouth with his napkin. "But your import company is doing fine, am I right?"

His eyes were big and sympathetic. Hugo didn't notice the sudden silkiness in his voice.

"Electro's doing as well as could be expected. It's mail-order, and that's a difficult business at best. And people don't know much about radio yet." He felt relieved that the conversation had turned away from Marie and her dressmaking girl friends. He even felt a faint flush of enthusiasm, as he always did when the subject turned to radio.

"You heard that last Christmas, Fessenden broadcast two musical pieces and a poem and they were picked up by ships a hundred miles away?"

"A sailor's life is never a dull one," Charles murmured.

"You've no imagination," Hugo protested. "That wasn't code, Charles, that was voice, that's the coming thing." He let his mind race for a moment. "Someday they'll broadcast symphonies, plays, even news and sporting events . . ."

Charles frowned.

"And you've got too much imagination, my friend—you're letting it run away with you. Who would pay for all of that? You'd be giving people something for free, throwing it away into the ether."

"It wouldn't be for free," Hugo objected. "You could broadcast advertising as well, companies would pay for that."

Charles raised an eyebrow. "You really think so? Your advertising would go in one ear and out the other, most likely. It wouldn't be like seeing an ad in the paper and coming back to it when you wanted."

He fished in his pockets for a few pennies to leave as a tip.

"So what are you going to do, Hugo? Your battery business is apparently going bust, and from your diet this past week, I'd guess Electro isn't doing all that well, either." He looked thoughtful, as if the idea had just occurred to him. "What you really need is an investor."

The difficulty with having Charles as a friend, Hugo thought sourly, was that he was so often right. And then he wondered if Charles was making an offer.

"I had a partner in the battery business, remember? He collected all the checks and I had to hound his father for the money."

Charles took his cane from the back of his chair and stood up. A young man who looked like he was going places, Hugo thought, admiring despite himself. And furthermore, a young man who looked like he had money. A good man to have for a friend in America.

He shrugged. "If you want to, come by my office sometime and we'll talk about it. It's at Thirty-two Park Place—right in Radio Row. I think you were there once before?"

Charles smiled wanly. "I remember it well, Hugo. It stank of ozone and varnish."

The room was quiet, and through the open window you could hear the coughing of automobiles and the occasional clip-clop of horses on the street below. Hugo was bent over the apparatus he'd hooked up on the worktable, a maze of wiring and batteries and a tube that glowed vaguely blue.

Charles looked over his shoulder, curious. "It all looks very impressive to me, Hugo. What does it do?"

"It's only one of the greatest inventions of the age," Hugo said, too enthusiastic to note how pompous he sounded. "It was invented last year—a De Forest Audion tube. It amplifies."

Charles stared at him, mystified. "Amplifies what?"

Hugo pointed at a meter at one end of the table. "This one measures the current going in, and that one"—he pointed to a meter at the other end of the table—"measures the current going out. Read the meters."

Charles looked at the dials, then nodded his head, still not quite understanding. "You're getting more out than you're putting in, I can see that. But what good does it do?"

Hugo straightened up and sighed, disappointed that his friend didn't see the possibilities.

"With a number of these in a series, you could amplify the current to almost any value you wanted, which means that your broadcasts could be received hundreds of miles away. That would be a great asset for sending messages to ships at sea. Or"—he suddenly smiled—"you could connect a microphone at one end and broadcast voice, like Fessenden did. With one of these, someday you'd be able to communicate with anybody else in the country who had one like it."

"They can do it now," Charles objected, unimpressed. "Almost everybody has access to a telephone."

"Ships aren't wired to each other, Charles. This doesn't use wires, that's why they call it 'wireless'."

For a moment, Charles was lost in thought.

"It wouldn't have to be one-on-one," he mused. "One person could communicate with thousands of others if they had something that would receive the signal." His face lit up. "Or the symphony you mentioned the other day. Not everybody would want to talk, but almost everybody would want to listen. You would have an enormous audience, Hugo." He frowned again. "All you have to do is figure out some way of getting them to pay admission."

He wandered about the room for a moment, pausing at a box that contained some heavy coils, dry cells, and various other electrical parts.

"What's this?"

Hugo walked over and began pulling out the equipment until Charles held up his hand.

"One demonstration's enough for today, Hugo."

Hugo reluctantly put the gear back in the box. "It's what I called the 'Telimco Wireless'—it includes both a transmitter and a receiver. I was selling them via the mails, seven dollars and fifty cents for the set. You could send and receive signals for more than a mile."

Charles knelt by the box and gingerly fingered the contents. "Did you sell many?"

Hugo nodded. "A fair number. Macy's and Gimbels carried them, F.A.O. Schwarz . . . and I advertised." He walked over to his desk and rummaged through a pile of magazines on it. "Here it is," he said proudly, "the *Scientific American*." He pointed to a page.

Charles took it and scanned the columns, frowning. "I can't find it."

Hugo ran his finger farther down the left-hand column, and Charles' frown deepened. "It can't be more than an inch deep, did anybody ever see it?" He squinted at the tiny type at the bottom: " 'Will work up to one mile. Unprecedented introduction prices. Agents wanted.' Did you ever get any agents, Hugo?"

Hugo looked uncomfortable. "None that really understood it. But the police showed up. They didn't believe it would work."

Charles raised an eyebrow. "But of course, it did."

Hugo smiled. "Of course."

"Did you ever promote it?"

Hugo turned up his hands. "No money."

Charles sat down in a nearby swivel chair and leaned his chin on the head of his cane.

"So what are you going to do, Hugo? You didn't make a fortune with your wireless, the battery company's not doing well, and here you are, selling electrical parts through the mail out of a dusty office in lower Manhattan. Not much of a future."

It was the type of assessment that Hugo hadn't expected from his friend, and it stung. He sorted through the magazines on his desk once again, took out a catalog and gave it to Charles without a word.

Charles flipped through it and handed it back, puzzled.

"Your catalog for the Electro Importing Company. So?"

Hugo leaned forward, once again carried away by his own enthusiasm.

"People are going to want these wireless devices, Charles, and they're going to want the radios that come after. They're going to want to listen to music that comes out of the air, and they're going to want to look at pictures that come out of the air, and they're going to want to see things that are happening anywhere in the world at the exact time they're happening." He paused to take a breath. "They're going to want to do all of these things, but they don't know it yet. So I'm going to make them know it. And I'm going to show them how they can make the devices themselves. I'm going to change the catalog into a magazine, complete with diagrams and instructions and information on what other people are making and doing."

Charles leaned back in his chair.

"I've often thought of starting a magazine myself," he said, reflective. "One on finance." And then he had another thought.

"But how are you going to get the money?"

"The catalog has a mailing list," Hugo said, trying to sound more confident than he felt. "I'll simply circulate the list, asking for people to send in subscriptions."

Charles looked scandalized. "You're going to ask people to send you money for a product that doesn't exist, that may never exist, and you think they will?"

Hugo nodded. "I think they will."

"I've never heard of such a thing," Charles said thoughtfully. "It sounds too simple, not quite . . . legal. No offense, Hugo, it just seems like there's too much trust involved." He stood up and wandered once more around the room, stopping at a bookcase to glance at the titles. He turned, smiling.

"Now I know where you get all your crazy ideas. I thought these would be technical manuals, but I see you read Verne and Wells, too. What are the German titles?"

Hugo was vastly pleased—here was another area of interest that he shared with his best friend.

"They're all romances, scientific romances. I'm very fond of them, even if they did give me nightmares when I was young."

Charles took one off the shelf and opened it at random. "You and Professor Lowell . . . do you really believe there are canals on Mars?"

"Maybe someday we'll go there and find out," Hugo said quietly. "But you probably think that's just another crazy idea, don't you?"

"I think a man will do almost anything he wants to do." And then a shadow passed over Charles' face that Hugo didn't see. "And maybe a few things that he shouldn't want to do."

* * *

Soup and crackers, Hugo thought bitterly. He was reduced to soup and crackers, and by the end of the week, he'd have to choose between food and rent. He could probably go back to the Roche battery people and offer his services as a consultant or a technician, but first he'd have to convince Mr. Roche he wasn't a spy for the competition. And with the Depression, Roche might not need help anyway. . . .

"You on a diet, Hugo?"

Charles had settled in the seat opposite him, turned to order from the waiter, then glanced back to Hugo.

"I'm sorry, my humor's misplaced. You're not feeling well or . . . ?" He ended the sentence delicately.

"I folded the Gee Cee Dry Battery Company yesterday," Hugo said dully. "I managed to pay off all the creditors, but it didn't leave much."

Charles looked dismayed. "You should have let them sue. That takes time, and meanwhile, you'd have some working capital."

Hugo held up his hand. "I'm not through yet . . . not quite." He took a folder from beside his chair and shoved it across the table at Charles, watching while he opened it and pulled out the magazine inside.

"It's what you call a 'dummy'," Hugo said after a moment. "It's something to show to potential advertisers."

"*Scientific Electrics,*" Charles said, quoting the title and frowning. "That's a little redundant, isn't it? Why not something that would appeal to the average reader, something more . . . modern?" He brightened. "Why not *Modern Electrics*?"

Hugo mulled it over for a minute, then nodded. "You're right, it's a better title."

Charles started dissecting the chicken on his plate, pleased at his suggestion and anxious to make more. "I like the title, Hugo, but the magazine's a little thin, don't you think? I should think you'd want to make a splash with something bigger. More pages, a larger size maybe."

"That would take a lot more money," Hugo said slowly.

Charles dabbed at his lips with his napkin, then paused with his napkin still at his mouth.

"You circulated the people who get your catalog?" Hugo nodded. "But nothing's come in yet?"

"A few dollars," Hugo said defensively. "But it's too soon."

Charles leaned back in his chair and thumbed through the dummy once again. "So it's still all a matter of money."

Hugo glanced out the window as a horsecar clopped past. "All a matter of money," he repeated bitterly.

"I have a suggestion," Charles said slowly. He reached in his coat pocket and pulled out a copy of the *New York American*, folded it to a page he'd marked and placed it flat on the table.

"Read it, Hugo."

Hugo scanned the quarter-page ad.

CHEMICAL FUEL CO. OF AMERICA.
SHARES $10 EACH.

This company has acquired the sole right to manufacture and sell a wonderful compound that when mixed with two parts ash and one part coal, produces from 50 percent to 150 percent more heat than can be secured from the best coal. . . .

"You believe this?" Hugo asked, surprised.

Charles grimaced. "I'm not a fool, Hugo. I investigated. The compound is some kind of a petroleum product—you were telling me about petroleum a few weeks back. They may be off on their figures, but I don't think by much."

Hugo looked at him blankly. "I don't know what you're suggesting."

Charles pointed at the bottom few lines of the ad. "Read the fine print, Hugo. They're offering a hundred-percent return in ninety days."

Hugo read the rest of the ad, then pushed away his half-finished bowl of soup. He was quiet for a long moment, hearing only the murmur of the diners around him. In the back of the restaurant, somebody had started up a gramophone with Billy Murray singing "Way Down in Cotton Town."

"They must be cheats and swindlers," he said at last.

Charles rolled his eyes.

"You don't know much about finance, Hugo. Read the other ads on the page—don't bother, I'll tell you. There's one for Concordia gold-mining stock at ten cents a share, and they're promising assays as high as two hundred and sixteen dollars a ton and that the stock will go up within a few days. They're cagey—they don't say by how much. And there's Barnes Copper at twenty cents a share and they guarantee twenty-five-percent return on your investment. And then there's one from Reall and Company, the bankers up on Broadway, offering Bell Telephone stock and reminding you that if you'd invested a hundred dollars in eighteen seventy-six you'd be worth a quarter of a million today."

He paused.

"Money makes money, Hugo. You may be right, these other companies are probably cheats and swindlers—with nickles and dimes per share, anybody can invest and probably nobody will investigate, because the money invested isn't worth the effort. But at ten dollars a share? Nobody's going to put money in the Chemical Fuel Company without looking into it, they have to be on the up-and-up."

"So how do you make *your* money, Charles?" Hugo asked softly.

Charles sighed. "That's a fair question, Hugo. But first you have to realize that money is like the waters of the ocean—it touches the shores of all the countries on the globe, and in each country it has a different value. Water is worth more than gold in a desert country, worth not much at all in a country covered with swamps."

He leaned across the table and looked Hugo directly in the eye.

"A dollar is worth so much here in the United States, Hugo. In a poor country, it's worth a lot more. There is a difference in value, and those who understand money can make a profit on that difference."

"Show me," Hugo said skeptically.

Charles reached into his wallet and took out a small piece of colored paper he threw on the table.

"That's an international postal-reply coupon, Hugo. They sell them in Italy and they sell them in Luxembourg, I'm sure. They're for prepayment of return postage. Now, the world cannot do without the international mails, right? So they all honor each other's postal rates. But postage is much cheaper in a poor country than in a rich one. These are cheap in most European countries. They can be redeemed for much more over here. I have an agent buy these coupons in Europe and I redeem them here. It's that simple. And the profit is all mine."

Hugo's head was swimming. "It's . . . illegal," he said at last.

Charles pushed the coupon toward him.

"Keep it, Hugo. Go to the post office and check it out. Look up the currency exchange rates. And then come back to me and apologize."

Hugo fingered the coupon for a moment, then folded it and put it in his pocket.

"The Chemical Fuel Company," he said slowly. "I don't have any money to invest in it."

Charles spread his arms expansively.

"I'll stake you, Hugo. Each of us will invest five thousand dollars in Chemical Fuel. By the end of ninety days, we sell our stock, you repay me and you'll still have five thousand dollars left for your new venture. How can you lose?"

For one of the few times in his life, Hugo felt close to tears.

"You would do this for me?"

"You're my best friend," Charles said warmly. He leaned

over and gripped Hugo's hand. "We newcomers to this country have to stick together."

It was when they were going out the door that Charles said, almost apologetically, "There's one minor detail."

A warning bell went off in Hugo's head, but he was so suffused with warm feelings toward Charles that he ignored it.

"My lawyers," Charles said. "When they draw up the agreement, they'll want some collateral. It's just a matter of form."

Hugo stopped abruptly, letting the diner behind bump into him. "I don't have any collateral. I don't own any property." He didn't try to keep the suspicion out of his voice.

Charles shrugged. "It's whatever will look good on paper, Hugo. Say Electro Importing, now that the battery company's been dissolved."

"That's everything I have," Hugo objected, balking.

They were outside now, standing in the sunshine and the warm breeze of a May day.

"Hugo," Charles said with a sudden firmness in his voice, "you have to face facts. For all practical purposes, Electro isn't worth anything at all. If you don't liquidate it this week, you will next week or the week after that. You can gamble on thousands of subscriptions coming through the mails, but I don't think you believe in that yourself— probably the most you get will be just enough to live on for the next ninety days." He cocked his head. "Don't you think it's worth the gamble? After all, it's going to be all my money."

He was right, Hugo thought, feeling slightly dazed.

"How can I thank you, Charles?" he said, overcome with gratitude.

Charles clapped him on the shoulder. "It's the least that one good friend can do for another."

Hugo sat in his chair behind the desk by the window and stared silently out at the rain clouds scudding over the rooftops across the street. There was a steady drumming against the windows, and a small trickle of water ran down the wall from a broken pane that had been patched with cardboard, now soaked and sagging.

"Tell me again, Charles," he said in a heavy voice.

Charles cleared his throat. He was seated in the other swivel chair, little rivulets of water running down the folds of his umbrella. Charles didn't seem nearly as devastated by the news as he was, Hugo thought grimly.

"It was in yesterday's paper," Charles said, clearing his throat once again. "I thought, of course, that you had seen it. The Chemical Fuel Company collapsed over the weekend—not enough money to pay the creditors. Or the investors."

Hugo was silent for a long moment.

"Cheats and swindlers," he said at last. "I told you, Charles."

Charles Ponzi said nothing. The eyes in the handsome face were alert and watching, but there was no sense of loss in them, which Hugo didn't understand. No sense of loss, no anger at the unfairness of it all, no apology for his own actions in urging a friend to invest. But as Charles had said three weeks ago, it was all his money.

"I'm sorry, Charles. For you to have lost so much."

Still no comment, only the watching and, oddly, the waiting.

"I will, of course, pay you back from the profits of *Modern Electrics* when I start publishing . . ."

"Yes," Charles said at last, clearing his throat, "that's something we have to talk about." Hugo frowned and tried to read beneath the bland expression on his poker face.

"You remember," Charles continued slowly, not moving his eyes from Hugo's, "Electro Importing was your collateral on the loan. That included *Modern Electrics*." He waved his hand. "And the contents of the office here. I'm afraid . . . they're no longer yours, Hugo. They belong to me."

Hugo came upright in his chair. "What do you mean?"

"Your collateral," Charles repeated in a suddenly harsh voice. He pulled a paper from his pocket and let it drop on the wooden floor between them. "There's your contract, Hugo, signed and witnessed. In exchange for the loan of five thousand dollars, I get Electro Importing, the magazine, this office and its contents, your lease . . ." He shook his head slightly, as if astonished at Hugo's naivete. "You must have read it before you signed it."

Hugo stared at him, seeing him for the first time. A young, dapper little man, handsome and charming. With eyes like a snake's.

"I'll take you to court," he said hoarsely.

"You do that." Charles retrieved the contract and read the heading at the top. " 'Adams and Grant, Attorneys at Law.' The best in the business, Hugo. You won't win."

Hugo stood up and took a step forward. Charles tapped on the floor once with his umbrella and the door abruptly opened. A policeman was standing just outside, his arms folded.

"It's time for you to leave, Hugo," Charles said casually. "Please take your coat, that's the only thing you own in here."

"You can't run the magazine," Hugo said in a tight voice.

Charles shrugged. "All I have to do is open the window and cry for an editor and I'm sure there'd be a dozen at the door in five minutes."

"You never invested a dime, did you?" Hugo suddenly asked.

"Of course I did," Charles said smoothly, and Hugo knew instinctively he was lying. "But the books of Chemical Fuel are under lock and key. I doubt that anybody will get to see them for months. And I'm not so sure that that kind of information would be in them in any event."

"You're a swindler," Hugo said heatedly. "You cheat your friends."

Charles looked surprised. "That's slander, Hugo, but

speaking in the abstract, I'd say one seldom succeeds in cheating one's enemies. A person's innocence is part of his charm, but it can also be his undoing. We all owe it to ourselves not to be . . : too innocent."

"Widows and orphans," Hugo cursed. "Your natural prey."

Charles shot his cuffs and stood up, glancing with distaste at the steady rain outside.

"Factory girls and fellow immigrants, Hugo. Incidentally, I really think you ought to look up Marie. She'd be most appreciative of a little sympathy just about now— you weren't the only investor."

He ran his hand over the dusty surface of the worktable, and there was a certain pride of possession in the movement. Then Charles turned and looked at him with the odd cock to his head that Hugo knew so well.

"I'm not a swindler, Hugo. I resent that." Hugo guessed that he was speaking for the benefit of the policeman at the door. "I'm a financier, and I make my money by studying market trends and investments. You came to me for help and I generously tried to help you. I offered to loan you money and you accepted. I suggested an investment and you agreed. As any good businessman, I insisted on collateral and drew up an agreement, which you signed. And all of that can be proved in a court of law. It's not my fault that Gee Cee Battery foundered, and it's hardly my fault that your scheme for a magazine is failing, or for that matter, that Chemical Fuel went under."

Charles waved his hand about the room.

"What I get in return for my time and money is a lease on a rundown office, a worktable, a desk and two chairs, your list of addresses, cartons of moldering catalogs, a bookcase of old books, and boxes of useless wireless parts. Not a very fair return on my investment in *you*, Hugo."

"Get out," Hugo said thickly.

Charles shook his head and nodded toward the policeman.

"No, no, Hugo—that's what I tell you." He pulled off his

gloves, shook the remaining water off his umbrella, and pointed toward the door. "Please leave, Hugo. I have work to do."

Hugo wandered the streets for hours, cursing silently to himself. He blamed himself fully as much as he blamed Ponzi, even more so. He should have been able to see through the man, his youth was no excuse. But that was the stock-in-trade of swindlers; they had the knack for making you like them, and believe in them. He'd have to remember that for the future.

He looked for work for two days—Roche had, predictably, turned him down. At noon on the third day, he found himself in the doorway of Rossi's and ducked in for a quick cup of coffee. His usual table by the window was vacant and he sat down, nursed his coffee, and stared out at the people on the street. There was no hope for it, he'd have to do the one thing he swore he would never do when he came to America. He'd have to send to his father for funds and he'd have to do it right away; he doubted that he could last for longer than a week with the money he had on him.

"Sir?"

Hugo, startled, glanced up. The man was well-dressed and apologetic. Hugo hadn't the faintest idea of what about, he'd never seen him before.

"You were in here a few weeks back," the man continued, easing into the empty chair at the table. "Discussing some investments with a friend. Do you remember?"

He would never forget, Hugo thought bitterly, and nodded. The man licked his lips, hesitating.

"I wondered if you knew of any favorable investment or company, your friend seemed so knowledgeable . . ." His voice trailed off.

Hugo stared at him blankly. He was well-dressed, obviously had money, and was anxious to invest it. He looked like the type who was interested in a quick return. And a healthy one.

"I'm not—" he started, then glanced out the window.

There was some sort of commotion in the street. He watched for a moment, then caught his breath as a man passed by wearing a harness and carrying an electrical apparatus on his back that Hugo recognized immediately. Hanging from the apparatus was a sign that read: PONZI'S TELIMCO WIRELESS! RANGE A FULL MILE! TRY IT NOW—ONLY $7.50!

Hugo turned back to the man in front of him. "There might be," he said bitterly. He reached into his wallet and pulled out the international postal-reply coupon that Ponzi had given him a few weeks before. "There's a consortium that deals in the imbalances in foreign currency and postal-reply coupons." He was thinking very quickly now, and invented a name on the spot. "The Securities Exchange Company. No doubt you've heard of it?"

"Of course," the man said. His eyes were glowing. "The return—how much of a return?"

"Why, you can double your money in ninety days," Hugo said sarcastically. At any moment his companion would realize he was being made a fool of, but he deserved it.

Suddenly there was a twenty-dollar bill on the table.

"I take it you and your friend are agents for the company. I'd like to invest."

Hugo stared at the money, his mouth open. Twenty dollars. It was twice as much as he had in his pockets, twice as much as he had in the entire world.

"Why, yes," he said slowly. "We've only just started." He searched his pockets for a scrap of paper. "This is an unofficial receipt, we should have the official ones tomorrow."

He scribbled the amount and his rooming-house address on the paper, and the man thanked him, shook his hand and left. Hugo stared for a moment longer at the bill, then reached for the menu.

"The fellow you were just talking to," somebody said. Hugo glanced up from the listing of steaks and chops and roasted chickens to stare into the face of another man, slightly older than the first but in most respects, his double. "I couldn't help but overhear. Ninety days to double your investment?"

This time a fifty-dollar bill graced the tabletop.

"I'm really not—" Hugo started hesitantly.

"My money's not as good as his?" the man interrupted, insulted.

The world was full of fools, Hugo sighed. Ponzi must have figured that out a long time ago.

"Of course it is," he said reassuringly. He scribbled out another receipt and sank back in his chair, deep in thought. He now had enough money to pay the first man his profit and he was ten dollars to the good. Two or three more investors like that and he could pay back the second man, or the third, or the fourth.

Halfway through his steak, he had the outline of the company firmly in mind, as well as a prospectus. He would open an office and place a small ad in the paper, but he was certain that news about the company would spread by word of mouth. All he had to do was to find a legitimate investment for his earnings. But there would be time for that.

He finished the steak and nibbled at one of the little cakes, deciding that the pink icing wasn't so bad after all. The audion tube and the Telimco Wireless and the canals of Mars were receding rapidly in his memory. . . .

Charles Ponzi finished checking the proofs on the latest issue of *Science and Invention*—he'd renamed *Modern Electrics* several years after he'd started publishing it. It had been amazingly successful, especially after he'd hired that editorial cartoonist away from the *Jersey Journal*. With his knack for machinery, the man had been wasting his talents at the paper.

He leaned back in his swivel chair and put his feet up on the desk, then lit up a cigar and fished in his wastebasket for the copy of the *New York Times* he'd thrown away that morning, too busy to finish it. He glanced at the

usual political machinations—he should have run for public office, he'd have been good at that—then turned to the
financial pages. The stock offerings were more reserved
now, but—he smiled to himself—there were still the usual
cheats and swindlers.

Then his fingers tightened and he read the headlines intently.

*Hugo Gernsback, creator of the "Gernsback Scheme," re-
leased from jail.*

He scanned the article quickly. How long had it been?
Almost twenty years now since he'd bought *Modern Electrics* from Hugo. Well, maybe "bought" wasn't the word.
But he had been a different man then, it had been a different life—one that he was glad he'd gotten out of. He
didn't really have the stomach for it, even then.

But Hugo. . . . He frowned. He'd misjudged him, he'd
felt sure that Hugo would borrow money from his father
and start all over again. Instead, he'd taken to "high" finance like a fish to water. Moved to Boston and started is-
suing stock certificates in a variation of the pyramid
scheme. Turned out Hugo had a silver tongue after all,
half the Boston police had invested with him.

Well, you could never tell what made a good man go
bad. . . .

He dropped the paper and bent over his desk, flipping
through the pages of a dummy for a new magazine. Great,
catchy cover, but he didn't care much for the title. It was
the first fiction magazine for the company and it needed
an intriguing title, something that would sum up the fantastic contents, a title that would be thrilling, astonishing. . . .

And then he had it. He searched in the desk drawer for
a black grease pencil and wrote across the top of the
dummy:

Astounding Stories of Super Science. . . .

David Gerrold has many arrows in his quiver. As a novelist, he has produced the classic *When H.A.R.L.I.E. Was One*, and the best-selling *War Against the Chtorr* series. As a television writer, he has dozens of shows to his credit, including "The Trouble With Tribbles," recently voted the best *Star Trek* episode of all time. As a short-story writer, he has been turning out hard-hitting pieces for better than twenty years. And as an editor, he produced some of the better anthologies of the 1970s.

In the following story, David inverts one of the more spectacular crimes of recent years, gets in some jibes at some of his favorite targets, and shows us a very different Charles Manson. . . .

What Goes Around
by David Gerrold

The fire blossoms outward, rosy petals of orange and black. The bullet spits. The sound pops softly in the sweating August night. Again and again.

It begins.

The door explodes. Horror invades, laughing wildly, screaming with invented rage at invisible monsters, nobody home here, just bodies, it doesn't matter—rage assaults the nearest target.

The screams become a nightmare chorus. On and on. Outrage and shock. The knives begin to work, plunging, tearing—rending first the clothes, then the flesh, and deeper still, into the heart of the beast, and from there into the fibrillating soul of the species. The wounds cut deep.

Bitterly the blades keep biting. Slender arms pump up and down, struggling with the dreadful work. Steaming blood pours forth, the muscles pull and strain. The bodies resist; it isn't easy—tendons, cartilage, muscles, bone, and spurting hot, wet blood; a fountain of gore—it isn't neat, it isn't pretty. Life fights back, it resists the assault; it struggles, fights, bites, kicks, screams, claws, shrieks, begs, wonders, pleads, gasps, and refuses to give up, even as it shreds away with dreadful ripping noises.

The gleeful cries go on and on. The harridans, the witches, cackle and laugh at the audacity of this vicious celebration. "Die, piggie, die!" The walls are splattered with scarlet slashes. Steel skitters along bone. Cartilage resists, then breaks. Bodies jerk, and still the blood pours forth, the baby slides wetly into dreadfulness.

Saturday morning.

The maid discovered the bodies. She ran screaming down the driveway to a neighbor. The police arrived in a squadron of gleaming vehicles, black-and-whites, and plainclothes—all with their lights blazing, some with sirens screaming.

The young detectives stood at the door of the sprawling house and stared in at the carnage—stunned beyond words—reluctant to enter, not knowing where to start. It was like a scene out of Hell. That was the metaphor, but it was insufficient.

"Who lives here?" one of them asked.

Another one turned away, gagging.

A third wrote down license numbers and began calling them in.

Few of them had ever seen anything like this in their careers. They'd heard about crimes of horrific violence; they'd seen the casebooks of a few. They'd never really expected to have to investigate one like this. Their training failed them, overpowered by their instinctive human revulsion.

But then the Chief of Detectives arrived and started barking orders. He barely glanced inside the house. He knew better. He didn't want to know. He didn't want the memories. He didn't want the dead things clogging up his vision, troubling his sleep.

The young officer came back from his black-and-white, holding his notebook open. "The pickup truck is registered to Charles Manson, white, male, age forty-two."

"Manson?" said one of the detectives, frowning. "Why does that name sound familiar?"

The Chief of Detectives grunted. "There used to be a rock star by that name." He turned to the officer. "Is this the same guy?"

"I don't know."

"Find out," he said—and groaned. Looking past the officer, he saw the arrival of the first carload of vultures. He recognized the reporters from the *Times*. Overhead, a news-chopper began clattering through the smoggy air, circling the site around and around. Up the hill, the neighbors were already out on their porches, shading their eyes against the morning sun and staring down at the tableau below.

The newspapers had a feeding frenzy. Banner headlines advertised the gory event as if it were important: **ROCK BAND MURDERED IN ORGY OF VIOLENCE**. Beneath, in smaller type, the article identified the victims: **Charles Manson and "The Family" Found Stabbed to Death in Manson's Bel-Air Home**.

The articles described the horror without being explicit: "Even veterans of the LAPD Violent Crimes Division were stunned by the carnage.

"Although officials at the scene refused to go on record about the apparent murder spree, it is believed that the Manson home was invaded by three or more knife-wielding individuals who stabbed all six of the occupants to death. A seventh victim was found shot to death in his car.

"At present, the police have not indicated whether or not they have any leads in the case."

The text went on to explain:

"Although generally unknown to the record-buying

public, Charles Manson and 'The Family' were fairly well-known in the Los Angeles underground club scene.

"One club-owner, who refused to be identified, said, 'Yeah, we knew them. They were bad. Loud and bad. That was why we booked them—as a kind of gag. We'd put them in as a spacer between two good sets. The kids hooted and jeered.

" 'Manson ate it up. He loved that shit. He'd get out there and scream at the crowds and they'd scream right back. He was a great warm-up. But, no—he never figured it out that no one took him seriously.

" 'You want the truth? Manson was an asshole. And the girls were pigs, pardon my language, but it's true. They were over-the-hill, overweight, out-of-tune, and ugly. If Manson liked you, he'd tell his girls to go to bed with you. I hate to think what he'd tell them to do if he didn't like you.' "

A sidebar article listed the Manson Family's history:

"The Manson Family made only three albums in their short-lived recording career. Their first, *We Are the Nightmare*, released in August 1969, attracted far more attention for the offensiveness of its language than for the quality of the music, most of which was shrieked rather than sung. *Rolling Stone* magazine gave it the lowest rating in its history, a ¼ star rating, and said the album was, at best, only good for breaking your lease. Nevertheless, the furor over the album's language guaranteed it enough sales to make it a cult item among radical punk rockers.

"Regarding *We Are the Nightmare*, band member Charles 'Tex' Watson freely admitted, 'Hey, man. We didn't intend this as music. It ain't supposed to be listened to. It's supposed be an initiation into the tribe. You have to inhale this deep into your mind, that's all. It's like, you know, a scream of consciousness. We don't want people sitting around and *listening* to this shit. We want them jumping up and down and shrieking with us. Like the hash-smoking assassins would pump themselves up into a killing frenzy before going out into the world to commit mayhem. Well, that's us. We're freaking fucking out.' (Watson was found shot to death in his car in the driveway.)

"Manson's second album, *Die, Piggies, Die!*, received an even worse critical drubbing. Cordwainer Bird, writing for *Rolling Stone*, opined that he hoped that the title of the LP indicated that this disk was a suicide note. 'Anyone stupid enough to buy this whiny piece of enervated bat-guano ought to have their ears ripped off their heads and stapled to the walls, where they can at least be useful as ashtrays. This record isn't even good enough be called crap. It's an insipid, puerile waste of vinyl, not even of interest to those morbid curiosity-seekers who like to stand around and gawk at the scene of a fatal accident.'

"Manson was so enraged by that review that when he was questioned about it on KPFK's late-night *Under the Rock* program, he erupted into a furious tirade. He threatened to cut out Cordwainer Bird's heart and eat it raw. It is widely believed that *Blind as a Bird*, the first of Manson's three singles, was written with Cordwainer Bird in mind. The lyrics, screamed in a near-incoherent rage, included these lines:

> " 'You don't know me! You don't know! You stupid
> motherfucking little dwarf, you don't know shit!'
> 'If I can't make you love me, then I'll make you
> hate me! But I won't let you ignore me!' "

"The resultant flurry of threats, lawsuits, and injunctions kept the album in the news long enough for it to sell a modest number of copies. Sludge Records (now defunct) even sold T-shirts labeled 'ONE OF THE MORBIDLY CURIOUS' to those who sent in ten dollars and a proof-of-purchase certificate.

"Curiously, it was Manson's third and last album that received the best reviews. *The Cage of Life* was released in 1972 and attracted almost no attention at all. Recorded entirely in Manson's garage, the LP has minimal production values, but the stark simplicity of the arrangements created a sense of the darkness of the LA club scene. The album's set piece, a brooding seven-minute dirge called 'Life Sentence,' tells the story of a man who has emptied his life of all value and now waits only for death. But by then, even curiosity-seekers had lost all interest in Manson and few copies of the LP even found their way into record stores."

The commentators *tsked*. They couldn't quite bring themselves to mourn Manson; there was nothing to mourn. He'd been a failure in life. He was, at best, a footnote; at worst, an embarrassing asterisk, a nothing.

What made him noteworthy now was not his life, but only his manner of leaving it. So they dwelt on that. They alluded to the rumors of mystic symbols written in blood on the walls of his home—his blood, his walls—and wondered who had been responsible and why.

They licked their lips and spent lugubrious tears on the unborn baby of Patricia Krenwinkle. They worried about Susan Atkins' last terrifying moments. They burrowed through the sordid details of the lives of Squeaky Lynnette Fromme and Leslie Van Houtin.

Perhaps the strange X's cut into their foreheads had something to do with the albums they recorded. The police spent hours playing and replaying the LP's. They paid particular attention to "Dyslexic Sadie" and "Smelter Skelter." They studied an underground video of the Family, trying to understand who these people were and why someone would want to murder them.

Charlie was the lead singer, with a voice as thin and unpleasant as February ice. Tex was the ax-man, posturing and posing—he would have upstaged Charlie were it not for Charlie's riveting, Rasputin-like gaze. The girls danced behind them, backing Manson's incoherent lyrics and Watson's pretentious gruntings with a ragged embroidery of artificial doo-wap noises.

In the meantime, the sales of guard dogs, security de-

vices, alarms, fences, cellular phones—and guns, weapons
of all kinds—jumped and kept on jumping. August turned
into September and the terror hardened into distrust and
bitterness. Whatever was out there remained unknown,
unidentified, uncontrolled. Would there be more killings?

Brooding late one night in an hour-long soliloquy,
Cordwainer Bird devoted one entire show to what he
called "the Manson phenomenon."

"It's not Manson," Bird began. "He was a nothing—a
gnat's fart, not worth the energy to talk about. He was one
of those little scuttlefish that comes out of the woodwork,
attracted by the light, but totally lacking any understanding of how to create the light in the first place.

"Yeah, right—" Bird said, jabbing his finger at the audience. "I'm an asshole for speaking ill of the dead, is that
your point? What do you think, bunky? The act of dying
automatically elevates a human being to sainthood? I got
news for you—Manson's music *sucked*. It sucked when he
was alive, it ain't gonna get any better now that he's dead.

"And his personal habits—? I'll tell you. He *smelled*.
Yeah, I met him. Three times. And you know what? He
was afraid of me. All those threats? He just did a little
shuffle and jive and dropped his head and wouldn't look
me in the eye. A fucking coward. A yutz.

"You know who he was? He was that skinny kid in the
ninth grade, the one who never got any hair on his chest
or under his arms or on his balls; the one who picked his
nose and ate the boogers when he thought no one was
looking; the one who had to be reminded to take a shower
once in a while because nobody ever explained to him
about deodorants.

"You know all those pictures of him making him look
like some kind of scary vampire bat? That was bullshit.
He was a scrawny little guy. Shorter than me! Shorter than
the average fire hydrant—a sunken chest, he looked like
he was suffering from terminal malnutrition. Yeah, he had
a great stare and he was incoherent, whacked out on

drugs and booze half the time, and you think that's the sign of a serious craftsman, the fact that he looked weird and you can't understand him?

"Okay—" Bird interrupted himself. "You want me to be compassionate. I'll be compassionate for two seconds. He had a lousy childhood. He can be excused for being an asshole, he had a lousy childhood. Okay, I'm through being compassionate. That's so much crap, it makes my gorge buoyant. *I* had a lousy childhood! Half the people in this room had a lousy childhood. So fucking what! We got over it. We didn't use it as an excuse to assault the people around us. We got over it. He didn't.

"So what's his claim to fame? No talent and he got himself murdered. And you people are gathering around, sniffing like jackals at a rotting corpse, pissing and moaning about how awful it was that these lives were snuffed out! What the hell—if it weren't for the fact that there's someone out there who is provably crazier than Charlie and his stupid Family, I'd probably want to shake his hand and thank him for improving the average IQ of the human race and removing some seriously sociopathic phenotypes from the gene pool.

"Y'know," Bird said, trotting up into the audience and sitting on the lap of a fat woman. She giggled in delight. "Y'know, if this universe worked the way it was supposed to—like if God had stuck around instead of taking off early for the weekend—Manson's name would be unknown to each and every one of us in this theater. He would have never made a ripple. He would have died forgotten. Instead, what do we get?" He leaped back to his feet. "The bloody awfulness of his death has turned him into a ninety-day wonder, a cultural icon. It's the goddamn Lindbergh baby all over again—only this time we've got CNN giving us hourly updates on how incompetent the Los Angeles Police Department really is. It's a bloody Frankenstein movie.

"How many of you are going to feel safe in your bed tonight? Yeah, none of you, that's right! That's why you do it. You love being scared. You love wallowing in other people's dreadful deaths, without ever stopping to think of the horror of it! Do you assholes know how much horror there is in the world? There's already more than enough for all of us! Why do you want to create more? What do you get from it?

"I'll tell you what you get—you get the feeling of power, the vicarious thrill of going along for the ride during a criminal act of mindless, stupid, thoughtless violence. You're not identifying yourselves with the ones who died screaming in the night—you're secretly recreating the act of murder, with yourselves playing the lead role as a modern-day Jack-the-fucking-Ripper. And by that singular deed, you align yourself with the disease, not the cure!

"Don't you give me that look, lady, that self-righteous, 'It's not my fault' look. I've seen you standing in the supermarket line, all of you, checking out the headlines in the *National Enquirer*. Oh, you don't read the *Enquirer*, right? So this speech is for everybody else. What do you read? *People* magazine? I thought so. Really socially uplifting material, lady. I'm not impressed. And who's that turnip sitting next to you, your husband? You, sir? When was the last time you read something that didn't have the dialogue in balloons?

"The horror isn't the murders, you idiots. The horror is that we've made such horrors commonplace in our society. These murders will be forgotten in two years, because somebody else will be murdered in some other place, some other way, and next time we'll have color video of it, and CNN will make some poor sucker rich because he was standing in the right place at the right time with his fucking camcorder turned on. Who really gives a shit about Charles Manson? None of you do. You just wish there was a video of him begging his killers for his life, so you could ride the adrenaline roller-coaster one more time.

"He was a weasel and he's dead, but the real assassins are the ones who keep him writhing on the knife!"

* * *

Around town, those who could reliably claim to have known him—*them*—now had stories they could dine out on:

"Oh, yeah, I knew him. . . . What was he like?" Shrug. "Actually, I never saw him get mad. Sometimes he could be a real charmer. He asked me to engineer an album for him, but nothing ever came of it—"

"The girls? They had a sleazy reputation. Yeah, it was true. If Charlie liked you, yeah, you could end up the meat in a pussy sandwich. But . . . it wasn't something you wanted to do twice. The girls were—it's hard to describe—I think the best word to use is *trayf*. It's a Yiddish word, yeah. It means *unclean*. I got a weird feeling off them, I can't explain it, but it was like being with dead meat. . . ."

"I got a friend whose cousin works in the coroner's office, and she said that the bodies were *dismembered*. The heart was removed from Manson's body and they still haven't found it. The baby was cut out of the mother—I mean, the things she said—it was sick. But they won't put it in the paper, because they're hoping to keep it secret, to help catch the killers."

"Okay, I'll tell you what I heard. I got this from the head of legal. He knows one of the detectives on the case. Anyway, the theory is that Charlie and his girls were having a wild party with some drug dealers, gang members, crack-heads, slam-bangers, whatever they're called, and it got out of control. Charlie tried to stiff them, offered them sex with the girls instead of cash, or maybe he tried to rob them, and the bangers took them down instead. It wasn't supposed to get that violent, but they were all strung out on drugs and you know—"

"No, I swear, this is God's honest truth. The caretaker was having a homosexual affair with Charleton Heston. Heston was there! While it was happening. But when they heard the screams, they climbed out a window and hid naked in the bushes. Then they snuck away. My step-brother is a public defender. He heard it from a secretary in the DA's office. The caretaker's lie-detector test was really dirty. They think the caretaker knows more than he's saying."

"Did you see this in the *San Francisco Chronicle*? Manson was a big L. Ron Hubbard fan. Now they think the Scientologists might be involved somehow—"

"You won't believe this, but I was invited up there a few times. Yeah, I could have been up there that night. Yeah, the rumor was that Charlie always had plenty of dope, that he grew it in the basement, that they were always stoned. But that's not true. They were beer drunks. They sat around drunk all day, watching TV. They watched reruns. They watched *Happy Days* and the *Brady Bunch* and the *Partridge Family*, all of those. Charlie loved them. They were supposed to be the nasty boys of rock, and the truth is, they were just a bunch of couch potatoes vegging out on the phosphors. It was boring, man. Stupid. Killing them was redundant. They were already dead from the neck up."

The investigative task force spread out across the city. Charlie's connections to the music community, the drug community, the gay community, the prison community, the science fiction community, the Scientologists, and the underground club scene were all investigated. Nothing substantial developed, but everything was pursued. Something had to fit somewhere; the crime couldn't have been simply a random happenstance. If a band of drug-crazed hippies could burst into anyone's home on a murderous killing spree, then what purpose was there to civilization?

Days stretched into months. No new leads developed. Old trails dried up. Publicly, the police said they were still investigating every possibility. Privately, they acknowledged that they were getting nowhere fast.

A panel of criminal psychologists and detectives appeared on the Cordwainer Bird talk show to discuss the apparent failure of the LAPD to produce substantial results. Bird had intended to focus on the issue of public safety, but instead allowed himself to be distracted into more speculation on the unsolved murders.

"What puzzles me the most," said one of the headshrinkers, "is the silence. There had to be at least three killers—probably more. The violence in the Manson house was . . . well, it wasn't describable. I was in Vietnam, and I never saw anything like this. But even assuming there were only three killers, that's three people who would know. More, if you include other gang members, family members—or anyone else who knew them and would have a reason to be suspicious. Whoever did it would have come home drenched with the blood of their victims. That couldn't have gone unnoticed. So, why haven't we gotten a call from someone's girl friend or neighbor or cleaning lady? A secret this big—it's got to break sooner or later."

Bird seized on this thought as the channel for the discussion that followed. "All right," he demanded. "What are the possibilities then?"

A forensic pathologist suggested, "The violence of the crime scene seems to rule out that it was an execution; but maybe it was an execution gone bad. In any case, if it was an execution, the killers were professional. They're probably out of the country by now. I'd look in the Bahamas, somewhere around there."

The first detective shook his head. "No, I think the killers are dead, at least one or two of them anyway. Maybe the victims fought back and the murderers died of their wounds later. Maybe they were killed in an innocent-looking car crash while they were trying to escape. Maybe they fled to Arizona or Nevada and were killed there. The best way to cover up an assassination is to kill the assassin too."

Bird spent the better part of the hour pursuing conspiracy theories, trying to puzzle out why anyone would want to murder a useless old has-been like Charles Manson.

Finally, at the end of the hour, he turned to the last of the detectives, an older man who'd sat quietly puffing his pipe, listening to everything and saying nothing. "What do you think?" he demanded.

The old man shifted his position in his chair, tapped his pipe on the ashtray, and spoke with deceptively soft words. "I think everybody's looking in the wrong place. I think the killers are already in custody," he said. "I think the LAPD picked them up on some traffic violation, found an old warrant for unpaid parking tickets, and put them away for a few months. Something like that. If they're a bunch of giddy kids—and that's my guess—then they've probably told their cell mates. And I'll bet that the cell mates are too terrified to say anything. That's what I think."

The following evening, Cordwainer Bird hosted a panel of psychics to see if they could solve the murders with their metaphysical prowess.

One psychic said that the murderer had red hair. Another said that the house was the target, that the murderers were trying to avenge a crime that the house had committed. A third claimed that the murderers had a supernatural connection with their victims, a connection that could not be explained or understood within the context of Euclidean geometry—that the lives of killers and victims were tangled in a web that went beyond the context of ordinary spacetime. Right.

Bird let them babble for twenty or thirty minutes before he angrily ordered them all out of the studio. Then he turned to his studio audience and delivered another of his scathing diatribes, this one about the human mind's inability to accept *"I don't know"* as an answer—that we will make up the most astonishing explanations and reasons and justifications, just so we don't have to live with the dreadfulness of having something in our lives feel *incomplete*.

"You supposedly intelligent human beings, educated and literate, will throw all of that rationality out of the window to become supplicants to a bunch of post-menopausal, self-important, unschooled, pretentious, posturing, posing old fools. These idiots don't know anything; they've conned themselves into believing they have some connection to the cosmic fluxes of the universe—and you idiots are so desperate to believe, you'll hang on every word, simply because you can't stand the pain of *not* knowing the answer.

"You wanna know the truth? When you don't know, you won't admit it. You got it hardwired that not-knowing means you're stupid. No, you got it worse than that. You believe that not-knowing is connected to your survival. So when you don't know something, you don't put yourself into a rational investigation, an inquiry, which is what a truly intelligent being would do. No, the evidence is that when you don't know something, you make something up. All of you—and then you pass your bullshit around as if it means something. And then you have the colossal gall to wonder why you're not producing results!

"You know what I think? I think the murderers are just like you. Just smart enough to understand the difference between rational and stupid, but not smart enough to recognize which side of the line you belong on. I think that when they finally catch the bozos who did it, we'll all be amazed at how small and pitiful they really are."

He was right.

Two days later, an ABC news crew, acting on its own initiative, performed an interesting experiment.

A driver, a cameraman, and two reporters started at the Manson house on Cielo Drive. They pulled out of the driveway and headed down the hill to Benedict Canyon, where they turned left to head out toward the San Fernando Valley. In the backseat, the two reporters began changing clothes. The cameraman taped the entire process.

When both reporters had completely re-dressed, the driver stopped the car. They were on a wide curve overlooking a fairly steep slope. Reporting on their regularly scheduled broadcast later that night, they said, "We assumed that the murderers changed clothes in the car. We thought to re-create that drive and see what we could discover. What we discovered was the place where they threw their bloody clothes away."

Three pairs of jeans, a flannel shirt, a USC sweatshirt, a blue T-shirt, and a black windbreaker were found on the hillside. Also a pair of tennis shoes and socks. All the clothes were blood-soaked.

The ABC news team knew better than to touch the evidence, but they brought back great shots of their reporters pointing at the clothes on the hillside and the forensics team bagging the evidence and carting it away.

The USC sweatshirt provided the break in the case. It was an expensive limited-edition shirt available only to members of Tommy Trojan's Homecoming Committee. Only thirty of them had been made. Armed with a new list of suspects, the detectives fanned out again. Anyone who couldn't produce their Homecoming sweatshirt was a suspect.

The list was narrowed to ten, then six, then three.

One of the young men contacted hadn't seen his shirt in months. His ex-roommate had apparently taken it with him when he'd moved out. "No, I didn't know him well at all. He was only here for a few weeks. I hardly ever saw him. He'd come in, crash for a few hours, then disappear again. A couple of times he brought his doper friends around, but I wouldn't let them smoke in here, so they stopped coming. He didn't have the second month's rent, so I told him to move out. When he did, he stole a bunch of stuff. It was real annoying, too. His dad was some rich director; he didn't need to steal my stuff. What's this all about, anyway? Does this have something to do with those clothes they found on TV?"

A bench warrant was issued for J. Michael Tate, also known as Joseph Tate-Polanski, the son of Sharon Tate and her ex-husband, Roman Polanski. Further investigation turned up the names of several of Tate-Polanski's frequent acquaintances: Marina Folger, Zbig Frykowski, and David Sebring.

Folger and Frykowski's whereabouts were unknown; they were presumed to be in Europe somewhere. David Sebring had died of a self-induced drug overdose three days after the Manson murders. It took a while longer for the LAPD to find Joe Tate. It turned out they'd had him in custody all along.

Joe Tate had been arrested on a DUI at the end of August. It was his third offense, the judge threw the book at him; he was still incarcerated in the county jail and would be for the next nine months.

When he was questioned by detectives, he readily admitted the killings. "It was the house, man—the house. My mom and dad lived there before the divorce. That was where I grew up. I was happy there—and then they sold it and he moved to Europe and she moved to New York, and I blame the people who bought it for breaking up our family. I wanted to get even, that's all. They had no right. I wanted to show them that they hadn't won anything at all. And I did. I don't feel sorry for them. They had it coming."

Cordwainer Bird had only a few more comments about the case. He tossed them off in his opening monologue the day after the verdict came down.

"Y'see," he said. "This was my point all along. Everyone was running around looking for grand conspiracies and strange connections. There weren't any. There never are. The universe is running by accident and God's on vacation. Stop looking for answers—even if there were any, you wouldn't understand them. Leave it be, you assholes. There just ain't no justice in this life—and that's that."

What would an alternate anthology be without an alternate Elvis Presley story? Fortunately, thanks to Walter Jon Williams, author of *Hardwired*, *Aristoi*, and several other well-received novels, you're not going to have to find out. . . .

Red Elvis
by Walter Jon Williams

Here it is, the white house south of the city on US 51. The Memphis Palace of Labor. The district is called Whitehaven and is tony, but the Palace itself sits on the highway opposite some ugly strip malls, a John Deere dealer, and a burger joint.

It's a big house made of Tennessee fieldstone, with a portico and a green lawn and some little mean shacks out back for the servants. It's not the sort of place you'd expect at all, not for the person who lived there. It's the sort of house a boss would live in.

There's a long, long line of mourners out front, stretching from the front door across the drive and for half a mile down Highway 51. The harmonies of a black gospel choir sound faintly from the interior.

Join the long, slow line of mourners who file past the coffin. Hear the music that rings somehow inside you.

Remember who the dead man was, and why you're here.

The boy knows that he has a brother who is just like him, except that he is an angel. They were twins— identical twins, because there was the same webbing between two of their toes—and the eldest lived and the youngest was born dead. And the boy's Mamma tells him that this fact makes him special, that even before he was born, he made his brother an angel.

But that doesn't mean that the boy can't talk to his brother when he wants to. His Mamma takes him to the cemetery often, and the two of them sit by the brother's grave and pray to him and sing songs and tell him everything that happened since they last visited.

The boy likes the cemetery. It's so much more pleasant than the family's little two-room shanty in East Tupelo, where the wind cries like a wailing haunt through the gray clapboard walls and the furniture needs mending and the slop bucket under the sink always smells poorly.

In the cemetery, the boy can always talk to his brother and tell him everything. In the cemetery, someone is always bringing flowers.

Something bad has happened and the boy has lost his Daddy. Men with badges came and took him away. He hears new words—there is "forgery" and "arrest," along with a word whose very utterance is an occasion for terror—"Parchman." Parchman is where Daddy is going, and a man named Orville Bean is sending him there. Orville Bean is Daddy's boss.

The boy screams and weeps and clings to his Mamma's leg. The men with badges told Mamma that the family has to leave the house. The boy always thought the house belonged to Mamma, but now it belongs to Orville Bean. Suddenly the gray two-room shack is the most precious thing the boy has ever known.

Mamma pets him and calls him by his special name, but the boy won't be stilled. Grandpa and Grandma, who have come to help Mamma move the furniture, watch the boy's agony with a certain surprise.

"That Mr. Bean sure is cruel," Grandpa says. "Boss don't have no mercy on a working man."

That night the boy prays to his brother to rescue Daddy, to fly him out of Parchman on angels' wings, but his brother doesn't answer.

* * *

Mamma's real name is Satnin, though everyone else calls her Gladys. She and the boy are never apart. She won't let the boy do anything that might hurt him, like swim or dive, or play with other children outside of Mamma's sight. He sleeps with Satnin every night so that nothing can harm him.

Satnin teaches him things to keep him safe. He learns to touch iron after he sees a black cat, and that if you have a spell cast on you, you can take the spell off with a Jack, which is a red cloth filled with coal dust and dirt and a silver dime. The boy learns that most dreams aren't true but that some are, and that Satnin's dreams are almost always true. When she dreams about something bad that's going to happen, she'll do something to prevent it, like make a cake, with special ingredients, that she'll feed to a dog to carry the bad luck away.

After Daddy comes back from Parchman, he gets a job in a war plant in Memphis, so he's home only on weekends. The boy spends all his time with his mother.

When the boy grows old enough for school, his Mamma walks with him to school every morning, then home in the afternoon. They still visit the cemetery regularly so that the boy can talk to his brother, who is an angel.

Sometimes the boy thinks he can hear his brother's voice. "I will always be with you," his brother says. "I am in Heaven and you are special and I will watch out for you always."

The boy is a Christian, which is good because when he dies, he will go to Heaven and see his brother. The boy and Satnin and Daddy go to the Assembly of God Church in East Tupelo, and they sing along with Daddy's cousin Sayles, who is in the choir. The Reverend Smith is a nice, quiet man who teaches the boy a few chords on the guitar.

In the Church, the boy receives his baptism of the spirit and gives away everything he owns to other children. His comic books and his bike and all his money. His Daddy keeps bringing the bike back, but the boy only gives it away again. Finally his Daddy gives up and lets the boy give the bike away for good.

"You are a good boy to give everything away," his brother whispers. "We will live together in Heaven and be happy forever."

The family moves to Memphis so that Daddy can find work. The boy is sad about leaving his brother behind in the cemetery, but his brother tells him that he is really in Heaven, not the cemetery, and the boy can still talk to him anytime he likes.

The family lives in the Lauderdale Courts, part of the projects run by the Housing Authority. Everyone in the projects works except for Satnin, who spends all her time with her boy. Daddy has a job at United Paint, but he can't earn too much or the Housing Authority will make the family move.

"They never let a workingman get ahead," he says.

The boy goes to Humes High School, where he's in the ninth grade. Mamma still walks him to and from school every day, but the boy has his own bed now, and he sleeps alone. He has nightmares almost every night and doesn't know why.

Sometimes he takes his guitar outside to the steps of the Lauderdale Courts and sings. People from the projects always stop what they're doing and form a half circle around him and listen. It's as if they're bewitched. Their staring makes the boy so self-conscious that he sings only after dark, so that he doesn't have to see the way they look at him.

He looks in the mirror and sees this little cracker kid in overalls, nothing he wants to be. He tries to make what he sees better. One time he has Satnin give his fine, blond hair a permanent. Another time he cuts his hair off except for a Mohawk strip down the middle.

One day, during summer vacation, the boy goes to the

picture show and sees *The City Across the River*, with a new actor named Tony Curtis. He watches entranced at the story of the poor working kids who belong to a gang called the "Amboy Dukes," and who wear flashy clothes and have their hair different from anyone the boy has ever seen. Tony Curtis's hair is perfect, long and shiny, winged on the sides, with a curl in the front and upturned in back. He talks in a funny jivey way, singsong, almost like he has his own language. It's like the language the boy's brother speaks in dreams.

The boy watches the movie three times.

Next day he goes to a hairdresser. He knows he'll never get the haircut he wants in a barbershop. "Give me that Tony Curtis cut," he says to the astonished beautician. The boy describes what he wants and the beautician tells him the cut is called a D.A. The beautician cuts his hair, but she warns him that his blond hair is too fine to stay in the shape he wants it, and sells him a tin of Royal Crown Pomade. The pomade darkens his hair by several shades but keeps it in place and makes it gleam.

The only place the boy can think to find the right clothes is on Beale Street. It's in the colored part of town where people are killed every week, then carried away so their bodies will be found somewhere else. The boy is a little nervous going there alone, but it's daylight and it looks safe enough, and as he walks down the street, he can see colored men dressed just as he wants to be, in raw-silk jackets dyed lime green or baby blue, with Billy Eckstine collars worn turned up.

The boy finds what he wants in Lansky Brothers' store. Pleated, shiny-black pants worn high on the floating ribs, with red or yellow seams. Double-breasted jackets in glowing colors, with huge vents and sparkles in them, big enough to move around in.

He spends all his money at Lansky Brothers.

Next time he looks in the mirror, he likes what he sees. Maybe everyone in Heaven looks like this.

* * *

In his nightmares, the boy is surrounded by enemies, all of them jeering and laughing at him. He fights them, lashing out with his fists, and often wakes with smarting knuckles from having jumped out of bed and punched the wall.

When the nightmares come true, he doesn't fight. He can't—there are too many of them, the biggest, toughest kids in school, surrounding him and calling him names. They say he dresses like a nigra pimp. They call him a sissy, a queer. He doesn't quite know what a queer is, but he knows it's bad. They threaten to cut his hair off. They knock him around every day, a jeering circle of crackers in overalls with muscles bulging out of their plaid shirts— they're everything the boy wants to get away from, everything he doesn't want to be.

In his dreams, he fights back, screaming wildly, sometimes running out of the apartment and into the hallway before he wakes. His mother makes him a charm to wear around his neck, a charm that smells of asafoetida and has a black-cat bone in it, but it doesn't keep the dreams away. His mother says he gets it from his father, who also has bad nightmares from time to time.

One day the other boys are pushing him around in the toilets. The air is blue with tobacco smoke. The boy has been bounced into the walls a few times and is being held in a headlock by one football lineman while another waves a pair of shears and threatens to cut his hair.

"I'd stop that if I were you." The voice comes from a newcomer, a big kid with a Yankee accent and the thick neck of an athlete. He's got a big jaw and a look that seems a little puzzling and unbalanced, as if his eyes are pointing in slightly different directions. His name is Schmidt and he's just transferred here from Detroit.

"You cut his hair," Schmidt says, "you better cut mine, too."

The big kids drop the boy and stand aside and mumble. The boy straightens his clothes and tries to thank Schmidt for intervening.

"Call me Leon," the big boy says.

The boy and Leon become friends. Leon plays guitar a little and sings, and the two of them go together to a party. Leon sings a Woody Guthrie song, and the boy plays accompaniment. Then the boy turns all the lights off, so he won't get self-conscious, and sings an Eddie Arnold tune, "Won't You Tell Me, Molly Darling." All the party noise stops as the other kids listen. The boy finishes the tune.

"Your turn," he says to Leon.

"Brother," Leon says, "no way I'm gonna follow that."

The boy sings all night, with Leon strumming accompaniment and singing harmony. The darkness is very friendly. The other kids listen in silence except for their applause.

Maybe, he thinks, this is what Heaven is like.

Leon is an orphan. His father died in a strike against Henry Ford just after he was born, and he'd moved South after his mother married again, this time to a truck driver whose outfit was based in Memphis.

Hearing the story of Leon's father dying after a beating by Ford strikebreakers, the boy hears an echo of his grandfather's voice: *Boss don't have no mercy on a workingman.*

Leon is always reading. The boy never had a friend who read before. The authors seem very intimidating, with names like Strachey and Hilferding and Sternberg.

"You heard Nat Dee yet?" Leon asks. He turns his radio to WDIA. He has to turn up the volume because WDIA broadcasts at only two hundred and fifty watts.

The voice the boy hears is colored and talks so fast the boy can barely make out the words. He's announcing a song by Bukka White, recorded in Parchman Prison in Mississippi.

Parchman Prison, the boy thinks.

Nat Dee's voice is a little difficult, but the boy understands the music very well.

* * *

The singer launches himself at the microphone stand like it's his worst enemy. He knocks it down and straddles it, grabbing it near the top as if he's wringing its neck. He wears a pink see-through blouse and a blazing pink suit with black velvet trim. His eyes are made ghostly with mascara and heavy green eye shadow. He's playing the Gator Bowl in front of fourteen thousand people.

The second he appeared, a strange sound went up, a weird keening that sent hairs crawling on the necks of half the men in the audience. The sound of thousands of young girls working themselves into a frenzy.

The sound sometimes makes it difficult for the singer to hear his band, but he can always turn and see them solid behind him, Leon mimicking the Scotty Moore guitar arrangements from the records, Bill Black slapping bass, and drummer D.J. laying down the solid beat that the singer's music thrives on.

The singer has finally wrung the mike stand into submission. He rears back perilously far, right on the edge of balance, and he hops forward with little thrusts of his polished heels, holding the mike stand up above his head like a jazzman wailing sax. He thrusts his pelvis right at the audience, and the long rubber tube he's stuck down his pants in front is perfectly outlined by the taut fabric.

The eerie sound that rises from the audience goes up in intensity, in volume. State police in front of the stage are flinging little girls back as they try to rush forward. All over the South, people are denouncing his act as obscene.

Incredibly, the singer is only one of the half-dozen opening acts for Hank Snow. But some of the other performers, the Davis Sisters and the Wilburn Brothers, complain that they can't follow him onstage, so he was given the coveted slot just before the intermission.

After the recess, the headliners Slim Whitman and Hank Snow will step onstage and try to restore the program to some kind of order. Some nights they have their work cut out for them.

The singer still has nightmares every night. Satnin persuaded him to hire his cousins, Gene and Junior Smith, to sleep in the same room with him and keep him from injuring himself.

When the singer finishes his act, he's soaked in sweat. He grins into the mike, tosses his head to clear his long hair from his eyes, speaks to the audience. "Thank you, ladies and gentlemen," he says. Then he gives a wink. "Girls," he promises, "I'll see you backstage."

The screaming doubles in volume. The singer waves good-bye and starts to head off, and then out of the slant of his eye, he sees the line of state cops go down before an avalanche of little girls as if they were made of cardboard.

The singer runs for it, his terrified band at his heels. He dives down into the tunnels under the Gator Bowl, where the concrete echoes his pursuers' shrill screams. The flimsy door to his dressing room doesn't keep them out for a second. His cousins Gene and Junior Smith go down fighting. The terrified singer leaps onto the shower stall, and even there, one frantic girl in white gloves and crinolines manages to tear off one of his shoes. The singer stares at her in fascination, at the desperate, inhuman glitter in her eyes as she snatches her trophy, and he wonders what kind of beast he's liberated in her, what it is that's just exploded out of all the restraining apparel, the girdle and nylons and starched underskirts.

He doesn't know quite what it is, but he knows he likes it.

Eventually reinforcements arrive and the girls are driven out. The dressing room looks as if it has been through a hurricane. Junior Smith, a veteran of Korea, appears as if he's just relived Porkchop Hill. The singer limps on one shoe and one pink sock as he surveys the damage.

Leon wanders in, clutching his guitar. The band's first impulse had been to protect their instruments rather than their singer.

"I wouldn't make no more promises to them girls," Leon says. He talks more Southern every day.

Hank Snow arrives with a bottle of Dr. Pepper in his hand. One of his business associates is with him, a bald fat man who carries an elephant-headed cane.

"I never seen nothing like it," Snow says. "Boy, you're gonna go far in this business if your fans don't kill you first."

"Junior," the singer says, "see if you can find me a pair of shoes, okay?"

"Sure, boss," Junior says.

Hank Snow points to the fat man. "I'd like to introduce a friend of mine—he manages Hank Snow Productions for me. Colonel Tom Parker."

The Colonel has a powerful blue gaze and a grip of iron. He looks at the singer in a way that makes him feel uncomfortable—it's the same look the little girl gave him, like he wants more than anyone can say, more than the singer can ever give. "I've been hearing a lot about you," the Colonel says. "Maybe you and me can do some business."

Colonel Parker does the singer a lot of good. He straightens out the tangled mess of the singer's management, puts him under exclusive contract, gets his records played north of the Mason-Dixon line, and gets a big advance from RCA that lets the singer buy his Satnin a Cadillac. Then he buys several more for himself and his band.

"I want to look good for this car," Satnin says. "I'm going to lose some weight."

Suddenly the singer is supporting his whole family. His Daddy quits his job and never takes another. Gene and Junior work for him. His Grandmother is living with his parents. Sometimes he thinks about it and gets a little scared.

But mostly he doesn't have much time to think. He and his band are on tour constantly, mostly across the South, their nights spent speeding from one engagement to another in a long line of Cadillacs, each one a different color and fronted by a half ton of solid chrome. Sometimes the cops stop him, but it's only for autographs.

"That Colonel, he's a snake-oil salesman for sure," Leon says. He's sitting in the shotgun seat while the singer drives across Georgia at three in the morning. "You better keep an eye on him."

"Ain't gonna let him cheat me," the singer says. The speedometer reads a hundred twenty-five. He laughs. "He sure is good with that hypnotism thing he does. Did you see Gene on his hands and knees, barking like a dog?"

Leon gazes at him significantly. "Do me a big favor. Don't ever let him hypnotize you."

The singer gives him a startled look, then jerks his attention back to the road. "Cain't hypnotize me any way," he says, thinking of the power of the Colonel's ice-blue eyes.

"Don't let him try. He's done you a lot of good, okay. But that's just business. He doesn't own you."

"He's gonna get me a screen test with Hal Wallis."

"That's good. But don't let the Colonel or Wallis or any of those tell you what to do. You know best."

"Okay."

"*You* pick your music. *You* work out the arrangements. You need to insist on that, because these other people—" Leon waves a hand as if pulling difficult ideas out of the air. "You've got the magic, okay? They don't even know what the magic is. They're just bosses, and they'll use you for every dollar you can give them."

"Boss don't have no mercy on a workingman," the singer says.

Leon favors him with a smile. "That's right, big man. And don't you forget it."

The singer buys the big white house out on Highway 51, the place called Graceland. Because he's on the road so much, he doesn't spend a lot of time there. His parents live out back and install a chicken coop and a hog pen so they have something to do.

On the road, he's learned that he likes the night. He visits the South's little sin towns, Phenix City or Norfolk or Bossier City, cruising for girls he can take back to his cheap motel rooms.

When he's home in Memphis, there's no place he can go at night—Beale Street is still for colored people. So he has the state cops close off a piece of highway for motorcycle racing. He dresses up in his leathers, with his little peaked cap, and cranks his panhead Harley to well over a hundred. He does incredibly dangerous stunts at high speed—standing up on the foot pegs with his hands outstretched, away from the handlebars; reaching out to hold hands with the guy he's racing with. He's a hairsbreadth from death or injury the whole time.

He thinks about the kids in school who called him a sissy, and snarls. When he's wound up the Harley and is howling down the road with the huge engine vibrating between his legs, he knows that the cry of wind in his ears is really his brother's voice, calling him home.

"What is this business?" the singer demands. "Some old burlesque comic? An Irish tenor? *Performing midgets?*"

"The Heidelberg Troupe of Performing Midgets." The Colonel grins around his cigar. "Great act. Know 'em from my carny days."

"*Carny* days?" Leon asks. "What're you trying to do, turn us into a freak show?"

The Colonel scowls at Leon. He knows who's put the singer up to this. "Why should we hire a rock act to open?" he says. "It costs money to hire Johnny Cash or Carl Perkins, and all they do is imitations of our boy anyway. We can get the vaudeville acts a lot cheaper—hell, they're happy to have the work."

"They'll make me look ridiculous," the singer says. His blond hair is dyed black for the movies he's making for

Hal Wallis. He wants badly to be the next James Dean, but the critics compare him to Sonny Tufts.

The Colonel chomps down on his cigar again. "Gotta have opening acts," he says. "Since nobody's gonna pay attention to 'em anyway, we might as well have the cheap ones. More money for the rest of us that way."

"That was something—" the singer begins. He casts an uneasy look toward Leon, then turns back to the Colonel. "We had an idea. Why do we need opening acts at all?"

Puzzlement enters the Colonel's blue eyes. "Gotta have 'em," he says. "The marks'll feel cheated 'less they get their money's worth. And you gotta have an intermission between the opening acts and the main show so you can sell drinks and programs and souvenirs."

"So we'll give them their money's worth *without* an opening act," Leon says. "We'll just play two sets' worth of music with an intermission in between." He looks at the singer. "The big man's willing."

"Hell, yes," the singer says.

"Save all the money you'd waste on those opening acts," Leon says. "And you don't have to pay good money to ship a dozen midgets around the country, either."

The Colonel considers this. He looks at the singer. "You're really willin' to do this?"

The singer shrugs. "Sure. I *like* being onstage."

"You'll have to do more than the five or six songs you do now."

"Plenty of songs out there."

The Colonel's eyes glitter. Everyone knows he gets kickbacks from writers who offer their songs to the singer. He nods slowly.

"Okay," he says. "This sure seems worth a thought."

And then his eyes move to Leon and turn cold.

Someday there's going to be an accounting.

The story in *Billboard* says that the singer has cut a special deal with the Army, that when he's drafted, he's going into Special Services and entertain the troops. It says he won't even have to cut his hair.

It's an absolute lie. The singer has an understanding with his draft board, that's true, but it's only that he should get some advance notice if he's going to be called up.

He hasn't even had his physical yet.

"Where is this coming from?" the singer demands.

Leon thinks for a moment. "This is *Billboard*, not some fan magazine. They must have got the story from somewhere."

"Who could have told them such a thing?"

Leon looks like he wants to say something but decides not to. The singer has enough on his mind.

Satnin is grieved and ailing. She's turning yellow with jaundice and nobody knows why. Her weight keeps going up in spite of the dozens of diet pills she takes every day. When her boy isn't with her, she stays drunk all the time. The thought of her mortality makes the singer frantic with anxiety.

The story about the draft keeps getting bigger. When the singer goes on tour, reporters ask him about the Army all the time. He can't figure out what's getting them so stirred up.

He keeps in touch with Memphis by phone. And when Satnin goes into a hospital, he cancels the tour and is on the next train.

She rallies a bit when she sees her boy. But within twenty-four hours, she fails and dies.

The next sound that comes from her hospital room is even more eerie than the sound of the singer's massed fans. Hospital personnel and bystanders stop, listen in rising horror, then flee.

The family is keening over Satnin. It's an Appalachian custom, and the good burghers of Memphis have never heard such a thing. The singer's powerful voice rises, dominates the rest of his family, his wails of grief echoing down the corridor. Waiting outside, Leon can feel the hairs rise on his neck. It's the most terrifying thing he's ever heard.

The funeral takes place in the big house on Highway 51. It's a circus. The gates are open, and strangers wander around the house and grounds and take things. The Colonel tries to keep order, but nobody listens to him. Reporters take the best seats at the service and snap pictures of everything.

The singer is frantic and crazed with grief. He keeps dragging people over to admire Satnin in her coffin. He spends hours talking to the corpse in some language of his own. Leon calls for a doctor to give him a sedative, but the doctor can't make it through the mass of people waiting outside the gates. The crowds are so huge that the state police have to close the highway.

At the funeral, the singer throws himself into the grave and demands to be buried with his Mamma. His friends have to drag him away.

Unbelievably, a reporter chooses this moment to ask the singer about the Army. The singer stares in disbelief.

"Ain't gonna go in no Army!" he shouts, and then his friends pull him away to his limousine. The doctor finally arrives and puts him to sleep.

The next day, there are headlines.

"We ain't at war," the singer says. "Why does anyone care about the damn Army anyway? Why cain't they leave a man alone?"

It's two days since the funeral, and the singer has spent the intervening time in a drugged stupor. He sits in a huge velour-covered chair in a room swathed in red velvet. Newspapers open to their screaming headlines surround his chair.

"Somebody's planting these stories," Leon tells him. "We all know that. And if you think about it, you know who it's got to be."

The singer just stares at him with drug-dulled eyes.

"The Colonel," Leon says. "It's got to be the Colonel."

The singer thinks about it. "Don't make no sense," he says. "Colonel don't make no money when I'm in the service."

"But he gets control," Leon says. "You can't look after your affairs if you're away. You'll have to put him in charge of everything and trust him. He'll have to renegotiate your RCA contract, your movie contract. When you get back, he'll be the one in charge."

The singer stares at him and says nothing.

"He's just some goddam carnival barker, brother," Leon says. "All he does now is arrange your bookings—anyone can do that. He isn't even a real colonel. He just wants to be the boss in the big house and keep you working in his cotton fields for the rest of your life."

"Orville Bean," the singer says. Leon doesn't understand, but this doesn't stop him.

"And you don't need the damn Army," Leon says. "All it does is protect bosses like the Colonel and their money. What's the Army ever done for you?"

"Ain't gonna go in no Army," the singer says.

"The draft board *has* to call you up after all this. The newspapers won't let them do anything else. What're you gonna tell 'em?"

"Have the Colonel work out something."

"The Colonel *wants* you in the Army."

The singer closes his eyes and lolls his head back in the big velour chair. He wishes everyone would go away and leave him alone. He strains his mind, trying to find an answer.

Make the Colonel do what you want.

The singer starts awake. He's heard the voice plainly, but he knows Leon hasn't spoken.

He realizes it was his brother's voice, calling to him from the Beyond.

The singer calls the Colonel on the phone and tells him that if he receives his draft notice, the first thing he'll do is fire Thomas Andrew Parker. The Colonel is staggered.

He says it's too late. The singer only repeats his demand and hangs up.

He manages to avoid seeing the Colonel for another week, and then the Colonel comes anyway. The singer agrees to meet him and wishes that Leon wasn't in town visiting his mom.

The Colonel walks into the den, leaning hard on his elephant-head cane, and drops heavily into a chair. He looks pale and sweaty and he keeps massaging his left arm. He explains that he's talked to every man on the draft board, that public opinion is forcing them to call the singer up. The Colonel has offered them colossal bribes, but it appears they're all honest citizens.

"Ain't changed my mind," the singer says. "You keep me out of the Army, or you and me are through."

"I can't," the Colonel protests. His powerful blue eyes are hollow.

"Then you and me are finished the second that notice gets here."

"Listen. There's a chance. The medical—" the Colonel starts, and then he gasps, his mouth open, and clutches at his left arm. His mouth works and he doesn't say anything.

Heart attack. His brother's voice. *Don't do anything.*

The singer knows the Colonel already had a heart attack a few years ago. He's old and fat and deserves exactly what he's going to get.

The Colonel's eyes plead with the singer. The singer just watches him. The Colonel begins moving slowly, his hand reaching for the elephant-head cane he's propped against a table.

Take the cane, the angel voice says. The singer takes the cane and holds it while the Colonel topples off his chair and starts to crawl toward the door. And then the Colonel falls over and doesn't move anymore.

"Ain't gonna have no more bosses," the singer says.

* * *

"Not gonna fight for no rich people," the singer says to reporters.

He doesn't give a damn about the firestorm that follows. He takes his motorcycle out onto the highways and blasts along at full speed and tries to listen to what his brother is telling him.

Leon tells him a lot, too. He reads him passages from a book called *Capital*. He explains about workers and bosses and how bosses make money by exploiting workers. It's everything the singer ever learned from his family, from his days as a truck driver after high school. Leon explains how he's a Marxist-Leninist.

"Isn't that the same as a Communist?" the singer asks. Leon's answer is long and involved and has a lot of historical digressions. But the angel voice that whispers inside the singer speaks simple sense:

Doesn't matter what people call it, it only matters that it's true.

There are bonfires out on Highway 51 now, the singer's records going up in flames. To the American public it looks as if their worst fears are confirmed, that the singer, driving girls into a sexual frenzy with his degenerate Negro music, is an agent of Moscow as well as of Satan. Outside the gate of the house are weeping girls begging him to repent. His brother's grave in East Tupelo is vandalized, so the singer has both his brother's body and Satnin's exhumed and reburied at Graceland.

Every booking has been canceled. The movie contract is gone. The singer doesn't care, because for the first time in his life, the nightmares are gone and he can sleep at night. The singer is going to Party meetings and making the members nervous, because crowds of reporters are still following him around and snapping pictures of everyone.

Johnny Cash and Jerry Lee Lewis tell anyone who'll listen that they're country singers. Ricky Nelson starts covering Dean Martin tunes. Little Richard goes into the church. Rock and roll is finished.

"Plenty of bookings in Europe, comrade," Leon says.

So the singer plays Europe, but he's playing clubs, not auditoriums or stadiums. His Daddy and Grandma stay home and take care of his house. The singer's European audiences are a strange mixture of teenage girls and thin intellectuals who wear glasses and smoke cigarettes. Gene and Junior Smith are still with him, protecting him from fanatics who might want to hurt him, or the strange, intense people who want to discourse on the class origins of his appeal. It seems to the singer that the Left doesn't understand rock and roll. Leon calmly says that sooner or later, they'll figure it out.

All the professional songwriters who kept him supplied with material are long gone. So are Scotty and the others who helped with the arrangements. He picks his own tunes. He has a new band, working-class British kids who worship the ground he walks on. The Party wants him to sing folk songs and songs about the Struggle. He obliges, but he rocks them up, and that doesn't seem to please them, so he just goes back to singing the blues.

He records in little studios in Italy and Germany that are even more primitive than the Sun studio in Memphis. He teaches them a trick or two—he knows how to create the Sun sound by putting a second mike behind his head and arranging for a slight delay between the two to produce Sam Phillips' trademark echo effect.

The records are carried into America in the holds of freighters. There's a surprising demand for them. There's even a story in the papers about a Navy sailor court-martialed for having some of his 45s in his locker.

His voice fills out. He's got three and a half octaves and he uses them brilliantly—his chest voice is powerful and evocative, his high notes clear and resonant. He wishes he had a bigger audience now that he knows so much more about the music.

Don't matter who listens so long as you sing it right, his brother says. The singer knows his brother always speaks the truth.

* * *

The singer is appalled by his tour of the East. It's taken him forever to get permission, and he's succeeded only because some kind of propaganda coup is necessary. Comrade Khrushchev has just built a wall in Berlin to keep out American spies, and he's demanded solidarity from Socialists everywhere.

Still, the singer can't believe the people he's got opening for him. Jugglers. Trained seals. A couple of clowns. A drill team from the Czech Army, and a couple of folksingers so old and so drunk they can barely stagger onto the stage every night.

At least there are no midgets.

With the tour is a platoon of big men in baggy pants and bulky jackets, supposedly there to protect the singer from counterrevolutionaries, but all they really do is insulate the singer from anyone in the countries he's touring.

Just like Colonel Parker, his brother whispers.

The audiences are polite, but clearly they like the jugglers best. The singer works like hell to win them over, but his real fans, the young people, seem to be excluded. At one point his rage explodes, and in the middle of a song he turns to Leon and screams, *"Look what you've got me into!"*

Leon doesn't respond. He knows there's nothing he can say.

When the singer returns to the West, he announces he's leaving the Party. His remaining audiences get smaller.

But he's singing better than ever. He gets together with French and British blues fanatics, men with huge collections of vinyl bought from American sailors, and he listens carefully. He knows how to take a minor tune, a B-side or a neglected work, and reinvent it, jack it up and rock it till it cries with power and glows like neon. And people with names like Dylan and Fariña cross the Atlantic to meet with him, to tell him how much he means to them.

He doesn't abandon the Left. He studies Marx and Gandhi and Strachey and Hilferding. He leads his band and followers in discussion groups and self-criticism sessions, American hill people and Yorkshire kids educating themselves in revolution. Leon suggests inviting others to run the meetings, intellectuals, but the singer doesn't like the idea.

Years pass. The singer's audiences grow older. He's disappointed that the young girls are gone, that he can't tease them and drive them mad with the way he moves.

And then rock and roll is back, exploding out of the sweaty-walled European clubs where it's been living all these years, blasting into the minds and hearts of a newer, younger generation.

For the first time in years, the singer hears his brother's voice: *Now's your time.*

The singer runs onto the stage, drops onto his knees as he passes the mike, slides across half the stage. He looks at the girls in the audience from under his taunting eyelids.

"Well . . ." he intones.

The eerie sound comes up from the audience again, adolescent girls in the thrall of a need they can't explain. The singer had forgotten how much he missed them.

"Well . . ." he sings again, as if he's forgotten where he was. The wail goes up again.

When he finally gets around to singing, he thinks he can hear his brother on harmony.

Most of his new audience isn't familiar with the old material, with the old songs and moves—it's all spanking new to them. And the new material is good, written by Lennon and McCartney and Dylan and Richards and Jagger, all of them offering their best in homage to their idol. They swarm into his recording sessions to sing backup or strum out chords. He isn't as popular as he once was—there's still a lot of resistance, and he doesn't get much airplay and is never invited to appear on television—but his new fans think the American Legion pickets outside his concerts are quaint, and his old fans have never forgotten him.

He hasn't forgotten much either. He remembers who shunned him, who helped when the chips were down. The few who dared to support him in public. He works to advance the Struggle. He not only marches with Dr. King, he gives him a bright yellow Cadillac so he doesn't have to march at all. He directs public scorn at the Vietnam War. FBI men in dark suits and hats follow him around and tap his phones. They can't do anything to him because he's never done anything illegal—in the confusion of the headlines and statements and his jump to Europe, his local draft board never actually issued his induction notice.

Outnumbering the FBI are the fans who camp outside his house, living there just as they did a decade before, people who seem to have a tenuous existence only in the singer's shadow. It's as if he's their god, the only thing that gives them meaning.

Only one way to become a god, his brother whispers.

He knows what his brother means.

When Dr. King comes to Memphis, it's only natural for the singer to climb on his bike and pay a courtesy call.

Maybe the magic will work one last time.

What was he doing on the balcony, exactly? Demonstrating his moves, jumping around, playing the clown for his bewildered host? Or was there a whisper in his ear, a soft murmur that told him exactly where the bullet would be found as it hissed through the air?

Bleeding, both lungs punctured, he shoves the confused Dr. King into the motel room and to safety. He falls, coughing blood, his moist breath whistling through the hole in his side.

King remembers, forever afterward, the peculiar inward look on the singer's face as he dies.

The singer remembers his baptism of the spirit, the way

he gave everything away. Now he's giving everything away again. He hears his brother's voice.

Welcome, his brother says, *to where we can live forever.*

You stand with the long line of mourners as it files up to the big white house. The singer's will was a surprise: there's an education foundation, and the house is to be renamed the Memphis Palace of Labor. It will become a library and center for research on labor issues.

File through a series of rooms on your way to view the coffin. Rooms so strangely decorated that they're like a window into the singer's mind. The Joe Hill room, the Gandhi room, the Karl Marx room. A pink bust of Marx sits in a shrine in the corner of his chamber, flanked by smoked-mirror glass and red-velvet curtains. Joe Hill—a life-sized statue of a noble-looking man in a cap and bib overalls—gazes defiantly at the scarlet velour walls of his chamber and at a piano gilded with what appears to be solid gold.

You have the feeling that the staid trustees of the foundation will redecorate at the first chance they get.

The singer lies in state under a portrait of the wizened figure of Gandhi, in a room whose walls seem to be upholstered in white plastic. Dr. King is chief mourner and speaks the eulogy. A choir from a local black church mourns softly, then spits fire. The crowd claps and stamps in answer.

And at last the moment comes when the huge bronze coffin is closed and the singer, Jessie Garon Presley, is carried out to be laid to rest in the garden. On his one side is his Mamma, and on the other his twin, Elvis, with whom he will live forever.

Katharine Kerr, author of *Polar City Blues* and *A Time of War,* is equally at home writing science fiction or fantasy, novels or short stories.

For her alternate outlaw, she has chosen one of our country's most rabid anti-Communists, Tailgunner Joe—and has given his story a curious twist. . . .

Cui Bono?
by Katharine Kerr

She is practicing the piano, playing Schubert, oddly enough, warbling along in her cracked alto with "The Earl King" when the doorbell rings. For a moment, as she lets her hands lie silent on the keys, she wonders if she's misheard, but again the ring comes, a large bronze sound in a small cottage. Barbara, perhaps, stopping by after church. She rises and walks to the door, opens it to sunlight and the smell of honeysuckle. She blinks hard against the glare before she recognizes her visitor, and even then she doubts.

"Uh, hello?" he says.

"It *is* you, Jack. My lord!"

Neither moves nor speaks for a moment. He stands as tall and straight as ever, as if he only pretends to wear vacation clothes, as if blue slacks and a green-striped shirt are really a uniform in some secret military. His hair, gray now but still thick, his face tanned to leather . . . but the blue eyes sparkle, as sunny as she always remembered them. And what is he seeing in her? A skinny gray woman in baggy jeans and a torn shirt. She turns from the door.

"Wait," he says. "I think I'm here to apologize."

"You think?"

He shrugs, palms up.

"I've learned things that make me think I was wrong, all those years ago. Please. Talk to me."

She looks past him to purple jacaranda and a painfully bright sky while her heart pounds, remembering what it meant to be young.

"Come in."

He follows her into the living room, stands looking around at the piano, the fireplace, the flowered couch and chair, the overflowing bookshelves, while she pulls the screen door to and latches it, leaving the other open for sun and air. She does not want to be shut into a room with him, not ever again.

"A real California bungalow," he announces.

"Yes. Would you like some iced tea? There's no liquor in the house, I'm afraid."

"No, don't bother." He perches on one end of the couch. "Sit down?"

She takes the chair opposite and nearest the open door.

"It's the Freedom of Information Act and all that," he says. "I read some things that made me wonder."

"You never were subtle, were you, Jack? Age doesn't seem to have taught you much about manners."

"Sorry." He actually blushes, a faint color along cheekbone and ears. "But, hell, do *you* want to make small talk?"

She laughs, but she can hear the bitterness in it.

"Let me guess," she says. "You're still in Army Intelligence?"

"Just retiring as a colonel, yeah." He hesitates. "Can I ask you which was your real name? Rose or Helen? Or neither?"

"Both. Rose's my first name, but Helen's the middle one, and so I went by that. Von Sussmann was my mother's maiden name. My real last name is Fergusson."

"Then, if you were using a fake name, you had to be in the Company. You were, weren't you?"

She considers lying, finds a lie automatically at hand, even now, after so many years without the need to lie. She refuses to lie to him again, not about this at least, no matter what trouble might come from the truth.

"I was, yes."

"Oh, Jesus. Then I do owe you. I owe you a bigger apology than I—" He stares at her, lips parted, mouth working.

"You believe me?"

"Yeah, of course I believe you. It tallies with everything. That's why I'm here, isn't it, because of the files I read? I mean, oh, Jesus! No manners at all, yeah. Helen—Rose—I'm sorry."

The wound she thought healed peels open to bleed tears.

"Damn!" She turns away, fumbling for Kleenex in her pocket, finds a crumpled wad to wipe her face with.

"I'm sorry. I should've worked up to it. But for days . . . well, weeks really . . . I've been trying to think of what to say. I mean, it took me a long time to even find out where you were. That friend of yours, Lisel, she's still around Washington, you know. And that was another clue. I mean, she wouldn't be working for a senator if you two were—well, what I thought you were back then."

"Nazi sympathizers? No, we weren't. Not at all. Lisel is just a friend of mine who happens to have a German name, just like I told you, not that you believed me. Or was it Commie spies? No, I don't remember you berating me for being a goddamn Commie."

He winces and slumps back on the couch, turning to look across the room.

"I was only twenty-four," he says. "An excess of zeal. What's that phrase from? Some play or other?"

"I don't know."

"Doesn't matter. Chalk it up to an excess of zeal. Jesus, if you'd only given me a hint—"

"I couldn't. You had to think . . . everyone had to think that I was a fossil, a loyal little member of the German-American Bund, hanging on to her Fascist principles, still dreaming of her Aryan warriors and her dead hero in the bunker."

"It sounds so damn silly now. And that crappy little organization you worked for. The Goethe Friendship League, wasn't it? It was like something out of a bad movie, Nazis trying for a comeback. I don't see how I could have believed it."

"Well, the war hadn't been over all that long." *Why am I making excuses for him?* she thinks. "It was what, fifty-three? Not even ten years."

"I still feel like a jerk. But anyway, a couple of months ago I was reading some old files, and they identified the League as a Soviet front. Pretty clever, coming up with a group that looked so far Right that no one would ever have suspected it marched on the Left. Oh well, sorry. Obviously your outfit figured it out. The file talked about a mole, too. Identified her as the secretary. I figured that had to be you, and, Jesus, I felt sick thinking of the way I screamed at you that night, calling you a traitor."

"It meant my cover was holding, didn't it?" Rose tries to speak lightly, to toss off the line like a movie heroine, but the wound aches and trembles her voice.

"I'm sorry. Rose, I'm so sorry I don't even know how to say it."

She nods, vaguely affirmative, reaches for words, finds only memories of how much she loved him; finds, too, her memories of that evening in his tiny office, painted government green, a table littered with papers along one wall, two chairs, Jack in one, herself in the other, facing each other in bright light. He was handsome then, in a crisp fifties uniform, thick stubble of blond hair, blue eyes glittering. In his rage, he barely blinked, until her own eyes hurt, watching him. And she, tall and awkward, convinced in her deepest soul that she was ugly, that she would always be ugly, that she would wander forever at the edge of other people's loves as she had wandered for years at the edge of his, listened as he harangued and snarled and tore what little heart she had into pieces.

"You gotta quit," he said. "You gotta quit tomorrow. We've got the goods on these guys, all right, and they're Fascists, plain and simple. If you don't walk out of there tomorrow, I'll know. I'll know what kind of traitor you are."

"It's just a job. It's about Goethe and literature and building bridges, Jack. All I am is the secretary."

"Bull. Just bull, that's all. If you don't walk out of there, I never want to see you again."

And he leaned back in the chair, arms crossed over his chest, and smiled.

Remembering brings back old habits of mind. For a moment, as she looks at the gray-haired man leaning back into the flowered cushions of her couch, she wonders if he's really working for Army Intelligence, if he's really come here to apologize, or if he's playing some other game for some other organization. Then she reminds herself that thirty years have passed since she was a someone, even a small someone, who might be important to affairs of state.

"Partly it was the times, wasn't it?" Jack goes on. "That writer, who was it? You remember? Anyway, some writer wrote a book called *Scoundrel Time*. That pegs it, all right. The scoundrel time. You couldn't trust anyone. I mean, with Tailgunner Joe taking aim at the Army. At Marshall, for crying out loud! At George Marshall, a real hero if there ever was one. I can still see him, the *Honorable* Senator McCarthy, him and his goddamned eyebrows, waving his goddamn scraps of paper around, claiming he had names."

"Point of order."

He laughs, and she smiles.

"You can bring back a whole era, saying that," he agrees. "Point of order. Jeez, it must not mean much to the kids these days. Doesn't to mine."

"Probably not, no. How many kids do you have?"

"Just two, both boys, good kids. One's in the Air Force, but I'll forgive him. At least it's not the Navy, huh?" He lets his grin fade. "Their mother's gone. Cancer. A couple of years ago."

"I'm sorry." She is, too, for this woman she never met, for living so long with someone as difficult as Jack, only to die early. "How awful."

He shrugs, starts to rise, sits again.

"You will forgive me?"

She would like to speak, to blurt out a fast "Of course," or perhaps even a second-thought bitter "No, never." She says neither, merely looks at him while she hunts for words. He misunderstands the wait.

"Well, I don't blame you. I acted like a bastard. Hell, I *was* a bastard to you that night."

"That's not—"

"But if I'd known who you were working for—" He shakes his head hard. "Scoundrel time. Couldn't trust anyone. Hey, maybe they said it about him, huh? An excess of zeal, I mean. Maybe some writer said that about McCarthy."

"Maybe so. A lot of people thought he was a hero, certainly."

"Well, in his own mind, I'm sure he was. Saving the country from the Commies."

Her surprise, her utter and complete shock that he would not know the truth, makes her laugh aloud. He stares, bewildered.

"Jack, have I been remembering it wrong? You were already in Army Intelligence then, weren't you?"

"Of course. Just a buck lieutenant, but I was. Why?"

Most likely they wouldn't have told him, she realizes, not his particular higher-ups.

"And of course your officers must have found out you'd been dating me. And here I was, this suspect girl with her German name and her German job." All at once something comes clear. "No wonder you were so angry that night."

"Well, yeah. Trying to protect my own backside did

come into it. But you're getting at something. What the hell is it?"

"Promise me that you'll never repeat what I'm telling you."

He goggles at her.

"I mean it, Jack. Promise."

"Okay. I promise." He's grinning, making an easy joke. "Unless it's a matter of national security."

"It is, but they know all about it already."

Again he stares.

"Well, here," she says. "Think for a minute about what things were like back in the late forties, early fifties. It's no wonder you didn't trust me, really. You've already said it—no one could trust anyone. But think about the way things were. Here was the whole country absolutely panicked about Communists. No one much thought about anything else for years. The entire government was paralyzed, really."

"Well, of course," he agreed. "Jesus, even the President was afraid to act. Eisenhower hated McCarthy. I don't care what any of those intellectuals say, I know it in my guts, he hated the man. But what the hell was he supposed to do? Speak out and have everyone start wondering about him? That would have been real bad for the country."

"Exactly. McCarthy had everyone terrified. Even your people. I don't suppose military morale had ever been that low before. Look at what happened to industries, key ones like computers losing important people. Either they were being blacklisted or they were resigning before they could be. Everyone remembers what happened in Hollywood because that's glamorous, but they were blacklisting scientists, too, and they meant a lot more to the country than actors."

"Yeah, and all those college professors, resigning rather than take a loyalty oath. You know, that made me so goddamn mad, that they wouldn't sign. I thought, yeah, they're Commies all right. But now, well, hell, you look back on things and you're not so sure. We might have lost some good people in with the rotten apples. And the suspicion and all that—yeah, you're right. Paralyzed, that's the word for the way the country was then."

"And what about our prestige in Europe?" she asked. "Right after the war, good lord, Americans were heroes. We'd saved Europe, and thanks to Marshall, we were rebuilding it. Everyone loved us, everyone wanted to be just like us. The Soviets had no prestige at all. In a few years, maybe Communism would have started to fade away, for all we know now. But then, all of a sudden, McCarthy came along, and we started acting like absolute fools in European eyes. Hasn't it ever dawned on you, Jack, how much prestige we lost, running around hunting for Communists under beds? We were the laughingstocks, not the Soviets."

"That poor little misguided bastard!"

"Misguided? What makes you think so?"

All at once he sits up straight, pure attention. She feels her mouth twist in a bitter smile.

"Think, Jack! When there's been a murder, what's the first thing the police ask? *Cui bono?* Who benefits? Well, somebody almost murdered America. Who stood to benefit the most? Whose hands did McCarthy play right into?"

"Oh, my God!" His voice drops to a bare whisper. "The Commies."

"Exactly. They both knew—your outfit and mine—they both knew perfectly well that the Soviets had planted moles all over the States. That's why McCarthy managed to get as far as he did, isn't it? He exposed a few unreliable agents for bait, people they wanted to get rid of, people who didn't know too much, and the intelligence community swallowed it whole. Our higher-ups assumed at the beginning that he was going to be useful."

"Things got out of hand kind of fast."

"Exactly. Very fast, and in a way that no one anticipated. What's the obvious answer? That he was working with the moles, not against them, to create a national panic."

"Jesus! Jesus H. Christ."

It's her turn to cross her arms over her chest, her turn to smile as he rises, begins to pace back and forth from the front door to the dining room and back again. All at once he stops, swirling on one heel to glare at her.

"Why didn't they tell the truth? After it was all over, I mean."

"What good would that have done the country? What kind of respect would Eisenhower have gotten from the public? What kind of faith in the government would the people have had if their own government had been duped? Besides, they might have panicked—you know, a sort of 'war of the worlds' effect. If McCarthy turned out to be a Communist mole, how could anyone trust anyone? We might have ended up with a constitutional crisis in this country. It looked possible then, anyway."

"Makes sense, yeah." He sits back down, shaking his head, letting his hands hang limp between his knees. "Jeesus!"

She lets out her breath in a long sigh and sinks back into the comforting cushions of her favorite chair. From outside comes the sound of a passing car, moving slowly. Birds are squabbling in the jacaranda tree. All at once she wonders if she should have spoken, wonders if her information will be taken back to some superior officer, both the information itself and the fact that she'd spoken of it. And wonders why she spoke—perhaps because this time, she's the one who has something to hold over him. Secret information has always meant power. Even old information brings a little bit of power in a relationship where—it seems to her—he always held her in his hand like a playing card.

"I mean, you're certain?" Jack looks up abruptly. "McCarthy really was a mole?"

"Certain? Well, honestly, can either of us be certain of anything that happened then? That's what I pieced together, and it makes a lot of sense, but for all I know, I was fed things in the hope I'd innocently pass them along."

"Oh. Well, yeah, that's true."

She looks away, remembering the final scene, played out for the entire country on television, such a new thing then, television, at the time of the Army-McCarthy hearings. Half of the entire country saw McCarthy settling into his chair, smiling around the chambers, reaching into his pocket and pulling out his usual scraps of paper. He was a good actor, Tailgunner Joe. He had lied for years about the names and the very existence of names on other scraps of paper just like that crumpled notecard. He showed no sign of fear, not a flicker, when he glanced down and saw written on that scrap his code name in the Soviet organization. The Pope, they'd called him. We hear the Pope is on TV. Those were the words on the paper—or at least they were if her information was accurate, if indeed Lisel had slipped such into his jacket pocket moments before the hearing began. Probably she had. He'd certainly broken later, when another army officer who believed in America as much as Jack did had leaned across a table down on the Senate floor. Oh yes, Joe had crumbled remarkably fast when that officer barked out his famous challenge.

"Have you no shame, sir?" She has spoken aloud.

"That's another one of those lines, yeah," Jack says. "Brings it all back. I heard that after the session ended, he went running back to his office and grabbed a bottle, guzzled about a quart's worth by the time he was done. Well, if that's true. But everyone knew he drank like a fish."

"Oh yes, everyone knew."

"What's that supposed to mean?"

"Nothing. His health started failing right after that, didn't it? Quite quickly."

"Jesus! You're not saying there was something in that whiskey, are you?"

"No, I'm not, as a matter of fact. Just an odd coincidence, I'm sure."

"Well, it took him a long time to die. But then it would. I mean, the people who'd hired him knew what they were doing. He wouldn't have dropped dead right away or anything suspicious like that."

"If anyone had hired him."

"Ah, come on, Rose! You're the one who's telling me—"

"A theory. Nothing more."

"You don't trust me, do you." It was not a question.

"Should I?"

He winces, rubs both hands across his face and through his hair.

"Maybe not," he says at last. "After the way I acted that night. But I swear to you, I'm not here for any other reason than to apologize. I mean, Jesus, Tailgunner Joe's been dead a long time now."

"Yes, he has. An awfully long time. But things are never going to be the same again here in America, thanks to him. Those wiretaps and the spying and the suspicion— it's still all out there. Do you think we'd have had Watergate if McCarthy had never existed?"

"Maybe not." Jack gets up and stands, hands shoved in his pockets, looking out the door. "*Cui bono?* I get your point. If he'd wanted to betray his country, he couldn't have done a much better job."

Rose watches him, merely watches for a long time, while the sound of another car on the street swells, then fades.

"Did he want to?" Jack asks abruptly.

"I've told you everything I'm going to. You're going back to Washington, aren't you? You've got all the files there. Dig for it if you want to know more."

"Bet they destroyed the important ones, if it was true."

"You'd think so. People do dumb things sometimes. Look at Nixon and his stupid tapes."

"Yeah, yeah, but there's something you're not telling me."

"What makes you think that?"

Jack sits down, heavily, on the edge of the couch so he can lean forward and study her face.

"Ah, forget it. Doesn't matter if there is or not. I meant it when I said that I came here to apologize. That's what matters."

He's right, Rose supposes. The past is gone, McCarthy buried. If indeed he's telling the truth about his contrition, then that truth, the truth of the moment between them here in this room in the eighties, is the only truth that can matter, that does matter now.

"I do forgive you," she says. "You couldn't know what I was, and I couldn't tell you. It was the times, I suppose, and the jobs we'd taken on."

"Thanks." Suddenly he wipes his eyes on his shirtsleeve, an awkward fumble of a gesture. "Ah, Jesus! Sorry. Means a hell of a lot to me."

Only then, seeing the damp of tears on striped cloth, does she truly believe that he found her to apologize and for no reason more. She waits, wondering how quickly he will leave, hoping he leaves soon, before he stays long enough to give his leaving the power to wound her once again.

"Well, hell," Jack says. "You want to go have lunch?"

"What?"

"Guess that's a lot to ask, after everything."

"No. I mean, well—maybe it is, but why?"

"What do you mean, why? Why go have lunch?"

"Yes, exactly."

"Because I haven't seen you for over thirty years, and you haven't seen me for over thirty years. Ah jeez, Rose. Can't we just sit down and talk?"

"Can we?"

She means the question seriously, and he takes it as such, letting her think, saying nothing till she's decided.

"Well, why not? Maybe that's all anyone can do now, talk things out and maybe heal the old suspicions."

"Yeah. Maybe so. The scoundrel time's over for us, anyway."

"Is it? I hope so, Jack. I really really hope so." Rose gets up quickly, heading toward the back of the bungalow. "I'll just put on some better clothes."

"Sure. I'm not going to take you out to lunch in those."

And in spite of herself, she laughs, hurrying out of the room before some tic of her face, some falsehood in her smile, can betray the final truth, the one she will never tell him, the one she hopes he will never learn. She was the agent who, in the end, passed along the code name to the CIA, used the code name, in fact, to buy immunity with. Her masters in the League trusted her, believing her one of them. One she had been, too, a fellow traveler on the Bolshevik way, an ardent believer in the people's revolution.

Not even her love for Jack would have made her betray that revolution, nor would any other love have made her leave the Party. But Stalin's crimes, the deaths, the purges, and the camps, above all, the camps—she remembers another wound, deeper than any Jack could hand her, one that will never heal, her sense of betrayal, her horrified disgust when she could no longer pretend that those stories, those reports, were merely the lies of the enemies of the people. From disgust blossomed searing hatred, the revenge-lust of a true lover scorned.

"No better than the Nazis," she whispers aloud. "Stalin was no better than the rotten Nazis. Thank God I saw it. Thank God I saw it in time."

And she weeps, just a little, while she pulls a dirty shirt over her head and drops it on the floor.

Judith Tarr, author of *Lord of the Two Lands* and *The Hound and the Falcon,* is one of our field's finest historical fantasists. Whatever the era or country in which she chooses to set her story, you can count on the details and the flavor being absolutely right.

As in this off-the-wall little story. . . .

Cowards Die:
A Tragicomedy in
Several Fits
by Judith Tarr

I know I'm top of the rock when Julia says she'll go to the Birthday Gala with me. Lucio and Cesco and Tonio and Little Thanaric all get smiled out to the wrong side of the door, but when I show up I get smiled in. Not that that isn't all I get, Julia being Julia and nose down in a book, but you spend a while around the capo's palazzo, you learn to tell when the luck's looking your way.

Lucio and Cesco take it like men, lay up for me when I'm coming back late from Vipsania's, but I'm as sober as a pontifex and I've been waiting for something to cut loose. Lucio gets a gap in his grin, Cesco gets his arm in a sling, I get satisfaction. Tonio's quieter, but that's no trouble, I've been saving up for a new taster, the old one was getting worn out. As for Little Thanaric, he's the kind to holler for tommyguns at sunup, but he gets called off on a rumble out Volaterrae way, so we make a deal to settle it when he comes back.

So here I am, dressed to the tens, zoot suit, reet pleat,

bullet in my buttonhole, and here's Julia, drop 'em dead at a thousand paces, with a handshake and a smile and a book under her arm. Her daddy being a traditionalist, her bodyguards carry the fasces and the axes, you know, rods to beat the marks with, axes to quiet them down, but they've got their nice long pieces too, looks like a new model, telescopic sights, I'd stop and ask but Luigi's coming up with the knife. He's a little bit too happy to do the ceremony, all he needs to do is touch the knife to my balls and give me the warning about getting too fresh with Julia, but he puts a jab in it that puts me damned near through Papa Julie's nice painted ceiling. I'm all set to kill him, but Julia says, "Marco, please. Not on the new floor."

So I'll gut him later, me and maybe Little Thanaric if he's game before we go at it with the tommyguns. Even Luigi's not as big as Little Thanaric. Luigi doesn't look too scared. He'll learn.

It's not so easy to put on a swagger when I've got to be bleeding through my best silk Arachnes, but Luigi's sneering and Julia's waiting for me to come over all polite and hand her into daddy's Rolls Armani. So what's a little blood for a lady like Julia? I hand her in, get in beside her, the engine purrs like Livia Augusta's tiger, and off we go to the gala.

Julia's daddy is a capo, a big capo, molto fortissimo, and we all know he'll be capo di tutti capi when Don Mario kicks it down to Tartarus. But Don Mario's still a bit short of kicking it, and Papa Julie's not in any big hurry, so it's all smiles and gladhands and eternal loyalties on Don Mario's birthday. The old bastard's looking healthier than Bootsy's horse, sitting up there in his box with just half a dozen muscleboys to keep the rest of us honest. We pay our respects, Julia being a stickler and her daddy being worse, and the old man is halfway down her cleavage and Luigi doesn't bat an eyelash. Me, I'd do something, but Julia shoves her book in my stomach, damn near knocks the wind out, and smiles at Don Mario and says, "Isn't he cute, Grandpapa? I love it when he gets all red and angry and the curl falls over his forehead and he looks so *protective*."

Don Mario laughs himself half into a fit. I'll kill something, by hades I will.

"There," says Julia, putting her hand on my arm. "There, Marco, I shouldn't tease." She smiles up at me, big brown eyes and soft yellow curls and never mind the rest because Luigi's there with his knife and a grin, no mistaking what would make him the happiest man in Rome.

I put on a smile and say as sweet as I can, "No, no, it's nothing. Look, here's Donna Livia to pay her respects, we'd better make room, isn't the show about to start?"

All right, so I'm talking too fast. It gets us out past Livia's tiger, which yawns and says something rude, but before I can think about giving the muscle the slip, there's one in front and one behind and we're being herded into Papa Julie's box. He's not there yet. Business, I suppose. He'd better make it before the lights go down or Don Mario will have a little bone to pick with him. Not that that's my worry, except for what could happen to Julia if Don Mario gets mad at her daddy.

I know better than to think we'll get into too much trouble up here with the whole of Rome staring right at us and Luigi standing just in knifing range, but I've got a few plans for when the lights are out. I make conversation with people who keep blundering in. Julia gets her nose in her book. The theater fills up clear to the sky. The antiaircraft guns are hiding behind the floodlights, but I know where I'm looking. I notice they're muzzle up. We haven't had anybody try to kill the capo in months, but it never hurts to be ready. A strafing run on the theater while he's at his birthday gala would be just the thing to spice up the show. They got Appy the Clod like that, a ways back, before everybody knew what an airplane can do.

I'm not expecting a bombing run tonight. It's all quiet, the dons are in their boxes—all but Papa Julie—and the lights are going down. Julia closes her book. She catches

my eye and smiles. I'm warm right down to Luigi's stab
wound, which I've sneaked a minute to check, and it's not
bleeding after all. She doesn't look worried about her
daddy, but then Julia never looks worried about anything.

Julia watches the show. I watch her. I've got my plans,
but it's a long night in the theater, and Luigi can't watch
me every second of it.

The show is spectacular, but I've seen it all before.
They've got an army of pygmies for the bloodsport finale,
mounted on ostriches, against an army of giants on gi-
raffes. The crowd loves it. I yawn. Julia wishes they could
have a nautical spectacle the way they did last year, but a
blonde in the next box over says, "Oh, no, that would be
too dull. Boats are so *slow*."

Julia likes the musical events better. They're putting me
to sleep, and she's leaning on the edge of the box, beating
time, and there's no snuggling up to her without Luigi
stepping in. He catches my eye once, when the soprano
starts to sing, and smiles.

No use to tell him it's the contralto who's the castrato.
Luigi's not up on the finer distinctions.

It's not going well, unless you count the way Julia turns
and smiles at me. She's swooning over the tenor, who's got
a face like a horse's, all sinuses, no brains, so I'm supposed
to swoon with her. I don't do a very good imitation, but
she's too wrapped up in the music to notice.

I start noticing it myself, not that I give a blue goose for
the tragicomedy, but I'm getting frustrated and Luigi won't
stop watching me. I know what the story's about, it's the
same one every year. *The Death of Julius Caesar*, and they
don't mean Papa Julie, unless they're getting symbolic for
a change. This is the first Papa Julie, the great Papa Julie,
the one who could have been Dictator of Rome if he'd
gone on the way he started, but Lucky Corny Sulla took
care of that.

This is the usual wheeze. Julie the C. and Lucky Corny
don't hit it off even when Julie's just a kid, so Corny tries
this and that, and when nothing works, he has the kid

nabbed and ever so carefully crushes his voicebox. So? you might say, if you're like Little Thanaric and don't care a brass ass for the classics. So back then everything ran on speeches. Oratory. People talked their way into power. And Julie, when Corny was done, could just about croak for his supper.

Being Julie, and being pretty sure Corny wasn't done with him, he went and hid right under Corny's nose, in the Subura in Rome. Where he could have died, him being a big man's son and groomed for a big man himself, but he was Julie the C. He ended up running every racket in the Subura, and that meant running most of the rackets in the empire. Corny was dead before Julie really got going, and maybe Julie helped him along and maybe he didn't. Big Pompey ran his course, Marco Antonio shacked up with his Egyptian piece, the Dirty Dozen Dictators carried on after Marco drowned in the Nile or got eaten by a crocodile, depending on who's telling it—and Julie the C. just went on and on.

So does the tragicomedy. Julie's a basso, he's not bad. The tenor's being the Nephew and Heir, Julie the Craps Queen, but this is Art, so he's calling himself Octavius. Takes about an hour to get him out of the gambling hall he's running off Shitlake Alley, get him through the Subura (with an aria at every streetcorner), and get him into the catacomb where Julie the C.'s been trying to die in peace. The tenor's not going to let him have that. I could tell them the Heir wasn't even there, he was busted for running a loaded-dice scam and they had to spring him after the old man popped off, but Art isn't interested in what really happened.

When it's finally over and they come out to take their bows, Julia holds out a hand. One of the muscle puts a rose in it. She stands up and wouldn't you know they're playing the lights around and one catches her, and she glows like Venus in her bathtub. Everybody looks up, including the tenor. She bows, smiles her brightest smile, and tosses the rose down to the stage. The tenor catches it, he seems to think he's the one they're all howling and cheering at, and he kisses the rose and bows and scrapes and kisses the thing again. You'd think he'd know when enough is enough.

Julia takes my hand. She says something I don't quite hear. She says it louder, not moving her lips. "Let's go, Marco."

"But," I say, "they haven't had the dancing yet."

I like that, see. The women don't wear much and the men are just furniture.

Julia's grip gets tighter. It almost hurts. "Marco, I want to go."

Well, if she puts it like that, I wouldn't be polite to say no. I'm just about to say so when the shooting starts.

"Oh, dear," says Julia. "Somebody jumped the gun."

That's so funny I have to laugh, which isn't all that smart when you're trying to get a woman down into cover and she's not having any, and there's a regular firestorm everywhere.

Well, not everywhere. Just the boxes. The crowd's screaming, but it isn't the we're-being-shot-at scream, it's the great-show-we-want-more howl. I can see them at it: Julia knocks me halfway over the edge of the box. She hauls me back, which says something for what she really thinks of me, and then the other muscle, the one who isn't Luigi, what's his name, Hiram, Habacuc, Hammurabi?, grabs me and throws me out the back and says, "It's a putsch, putz."

I know enough Judean to figure that out. The swear-word isn't enough to get my blood up, and anyway Julia's still got a grip on me and we're hustling through Hades. They call the back passages that, and it looks like it. The lights are down, emergency reds on, people screaming and running. Julia's not moving all that fast. Just fast enough to get us out with breath left to run for it. The muscle's in tight around us.

"Putsch?" I say to Hiram. Herschel. Whatever. "Who—"

Hammurabi looks disgusted. "She always picks 'em for

looks," he says to Luigi. Luigi is busy being point man. Habacuc decks a beefy type who just happens to be carrying a bicycle chain.

So I'm slow. I'm not stupid. "Papa Julie's making his move," I say.

Nobody gives me the laurel for genius. Julia pulls me around a corner, and there's a door, and muscle in it. The whole lot of us tumble out into a car that's not the Rolls, somebody's been smart there, and the doors slam and the car takes off.

It's smooth. It's fast. It makes me so mad I dive for the door and start wrenching at the handle, with muscle on me like crocodiles on old Marco Antonio, and him being my main ancestor of record I say I'm entitled to it. I'm thinking I should have taken that nice little numbers racket in Alexandria that Uncle Marcello had all ready for me, instead of holding out for a gig in old Rome, except then I wouldn't have met Julia. For all the good that's doing me right now.

"I ought to be back there!" I yell. "I want my piece of the action."

"Don't worry," says Julia. "You'll get yours."

I don't even want to know what she means by that. Luigi lost his knife somewhere, or he's decided he's got other turbot to fry. Meanwhile every capo in Rome is getting shot to pieces, including Don Mario, who should have known better.

Well, maybe he did. A capo knows when to go, and how to go in style. I won't be surprised to hear he went down face forward, giving the gladiator's salute to Papa Julie.

Palazzo Cesare is quiet. The riot shields are up and the muscle's deployed, minus me. Julia's reading her book. I take a look. It's Viddy the Nose, I should have known, his good old *How to Win Girls and Influence Bosses*, and look where that got him. He got too up close and friendly with another Julia, ended up Exhibit A in an iceberg off Cape Boreas.

"Well," I say when the clepsydra in the atrium dribbles midnight, "I'd better be going. It's getting late."

Julia hardly looks up from her book. "You can't do that. We're sealed in."

"I can get out," I say.

"Don't," says Julia. She's not even looking at me, but I stay where I am. I won't say I'm nervous. I'm as bored as hades, is what I am. I think about knocking Julia over and giving her what she's been begging for since the day I met her. It isn't Luigi that stops me. It's thinking that she stood up right before the shooting started, and if that wasn't a signal then I'm Julie the C.

"You might have got killed," I say.

She sighs. I've interrupted her once too often, but this time at least she looks at me. "I might have," she says. She's cool. She's calm. She looks good enough to eat.

I'm not going to tell her that. So I say, "I'd hate it if you had."

"Good," she says.

"I want a piece of the action," I say.

She puts her book down. I take a deep breath. I'm ready for anything, except for what she does. She decks me with a neat left jab. "That's for being stupid. And this," she says, bending over me and kissing my nose, "is for being adorable. Daddy says your family owns half the rackets in Alexandria. Why doesn't it own all of them?"

"Because your daddy owns the other half," I say. I'm proud of myself. It's not easy to be cool when you're flat on your back and Julia is sitting on your stomach discussing your prospects. And there's Luigi. Jove knows where Luigi got to.

Julia smiles. "Then you do think a merger is just the thing for all of us."

Actually I don't. "I'm not out for your money," I say.

"Of course you're not. You're out for my body." She pats her assets fondly. "And I'm out for yours. Not that I have

any illusions, you understand. In ten years you'll be fat
and bald and I'll be just hitting my stride. We'll agree to
separate arrangements then, I'm sure. Meanwhile we'll enjoy what we've got while we've got it."

"No," I say. "I'm not on the market."

She narrows her big brown eyes. Amazing how small
and mean they look all of a sudden. Just like her daddy's.
"A prior engagement?"

Now I know where Luigi is. He's right behind her. He
has his knife again, or one just like it. He's smiling.

"You don't know Cleo," I say.

"I think I do," says Julia. "Miss Respectability? Blue-
stocking of the Year?"

"She's not that bad," I say. "She and my pater have a
racket going that would make even your daddy sit up and
beg."

"Oh," says Julia. "That. My daddy says he's going to
have to marry her himself if she keeps up, or ice her himself, whichever comes first. Really, Marco, I can't understand why you're so dense. Daddy has the pontifex on
call, and the contracts are all drawn up. Do you want to
stand up for your wedding like the fine upstanding young
man you are"—right, and so's my little man, who doesn't
care about anything but the prime assets parked right in
front of him—"or are you going to be difficult?"

"Difficult dead," I ask, "or difficult in chains?"

"You're no good to me dead," says Julia.

I have to give it to her. She has all the angles covered.
Including, eventually, mine. By that time Luigi isn't there.
I can't see anybody else, either, but knowing the help I figure the walls have eyes. It never stopped me before. It
might stop me now, but Julia's got her own opinion about
that.

Cowards die every time they turn around, old Julie the
C. said, and the real guts just throws itself on its sword.
Julie had a point, I always thought, but that was before I
knew Julia. Swords aren't what she has in mind.

"I picked you, you know," she says in between rides

around the course, "because you have such a sweet face. And wonderful connections in Alexandria. *And* you aren't half as dumb as you look. I like that in a man."

"Urg," I say.

"You're going to be capo di tutti capi when Daddy kicks it," she goes on. "You've got a lot to learn, of course, but you'll learn it. I'll see to that."

I don't say anything.

Julia smiles. She melts me right into the rug. Egyptian. Antonio and Antonio, Shippers. Twenty thousand sesterces if it's an as.

Old Julie the C. doesn't have a line for people who die twice. Once for Hades, and the later the better. Once for Julia. What does that make me? Half a coward?

I ask Julia. She laughs. She doesn't say what she thinks I am. Not till a lot later, and then I almost don't catch it.

"It makes you a capo," she says. "My capo. All mine."

I'm top of the rock. Just so long as it's not Tarpeia's—the one they throw people off of. People who go too far. People who get in Papa Julie's way. Or in Julia's.

It's better than swords, I suppose. Or crocodiles. I think about it while she nibbles my ear, and that's not easy but I manage. After a while I shrug. I feel a grin break out. "Well," I say. "All right. Why not?"

"There's my Marco," says Julia.

Dean Wesley Smith is what we call in the trade a Triple Threat: as a writer, he has produced excellent work at all lengths, from novel to short-short story; as an editor, he was responsible for the brilliant novella series from Axolotl Press; and as a publisher, his Pulphouse Publishing Company is a force to be reckoned with.

For this anthology, Dean has chosen to write about a most unusual outlaw, one who was never found guilty in court but was banned for life from the sport of baseball. One Shoeless Joe Jackson, by name. . . .

Black Betsy
by Dean Wesley Smith

Eleven in the morning, December 5, 1991. The time and the day stuck in my head like the memory of my first kiss or the memory of my dad dying. The weather that morning had turned unseasonably cold. Not baseball weather at all. A storm coming down the West Coast from Alaska was projected to bring four inches of snow to the valley floor, and light snow was already falling. The storm would eventually drop almost a foot of snow and shut down the schools for two days. But that wasn't what I remembered about December 5, 1991. What I remembered about that morning was Edward Toole. I turned on the jukebox that morning and sent him back to 1951. Back to a time when baseball was important to him, and to one other very special man.

I had just finished the morning bookkeeping for the Garden Lounge, made the deposit from the night before, and started the prep work for the day. Light snowflakes swirled in a whirlwind just inside the front door as Edward entered. He brushed off his coat, stamped his feet hard twice, and then moved through the empty tables toward the bar. He was a big man, thick shoulders, thick waist, with thinning brown-and-gray hair, and dark, brooding eyes. He was the last person I would have expected to show up in the Garden at eleven in the morning. He worked as a house lawyer for the big computer firm to the south of town. He had a wife, two boys, and was the town's Little League baseball coach. His usual drink was bourbon and water, with a twist of lemon. He never had more than three in any given night, and never before five.

He didn't look up as he approached the bar, which was also rare. Usually he was one of the most open and smiling people who came through the door.

"Morning, Stout," he said quietly as he pulled out a bar stool. He took his coat off and draped it over the stool, then climbed onto the stool closest to where I was working at the well. I had been cutting fruit, so I still had limes, lemons, and oranges scattered on the waitress station next to him.

"Edward," I said. "Good to see you. Out of the office early today. Heading home before it gets too deep out there?" I wiped the lime juice off my hands and slid a bar napkin in front of him. "What can I get for you?"

"The usual," he said, then swung around on the stool and faced out over the empty lounge. "You know," he said, seeming to stare off at the front door, "this place looks the same during the day as it does at night." He laughed. "Even the same smell of smoke and cleaner. For some reason, I thought it would be different."

I glanced around. The Garden was a small bar by current standards. More like a neighborhood bar in the old fifties tradition. It had a dozen vinyl booths, six tables, and a bunch of plants, mostly fake ferns. The walls were a natural wood, dark brown, and the carpet was the same dark brown color. The old oak bar, in front of a mirror and glass racks, filled the wall opposite the front door. A classic jukebox was framed in real plants to the right of the bar. Except for Christmas Eve, the jukebox was never plugged in. Background music was supplied by the stereo hidden behind the bar.

Most of the customers said the Garden felt comfortable, like an old sweater. For me, it had been home for five years. And since I had never been married, my regular customers, like Edward, were the only family I had.

I cut a twist off a fresh lemon, slid it along the edge of the glass, dropped it into the golden bourbon, and set the glass on the napkin in front of him.

He twisted around to face me, holding a strained smile in place. "I suppose," he said, "since there are no windows, there would be no reason for this place to notice the time of day. I just hadn't thought about it before." He picked up the drink, nodding thank-you, and downed half of it.

In all the years I had been serving him, I had never seen him do anything but sip bourbon. Not even the night his Little League team won the state championship. "Everything all right on the home front? Carol and the kids?" I asked, picking up a lime and going back to slicing.

He finished the rest of the drink and slid it toward me for a refill. "They're fine. Or at least they were this morning." He paused for a moment, then said hesitantly, "But I just got fired."

"Holy shit! You're kidding."

Edward gave me another strained smile as I picked up his empty glass and moved to refill it. "Wish I was. Seems I made a bad choice a couple months back. Since what I did seems to be unethical, they had no choice but to fire me. And it seems that the State Bar will yank my license to practice law, too."

I finished making the drink in silence and placed it in front of him. "It was that serious?"

He nodded. "Mostly stupid on my part. I guess I knew better. Just wasn't thinking."

I stood across from him, waiting for him to continue. Tell me what he had done. He took a sip of his drink, looked up at me and asked, "You ever hear of Shoeless Joe?"

"The old baseball player they made the movie about?"

Edward nodded. "That's the one. I had a chance to meet him once, back when I was fifteen. Back in nineteen fifty-one in South Carolina. But I was too afraid to go into his bedroom with my baseball coach and two of the other players. In those days, I really wanted to be a professional ballplayer when I grew up, and everyone knew that Joseph Jefferson—Shoeless Joe—Jackson was the best left fielder to ever play the game. And one of the best hitters ever. I guess as a kid I just didn't have the courage to meet him. He died two days later, and I always blamed myself."

I slowly shook my head, took a deep breath and looked down at the fruit I had been cutting. None of this was making sense. But sometimes that was what a bartender had to expect. When customers needed to talk about problems, very rarely did they make immediate sense. The best thing a bartender could do was just keep them talking until they talked themselves out.

"You blamed yourself?" I asked. "Why? How old was he?"

"He was sixty-three. And he was sick. I know all that. He died on December fifth. Forty years ago today. Interesting, huh? That I would get fired on the same day. I think it is a sort of poetic justice."

"But if he was sixty-three and sick, why would you blame yourself?"

Edward took a deep breath and looked quickly around the bar, as if to make sure no one could hear him. Then he looked me right in the eye and said, "I stole Black Betsy. His bat."

Edward sipped on his entire second drink, and he sipped his third through the lunch crowd, and a fourth up until we were alone again at two. During that time, we talked about what caused him to get fired, how stealing Shoeless Joe's bat from his house had caused him guilt for forty years. During lunch, Edward and two other regular customers filled me in on the entire Black Sox scandal of the 1919 World Series. I learned how Shoeless Joe was the leading hitter for that series, with a .357 average. How he played errorless ball for the eight-game series, yet was still thrown out of baseball for agreeing to take five thousand dollars to throw the series.

I learned about Comiskey Park, the White Sox, and Commissioner Kenesaw Mountain Landis. I learned about the seven other players who were thrown out with Shoeless Joe, and about the Ten Day Clause in the old player contracts that led to the entire mess.

I also learned that Edward was a haunted man. He was haunted by a mistake he made as a kid. For his entire life, he continued to make the same sort of bad decisions and mistakes. I also learned that he knew when he entered college that he really didn't have the talent to be a professional baseball player. He truly loved being a lawyer, yet never lost his love for baseball, or regretted not playing it for a living.

At some point during that three-hour period, I decided to break one of my own rules. I would plug in the jukebox and give Edward a chance to correct that one big mistake.

The jukebox in the Garden Lounge was a time-travel device.

Actually, every jukebox is a time machine in a limited fashion. When a song is played on a regular jukebox, a person sort of travels back to the time and the memory associated with that song. The Garden jukebox does almost exactly that, with one major difference. It physically takes the person to the memory and allows that person to be there inside his former body for the length of the song. He is actually there, smelling, tasting, and feeling the past.

And they can change it, too. Which is why I allow myself to plug the jukebox in only on Christmas Eve, and then only for a few close friends every year. Changing the past is way too dangerous. And I have lost a couple of good friends because of it.

I inherited the jukebox with the junk in the basement of the first bar I tried to own. Ten minutes before the bank came in to close me down, I hauled the old jukebox out of the basement and into my garage at home, figuring I had the spare time to fix it up. When I got around a year later to opening it up, I discovered a bunch of stuff inside that didn't belong in a normal jukebox. Stuff that seemed far beyond my limited electrical ability, so I just cleaned off the dust, fixed the electric cord, which looked as if someone had ripped it from the back of the machine, and turned it on.

Luck had it that the only forty-five I had around the house was a recording of a song that reminded me of the night I almost asked Jenny, the only woman I had ever loved, to marry me. It had been her favorite song. I had the record in a box in the garage, together with pictures of· her, and hadn't listened to it in years.

I fired up the song and the next thing I knew, I was with Jenny. I could feel my fingers touching her hand. I could smell her light perfume. I licked my lips and I could taste the faint cherry from her lipstick. I was there, fumbling, trying to get up enough courage in my twenty-three-year-old body to ask her to marry me. Yet I was also there as a thirty-seven-year-old man, with the clear memory that I had not asked her. And the next week she had left me to go back to college, and eventually to another man.

I sat there beside her, stunned, not talking, until the song ended and I found myself back in my garage.

The next day I finally got up the courage to play the record again, and ended up sitting next to Jenny again. And again at the exact same time and place. That was where my memory from that song took me. That second time, I almost asked her to marry me. Almost. It would have changed my life and my future. And I had no idea what that would have meant. My life really wasn't so bad.

I have never had the courage to play Jenny's song again, even though it is on the jukebox, waiting.

Since then, every Christmas Eve I have given a few close friends the opportunity to go back and relive one memory. Sometimes they change something back there and don't return. But most of the time they pop back into the bar as the song ends. Sometimes laughing, sometimes crying, but always more content than before they played the song.

Now I was going to break my own rule. I was going to plug in the jukebox on December 5, 1991, and give Edward a chance to change his past and his life. I just hoped I was doing the right thing.

"Well," Edward said, looking around as the last lunch customer went out into the blowing snow. "I suppose it's time for me to go home and tell Carol the news." He shook his head. "Damned if I know what we are going to do. I have never been fired before."

I sat two dirty glasses in the sink and took a deep breath. "Humor me for a moment. What do you think would have happened if you hadn't stolen that bat?"

Edward shrugged. "I would have slept a lot better over the years, that's for sure."

I nodded and went on. "You have a song, or style of song, that reminds you of that time you went to see Joe?"

Edward thought for a moment, then nodded. "Big-band stuff. You know, like Dorsey. My mom was always playing it, and I remember a record player on low with one of those bands playing on it when we visited Joe's house. Why?"

I pointed at the Wurlitzer jukebox to the right of the bar. "You ever have a song take you back to a memory?"

"Of course. Who hasn't?"

I moved out from behind the bar, reached in behind the polished chrome of the jukebox and plugged the cord in. A soft whirring came from inside, and I could feel my stomach tightening. I always felt sick every time I turned on the jukebox. The sickness of dread, of worry. The sickness of fear, like going into a bad situation, or knowing the moment before you are going to get hit that you will get hurt.

I stood and faced Edward as the green, red, and yellow lights flickered on, casting an odd rainbow on the floor and nearby booth. "I know you won't believe me, so just listen. This jukebox can take you back to that memory of Shoeless Joe."

Edward laughed. "I don't need a machine to do that. It's with me every day."

"It will actually take you there. Maybe this time you can leave the bat."

Edward looked at me for a moment, then snorted. "Right." He picked up his drink and downed it. Then reached into his pocket for his wallet. "I think I had better be getting home. Music there to face for sure."

"I told you that you wouldn't believe me. Instead, just humor me. Play one song. Do that and the drinks and lunch are on me. I will even supply the quarter." I held up a quarter for him to see.

He looked around at the empty bar. Then, after a long moment, he shrugged. "Stout, people said you were a strange bird. Now I guess I know why." He moved over to the jukebox, taking the quarter from me as he did.

"There are a number of big-band tunes on there. Pick the one that reminds you the most of that moment you took the bat."

"Will do," he said, shaking his head.

I watched him as he looked over the selection, then dropped the quarter into the slot and punched the buttons. The jukebox clanked and then the sound of a small motor came from inside, followed by a bunch of clicks.

Now I felt as if I wanted to throw up. What happened if he changed something really major? Something that cost a lot of lives. Every damn time I plugged in the jukebox, that fear hit me like a hammer.

I took a deep breath, placed both hands on the bar in

front of me and faced him. He was a friend. He deserved the chance. "Just think about that moment in Joe's house," I told him. "And remember while you are there, that you have only the length of the song that is playing. Not one moment longer."

"Sure," he said. "And then . . ."

The song started and Edward faded from the bar and was gone.

I took a deep breath and moved over to the well as the Jimmy Dorsey Band filled the room with the sounds of the past. I was going to break another one of my rules.

I needed a drink.

Big-band music played softly from an old record player in the cluttered dining room. The house smelled musty and closed in, with a faint medicinal odor that seemed to coat everything. A big overstuffed couch with doilies on the arms filled one wall. Glass cabinets crammed with old trophies and pictures filled another. Outside, it was a cold December day in South Carolina.

In front of the glass case was a round umbrella stand. In that stand were five baseball bats, including a black one. Edward stared at that bat for a moment, not really understanding what it was, then glanced around the living room.

"Wow, Stout. You can really pull off an illusion." As he said it, he realized his voice didn't sound right. It seemed too high, and at a different pitch. He glanced down at his younger body, the heavy coat, the boots, and the memories came flooding back. The memories of coming into Shoeless Joe's house with Coach and Dave and Johnny just a few minutes before. Yet those memories were overlaid by the forty years of the future, and by the very real memory of just getting fired from a job he really loved.

"Stout! How—"

The sound of laughter came from the back room over the top of the music. Stout had been right. Somehow he was here, yet he wasn't. He couldn't be here. He was mar-

ried, with two kids forty years in the future. He reached
out and touched the arm of the couch. It felt real.

He looked around again, then moved over and pulled
out the black bat. It was heavy and a little cold to his
touch. The grip was rough with the old tape and felt almost sticky. Black Betsy. Joe's favorite bat.

He remembered looking at it forty years ago, then slipping it up inside his big coat and going out the front door.
He had stashed the bat in a large bush and waited for
Coach and the others to come out. They had ribbed him
a little about not going in to see Shoeless Joe, but not
much. Mostly they just talked about how exciting it was
to meet Shoeless Joe and how he couldn't have really
thrown the series.

Edward had gone back that night and picked up the
bat. He still had it, up in his attic forty years later.

Young Edward turned the bat over in his hands and
looked at the initials S. J. carved in the handle. Many a
night over the next few years he would hold that bat and
run his fingers over those initials. He did so again now, his
young self treasuring the feel, his older self hating it, the
two emotions battling inside his head and stomach.

The fight lasted for only a moment, but it seemed much
longer. Finally the forty-year-old memories won and he
dropped the bat back into the umbrella stand.

It was as if the weight of an entire life lifted from his
shoulders. "Thanks, Stout," he said to the air. He took a
deep breath and let it out. It was time to face a few more
things. The song was still playing, so with one last look at
Black Betsy, he turned and headed for the back room.

Shoeless Joe's bedroom was filled with a huge dresser
and a big old metal bed. The drapes were open to the gray
December day. Joe was propped up on pillows and he was
laughing. To Edward he looked like a skeleton, with large
ears, an even bigger nose, and eyes that seemed to sparkle.

As Edward entered, Joe looked over and nodded.

"Glad you came in," Coach said and motioned for
Edward to move up beside the bed. "Edward, this is Shoe-

less Joe Jackson. Mr. Jackson, this is Edward Toole, one of
my better players." Joe smiled and stuck out his hand.
Edward shook it. Joe's grip was strong, but the skin was
dry and rough.

The older Edward wanted to scream and shout for joy.
He was actually meeting Shoeless Joe Jackson. Actually
shaking his hand. But his fifteen-year-old self was too embarrassed to talk. This time, the young self won.

"Nice meeting you, Edward," Joe said. His voice was
deep and powerful and, coming from the thin body, it surprised Edward.

"Nice meeting you, sir," Edward stammered.

Joe smiled as if he understood. And just maybe he did,
because for a moment he looked into Edward's eyes. Then
his smile slowly turned to a frown. He shook his head and
looked around. "I suppose you all are wondering the same
question that everyone wonders. Did I really throw the series?"

"Sir," Coach said, "I made the boys promise to not ask
about that."

Joe waved a large thin hand in dismissal. "That's all
right. After thirty years, I have sort of got used to it."

In the other room, the song was almost finished.

Joe looked directly at Edward. "Sometimes you make
good choices and sometimes you make bad ones. Just like
in a ball game. And with every play, you must live with
the choice. Sometimes only to the end of the inning.
Sometimes for much longer. You understand me?" He was
asking Edward directly.

Both young and old Edward could do nothing but nod.

The song had very few seconds left.

"I made a bad choice and it cost me," Joe said. "But I
tried from that day forward to make good choices. And I
kept on living. Just like in a game, you must keep on playing, no matter what the mistake. What I learned is that
you don't ever give up."

Edward nodded. "Thank you, sir." And Edward's older
self added, "More than you will ever know."

The song ended, and forty years of future memories slipped from the young Edward as Shoeless Joe nodded and smiled.

The last notes of the big-band song echoed around the Garden Lounge.

Edward did not reappear.

I let go of the warm chrome of the jukebox where I had been holding on to make sure I remembered Edward. He didn't come back, so he had changed the past somehow. He probably didn't take the bat this time, and that had changed his present in some way. Now maybe he hadn't got fired. Or maybe he had never taken the job with the computer company in the first place, or he had never become a lawyer.

Anything could have happened, and I would not even have remembered him being in the bar this afternoon if I hadn't been holding onto the jukebox when the song ended. My memories would have switched over to this new world. But by touching the jukebox, I could remember the old world. And Edward.

I couldn't resist the temptation to go to the phone book and see if Edward's name was still in there. It was, only it also had an office number with it beside his home phone. It looked as if he had hung out his own shingle in this world. I hoped that meant he was happier. I finished my drink and went back to cleaning up from lunch rush. If he didn't show up after five, I would check around. Until then, there wasn't anything I could do but wait.

At seven minutes after five, Edward walked through the door. He looked the same, except that he wasn't wearing a suit. Instead, he had on a casual dress sweater and golf slacks. He smiled and waved as he came through the door, and I waved back and started to make his normal drink.

There were about twenty of the regulars in the Garden and he stopped for a moment to talk to a few of them at the first table. So by the time he was on the only empty stool to the right of the waitress station, I had the drink in front of him.

"Quick as always, Stout," he said. Then he held up the glass with the bourbon and a twist and looked at it. "But what's this? You forget after all these years that I drink vodka tonics?"

A couple of the others at the bar laughed, and I laughed right along with them as I took the drink back from him. "Just not with it today," I said, trying to act as normal as I could even though my heart was pounding as if I had just run a hard five miles. I had about six hundred questions I wanted to ask him. Yet I knew he wouldn't understand a one of them.

I fixed him a new drink and slid it in front of him. He held it up and looked at me. "To Shoeless Joe Jackson," he said, making a toasting motion, then sipping his drink.

"Shoeless Joe?" I asked, somehow keeping my voice from shaking. "Wasn't he the one they made the movie about?"

Edward laughed. "You know, Stout, you have said that same thing every year. It's December fifth, forty years from the day Shoeless Joe Jackson died. Don't you remember we toast him every year on this date? He was the greatest left fielder to ever play the game." He paused for a moment, smiling to himself.

"Oh, God," one of the regulars down the bar said, shaking his head. "Here we go again."

Edward just kept on smiling. "You know," he said, "I met Shoeless Joe once."

Robert Sheckley has been delighting science fiction audiences for more than four decades now. I don't think there's any question but that he is acknowledged to be the finest humorist ever to grace our field, and I personally consider his *Dimension of Miracles* to be one of the half-dozen best science fiction novels ever published.

Here he gives us not one alternate outlaw, not two, but a whole town's worth.

(Which town? Read on. It won't take you long to figure it out.)

Miranda
by Robert Sheckley

It was quiet that morning in the little town of Cicatrice, California. It was especially quiet in the vicinity of the First National Trust Bank, the only bank still open in Cicatrice that year. The other two had gone under a couple of years earlier, during the worst of the Depression. That had been a bad time. But not much had happened since then. And no one was expecting the dire events that were shaping up so imminently as three cars drove into town from nearby Route 66.

As the three cars were parking, we may note that the lighting in the streets of Cicatrice was sepia that morning in October. The town seemed almost deserted. What few men there were, walking about and nodding to friends—for this was not a large town and most people knew each other—were for the most part wearing tan polyester suits and two-tone shoes and snap-brim hats. There weren't many women on the street, either, that day in October, but those who were there had on careworn yellow and blue sunsuits that accentuated their stretch marks and did nothing to hide their flab.

Since the cars are still parking, we have time to note that in those days, Cicatrice was considered the fashion nadir of America. The worst of current tastes were wildly popular here, with the result that even when people were in style in Cicatrice, they looked tacky all over, but especially in terms of hem length. Maybe the fact that most of the local people bought their clothing at the Five and Dime had something to do with it, K-mart not having yet been invented.

The first of the three previously mentioned cars parked opposite the bank. It was a '33 Pontiac, colored a dusty gray. The man driving it was handsome in a distinctly Latin way. His hair was prematurely gray. He had a cunning little mustache. He wore a light-gray suit, sharply cut. His name was Caesar Romero. He was a bank robber.

The woman sitting beside him in the front seat was a good-looking Latin type. She had a big mouth with a lot of lipstick. She wore a complicated-looking black-and-green skirt with ruffles and a bolero top of distinctly foreign appearance. She was tanned, or maybe medium brown was her natural coloration. It was hard to tell with foreigners what was their natural coloration and what was suntan, especially when the background lighting was sepia.

This woman wore a big bandana hat with a bunch of yellow- and black-striped bananas on it. The hat also featured a bunch of deep red cherries that matched the woman's dark red lipstick. Her name was Carmen Miranda. She, too, was a bank robber.

"Are you sure this is the right place?" Carmen asked. She was speaking her native Portuguese, the only language she spoke without accent. The man to whom she spoke, Caesar Romero, was able to follow her only with difficulty. Caesar was a Cuban, a Spanish-speaker, and his English was impeccable. The Spanish have always had trouble with the Portuguese, and now was no exception.

But Caesar had no trouble understanding Carmen herself. They had met some months earlier in New York, where she had been trying unsuccessfully to join the Rockettes and he was doing stand-up comedy at the Spanish Harlem Roxy.

"Of course it's the right place," Caesar Romero said. "This is the place the Professor cased for us." Caesar was alluding to Harry Houdini, an unsuccessful magician who set up bank jobs for a cut of the action.

"It doesn't look like much," Carmen said.

"It'll be fine," Caesar assured her. He took the Shell road map out of the glove compartment and unfolded it. There was a big penciled cross where Cicatrice appeared, right there on Route 66 at the bottom of California. The Professor had scrawled on it in pencil—and this was mentioned in newspaper accounts later—"Only bank in town, can't miss it."

"Something I don't like about this setup," Carmen said, looking around at the town.

"Looks all right to me," Caesar said. "There's not a cop in sight."

"I still don't like it."

"What's the matter, Carmen?" Caesar asked. "You having a *bandofersiero*?" He was referring to the spirit of Consternation in the Molambo religion—of which Carmen was an adherent—as the function that brings second sight and heartburn.

Carmen sighed and shook her head. The bananas on her chapeau rustled faintly. "I don't know," she murmured.

"This bank job is the chance of a lifetime, babe," one of the men in the backseat said. His name was John Garfield. He was new to Carmen's gang. He spoke roughly, but projected an air of great sympathy. He was an out-of-work actor. Carmen liked him, but she wasn't sure she trusted him. And she really wondered about this friend of his, sitting beside him in surly silence, this Charles Laughton person. What a weird-looking guy to have as a partner.

The other two cars pulled in behind them and parked at the curb. Carmen had decided to use plenty of help for this job. In one of the cars, the Nash, was a small-time grifter from Wisconsin named Edward G. Robinson. With him was his partner, an Easterner named Humphrey Bogart.

Carmen didn't know anything about those two. They had been vouched for by her old friend, Sherman Billingsly, owner of Shermie's Beanery, a joint on New York's West Fifty-third Street where Carmen often ate.

In the other car were two old friends, small, sinister Allan Ladd, and his partner from Brooklyn, big, tough William Bendix. They parked their Packard behind Bogart's Ford, which in turn was parked behind Carmen's Studebaker.

By prearrangement, all of them met five minutes later at a back table in the Rosebud Luncheonette & Diner, across the street from the bank.

"Well, Carmen, what do you think?" Bogart asked with his wiseguy smirk and the faint lisp that had prevented him from becoming an actor.

"It looks pretty good," Carmen said. But there was no confidence in her voice.

"So let's get to it," Bendix said, straightforward and insensitive, slurring his vowels in a humorous way that nobody laughed at.

"You all know what to do?" Carmen asked. The men nodded and grunted and drank coffee.

They trusted Carmen. This wasn't her first bank job. Ever since coming up from Rio de Janiero, a poor girl from the favelas with her eyes full of stars and her heart full of sambas and cotton candy, she had been pulling bank jobs, first in New York, then all over California. She had emblazoned a trail of blood and bucks across the state, and the newspapers had written lurid stories of her carryings-on in the gilded and overpriced watering troughs of Beverly Hills. But the truth was, at night, after work, Carmen usually went to the movies, sometimes alone, sometimes accompanied by the gallant Caesar Romero, sometimes by Alice Faye, a waitress in the Hollywood Piggly Wiggly with whom she had struck up a friendship.

In the company of these friends, but more often alone, Carmen watched the stars of the silver screen and wished with all the passion of her carioca heart that she could be one of them.

But fate had decreed otherwise. This was what life had brought her: sticking up banks, watching movies and, sometimes, entertaining her gangster friends with little songs and dances.

Back in the cafe: "Anyone see any police out there?" Carmen asked.

"The coast is clear," grunted Edward G. Robinson.

"All right," Carmen said. "Let's do it." She got up. Caesar paid the bill for all of them and then went outside.

No cops in sight. The town of Cicatrice was as quiet as a tomb. It looked perfectly safe. Yet despite this, Carmen was haunted by a vague sense of apprehension. She ignored it. Sometimes you just have to ignore your apprehensions. Otherwise you'd never get out of bed.

Carmen leading, the eight robbers walked inside the bank. They took up positions where they could keep an eye on everything, including the street as seen through the big plate-glass window. Carmen went up alone to the single teller's cage.

There was a nameplate on the counter. The teller's name was Adolph Menjou.

"Good morning, ma'am," Menjou said. "What can I do for you?"

"You theenk ees a nice morning?" Carmen said with her broadest smile.

"Sure looks nice to me," Menjou said. His eyes twinkled. He was the soul of bonhomie. Carmen, a fool for suave, mustached Europeans, almost regretted robbing such a nice-looking man, until she reminded herself that the money wouldn't come out of his pocket.

So she said, "Well, let's try to keep eet a nice day, hah? Just don' make no sudden moves, hokay, boychick?"

Opening her purse, Carmen took out a long-barreled .44 revolver. It was a big, clumsy weapon, and she had asked the other gangsters many times to get her something smaller, but they always forgot to. She would have liked one of those snub-nosed police guns that cops sometimes carried in movies, a nice pearl-handled one that would fit inside her garter. But it had been too late to get one for this job.

Carmen quickly checked the pistol's firing hole, or whatever it was called—she had no head for technical English. Sometimes the firing holes got plugged up from stuff in her purse. Once she'd found a lipstick jammed into the muzzle or nozzle or barrel or whatever it is you called the firing hole. But this time, it was clear.

Carmen brandished the gun. "See thees?"

Menjou's eyes widened slightly, but his voice was steady as he replied, "Yes, ma'am!"

"I want money!"

"Certainly," Menjou said. "I'll just wrap this up for you." He reached down and scooped up the bills in his till. They might have come to fifty dollars.

"I don' want that chicken feed," Carmen said. "What I'm after is the payroll for the Clarkson mine."

"Yes, ma'am!" Menjou said. "You're very well-informed, miss!"

"I get around," Carmen smirked. "Gimme the payroll!"

"I don't have it here in my cage," Menjou said. "They wouldn't trust anything that important with me. Even if I have been with the bank for almost thirty years." He shook his head, pulling himself out of the sudden dismal mood that had descended on him. "I'll have to get the payroll from the manager."

"Just make it queek," Carmen said.

While this was going on, the other bank robbers had fanned out and were covering the bank's two customers, as well as the temporary secretary-typist from nearby

Canobie. Since at that moment there were seven gangsters and only four civilians, the task was not onerous. The bank robbers had a variety of guns. Allan Ladd carried a nice walnut-handled luger that he'd taken off a sheriff when they'd pulled the Black Dahlia job in Possum near Sacramento. Caesar was looking good with a double-barreled shotgun that he drew out from beneath his long yellow riding coat with an elegant gesture. The others had the more usual-looking .38 caliber revolvers.

The two customers and the typist had been shocked into silence by this turn of events. They stayed cool. But a new arrival, a tall blonde named Betty Hutton, stepped into the bank, took one look at the drawn firearms and began to scream. A man, whose name was Richard Widmark, came in just behind her, sized up the situation and quickly slapped Hutton's face, shutting her up. He hissed, "Whadda ya wanna do, get us all killed?"

Hutton, very blonde, a little on the large side but nice, looked up at him quizzically. "Haven't I seen you some-place before? What do you do for a living?" Widmark, who was a sales agent for Mill Valley Feed, and a little sensitive about the subject, did not dignify her remark with a response.

And now the bank president, a dapper foreigner in cut-away coat and fawn slacks, came out from an inner office. He had on gray silk gloves, which he peeled off slowly. His name was Tuhran Bey. He had just been transferred here from Allahabad. First day on the job and this had to happen.

"What seems to be the trouble . . . ?" He saw the drawn guns and froze in his tracks.

Carmen said to him, "Leesen, Mr. Bank President, we want the Clarkson payroll and we want eet quick. You give it up, we don't kill nobody, see? Otherwise it's aye bam bam bam, aye, carramba, adios la musica. You hear what I'm saying to you, Chico?"

"There will be no need for violence," Tuhran Bey said

quietly. "Quick, Adolph, go into my office and get them the Clarkson payroll."

Menjou hesitated. Allan Ladd prodded him in the back with the luger. Menjou hurried to Tuhran Bey's office, followed by Ladd and John Garfield. Menjou went directly to the big black safe in the corner by the hat rack, dialed in the correct digits, swung open the safe door and, reaching in, took out a canvas bag on which were stenciled the words, "Clarkson Mine Payroll."

He handed the bag to Carmen. She took it and said, "Thank you verry much, Mr. Bank Teller!" and handed the bag to Romero, who hefted it and grinned.

"Let's go!" Carmen said.

The criminals, guns at the ready, backed out of the bank. The last to go was Carmen.

She paused in the doorway and smiled wide and handsome for the people. She opened her mouth; her attention turned to an invisible orchestra. She sang, "Ay yi yi yi I like you very much!" It was her mark, her signature, her leitmotif, her shtick, and it had made her famous among gangsters. Sadly, it was to be the next to the last time it would ever be heard.

Out in the street, William Bendix yanked the canvas bag away from Caesar Romero and ripped it open. He'd had his doubts about Tuhran Bey and now he was going to find out. Inside the bag, he found neatly banded stacks of cut newspaper. "We been robbed!" he cried.

The bank robbers gaped into the canvas bag, then looked at each other with disordered gaze of wild surmise. The word "betrayal" was about to be heard. But who had set them up? Alas, there was no time to consider the question, which, under the circumstances, was academic.

Carmen was the first to react. "Ve been tricked! Quick, into the cars!"

But already it was late, very late. Policemen suddenly came forth from behind buildings and out of alleys, from out of shoe-shine joints and pool halls, and there were some state troopers among them, tall and severe in their

. uniforms of well-tailored tan. More and more cops came pouring out of beer halls and dime-a-dance places. These men were drawn from every town and city between Bakersfield and West L.A. It was the most elaborate trap the Feds had set up since they killed John Dillinger at a theater in Chicago.

"Drop those guns, Carmen!" Police Captain Jack Hawkins cried. "You and your thugs haven't got a chance. Surrender while you can!"

The beautiful Sambaiste with the Baian clothing and the banana-heavy headdress glared defiance at the clean-shaven young upholders of the law. "You'll never get me alive, choppers!" Carmen shouted back, in the excitement losing some of the subtler points of the English language.

But Carmen was past the silliness and inadequacy of words. The beautiful and remarkable Sambiaste from faraway Brazil stood poised with her .44. The police poised back, and there was a moment of standoff until suddenly bullets began filling the air like hailstones on a dark New England day.

Bullets ricocheted off building fronts and startled the sparrows squawking from the telephone wires. Bullets swept the street like chaff driven by a cold wind from hell. Bullets ricocheted off signboards, broke the windows of cars, slammed into telephone posts, punched holes in storefronts. Bullets pecked at the gangsters like flocks of crazed and malevolent birds.

The gangsters tried to take cover. They ducked down behind vintage Studebakers and Packards, attempting to escape the hail of fire from hell. The gangsters whirled, ducked, dodged, fired back, swore, cursed, staggered to and fro, jerking mightily whenever a slug bonked into them. The gangsters dodged and ducked and whirled and ducked, but it was no use. The cops, aided by grim-jawed Federal men, poured in a dense and accurate fire. And, not content with the usual small arms, the agents of the law now augmented the already hellish fire with suddenly produced tommy guns, and with Johnson guns, and even with the new and dreaded J. Edgar guns.

Slugs zinged up and down the street like mouse droppings in a hailstorm. There was only one possible result: the multitudinous slugs from the various and multifarious weapons chopped down the gangsters, burying them, as it were, beneath the bodies of countless copper-jacketed metallic hornets.

One by one the gangsters caught it, crumpled, and cashed out. William Bendix looked up in surprise as the first bullet of many hit him. He died comically. Allan Ladd was cool when he took his. Caesar Romero had a sneer on his lip when they cut him down, but no matter what way they chose to go, they fell, all of them, blood-laced dancers in the ballroom of hell, going down to dusty death, where Antony and Cleopatra were there to welcome them in the name of the damned. Or so it is believed.

Carmen spun and danced on the targeted sidewalk as steel fire clattered around her, and the bullet-torn bananas on her hat of great beauty seemed to shriek in their own mortal agony as slugs tore through them. Four times Carmen shot Rooty-Toot, her long barreled .44, blazing death in all directions. She stood there for a moment, a Latin Brunhild in an Anglo-Saxon Götterdämmerung, and in that moment, she was magnificent. Then, engulfed and overwhelmed by the thousand blows of the police ambuscade of dire import, she crumpled to the sidewalk.

For endless seconds the firing went on, causing the bodies of Carmen and her gang to jump and dance on the pockmarked and blood-streaked pavement. After a few more minutes, the cops desisted from their firing, and now they just stood there, some of them panting slightly, watching, waiting.

Carmen lay in the dirty street, bullet-ridden, stitched to a fair-thee-well, a goner. She gasped for breath, for life, and as her soul hovered between earth and heaven, her vagrant eye caught sight of the marquee of a nearby movie theater. There in big letters were the words, "Tonight

Only! Robert Sheckley and Gail Dana Star in *They Made Us Stars!*"

Carmen smiled bitterly. She had always wanted fame and stardom. Life, or fate, or chance, or whatever it was, had decreed otherwise. She knew she would have been good. She and her friends, Caesar, Johnny Garfield, Allan Ladd, would have been just as good as those other people, the famous ones, the international stars like Sheckley and Dana. It was a trick of fate that had made her an unknown bank robber instead of a famous star named Carmen Miranda. No doubt it was related to that same stupid trick of fate that puts other people's names up in lights instead of one's own.

Well, Carmen was in the lights now. Floodlights from official cars, flashlights from reporters, who had gathered like vultures around the corpse of a newsworthy kill.

What was there left to say? Only this. Carmen mustered a smile. And she sang, "Aye yi yi yi yi I don't like this very much!"

And then she died.

Allen Steele, author of such excellent novels as *Orbital Decay* and *Labyrinth of Night,* took the notion of alternate outlaws to mean something quite different: a story of historical outlaws in an alternate setting. . . .

Riders in the Sky
by Allen Steele

St. Louis, Missouri: August 30, 1874.

The Missouri Pacific airship *Ulysses S. Grant* hovers beside the tall, wrought-iron mooring tower, its gray-canvas envelope rippling slightly in the morning breeze wafting off the Mississippi River. A packet steamer cruising downstream toots its horn twice as it passes the aerodrome: a small crowd, dressed in meeting clothes for Sunday services at the nearby Episcopal church, gathers around the outer edge of the dusty field to watch the weekly launch of the skyship.

At the bottom of the lowered gangway beneath the gondola, a uniformed conductor, Emmett Riley, snaps the tickets of the last few passengers to board the craft. Wealthy cattlemen, bankers, grain speculators—they're the only ones who can afford the extravagance of a thirty-dollar ticket to Kansas City. Some of them seem to think they're boarding a Pullman coach; a burly gentleman with muttonchop sideburns is puffing on a fat cigar as he extends his ticket to the conductor. Without a word, Riley snatches the stogie from the other man's mouth, drops it to the ground and stamps it out under his shoe.

"Positively no smoking allowed, sir," Riley says. "In fact, I must relieve you of your matches before you can board."

The businessman protests, loudly proclaiming his God-given right to smoke wherever he God-damned well pleases, but the conductor remains adamant. For the safety of the airship and its passengers, no flammable substances are allowed aboard the *Ulysses S. Grant.* "God-damned Irish," the banker mutters under his breath, but in the end, he surrenders his tin matchbox to Riley before he stalks up the gangway steps to the passenger cabin just aft of the pilothouse.

The conductor shakes his head as he holds out his hand to the last two men in line. "Some people have no common sense whatsoever," he murmurs.

"I quite agree," says one of the men. He's tall and slender, with a dark, bushy beard, wearing boots, a bowler hat, and a long linen duster; Riley notes that his eyelids are constantly batting, as if suffering from a nervous tic. He puts down his cloth carpetbag as he digs his ticket out of the pocket of his greatcoat. "One shouldn't be flying if one can't respect simple rules. Isn't that right, Jonathan?"

The other man—older and more heavyset than his traveling companion, with lighter hair and a trim mustache— grunts distractedly. A horse-drawn buckboard is parked beneath the baggage compartment in the rear of the gondola; he's intently watching the ground crew as it hoists a padlocked strongbox from the buckboard through the open hatch.

The first man coughs. "Jonathan . . . your ticket?"

The second man turns around quickly. "Uh, yeah . . . sure, Tom." He pulls a ticket from the pocket of his duster; his hand is trembling slightly as he gives it to the conductor.

The conductor smiles but says nothing as he snaps the ticket. Aeronautics still makes many people nervous; as tough as this character looks, his knees are visibly shaking. He watches the two young men—brothers from the looks of them, probably stockmen—as they climb the gangway to the passenger compartment. Riley folds the ticket stubs into his coat pocket and climbs up the stairs, where he cranks up the gangway and shuts the hatch.

A few minutes later, the pilot extends his left arm out his window. "Contact!" he yells as he drops his hand.

Two men standing on either side of the airship grasp the long blades of the port and starboard propellers and yank them down. The twin 200-horsepower internal-combustion engines, manufactured in France by the Giffard Sky Ship Company and brought to America aboard steamships, roar to life.

Horses whinny in terror and dance backward as an artificial wind, malodorous with gasoline fumes, rips across the dusty aerodrome, tearing caps off the heads of the other ground men holding the taut mooring lines. On another hand signal from the pilot, the mooring-tower cable is detached; the men on the ground simultaneously drop their lines and race away from the airship.

For a moment, the dirigible hovers above the aerodrome, severed from all contact with the earth, yet still close enough for its lower rudder to lightly touch the ground. Then the engines are throttled up, and the nearby crowd, their eyes stinging from the windswept dust thrown in their faces, gapes in awe as the leviathan slowly rises into the sky.

The *Ulysses S. Grant* ascends to its normal cruising altitude of one thousand feet; then the pilot twists the rudder wheel as the copilot steps on the elevator pedals. The mighty airship turns its blunt prow westward and commences its journey across the Missouri plains to Kansas City.

Back in the cabin, most of the fifteen passengers are staring out the beveled windows, watching as church steeples and the rooftops of five-story buildings recede beneath them. The banker who had argued with the conductor about his cigar has doubled over in his seat in the front of the cabin and is getting violently ill. The conductor snatches up a pail and a wet washrag before he rushes down the aisle to tend to him.

As Riley passes the two men who came aboard last, he notices that although the one called Jonathan has his eyes tightly shut and is holding fast to his armrests, his brother Tom has pulled a pocket watch from his vest and is studying it.

Riley shakes his head as he pushes the pail beneath the sick passenger. There's always some fool who complains if he's not in Kansas City in eight hours, just as the company broadsheets have promised. Not so long ago, he would have been lucky if he had been on the other side of the state in eight days, let alone eight hours. . . .

And only then if his train or stagecoach hadn't been intercepted by highwaymen.

Five hours later, the *Grant* is close to the town of Lexington, following the Missouri River toward Kansas City. It's shortly after one o'clock; the conductor has just cleaned up after a mid-flight lunch of sandwiches and bottled lemonade and has settled down in his seat in the rear of the cabin. Most of the passengers have become bored with watching the passing scenery; despite the omniscient engine roar, some have fallen asleep. The air inside the cabin has become hot and uncomfortable—the passengers have closed their windows against the constant wind and noise—but Riley pays it little mind. In another three hours, the airship will land in Kansas City. Maybe he can catch a few winks before landing. . . .

Just then one of the passengers—Tom, the one who has been carefully studying his watch throughout the journey—suddenly rises from his seat. He picks up his valise with his left hand, grasps the brass ceiling rail with his right hand, and begins to walk toward the back of the cabin. At first the conductor thinks he's heading for the lavatory—a small anteroom next to the galley where the chamber pot is located—but instead, he walks past the door.

A few moments later, his companion also stands up. A little less easily than his brother, Jonathan starts to walk the opposite way down the aisle, in the direction of the pilothouse.

Only a couple of the other passengers, drowsy with the

heat and noise, take note of their actions, but Riley is astonished. After all, there are placards posted throughout the cabin. *Please! For Your Safety, You Must Remain in Your Seat Unless Escorted by the Conductor!* And, as this man himself observed, those are the rules.

As Tom approaches the rear of the cabin, Riley stands up and steps into the aisle, blocking him before he can go any farther. "Excuse me, sir," he says politely, "but you and your kin cannot tour the ship just now. If you'll please . . ."

His voice trails off. For the first time, he sees the man's eyes: blue and cold, not unlike the surface of the Atlantic as he saw it from the deck of the sailship that brought him over from his native Ireland twenty-two years ago, and just as menacing. . . .

In that instant, the passenger's right hand leaves the ceiling rail. It slips beneath the hem of his long coat . . . and then, in a single swift motion, the hand reappears, and clasped within it is a Colt navy revolver.

Riley freezes as he stares down the bore of its seven-inch barrel. Although the click of the hammer is subdued beneath the thrum of the engines, the conductor hears it as clearly as if it was the crack of doom.

"Take me to the baggage compartment," the gunman says softly. "Do it now, y'hear?"

Riley slowly looks up at him. All at once everything falls together in his mind. "Oh, sweet Jesus," he whispers. "You're him . . ."

The man scowls at the conductor. "Don't use His name in vain. Not on the Sabbath."

Then the slightest hint of a smile creases the bearded face. "But if you want," he adds, "you can call me Jesse."

The hijacking of the *Ulysses S. Grant* on August 30, 1874, by Jesse and Frank James marked the beginning of a short, yet fascinating, part in the history of the American West. The exploits of the outlaws who dared rob airships in flight has been romanticized countless times through novels, TV shows, and movies, albeit wildly inaccurate for the most part.

If one were to believe popular fiction, airship robberies were a constant danger; in fact, only three successful hijackings were committed between 1874 and 1882, although there were a dozen or so unsuccessful attempts. No airship ever crashed or exploded during a holdup, nor were any beautiful women ever abducted at gunpoint by masked bandits—in fact, women and children were prohibited from riding in airships until 1897.

Nonetheless, both history and fiction agree on one point: it was Frank and Jesse James, along with other members of their gang, who invented airship robbery, and it was the murder of Jesse James that brought the era to a close.

In retrospect, it is only logical that the invention of dirigibles would have naturally led to airship hijackings. New technologies tend to breed criminal activity as a side effect, just as the recent proliferation of computers has led to computer crime, whether it be by organizations specializing in wire fraud or by teenage hackers hacking into sensitive databases. In this case, it was the invention of the dirigible in France by Henri Giffard in the 1860s.

Giffard took unsteerable hot-air balloons, developed in the late 1700s by the Montgolfier brothers, and redesigned them as semirigid envelopes pumped full of hydrogen. Giffard's early steam engines were too heavy to allow more than one person as a passenger, but with the assistance of the Brazilian inventor, Alberto Santos-Dumont, Giffard married the lighter and more efficient internal-combustion engine to their fuselages, and thus the modern airship was born.

Giffard's dirigibles were seen only as a novelty in France, but they were noted with great interest by the American ambassador, who saw their military potential. He alerted the United States War Department, and within a few months, scientists and generals from America traveled to Paris to watch one of Giffard's "steerable balloons" fly circles above the Champs de Elysses and drop simulated bombs into the Seine. The Americans were suitably impressed; the Civil War had just begun, and the War Department was desperate for a tactical edge over the Confederate States. On advice of their envoys, it hastily contracted Giffard to immediately construct two "sky ships" for the Union Army.

Giffard's dirigibles, the *Boston* and the *Potomac*, were not delivered until the war was close to its end, but they performed well in many ways: reconnaissance missions above enemy lines, delivering supplies to troops in hard-to-reach places, taking key officers from one combat zone to another in less time and with greater security than even unoccupied rail lines could manage. Although the *Boston* exploded in midair during Second Bull Run after being hit by Confederate mortars, the *Potomac* earned an indelible place in history as the aircraft that escorted Abraham Lincoln to Gettysburg; during the flight from Washington to the battlefield, Lincoln found the peace of mind to compose his most famous speech on the back of an envelope.

After the war, popular speculation ran wild about the possible uses of skyships, ranging from airborne buffalo hunts in the Dakotas to improbable dime novels about Frank Reade's exploits on the moon. However, the only private companies that could muster the capital necessary to develop dirigibles as passenger aircraft were the railroads. They needed a vehicle that could safely transport people and small cargo across the most dangerous territories in the West—particularly the state of Missouri.

Labeled by the *Chicago Times* as "The Outlaw's Paradise," the western parts of the state had become overrun by bandits. Like the James and Younger brothers, who were veterans of Quantrill's Raiders, many of them were former Confederate guerrillas who had continued their outlaw lives after the war, often with the aid of Confederate sympathizers among the local citizens. Stage holdups had become almost commonplace, and desperadoes had recently learned how to derail iron horses. Although no one in the rail companies seriously considered replacing locomotives with dirigibles, they realized that dirigibles offered a viable alternative for the gold shipments that frequently needed to be sent to the Western settlements ... and, likewise, there was money to be made from selling seats to well-to-do travelers who wanted "scenic" (that is, safe) passage across the badlands.

In 1872, the Giffard Air Ship Company delivered the first commercial skyship to the Missouri Pacific Railroad: the *Ulysses S. Grant*, two hundred and eighty feet long, complete with a railcar-like passenger cabin and a small baggage compartment. It was scheduled to provide weekly service between St. Louis and Kansas City, weather permitting. Broadside advertisements proclaimed it to be "The Epitome of Grandeur and Comfort, Unstoppable by Neither the Forces of Man Nor Nature."

As always, one man's hubris is another man's insult, and the man who was insulted was none other than Missouri's most infamous outlaw, Jesse James.

History doesn't record which member of the James-Younger gang came up with the idea of hijacking the *Ulysses S. Grant*. Most of the dime novels of the time said that it was Jesse's brainstorm; in later years, Cole Younger would assert that he was the one who had thought up the scheme. Most historians tend to discount both notions; Younger made many such unverifiable claims to Jesse's fame, and the authors of the *Wide-Awake Library* were the least trustworthy of sources. Conventional wisdom has it that Frank James was the smarter one of the brothers, and logically would have been the one who devised the scheme, despite eyewitness accounts of Frank's obvious nervousness during the first hijacking.

As for Frank James himself, he remained laconic on the subject, except to once supply a motive during an interview with a *Kansas City Times* reporter near the end of his life. "If they thought they could fly a skyship named after that sonofabitch Grant over Missouri," he said, "they had another think comin'."

* * *

While Frank went into the pilothouse, where he pointed his revolver at the two pilots and demanded that they immediately land the airship, Jesse forced Emmett Riley to lead him into the cargo compartment. There the hapless conductor was tied up with ropes from Frank's bag.

When that was done, Jesse cranked open the cargo hatch. He then pulled out of his valise a long flag made of red- and blue-dyed bedsheets, weighted at one end by a small bag of buckshot. As the airship began to descend, Jesse dropped the flag through the hatch. Then he took a seat on the strongbox and patiently waited for the airship to land.

The plan was cunning both in its simplicity and its exquisite timing. The remaining members of the gang—Jim, Bob, and Cole Younger, along with Bill Stiles, Sam Wells, and Clell Miller—had been waiting on the outskirts of Lexington, which the gang already knew from newspaper stories would be one of the towns the *Grant* would fly over. Since, through the same highly detailed accounts, Jesse knew just how fast the dirigible would travel at cruising speed, he was able to accurately time the journey, using his pocket watch to estimate the air speed and sighting well-known local landmarks to double-check his bearings. The flag was dropped to alert gang members on the ground that he and Frank had taken control of the airship; all they had to do was ride to where the *Grant* finally touched down.

As it turned out, the bandits were already waiting for the *Grant* when it landed in a cow pasture on the banks of the Missouri, just across the river from Lexington. So deftly was the hijacking handled that the dozing passengers were unaware that a holdup was taking place, and even when the *Grant*'s gondola was skirting the treetops, many assumed that the airship, like the locomotives they were more accustomed to riding, was simply stopping to "take on more coal," as one passenger later told a reporter from the *St. Louis Post*.

Meanwhile, a group of Lexington citizens, having spotted the airship's unexpected descent, rode on horseback or in carriages to a bluff across the river from the landing site. There they watched in bafflement as a small group of horsemen grabbed the airship's dangling moorlines, lashed them to trees, then drew their guns and climbed up the lowered gangway into the gondola.

By all reliable accounts, the first airship robbery was peaceful. While Frank held the pilots at bay and Jesse relieved the baggage compartment of its strongbox, the three Younger brothers made their way through the cabin, taking jewelry, watches and cash from the startled passengers at gunpoint. The only passenger spared from robbery was one Hiram Taylor, a cattleman whose Virginia accent betrayed him as a Southerner. Upon discovering that he was a Confederate veteran from Lee's army, Bob Younger handed back the silver watch he had just taken.

In less than fifteen minutes after landing, the gang rode off into the forest, having done its job of robbing the airship of two thousand dollars in gold and currency, plus whatever had been taken from the passengers. They left behind sixteen cowed men, an undamaged dirigible, and a new legend in the annals of history.

As newspaper headlines screamed the story from New York to San Francisco, it wasn't only the Missouri Pacific Railroad that was worried. Three other dirigibles had already been purchased and put into service by other railroad companies, and more had been contracted for, all on the assumption that they were untouchable by highwaymen. Now that claim had been put to the test and had failed.

One of the reasons why the James-Younger gang had gained so much notoriety was that the public had little sympathy for the railroads in the first place. The railroads were perceived as being run by cynical, greedy carpetbag-

228   Allen Steele

gers from the East, getting rich at the expense of hardworking Westerners; the fact that the James-Younger gang
had killed many men during their railroad holdups was
conveniently overlooked by the reporters who had lauded
Jesse as the "Robin Hood of the Plains."

The additional fact that many of these railroad and
bank robberies had not been performed by the James
boys, but instead by anonymous bandits claiming to
be them, didn't prevent the railroad men from getting
alarmed. Although the Missouri legislature had appropri-
ated ten thousand dollars for the hiring of the Pinkerton
National Detective Agency solely for the purpose of appre-
hending the James gang, the Pinkertons had already been
foiled many times in their attempts to apprehend the
James and Younger boys. Eyewitness descriptions of Frank
and Jesse James were confused to the point that no reliable drawing of their faces had ever been made, thus allowing the outlaws to walk the streets of Kansas City and
St. Louis with impunity.

Indeed, on more than one occasion, either Frank or
Jesse had shared barroom tables with Pinkerton operatives
who were searching for them, and undercover agents who
dared to ride into Jesse James' native Clay County to ferret
out the gang were often found shot dead by the roadside.
Likewise, no one in the rural Missouri countryside was either disloyal or brave enough to disclose the locations of
their hideouts, despite the two-thousand-dollar bounty
Governor Silas Woodson had placed on their heads.

Within a month of the *Grant* hijacking, a second dirigible was robbed in flight: the *Andrew Jackson*, operated by
the Louisville and Nashville Railroad, was taken over by
three masked bandits and forced to land just outside of
Bowling Green, Kentucky. Although the modus was virtu-
ally identical to the *Grant* holdup, there was little reason
to believe that the James-Younger gang was responsible for
this second assault. However, the *Nashville Banner* charged
Jesse James with the *Andrew Jackson* hijacking, and that

unproven allegation was faithfully reprinted in newspapers across the country.

Whether or not it was the James-Younger gang or copycats, the railroads took quick measures to prevent a recurrence of the hijackings. Deadbolts were installed on the inside of the pilothouse door, allowing the pilots to lock themselves in their compartment before takeoff. Latchkey locks were installed on the cargo compartment hatches, with the key entrusted to the copilot.

The Missouri Pacific, fearing a repeat of the August 30 hijacking, furthermore hired armed guards to ride in the baggage compartments of the *Ulysses S. Grant* and, several months later, its new airship, the *Prairie Viking*. It also issued two-shot derringers to its conductors. However, the guns were little more than a bluff; on the urgent advice of the Giffard Air Ship Company, neither the guards' rifle nor the derringers were allowed to be kept loaded while in flight. The company was rightfully concerned that a stray bullet within the cabin could pierce the skin of the hydrogen-filled gasbags in the dirigible's envelope and thus cause an explosion. The railroad counted on that bit of scientific minutiae being lost on the public when it allowed newspaper photographers to shoot pictures of rifle-toting guards posed on the gangway of the *Prairie Viking*; the point was to reassure passengers and to make robbers think twice about hijacking any more airships.

The ruse worked for a while. During the rest of 1874 and early 1875, there were no more successful skyship robberies. In July, 1875, two men attempted to rob a Southern Pacific dirigible en route from Austin to San Antonio. They used an ax to break through the hatch of the baggage compartment, only to be confronted by the rifles of two Texas Rangers riding shotgun in the aft hold. The would-be robbers were apprehended without a shot being fired, but that wasn't all; in the fashion of true Texan justice, the passengers mobbed the bandits as soon as the dirigible safely landed in San Antonio and hauled them to a nearby oak tree, where they were lynched within minutes. The railroad companies made certain that news of the failed hijacking and the grisly fate of the perpetrators was spread wide and far.

For another twelve months, there were no more attempts on dirigibles. Then, on July 7, 1876, the James-Younger gang struck again. And this time they got away with one of the most daring robberies in American History.

On that morning, the *Prairie Viking* lifted off from the Kansas City aerodrome and turned southeast; in its locked baggage compartment were two express safes containing fifteen thousand dollars in gold and currency. As usual, there was an armed guard in the baggage compartment, and the door to the pilots' gondola was locked from within.

It was supposed to be a routine flight to Memphis, Tennessee, yet less than an hour after the skyship departed from Kansas City, three men stood up from their seats, pulled revolvers out of their coat pockets, and calmly informed the conductor and passengers that they were being hijacked.

The conductor, John Blackman, surrendered his derringer on demand, but then told the bandits that the baggage compartment was locked and the only available key was in the pocket of the copilot, who was locked inside the gondola. "Sorry, boys," he said, "but you might as well put away your pistols and sit down. This ship won't land until we reach Memphis."

It was then, according to witnesses, that one of the robbers—later identified as Jim Younger—cocked his revolver and pointed it straight at the ceiling. "I'm not asking you to land, mister," he said, "but if that's the way you want it . . . then we'll land."

Blackman knew exactly what the bandit meant. A single gunshot through the ceiling would cause a hydrogen explosion in the gasbag directly above the cabin, and the *Viking* would go down in a fiery crash. Perhaps it was a suicidal bluff, but Blackman couldn't afford to risk the lives of his passengers by calling it.

While one of the passengers, a Presbyterian minister, began to lead the others in prayer for their lives, the conductor was marched to the aft end of the cabin, where he knocked six times on the hatch, the standard "all clear" signal for the guard within. The guard, Joseph Potts, apparently believed that a lunch pail was going to be passed to him; he unlocked the hatch and pushed it open, but barely had time to raise his unloaded Winchester before Cole Younger thrust a bowie knife into his chest.

Blackman thought that the bandits' next move would be an attempt to make the pilots land the airship, yet none of the desperadoes made a move toward the pilothouse. While Jim Younger held the conductor and the hymn-singing passengers at bay, Cole Younger and a new member of the gang, Hobbs Kerry, hauled the overstuffed carpetbags they had carried aboard the *Viking* back to the baggage compartment. Again, a flag was dropped out of the open aft hatch; a few moments later, Hobbs Kerry and Cole Younger shoved the two safes through the hatch, where they plummeted to the rolling Cooper County countryside a thousand feet below.

What happened next astonished everyone aboard. While the three men took turns keeping the passengers at gunpoint, each bandit pulled large bundles of sewn-together bedsheets out of the bags. Long ropes had been knotted around the corners of the sheets; each of the trio carefully uncoiled the ropes, wrapped them under their chests and around their shoulders, then took the bundles in their arms.

Then, to the horror-stricken cries of Blackman and the passengers, each bandit stepped through the cargo hatch and out into empty space. "See you 'round, squareheads!" Cole Younger was heard to yell before he leaped into oblivion.

Blackman rushed to a window, believing that he would see the three men plummeting to their death. Instead, he saw three giant "handkerchiefs" gently wafting downward on the warm summer breeze. Suspended beneath each one was a man, holding onto the ropes, screaming rebel yells that could be heard above the thrum of the engines.

The pious Presbyterian minister muttered a blasphemy as he watched this ungodly sight. Meanwhile, the two men in the pilothouse were wondering what on earth was going on back in the cabin. Unwilling to disobey company rules, though, they refused to unlock the pilothouse door until they arrived in Memphis some seven hours later; by doing so, they unwittingly allowed the James-Younger gang to make the best of a clean getaway.

Yet it wasn't a perfect crime. Although Jim and Cole Younger landed safely outside Otterville, where they were picked up by the rest of the gang—who, by then, had already recovered the two safes and hidden them in the woods—Hobbs Kerry was less fortunate. He got an arm tangled in his ropes, which caused his rudimentary parachute to veer far away from the others. To make matters worse, he broke his left leg upon touchdown. Then, just to prove that bad luck runs in threes, he was discovered hobbling through the bean field of the shotgun-toting farmer who had spied his descent and wasn't about to accept his feeble excuses.

Kerry was hauled in the back of a buckboard to Sedalia, where he was thrown in jail. Suffering considerable pain from his broken leg and scared of being hanged, Hobbs Kerry broke down. He told the entire story to the sheriff and, later, a reporter from the *Kansas City Times*.

It turned out that Frank James had masterminded the plan. Gaining inspiration from the flight of dandelion seeds, he had persuaded his and Jesse's mother, Zerelda Samuel, to sew together a "sky sock" of old sheets. After Frank himself successfully tested the principle by jumping off a tall Missouri River bluff, he convinced the other members of the gang that they could pull off the robbery.

It had taken nearly a year for the gang to perfect the plan, during which time Jim and Cole Younger had proven themselves to be the gang's best jumpers. Although he was willing to leap out of an airship with his brothers, Bob Younger's acrophobia ultimately got the better of him; at the last minute, Jesse decided that Bob would join him as part of the group that would wait outside Otterville for the signal flag. Kerry himself volunteered to substitute for Bob, figuring that he would prove himself to the rest of the gang by taking on the most hazardous part of the mission.

Hobbs Kerry's confession established that the James-Younger gang was responsible for the robbery of the *Prairie Viking*. Once again, railroad officials seethed while the telegraph wires hummed with the news of the latest exploits of Jesse James and his gang.

Next time, they quietly swore amongst themselves, we'll get the bastards. No matter what it takes, we will stop them.

And so they did.

On September 7, 1876—exactly two months after the holdup of the *Prairie Viking*—the Great Northern airship *Jupiter* lifted off from the aerodrome in Des Moines and turned due north toward Minnesota. Although the airship served Minneapolis and St. Paul, it was scheduled to land in the small town of Northfield, about thirty miles south of the twin cities, where passengers heading to the cities would board a short-line train to their final destination.

There were two reasons for this oddity. First, the Minneapolis City Council had voted against leasing land to the railroad for the building of an aerodrome. The *Jupiter* itself lived up to its name. The largest skyship of its time, it was four hundred feet long, propelled by two 350-horsepower engines, with a passenger seating for up to fifty people. Minneapolis citizens disliked the idea of such a behemoth buzzing over their city, and thus had voted down a proposal to build an aerodrome within their county. In this they had been aided by the local steamboat companies, which had foreseen competition from an aerodrome so close to their Mississippi River ports.

Northfield businessmen took advantage of the injunction. Stating that an aerodrome would help boost business in their community, they had prevailed upon the townspeople to let the Great Northern Railroad build its dirigible field near the train station. The most prominent beneficiary of the aerodrome was the First National Bank of Northfield, which believed that regular skyship service would help ensure the safe arrival and departure of express safes. As a result, the *Jupiter* always carried a large safe in its baggage compartment, often containing as much as two hundred thousand dollars, from both the Northfield bank and those in Minneapolis and St. Paul.

It was a target too tempting for the James-Younger gang to pass up. Emboldened by the success of the *Prairie Viking* holdup, they made plans to rob the *Jupiter* in just the same way. Unfortunately for them, the Pinkerton Detective Agency had already second-guessed them.

The denouement is well-recorded in history, popularized to this day by scores of novels and movies. Four members of the gang—Clell Miller, Charlie Pitts, and Jim and Cole Younger—boarded the skyship in Des Moines, carrying with them the carpetbags containing their "parachutes." Frank and Jesse James, along with Bob Younger and Minnesota native Bill Chadwell, had already journeyed north to the drop zone in the forest just south of Northfield, where they would retrieve the safes and rendezvous with the other gang members once they parachuted to safety.

What no one in the gang realized was that for the past six weeks, half of the passenger seats in the *Jupiter* had been occupied by Pinkerton agents posing as traveling businessmen, their expenses paid by a conglomerate of railroad companies that wanted to see the robberies halted. Already, twenty-five Pinkertons had taken the round-trip flight six times between Des Moines and

Northfield, pretending to read books and newspapers while they suspiciously eyed every person in the cabin.

"It was a long shot," Allan Pinkerton said later, "but it certainly paid off in the end." On that day in early autumn, the patience of his operatives was rewarded.

Shortly before the *Jupiter* began to make its descent for approach and landing in Northfield, Miller, Stiles, and the two Youngers stood up as one. As Cole Younger began to march down the long aisle toward the baggage compartment, the other three men began to spread out through the cabin.

According to eyewitness accounts, Miller and Stiles made the fatal error that tipped off the Pinkertons; before Cole gave the prearranged hand signal, they reached into their jackets and began to pull out their guns. Yet the pistols had barely cleared their pockets before two detectives leaped to their feet behind each man, pulled out their derringers, and shot both men in the back from a range of less than five feet.

As Jim and Cole Younger reacted to the gunshots, they went for their own guns . . . only to find themselves surrounded by nearly a score of Colt revolvers, all aimed directly at them.

Cole already had his hand on his pistol. According to popular legend, he whipped it out of his pocket and pointed it to the ceiling. "How many of you are ready to go to Hell?" he asked.

The nearest Pinkerton stared at him down the barrel of his Colt. "We all are, sir," he said evenly, "but you'll get there first."

Cole Younger stared back at him for a minute, then carefully uncocked his gun and dropped it on the seat beside him. Jim Younger simply sighed and raised his hands to the ceiling.

A thousand feet below, Frank and Jesse James realized something had gone wrong in the plan when the *Jupiter* cruised overhead without a flag being dropped or a safe falling out of the hatch. They had only begun to climb into the saddle, though, when three men appeared in the woods and opened fire upon them; a Northfield sheriff's posse, patrolling the forest at the behest of the Pinkertons, had spotted the smoke from their cookfire and had homed in on them. During the ambush, Bill Chadwell was killed by a bullet through the chest, while Bob Younger was severely wounded and left behind to be arrested.

When the *Jupiter* landed in Northfield, Jim and Cole Younger were put under arrest. Although they expected to be hanged, they were put on trial with their brother Bob and sentenced to life in prison. Photos of the bodies of the other gang members became the subject of popular postcards.

Out of the entire gang, only Frank and Jesse James escaped. It would be six long years before either of them would be seen again.

In the absence of the James brothers, the world moved on around them as if they had never left.

As usual, a number of bank and train robberies were committed in their name, although it's doubtful that either one of the brothers was responsible. Their notoriety superseded them so that every cow-town bank stick-up or train derailment by masked men was ascribed to Frank and Jesse James. The reward for their capture, dead or alive, was raised to five thousand dollars, while newspapers made lurid claims to Jesse being spotted during robberies in places as distant as Mexico, Virginia, and South Carolina.

In the meantime, other gangs attempted to emulate the James boys, but none of them mastered the finer nuances of skyjacking. More than once, bandits leaped from airships with homemade parachutes, only to have their arms and legs tangled in the ropes or have the chutes themselves rip open; some of these robbers were buried where they were found. Two more were apprehended before they boarded the craft. On one occasion, a gunman was overcome by the passengers and almost beaten to death until the conductor pried them off the poor man.

Each time, newspapers claimed that Jesse James had been arrested or killed, only to have the truth revealed by positive identification of either the jailed prisoners or the bodies in the local morgue. It wasn't until April 3, 1882, that Jesse James turned up again. This time he couldn't ride or parachute to safety; he was found dead on the floor of the bedroom of his house in St. Joseph, Missouri.

As it turned out, he had been living a quiet existence as Thomas Howard, a wheat speculator who had moved from Nashville, Tennessee, only six months earlier. His killer was a young man named Bob Ford.

According to Ford, Jesse had recently decided to return to airship robbery, and had recruited Bob and his brother Charlie to be members of his new gang. Jesse didn't know that the Ford brothers had already struck a deal with Missouri's new governor, Thomas Crittenden; for the reward of five thousand dollars, Bob Ford had agreed to assassinate Jesse James.

Bob and Charlie Ford had been houseguests of Mr. Howard for the past several days, waiting for their chance to strike. Only that morning, over the breakfast table, Jesse had hinted at his next planned heist, the hijacking of the Union Pacific airship *Abraham Lincoln* out of Omaha, Nebraska. When he walked into the adjacent bedroom to discuss the plan in more detail, Bob and Charlie had followed. When Jesse stood up on a chair to straighten a picture frame, Bob had shot him through the back of his head.

Frank James didn't remain at large for very much longer. Six months later, on November 5, he formally surrendered himself to Governor Crittenden, during a prearranged press conference in the governor's office. As it turned out, Frank James had also been hiding out in Nashville, under the pseudonym of B. J. Woodson. Although he was subsequently brought to trial in Independence, Missouri, for the hijacking of the *Prairie Viking*,

the jury—comprised mainly of Confederate sympathizers—acquitted him of all charges.

Frank James lived comfortably for the rest of his life by
merchandising his past. He lectured before packed houses,
published his memoirs, and fired the starting gun at many
airship races. He died at age seventy on the set of a Hollywood silent movie, *The Great Airship Robbery*, for which
he had been hired as a technical advisor.

By then, the age of the skyship was all but over. Following the *Liberty* disaster of 1908, when a careless match
struck by a pipe-smoking passenger caused the explosion
of an airship over Lakehurst, New Jersey, Congress passed
laws that prohibited the use of inflammable hydrogen in
dirigibles. Because of this, the rail companies were forced
to resort to helium as the lifting property; this in turn
caused fares to rise, since the use of helium meant that
fewer pounds could be lifted. In the long run, it spelled
the end of the skyship business; before 1915, airplanes replaced dirigibles as the principal means of air travel. The
railroads retired from the industry, and airship robberies
became a cliché left over from the last generation.

The Jesse James house still stands today in St. Joseph,
maintained as a state historical landmark. The rooms are
carefully preserved just as he left them, including the bedroom where he was shot from behind by Bob Ford. The
chair on which he stood lies in place on the wooden floor,
and on the wall above it is the askew picture Mr. Howard
was straightening at the moment of his death.

It is a framed lithograph of the skyship *Prairie Viking*.

Jack Nimersheim was making a comfortable living as the author of more than twenty books on computer science, along with four monthly columns in major computer magazines, when he decided that it was finally time to try his hand at his first love, science fiction. That was two years and sixteen very successful stories ago, and it looks like Jack, a 1994 Campbell nominee, will be writing well-received science fiction for years to come.

This striking little tale is told by perhaps the most famous unidentified man of the past half-century.

#2, With a Bullet
by Jack Nimersheim

Lone gunman, my ass! Jack was bigger than life. No one person working alone could have brought him down, I don't care what the official reports say.

It took a posse of Texas Rangers to close the book on Bonnie and Clyde. A virtual battalion of Federal agents lurked outside a Chicago movie theater, waiting to ventilate Dillinger. Ness needed the resources of the entire Treasury Department to vanquish Capone. Even then, he only managed to ship him up the river for eleven years—on a wimpy tax-evasion charge, for Christ sake.

All of them were bush-league compared to Jack Kennedy.

And now the government expects people to believe that one dedicated agent ended Kennedy's crime spree. Bullshit!

There may be a more diplomatic way to express my skepticism, but why compose a civilized sentence when a single eloquent word will do?

Look, I'm not one to speak ill of the dead, but Jack

Kennedy was a crook. The media may have embellished his exploits, as the media feel obligated to do, but underneath it all, he still made his living breaking the law. Plain and simple.

I'll admit, most of his ill-gotten gains ended up in the hands of people who truly needed it. That's how he earned his *nom de crime*, "The Twentieth-Century Robin Hood." (Why must we Americans always look to England for romantic images? Surely our own considerable history can provide comparable inspiration.) According to the latest estimates, however, the total take from his criminal operations exceeded five billion dollars. If he kept a mere one tenth of this for himself, his personal fortune easily surpassed that of the "affluent elite" he constantly asserted were his only prey. And let's not forget, a lot of people died—upward of two hundred, by some accounts: cops, criminals and civilian casualties—during his brief but bloody career.

From the very beginning, Kennedy captured the imagination of the American public. No one can deny this. His boyish charm, rugged good looks and privileged upbringing would have guaranteed celebrity for almost anyone, in almost any endeavor. The irony of these attributes defining a thief and a thug made him irresistible to the press. And make no mistake about it, Jack knew how to manipulate the press. Especially television.

Who can forget his admonishment to "the common folk of America," as he called them, during that amazing *Person to Person* interview Edward R. Murrow arranged to conduct in a secret location, while Jack still sat atop of the FBI's most-wanted list? Along with millions of others, I watched in wonder as he looked directly into the camera and announced, "Ask not what I have done to this country, but ask what this country has done to you."

Even the normally unflappable Murrow could not think of a suitable rejoinder for this little gem.

When Jack was good, he was very good; I'll grant him

that. It was when Jack was bad that people, including those "common folk of America" he so desperately wanted to impress, had to keep one hand on their wallet and one eye cast suspiciously over their shoulder.

The point is, I don't want you to misinterpret my opening observation. I have no great respect for Jack Kennedy. As I stated earlier, he was a criminal. Nevertheless, he *was* a criminal genius. The very idea that he could be taken out by a single individual is ludicrous.

And yet, this is precisely what the government would have you believe. The critical question then becomes, Why?

I have a theory about that. Neutralizing this larger-than-life villain required the creation of a hero who was larger still. Allow me to explain.

Despite the crimes he committed, the life he lived, people were fascinated with the "Boston Bandit," another one of Jack's popular nicknames. More than a few enterprising entrepreneurs fattened their bank accounts hawking Kennedy memorabilia. Adults flocked to boutiques and bargain-basement sales to purchase "Kennedy, the King of Krime!" or "Just Do It, Jack!" T-shirts. Teenagers bought more than ten million copies of "Jumpin' Jack Cash," a hastily produced parody of the popular Rolling Stones' song with the lyrics appropriately modified to glorify a more menacing milieu. One sicko even produced a line of Jack Kennedy trading cards. Each one graphically depicted a different murder attributed to Kennedy. Kids snapped them up by the carton, which didn't even include a block of stale bubble gum. Evil, it appears, is somehow less abhorrent when it wears a seductive face, displays a sophisticated demeanor.

You see Washington's conundrum, don't you? America, a country starved for idols and icons, had discovered a new hero. There was only one catch. He was a total miscreant. Welcome to the era of telegenic malevolence.

Even more ominous than the psychological impact of

Kennedy's popularity were the physical perils it posed. A thin line divides adulation from emulation. The potential threat of so-called "copy-cat crimes" could not be ignored. Already, some kid in Arkansas had committed a series of robberies that bore a striking resemblance to some of Jack's more celebrated escapades. Additional incidents of a similar nature were bound to follow, unless the authorities discovered some practical way to remove the patina from Kennedy's charisma.

Enter, the lone gunman.

Talk about icons! This one is deeply ingrained in the American psyche, even if the image is often more metaphor than fact.

Wyatt Earp single-handedly cleans up Dodge City. Teddy Roosevelt takes on the corporate giants of his day and bullies them into submission. Jackie Robinson challenges institutionalized racism and emerges victorious from the Dodgers' dugout. Davy Crockett and the bear; Daniel Boone and the Indians; Lincoln and the slave owners; Lindbergh and the Atlantic Ocean. Paul Revere, Patrick Henry, Johnny Appleseed, Susan B. Anthony. Our nation lionizes the individual who overcomes supposedly insurmountable odds to achieve some seemingly unattainable goal.

It always has. It always will.

America's penchant toward hero worship contributed in no small measure to Kennedy's own fame. The way I figure it, some bureaucrat somewhere must have seen the logic in exploiting this same attitude to deflate his stature.

But it won't wash. Not over the long haul.

People will begin to doubt, for suspicion is also an American obsession. Over time, the hairline cracks in the government's story will develop into major fissures. Someone will poke. Someone else will prod. Already, a D.A. in New Orleans has begun to suspect the truth. He's only the first. Others will follow.

The intricate framework of official lies is bound to weaken. Ultimately, it will collapse.

All I have to do is bide my time, wait for just the right moment to come forward. Then, everyone will know who I am. And they'll understand what I was doing on that grassy knoll . . . one cold November morning in Dallas.

Janni Lee Simner is one of the hot new authors on the science fiction scene, with half a dozen well-received stories out during the past year.

For her alternate outlaw, she has chosen a man who certainly had the skills to do just about anything he pleased: The Great Houdini . . . .

Learning Magic
by Janni Lee Simner

"I never thought I'd see the day," Papa yelled, shaking his fist in Ehrich's face, "that you'd be arrested for stealing."

"It was just a stupid old scarf," Ehrich said. He met Papa's eyes without flinching. "And I wasn't arrested."

"Only because I paid the manager three times what it was worth. As if I can afford to throw such money away. Even then, it was all I could do to talk them out of locking you up." Papa shook his head. In the lamplight, his face looked old and pale. "Ehrich," he said, "what am I going to do with you?"

Ehrich didn't answer. He stared past Papa, toward the kitchen doorway. His sister stood there, watching them both. Gladys' hair was pulled back from her face into a tight bun, and her brown eyes were wide. Ehrich glared at her, and she turned away.

Papa sighed. "Your poor mama," he said. "She must be rolling over in her grave."

"You leave Mama out of this!" Ehrich snapped. His voice cracked. "Mama has nothing to do with it." He bolted across the room, shoving Gladys aside and running into the dark hall. Papa yelled after him, but didn't follow.

Ehrich ran to his bedroom and threw himself down on

the bed. He pounded his fist into his pillow. "It's not fair," he said. "It's not fair."

Ehrich hadn't even been there when it happened. When Papa moved from Wisconsin to New York, Ehrich had followed, helping earn money to send for the rest of the family. From the moment he'd left, he'd regretted it. He'd missed Gladys and his brothers, but most of all, he'd missed Mama. He'd longed to smell her cinnamon-apple smell, to look into her chestnut eyes, to talk to her again.

He never got the chance. When the train finally arrived, one bright autumn morning as the leaves were starting to fall, Mama wasn't on it. There'd been a crash, just outside Chicago, and the train had derailed. Twenty-seven people had been killed. She'd been one of them.

There must have been a way to save her. If Ehrich hadn't left Wisconsin, if he'd been on that train—somehow, he would have found it. He threw the pillow across the room. It hit the wall with a thud.

He stood, reaching up to the dresser and lighting a small candle. Yellow light filled the room. The bed and battered dresser were against one wall, a window and wooden wardrobe against another.

Ehrich knelt by the dresser, opening the bottom drawer. The bed and the other two drawers he shared with his brother Dash, but the bottom one was his. That was where he kept his magic.

It was filled with books, and with the odds and ends he needed for his tricks—bits of rope, tattered cards, a penny that always came up heads. Some of the tricks were easy, like the sliding wooden box that made coins disappear, or the cards that changed suit in his hands. Others, like opening locks without keys, or wriggling out of tied ropes, took more work. Ehrich practiced over and over, until he got them right.

He paid for his equipment when he could. When he couldn't, he took it anyway. Today he'd been stupid and gotten caught.

He'd been working with one of Gladys' old green

scarves, making it appear and disappear between his fingers. He'd wanted to make it change color, too, but he needed a second scarf for that. Gladys didn't have any other colors, and the handkerchiefs his father and brothers carried were too thick. Mama had a blue kerchief she'd worn when she went out, but they'd buried her in that. Ehrich had searched through all of Gladys' drawers, and Papa's as well, but he hadn't found any others like it.

That was why he'd stolen one. He'd made the mistake of going someplace where the manager knew him, and then he'd left too soon, making the man suspicious. He'd have to try somewhere farther away.

Ehrich closed the drawer. He put out the candle, then grabbed his coat and cap from the wardrobe.

"Harry? Harry, where are you going?"

Ehrich whirled at the voice. It was Gladys, her small figure outlined in the doorway. With one hand she shaded her eyes, trying to see into the dark room.

"Don't call me that," Ehrich snapped.

"It's the only way to get your attention," Gladys said. "You didn't hear me before."

Ehrich shrugged. Harry was the name he'd used when he'd first arrived in New York. He'd already started studying magic; back then he'd wanted to perform one day. Ehrich Weiss didn't sound like a performer's name, so he'd chosen Harry instead, Harry Houdini. He'd dropped it when Mama died. He had more important uses for his magic now.

"Where are you going so late at night?" Gladys asked.

"None of your business."

Ehrich saw his sister stiffen. He didn't care. She was younger than he, only thirteen. She couldn't tell him what to do.

Ehrich turned away from her and opened the window. A gust of cold wind blew in. The air smelled of frost, even though it was only October. He climbed out onto the fire escape. Icy rain fell, and the street below glistened. The overcast sky reflected orange light. From inside, Gladys called him again.

Ehrich slammed the window shut and started down the fire escape. His footsteps echoed on the metal as he walked.

He would get a second scarf, and he would practice the tricks until he got them right. He'd work his way through all his books, and when he finished, he'd find more. He'd steal whatever he had to, and he'd make sure he didn't get caught. If he were arrested, he wouldn't be able to practice his magic at all. He couldn't let that happen.

Because although the tricks he'd learned so far were tricks he could explain—he hid the cards up his sleeves, he undid the locks with small pieces of wire—there was another kind of magic, magic that worked on its own. Not the magic that mediums used when they pretended to talk to the dead; Ehrich had been to enough seances to know that they were as fake as any card trick. Besides, he didn't want to just talk to Mama. He wanted to bring her back. Even the mediums admitted they couldn't do that. But if Ehrich practiced long enough and hard enough, maybe he'd find the magic that could.

Ehrich walked through the city, far enough from home that no one would know him. The rain froze as it hit the ground, and the cobblestones were slippery under his feet.

He came to a cluster of stores. Each had its own smell—the stiff scent of leather, the tang of old fish, the grimy smell of newsprint. Most of the buildings had apartments above them; some rose four or five stories high.

At the edge of the cluster, Ehrich found a small Five and Dime. A sign painted over the door read "McMurty's." The apartment above it was only one story. Probably just the owner's family lived there, and maybe a boarder or two. Ehrich turned the doorknob. Nothing happened. He stood there, staring at the door, ignoring the cold metal against his palm. No light came through the high windows, and he realized that the store was closed. He hadn't even thought about the time when he'd left.

He glanced about. The other stores were dark, too. The only light came from the gas lamps lining the street, and the street itself was nearly empty. A scowling old man, his collar turned up against the rain, walked briskly past. In a doorway farther on, two small boys lay huddled together, sleeping.

Ehrich sighed, and his breath came out in a puff of mist. He'd been stupid again. Now he'd have to come back tomorrow. He turned to walk away.

And turned back again. If he wanted magic, why not use magic to get it? He felt through his coat. In his left pocket, he found a piece of bent wire.

Bracing his hand against the doorknob, Ehrich pushed the wire into the lock, feeling for the mechanism. His fingers were numb in the cold air. The pick flew from his grip, and he had to bend down to retrieve it.

He tried again, more slowly this time, concentrating as much on holding the wire as on releasing the lock. He heard a click, and he knew he had it. He opened the door and stepped inside, pulling it shut behind him.

The room smelled of mildew and damp wood. It was dark, with only the glow of the gas lamps shining through the high windows. Ehrich waited for his eyes to adjust. By the faint light, he could make out rows of wooden shelves, crammed close together.

He started down one of the narrow aisles, past jumbles of cracker tins and bottled medicines. The shelves extended above his head, and the highest items were beyond his reach.

On the other side of the room, where the aisle ended, Ehrich found a small, open area. In one corner, a cash register wobbled on an uneven table. In the other, there was a closed door, probably leading upstairs, or into a storeroom.

Ehrich turned to the next aisle, fumbling through a box of belt buckles and shell necklaces. Higher up, he discovered a pile of men's handkerchiefs. He stretched his neck back to see the top shelf. Crammed between a sack of seed packets and a pile of magazines, he saw a small wooden box, overflowing with women's scarves.

Ehrich stepped onto the bottom shelf, holding the shelf above it with one hand and grabbing the box with the other. The wood creaked under his weight. He jumped down and rummaged through the box.

Some of the scarves were coarse linen; others were smooth and fine, like silk. Ehrich held each one toward the windows, straining to make out the colors. He came to one that was pale blue, just like Mama used to wear. It felt light and gauzy. It would be perfect for magic. Ehrich smiled and shoved it into his pocket.

He threw the rest of the scarves back into the box. Taking the box in both hands, he stepped back onto the shelf.

There was a creak, and then, without warning, a loud crack. Ehrich crashed to the floor, banging his head on the shelves behind him. The box fell after him, and dozens of scarves fluttered softly to the ground.

For a moment, Ehrich couldn't move. His head throbbed. Splintered wood and swirls of cloth were everywhere. He remembered the noise the wood had made when it broke, though, and he knew he had to get out quickly, in case someone had heard. He pulled himself to his feet. The room started spinning, and he held out both arms to steady himself.

"Stop right there!"

Ehrich froze. The woman's voice came from directly behind him. She must have come from the apartment. Orange light spread through the room, and he knew she'd lit a lamp. Slowly, he turned around.

It was only a girl, fourteen or fifteen at most. She stood in the open space at the end of the aisle, wearing a white cotton nightgown that brushed the floor. Her hair fell to her shoulders in brown waves, past a high collar embroidered with purple flowers. In one hand she held the lamp; in the other, a small pistol.

"Don't move," the girl said. "I'll shoot." Her hand wavered as she spoke, and Ehrich realized she didn't mean it. Since she'd come down alone, maybe she was the only one in the building.

"Where are your parents?" Ehrich asked.

The girl's grip on the gun tightened. Her face tightened, too, with a scared, anxious look. "They'll be right back," she stammered. Then she realized what she'd said, and her face went pale.

Somehow, Ehrich had to get the gun. He took a step forward. She raised the gun higher and backed away. Ehrich took another step. Her hair reminded him of Gladys, when she let it down at night. And her eyes—

Ehrich swallowed. Her eyes were small and chestnut-brown, just like Mama's.

Another step, and he smelled the lilac scent of her perfume. That wasn't right. Mama smelled of cinnamon and fresh-baked bread. The person standing here was just a girl, younger than him. Mama was dead. Nothing he could do would change that. Not unless—

Ehrich's stomach tightened. Maybe it was time to use his magic.

He reached into his right pocket. The scarf felt warm against his fingers. He crumpled it to a ball in his fist.

He arced his left hand upward, in front of the girl's face. She jumped at the motion, and the gun clattered to the floor. Ehrich hadn't planned on that, but real magic was supposed to do things you didn't expect. He scooped up the gun with his left hand and pulled his right hand from his pocket. He brought both hands together and quickly threw them open. If he did the trick right, he knew, the scarf would seem to come out of the air.

The blue cloth flew from his fingers. The girl gasped, and Ehrich knew the trick had worked. She didn't move, just stared at him out of frightened eyes. Mama's eyes. "What do you want?" she asked.

With his right hand, Ehrich grabbed the scarf from the

floor. "Put it on," he said. His voice sounded strange, even to himself.

The girl shook her head. "You're crazy," she said.

Ehrich lifted his left hand, the one with the gun. His aim didn't waver. "Put it on," he said again.

The girl opened her mouth to say something, then looked at Ehrich and shut it. She took the scarf and pulled it over her head, knotting it tightly around her neck.

The scarf hid her hair. Her face was still too young, but if Ehrich focused on the brown eyes, the blue kerchief, he could almost ignore that. He stood very still, waiting for the real magic to come and finish what he'd started. He heard a click from the front door, but he ignored it. "Mama," he said, reaching out to touch her cheek.

The door flew open, letting in a burst of cold air. Ehrich didn't even turn around. The smell of lilac had faded beneath cinnamon and fresh-baked bread, and Mama's trembling cheek was soft beneath his fingers.

"Daddy!" Mama pulled away from his touch. She brushed past him, running to the door. Ehrich whirled around after her.

A man stood in the doorway. He was taller than Ehrich, and heavier, with dark blond curls cut close to his neck. Mama ran into his arms. That didn't make any sense at all.

The man pushed Mama aside and started toward Ehrich. The room began spinning, faster than before. Ehrich didn't know what the man wanted, but he knew that the magic was leaving. His stomach lurched. He couldn't lose Mama, not again.

His grip on the pistol tightened. He cocked the trigger and fired. There was a high scream, but the man kept coming. Ehrich fired again. The man crumpled to the floor.

The pistol fell from Ehrich's hand and he slid to his knees. For a long moment, he knew only the acrid smell of gunpowder.

When the smell faded, the room was silent. The man lay on the floor in front of him, very still. That was good. Ehrich climbed over him and started looking for Mama.

He found her lying behind the door. Her brown eyes were open, staring at the ceiling, and her hair fanned about her head like a halo. Ehrich knelt by her side. He touched her cheek, ran his hand down to the collar of her nightgown. He felt something sticky beneath his fingers.

A bright red stain was spreading across the white cotton. Ehrich stared at it, stared at Mama lying on the floor. He couldn't stop staring.

The scarf had fallen from her head. Ehrich picked it up. Closing his eyes, he brushed the soft fabric against his face. It smelled faintly of lilac.

That wasn't right. Mama smelled of cinnamon. Ehrich opened his eyes and looked down again. A girl lay on the floor, fourteen or fifteen at most, in a bloodstained nightgown. Mama hadn't come back. The magic, real magic, hadn't come after all.

Ehrich turned away. A sob rose in his chest, and he fought it. He jumped to his feet and ran out the door. The icy rain had turned to snow, and it fell in large wet flakes that numbed his cheeks. Ehrich didn't care. He kept running.

"Mama," he called. "Mama." He began to cry—hard, choking sobs—and the sound echoed down the street as he ran.

Snow fell through the night, but morning dawned clear and cold. A light wind blew, pushing swirls of white along the cobbled street. Ehrich's shoes were soaked through, his coat wet and dripping, but none of that mattered. He'd run most of the night, trying not to think about what had happened. He'd killed Mama. He'd killed a fifteen-year-old girl and her father. Either way, the magic had failed. Mama was dead.

Now, as he shuffled home through the snow, he felt strangely calm. There was a hollow, aching space inside him, but that was okay. The emptiness protected him. For the first time all night, he couldn't feel, and he didn't want to cry.

He thought about taking the fire escape to his room, but decided he didn't care whether Papa knew he'd been gone or not. He climbed the front stairs to the apartment, opened the door, and stepped inside.

Gladys sat in the kitchen, her head in her hands. She looked up as Ehrich entered. He could tell she'd been crying. He wondered why.

Her face hardened when she saw him. "Where were you?" she yelled. "Papa's out looking for you, you know. What'd you run off like that for?"

"None of your business," Ehrich said. He tried to walk past her, but Gladys grabbed his coat and wouldn't let go. She stared at him, waiting for an answer. Her brown eyes flashed with anger.

Ehrich opened his mouth to say something, then closed it again. He looked at Gladys' eyes. They were like Mama's eyes, too. He wondered why he hadn't noticed before.

But her dress was green, and her hair was light brown. That wasn't right at all.

Ehrich felt into his pocket. The scarf was still there, as damp as his coat. He took it out and brought it to his face. The lilac scent was gone, replaced by the dank smell of mud and snow.

He'd used all the magic he knew, but Mama hadn't come back last night. That didn't mean she would never come back. There would be other chances. Next time maybe he would get it right. He smiled.

"What's so funny?" Gladys demanded.

It's all right, Ehrich wanted to tell her. Mama's coming home. But instead, he just jerked the coat free from her hands and started to his room. Gladys yelled after him, but Ehrich kept walking.

He went straight for the bottom dresser drawer. Somewhere, in all the books and tricks, there was real magic. He would find it. He knew he would.

He crumpled Mama's wet blue scarf into his palm, reached into the drawer for Gladys' dry green one, and started practicing.

Here's Tappan King—novelist, story writer, editor—with a unique vision of the greatest pirate who ever lived. (And who, under other circumstances, might well have been the Queen of England.)

The Crimson Rose
by Tappan King

A fair wind blew west toward Hispaniola, setting the sails of the *Isabella* cracking, sending the ponderous galleon flying over the foaming waters of the Spanish Main. His Royal Highness Charles, Crown Prince of Spain, Portugal, Great Britain and the Netherlands, paced restlessly back and forth upon the bridge, scanning the far horizon for land, wishing mightily that this dismal voyage would soon be over.

It had been more than two months since the *Isabella* had departed Seville. Though Charles had only recently attained his seventeenth year, his father, King Philip, had decreed that the young prince should make a progress of the Spanish colonies in the West Indies, believing it was not too soon for his son to assume some of the duties attendant to his station.

Charles, who had been sent abroad to Oxford the previous fall, immediately protested the order, dispatching an impassioned letter to his father, the king, arguing that the voyage would be disruptive of his studies. And, indeed, there was an element of truth in his contention, though the studies the young prince had in mind were drinking, brawling, gambling, and wenching, not history or theology.

For Charles, freed from the oppressively pious atmosphere of the Escorial, his father's monastic palace in New

Castile, had lately fallen in with a crowd of wellborn young rakes and libertines who often slipped away incognito to London to frequent the fashionable new taverns known as "charter houses," which had sprung up overnight right under the nose of England's grim Lord Protector, the Duke of Alba. These disreputable establishments offered not only beer, ale, wine, and brandy, but more exotic substances as well, such as coffee from Arabia and the bittersweet Mexican beverage known as "chocolate." Some boasted smoking chambers, where one could purchase pipes filled with Indian tobacco, a sweet hemp resin called *bhang*, the coca leaf from Peru, even opium from Cathay.

Many of these houses had gaming rooms, which also served as impromptu brothels. The "Bloody Duke" had condemned these establishments as breeding grounds for heresy and sedition, and rightly so, for the headiest brew served there was the free play of ideas, the open discussion of topics forbidden by the Church and the Crown. It was understandable, therefore, that Prince Charles would be reluctant to leave such exquisite worldly pleasures.

But King Philip was unmoved by his son's entreaties and summoned Charles home to prepare for the journey. And so, when the winds freshened in June, the prince made passage aboard the *Isabella*, the flagship of a flota of some twenty ships bound for Santo Domingo, by way of the Canary Islands.

Despite all the comforts provided for him, Charles found life at sea barbaric. His cabin was cramped and unsanitary, his servants were surly and resentful, the food was barely edible, and the ship's motion left him constantly queasy. To make matters worse, there was no one to talk to. The ship's captain, Don Pedro Dominguez, was a bully and a drunkard, and his crew were haggard wretches, fearful of their captain's moods. Even the soldiers who guarded the prince's person were sullen souls who could never be tempted into a friendly game of bones.

If not for the ship's pilot, a genial young Portuguese

sailor named Gilberto Nunes, Charles would have been out of his wits with boredom. The pilot became the prince's fencing partner and sole confidant. Mornings, Charles would often join Gilberto at the wheel for coffee and conversation. And at night, the pilot and the prince would sit on the aft deck under the stars, smoking tobacco or hemp and engaging in idle talk about the ways of the world.

It was on one such night that the pilot told Charles he was considering leaving the *Isabella* when it docked in Santo Domingo. "I live each day in fear of my life," he told the young prince. "The pirates grow bolder each year. There are those who say that they will rule this sea a few years hence."

"Little chance of that!" scoffed Charles. "Spain has the greatest navy in all Christendom. Any bravo who dared to challenge the Crown would soon be brought to heel."

"With due respect, you do not see the Indies as we do, Milord," said the pilot. "There is a saying here: 'There is no law beyond the Line.' We are many leagues from Spain. Your father is preoccupied with adventures in Europe. He has stripped these coasts bare of defenses to fight his many wars at home. Already there have been attacks against the treasure houses at Venta Cruces and Nombre de Dios. It is but a matter of time before they attack the flota itself."

"If they do, they will soon regret it," said Charles. "Look around you, Gilberto. We are guarded by a half dozen of the finest warships ever built. Surely there is no force in all the Indies that could stand against such might."

"I pray you are right, Milord," said the pilot.

But that night, as Charles drifted off to sleep, he found himself half-hoping that a pirate ship would dare to attack the fleet. It would certainly break the tedium of the voyage and give him a story to tell that none of his companions in London could match. No such misadventure occurred, however, and as midsummer approached,

Charles found his dreams were filled not with thoughts of bloody battles, but of firm ground and fresh food and lovely ladies. The landing at Santo Domingo could not come soon enough for him.

As July drew to a close, Charles could scarcely contain his impatience. It was reckoned that they would come in sight of Hispaniola on this day, and Charles had risen early in the hope of being the first to make landfall. As he stood on the bridge, shading his eyes from the glare of the sun, he saw a glint on the horizon and turned to alert Gilberto. But before he could speak, there was a shout from the crow's nest above.

"Hard about!" the pilot cried. Above him, dozens of sailors began to swarm about the rigging, trimming the sails. The *Isabella* heeled over to starboard and began to point up into the wind.

"What is happening, Gilberto?" Charles demanded.

The pilot turned gravely to the young prince. "It is as I feared, Milord," he said. "We are beset by pirates."

Then Charles heard a triumphant shout and looked up to see the pirate chief swinging across to the *Isabella* on a stout halyard and dropping to the deck below him with catlike grace. A moment later, their eyes met, and the young prince's guts clenched in fear.

"So, this is the good-for-nothing Prince of Spain!" said the pirate, a slight smile touching his lips. "Well," he amended quickly, appraising the young prince with a calculating gaze, "not good for nothing, surely! I'd say he's worth at least fifty thousand pounds to King Philip—more perhaps, if we ransom him a piece at a time!" The pirate's men laughed aloud at this last statement, though Charles himself could not see the humor of it.

Charles stood as still as a statue, curiously unafraid, as the pirate chief slowly began to climb the ship's ladder toward him, aiming his pistol at a spot a few inches above the young prince's heart. Charles's hand fell upon his sword. He drew it slowly, almost without thinking, holding the gleaming blade at guard before him.

The pirate chief snapped his fingers twice. "Tupac! Diego!" Two of the pirate's lieutenants, one a sharp-faced native, the other a massive black man, began to follow their leader up the steps, swords drawn.

As the pirate chief drew near, Charles was surprised to observe that he was a smaller man than his great voice and bold demeanor had at first suggested. Indeed, he was shorter than Charles himself, and his frame was lithe and slim. And instead of the hairy face and swarthy complexion one associated with a proper pirate, this fellow was boyish, smooth-cheeked and fair, with wispy copper ringlets and skin the color of milk. His face looked oddly familiar. But there was no mistaking the deadly intent in those pale, cold eyes.

"You may take me if you can," the prince shouted in a voice that nearly cracked, sounding bolder than he felt. His heart was racing wildly. "But know this. I will sell my life dearly!"

The pirate chief's laughter filled the air. "He's got spirit, I'll give him that."

"Come closer, and I'll show you spirit," Charles said recklessly, sword raised.

With a flash of steel, the pirate chief swiftly drew his own sword, tucking the pistol in his sash and gently tapping the tip of the prince's weapon with his own. Then there was a furious clash of blades, and Charles was fighting desperately for his life, trying to remember everything his instructors had ever taught him as the pirate beat him back against the railing. As the prince spun to parry a wild thrust, he glimpsed a dusky shadow out of the corner of his eye. He felt a searing pain above his temple, and then was overcome by darkness.

"Your Highness?"

Prince Charles rolled over in bed, pulling the bedclothes up about his head to avoid the harsh light of the lamp. "Go 'way!" he snarled. His slumber had been disturbed by a preposterous dream in which he'd been taken prisoner by pirates in the Indies, and he was determined to make up for the lost sleep.

"You must wake up, Your Highness." The voice was sweet and clear, but with a strange accent. Charles rolled over and sat up. His head throbbed and he felt sluggish, as if he'd been drugged. A young woman about his own age was watching him from the foot of the bed.

He stared in wonder at the lovely apparition before him. She was tall and slender, with unbound hair like an ebony waterfall, skin the color of oiled oak, and eyes as dark as night itself. Her simple white-linen gown was cut low and fitted close, revealing a muscular figure. A heart carved of a single sapphire hung at her bosom. Her feet were bare.

"Where am I?" asked the prince.

"Hy Brasil," the young woman answered.

Charles blinked, but the apparition did not vanish.

"You must wake up," she repeated insistently. "Here. Drink this," she said, setting a steaming mug on the nightstand beside the bed. "It will help to revive you." Charles's nose told him it was filled with hot, spiced coffee. He held the mug in both hands and took a sip. It was bolder than any brew he'd tasted in London, setting his blood racing and chasing the cobwebs from his brain.

When he could at last take his eyes from the young woman, he stared about in equal wonder at his surroundings. The room was a curious combination of the refined and the rustic. Its walls were made of polished logs, laid one on another, and its ceiling was a high arch of stout branches, thickly covered with wide, green leaves. The great canopied bed in which he lay, and the fine furniture about the chamber's walls, were ornamented with gilded carvings of fantastic beasts, but the rugs on the floor were of native weave in outlandish hues. The ewer on the nightstand was made of the finest china, but the bowl beside it was roughly hewn of wood, and heaped with ripe fruits of a kind he had never seen before. Hanging from the rafters was a massive wicker cage that contained an enormous parrot, whose plumage was a riot of greens and reds and yellows. Outside an open window, he could see moonlight dancing on a wide harbor, and he could hear the sound of faraway music.

"You must dress now, my lord," she said. "You are expected on the half hour."

"Expected?" asked Charles. "Expected by whom?" The prince was about to swing his feet to the floor when he realized he was naked, and was overcome by an unexpected wave of modesty, hastily pulling the feather bedding close about him.

The young woman lowered her gaze. "I may not say. There is clothing for you on the chest at the foot of the bed. I . . . I will wait for you outside."

Charles was about to reply, but she had already withdrawn from the chamber without a sound. The prince rose, wincing slightly at a tender spot on the side of his head. The sultry air from the window was balmy against his naked skin, and faintly scented with sweet blossoms.

On the chest was a lavish set of garments made of cream-colored silk—doublet, hose, blouse, waistcoat, cloak—with soft, tan kidskin shoes and a matching cap with a single white feather. He dressed quickly, regarding himself in a great polished glass that hung upon the wall. The clothing fit as if tailored for him by hand. Even at the formal state occasions of his youth, he had never been attired in such finery.

He stepped out of the bedchamber and found the young woman waiting for him in a small sitting room.

"Come," she said. "We must be going now. Follow me."

Charles followed the young woman down a long covered passage lighted with flaming torches. It led to an immense wooden quay that curved around a quiet cove, where a row of longboats was docked. Beyond, through a narrow strait, he could see a larger harbor, where the ships of the pirate fleet were moored. He thought he could make out the *Isabella* in the far distance. Ahead, the woman was walking along a wide mall planted with flowering shrubs, headed toward a great manor house. It was a massive building made of rough-plastered stone, with wide porches and high gables that seemed out of place in this lush wilderness. One wing was still incomplete, its scaffolded walls half-covered with a slip of mortar and shell.

The young woman paused before the main entrance, a pair of heavily carved wooden doors at the top of a short flight of steps, guarded by a pair of natives in barbaric livery who bowed low as Charles entered. Once inside, the prince halted, staring in astonishment at the vista before him.

If not for the sultry heat and tropical flora, he might have been in one of the grand houses of London or Madrid. He stood in a broad entrance hall decorated in opulent splendor. Its floor was tiled in black and white marble, a five-petaled rose of coral and pearl inlaid in each tile. Its ceiling was ablaze with a half-dozen massive golden chandeliers, each alive with creatures from the sea—dolphin and narwhale, mermaid and kraken. And along the walls were rich murals depicting scenes from history and legend: King Arthur and his knights, Roland winding his horn, St. George and the dragon, Henry V at Agincourt. It reminded Charles more of the summer home of some unknown prince than the lair of a black-hearted pirate.

A bejeweled clock on a nearby table began to chime the hour. "This way, please!" called his guide urgently, standing beside an open door to the left. Charles entered quickly, finding himself in a great library lined with hundreds of bound books. He hardly noticed when the door closed firmly behind him. Before him stretched a long table lit by tall silver candelabra, covered with maps and charts and instruments of polished brass. As he came closer, he could see that the surface of the table itself held a map of the world picked out in wood and ivory inlay. Though he was dazed by the magnificence of the cham-

ber, Charles could not help but note that every aspect of
the room, from the lush draperies to the line of blazing
sconces, to the huge portrait hung upon the far wall, was
cunningly devised to draw attention to the far end of the
table where the pirate chief stood, back to the door, smoking a long tobacco pipe and regarding a great globe upon
a bronze stand. The pirate was dressed this evening more
like a lord than like a brigand, in a long, black-velvet coat
embroidered with hundreds of tiny seed pearls. His mane
of coppery hair, as long as an Irishman's, cascaded from
under a rakish black-silk bonnet, and a gaudy but lethal-
looking sword hung at his hip.

"You're late, nephew," the pirate said, turning swiftly
about. The young prince gaped. Beneath the rich coat was
a sumptuous gown of elegant black satin, trimmed in silver brocade, which ended in a broad farthingale. Its bodice was cut almost to the navel, revealing an ample
expanse of delicate white flesh that left no doubt but that
his host was a woman.

"I said, you're late!" The young prince was so transfixed
by the spectacle before him that he could scarcely reply.
She drew on her pipe, a slight smile curving her lips. She
was clearly amused by the young prince's consternation.

"God's death!" the woman continued. "Are you bereft of
common courtesy, or did that clout on the ear Diego gave
you addle your wits? Speak, lad, if you value your life!"

"I . . . I don't know what to say," stammered the prince.

"That's evident," the woman replied with a hearty
laugh. "You might begin by giving your Aunt Bess a kiss,
as you used to do when you were a child."

"Aunt Bess? I'm afraid I don't understand . . ."

"I had credited you with more wit, boy. Before you
stands your mother's sister! Elizabeth, daughter of your
own grandfather, King Henry!" She jerked a thumb at the
painting upon the wall, and Charles suddenly recognized
it as a portrait of Henry VIII, his mother's father. The
woman stood for a moment at the same angle as the old
king, as if to enhance the resemblance, then strode for-

ward, offering Charles a rouged cheek. As she drew near, the young prince caught the musky scent of her body, mixed with sweet perfume, and noticed the faint tracery of lines on her face, barely visible beneath her powder.

"Elizabeth?" repeated the prince. "But I had thought— my father told me you had perished at sea!"

"Aye, he would say so," she replied. "But I survived, no thanks to Philip—or to the Bloody Duke of Alba, may God strike him dead!" She paused, as if suddenly aware of her outburst, then smiled winsomely, taking Charles's arm with her long, slim fingers and drawing him over to a small couch nearby. "But I forget my manners. Come, sit here beside me and allow me to offer you refreshment," she said, patting the place beside her.

As Charles sat down, Elizabeth snapped her fingers and a servant appeared from the shadows, a native, by the look of him. "Bring us coffee and brandy," she said to him, "and a plate of those delightful sugar candies that Juana made this morning."

The servant vanished and returned a moment later with a silver tray covered with elaborately fashioned confections. Elizabeth's eyes sparkled as she plucked one from the assortment. "We will be dining soon," she said with a conspiratorial whisper, "but I never could resist an opportunity for sweets." She popped the tidbit in her mouth, licking the sugar from her lips, then pressed one to his own. He opened his mouth and swallowed it, tasting an extraordinary medley of flavors—sugar and cinnamon and cocoa and rum. His eyes widened, and she clapped her hands with delight. "Excellent, is it not?"

"It's remarkable," he answered, shaking his head in wonder. "I've never tasted anything quite like it . . . Aunt Elizabeth."

"Come, now! Call me Bess! And I shall call you Charlie, just as I did when you were a child," she said, plucking another sweet from the tray. "You'll find we enjoy here in New Albion all the luxuries you were used to in Europe— and a good many new ones besides."

"New Albion?" asked Charles. "Where is this place?"

"We are on the northeast coast of Brasil, not far from Panama," Elizabeth replied, "in a place once known as Cartagena, or New Carthage—though I have since rechristened it after that land which was once my home."

The servant reappeared with a service of brandy and the strong, spiced coffee Charles had tasted earlier. When he'd eaten and drunk his full, Elizabeth took his hand and fixed his gaze with hers.

"I have a grim duty to discharge, Charlie," she said. "And it is best done quickly. Not long ago, you said your father had told you I perished at sea. Now I must tell you the bitter truth of that black day, and it is this: The Duke of Alba, Lord Protector of Great Britain, plotted my death, with the full knowledge and consent of your father, King Philip."

Charles stiffened, pulling his hand away. "I cannot believe it," he said.

"Yet it is true," she answered. "Shortly after your birth, there was an uprising of my supporters in the North, protesting the harsh rule of the Roman Church. Philip ordered Alba to England from the Netherlands to put down the revolt. The Duke accused me of fomenting the insurrection and demanded my execution, but the Parliament would not approve it. So Philip exiled me off to Flanders to stay with the emperor's mannish sister, Mary, until the fires of rebellion had cooled.

"But Alba conspired in secret to have me killed. He placed a faithless servant upon the ship with orders to poison me three days out from land, and then to set the ship afire. Had God not been watching over me that day, I would have perished. But my counselor, Doctor Dee, had drawn my horoscope that morning, and it warned me of the treachery. I discovered the brew that contained the poison and sought the aid of a brave young sailor, Francis Drake by name, who slew my would-be murderers and commandeered the ship. When I did not return, Philip and Alba thought me dead, and I did nothing to dissuade them from the notion. In time, we reached the Indies, where I have remained since."

"What you speak of is murder," said Charles coldly. "My father would not be party to such a crime."

"I would not have credited it myself had I not seen it with my own eyes. But as it happens, I have evidence of Alba's treachery, and Philip's, bought at great cost." She reached into her bosom and pulled out a small key. With it, she opened a drawer in a nearby table, drew out a tattered sheet of paper and handed it to the prince. "My death warrant, in the Bloody Duke's hand, endorsed by your father, King Philip!"

Charles stared long and hard at the letter. He recognized Alba's dark, spidery hand, and his father's seal and sigil looked genuine. It gave grim support to her grisly tale.

Elizabeth placed her arm about the young prince's shoulder. "It is not such an uncommon thing, Charlie," she said with a bitter laugh. "Kings often kill queens and princesses when it suits them—and princes, for that matter. Did not my own father bury five of his wives? Did not your father order the death of your own mad half-brother, Carlos?"

Charles stared mutely at her, unable to answer.

"And that is the reason you are here, dear Charlie," Elizabeth said with a sad smile. "I have thus far escaped King Philip's notice, but that time is ended. Soon we will clash here in the Indies. I need an assurance that he will not turn his hand against me again. You will be that assurance."

"I don't understand. How can I guarantee your safety?"

"I'll be plain, Charlie. I mean to ransom you. Forgive me for it, but you must understand that my plight is desperate. Tomorrow I will send the *Isabella* back to Seville with a letter, making this demand: King Philip must send me without delay a Letter of Patent, in his own hand, granting me full right and title to these lands I now hold, and pledging that he will not attack those territories. In guarantee of that pledge, he must also send me the sum of one hundred thousand ducats in gold. If he agrees to this, I will return his ships to him unharmed, along with those passengers who remain alive . . . including you, Charlie."

"But what if he does not agree?" asked Charles, though he knew well what her answer would be.

"He will," she said gravely. "He must!"

She rose suddenly. "Come! Let us not dwell on such unpleasant matters. Rather, let's celebrate our happy reunion. My cooks have prepared a modest repast of the local provender. I'll wager you'd enjoy some decent food for a change, would you not, Charlie?"

"I would at that," said the prince, grateful himself to take leave of unpleasant matters.

Elizabeth entwined her arm around his and led him to a magnificent dining room where a sumptuous selection of choice viands were laid out on a fine table covered in white linen. Charles noticed that a third place had been set at the table. He was about to ask about it when the door opened and a figure entered.

Standing in the doorway was the young woman who had awakened him earlier. But now she was dressed not in a linen shift, but in an exquisite white gown of brocaded silk. Her dark hair was pulled back under a sparkling tiara, and she held in her hand a fan of carved ivory.

"Allow me to present my goddaughter, the Lady Catherine Drake. Kate, this is His Royal Highness, Charles, Prince of Spain."

"Good evening, Your Highness," Kate replied, her eyes wide in feigned innocence. Charles stepped forward, taking her hand. She curtseyed low. Impulsively, Charles raised her hand to his lips. Elizabeth regarded the two intently for a moment, then gestured to the table.

"Come, come! Let us sit down," she said. "I, for one, am famished!"

They sat together. As the meal progressed, Charles found his attention divided between his bold, vivacious aunt and the beguiling young creature at his side. Eliza-

beth's account of her adventures in the Indies bordered on
the fantastic, but Kate's dark eyes kept drawing his gaze.

"Tell Charles the story of how you became a pirate,
Mother!" Kate said when they'd eaten their fill.

"Very well, Kate, I shall." Elizabeth rubbed her palms
together, warming to the tale. "My dear Francis Drake was
a fine sailor, and he soon distinguished himself well in the
reaving trade. Over time, he proved himself a better com-
mander, and as ships fell to him, he began to assemble his
own fleet of privateers, often harrying the Spanish and
Portuguese ships on behalf of the Dutch and French,
sometimes taking prizes for his own. Eventually he became the most feared pirate in all the Caribbean. I was at
his side through it all, at first staying in port to guide his
affairs, but later joining him as a crewman on his voyages.
It was he who took Cartagena in a single night, with the
help of my own wit and advice, and held it fast against all
attempts to retake it."

"It was about then that I was born, was it not?"

"Yes, child," said Elizabeth indulgently. "God in his wisdom had chosen to make me barren, so I could not give
my Francis the child he so desired. That he found in a native woman, though a Christian, named Maria, whom he
took as a lawful wife. Like your own mother, Charles, the
girl died not long after her only child's birth, and I cared
for her as if she were my own daughter.

"Five years ago, my beloved Francis returned from a
raid gravely wounded. He perished from the fever shortly
after, despite all my efforts to save him. His men, who
loved me well, conferred, and agreed that I should lead
them in his place. In the years that followed, our ventures
have met with much success, and I have built a goodly
kingdom here on this favored coast."

"Do you ever think of returning to England?" asked
Charles.

"As what? A pretender? A rallying point for rebellion?
I think not. Alba would not let me live long in that land."
Elizabeth sighed. "As Seneca cautions us, it is best to suf-

fer what we cannot mend. I will confess that once all my
thoughts were of that isle, but I have made my peace with
God's plan for me. In this land, I am both prince and
princess—and Pope besides. The natives here have a kind
of superstitious veneration for me, which I do not discourage. And why not?" She laughed. "Mine own mother
was a witch, or so 'tis said!"

The conversation lasted well into the evening, and
Charles was reluctant to leave the company of these two
extraordinary women. But when wine and fatigue began to
overcome him, Kate escorted him back to his cottage. Her
face haunted his dreams that night.

The next morning he began the exploration of Elizabeth's realm, with Kate as his willing guide and companion. The harbor town of New Albion was much larger
than he'd at first suspected, with hundreds of houses of
wood and mortar, a large church, and a busy market
where a wide assortment of goods could be bought or bar-
tered.

Elizabeth's own dwelling was magnificent, adorned with
many objects of great beauty and surrounded with lush
gardens and fountains. There was also a well-equipped
stable, with some of the finest horses Charles had ever
seen. On many mornings he would go riding with Elizabeth and Kate along the strand, or through the sun-
dappled corridors of the forest.

One morning Elizabeth took Charles and Kate on a ride
through her plantations south of the city. They traveled at
a leisurely pace, stopping frequently to rest and refresh
themselves at small shelters set up beside the fields. Their
course took them over the top of a high ridge, where they
halted their horses and gazed down into a lush valley below.

"As you can see, Charlie, I have done well with my little plot." The slopes of the hills before them were thickly
planted with coffee and cacao beans. The fields below held
row after row of tobacco and coca leaves, and vast tracts
of cane sugar.

"Why, there is more treasure here than all the gold in Mexico," exclaimed Charles, who knew the price his mates in London willingly paid for such rare delights.

"Indeed there is," said Elizabeth with some pride. "And I hope soon to trade with the Spice Islands as well. If this commerce continues, I will soon be wealthier than even the Genoese and the German bankers who bought your grandfather's emperorship for him and pay your father's armies. With such resources, I might one day make this kingdom a second Camelot, a New Jerusalem here in the New World."

Her bold vision set Charles's imagination afire. How thrilling it would be to carve a new empire of one's own, rather than to wait for someone to die in order to inherit a contested one.

Some time later, Elizabeth arranged a hunting party on Charles's behalf, seeking the white-tailed deer and wild boar with which they'd stocked the forest west of the city. She appeared that morning in men's garments, accompanied by a retinue of bare-chested native beaters whose skins were tattooed with strange-looking symbols.

That wilderness was denser than any wood in England or Spain, and Charles would soon have been lost had he not followed Elizabeth closely. After a morning of fruitless pursuit, they heard a rustling in the thicket, and Elizabeth dropped from her saddle, gesturing toward the high grass ahead. The beaters fanned out, encircling the prey, and began to create a great noise with their big wooden rattles.

"There, Charlie!" she cried aloud. "There's a fine one for you! Make yourself ready!" Charles, who had never stuck a boar himself, clutched his pike closely, waiting for the beast's charge. A moment later, it erupted from the brush, and the prince jabbed it hard in the side. The swine bellowed and turned on him, pulling the pike out of the prince's grip, ripping his coat and grazing his flesh with its tusks. It was turning to charge him again when Elizabeth stepped forward and transfixed it with her lance.

A moment later, her attendants struck off its head with their broad, sharp knives.

"Well done, Charlie!" said Elizabeth as she bandaged the prince's wound. "That was great sport, eh, lad? By God, I wish I had a son such as you to hunt with!" Charles felt weak with blood loss, but exhilarated as well, and strangely flattered by the pirate queen's words.

As he was taking a stroll along the quay one windy morning a few days later, Charles came upon Elizabeth, dressed in her captain's garb, staring out to sea. Her pirate fleet was massing in the outer harbor, readying itself for another raid.

"In four days' time we sail for Rio de la Hacha, Charlie, there to intercept a shipment of silver bound for Havana," she said. "I must confess, I grow weary of a pirate's life. It is a young man's game, and I am no longer as young as I was. I would rather live here as a proper prince and let others do my fighting for me. This is a lawless country, Charlie. With greater means, and God's help, I'll wager I could bring justice to this region."

"It would take a great force indeed to tame the Indies, Aunt Bess."

"I might have such a force in a few years. Many of the privateers here in the Indies would sail under the Crimson Rose if I could pay them well enough. Together, we could make an armada of four-score ships to keep the rest in line. And I could marshal a considerable army as well. Two thousand white men already call me their leader. My good lieutenant, Diego Mandinka, was an African prince in his own land. He could muster a force of some one thousand escaped Negro slaves—*cimarrones*, they call them—who know these jungles better than any man alive. And Tupac Amaru, who bested Alba's cousin Francisco, Viceroy of Peru, commands an irregular army twice that size."

Elizabeth turned back to the sea. "But men must eat, swords must be forged, and ships mended, and that takes silver. Until then, I must earn my keep the best way I can.

I will be gone for three weeks. Two, if all goes well. I must ask a pledge of you, Charlie."

"What sort of pledge?" asked Charles warily.

"I think you will agree that I have treated you with courtesy and trust these past few weeks, Charlie. I ask you to do the same to me. First, I will ask you to look after my Kate while I am gone. She has little fit company these days, and I feel certain that she likes you. I do not think you will find this request too hard."

"Not at all!" said the prince.

"Good. But I must ask more of you. I charge you by your honor not to escape while I am gone, nor to harm any man here. It will go hard for you if you do. My men will do my bidding even in my absence, and they have orders to take your life if you attempt to escape. Give me your word on it, Charlie. I have come to like you, and would hate to lose you."

"You have my word," said Charles. This pledge was not so hard to give, either, since the prince did not much wish to die himself.

After Elizabeth's departure, the days fled past in blissful succession. Though Charles knew on some level that the *Isabella* would return any day, he put the thought out of his mind, enjoying the life of a grandee in a jungle kingdom. He and Kate spend most of their days together, for she delighted in showing him the wonders of this strange kingdom, and to be in his company.

When Elizabeth returned at last from her expedition, laden with silver, preparations began for her birthday celebration. The date was known—the seventh of September—though none knew her true age for certain. Charles speculated that she was nearly forty, since he recalled that she had been in her mid-twenties at the time of his own birth. But Kate thought that seemed too advanced an age for a woman of her vitality.

A great pavilion had been erected in the town square for the celebration, and all of New Albion's many citizens, who numbered in the thousands, turned out for the festivities. A banquet table had been set up on a raised dais, laden with rich delights. Charles was given a place of honor to Elizabeth's left, with Kate on her right. All during the evening, the two young people stole glances at one another while the celebration continued. They watched an almost endless procession of entertainments, plays and recitations, musical performances and dancing, even a joust with lances and a display of fireworks over the harbor.

When the entertainment was done, the floor was cleared and Elizabeth led Charles out into the center of the arena. The musicians struck up a festive jig, and the pirate queen began to dance with gay abandon, whirling about Charles as he struggled to keep time. Shortly afterward, when her African lieutenant, Diego, stepped between them and began to dance with Elizabeth, Charles found himself partnered with the lovely Kate. Their hands joined and their eyes met, and he danced with her late into the night. The threat of his death, and indeed, the existence of the whole world, were far from his mind.

Charles woke suddenly, unsure of where he was, roused by an anguished cry. Kate stood by the window, her body racked with sobs, dressed only in one of his cast-off shirts. He threw the bedclothes back and went to her, encircling her with his arms and kissing her.

"What is it, my love?" he whispered, tasting the salt of her tears on her cheek.

She pushed him away. "Look for yourself," she said angrily. "The ship is here!" He looked past her. He could make out the shape of the *Isabella* in the outer harbor, moored at anchor, and his heart sank. In the two long months since the ship had departed New Albion, Charles had lived a life almost free from care. Though the constant presence of Elizabeth's soldiers reminded him that she held his life by a thread, he had almost convinced himself that her threat was only a bad dream. But the sight of the

Isabella, and the tears on Kate's cheeks, brought it all home to him again.

"Why do you weep, dear Kate?"

"You know well why, Charlie. Today I will lose you!"

"What do you mean?" he said, taking her hand in his.

"If your father, the king, has paid your ransom, you will leave me and return to the arms of one of your painted London women. And if he has not, Elizabeth will have you killed. Either way, I will lose you forever!" She pulled her hand away, wrapping her arms around her body. "Sometimes I think I would rather have you dead than in the arms of another woman, Charlie!"

He swept her up in his arms, silencing her with a kiss, not sure if she spoke in jest, if it were the lady in her blood or the savage who spoke. "Let us not spend our last moments together in quarreling," he said, kissing her firm brown neck. For a moment, she resisted him, but he held her fast. Then she began to pull him toward the bed, her kisses hungry and demanding.

An hour later, Charles stood beside Elizabeth on the Calita, the narrow spur of rock that enclosed the outer harbor, watching a small pinnace rowing toward them from the *Isabella*. Diego stood close behind them, a large matchlock cocked and ready in his hand. As the boat approached, Charles could make out two corseletted soldiers armed with pikes in the bow, and a slim man in dark robes standing in the stern. Tethered to the pinnace was a small flatboat, covered with a dark cloth.

"By God's teeth!" said Elizabeth. "It's Count Feria, Philip's old envoy. I had thought you dead long ago, you old goat!" she called out.

"I had thought the same of you," the old man called back in flawless English. "Would that our reunion had come under better circumstances, my lady."

"In my day, Feria was the craftiest of Spain's diplomats, Charlie," she whispered. "I do not trust him." Then she spoke aloud. "You were to come alone, Feria," she said.

"How can an old man as feeble as I handle such a great

ransom alone? I need these strong young men to help me."

"You have the gold, then?" asked Elizabeth.

"It is here," he said. Feria bent down stiffly and pulled back the drape from the barge. Stacks of gold ingots gleamed in the morning sun. "I trust the prince is well."

"He is here," Elizabeth replied. At a signal, Diego thrust Charles roughly forward. "How do I know you have not brought me gilded lead, Feria?"

The count regarded the prince intently across the few yards that separated them. "How do I know you have not brought me an impostor? It seems we must trust one another at least to this extent, my lady. Send the boy to us, and the gold is yours."

"Leave the gold and I will give you the boy," said Elizabeth. "I believe you have a letter for me as well."

Feria nodded, reaching slowly into his robe. He drew out a packet sealed with wax and held it up for her to see. "It is yours for the taking, my lady."

"Have your men throw out their arms," said Elizabeth. Feria's face hardened, but then he nodded again. At a signal from the old man, the soldiers complied, throwing their pikes and swords onto the beach, and a moment later, their daggers as well. Elizabeth began to walk forward. Diego followed, pushing Charles before him at gunpoint.

"Have your man withdraw," said Feria, gesturing toward Diego with his chin. "Just you and the prince." Now it was Elizabeth's turn to pause. A moment later, she nodded, and she and Charles closed the distance to the water's edge. As they approached, Feria stepped carefully out of the pinnace, with the aid of one of the soldiers. A moment later, the three were face to face, barely a sword's length apart.

"The letter, Feria," said Elizabeth. The old count held the packet out to her. As he stepped past the prince, he took the young man's arm as if to steady himself.

"Be prepared to run," he whispered in Charles's ear. "I

will not be coming with you." A moment later, he had pulled a dagger from his cloak and was plunging it toward Elizabeth's breast.

Charles turned, saw the flash of the knife, and in that instant his hand clutched the count's wrist, checking it just in time. Elizabeth, shaken, staggered backward into Diego's arms. Feria fought the prince with desperate strength, turning the blade toward him. Then, with a whispered prayer, the old count slashed it down across his own forearm. Blood spurted, soaking Charles's shirt, and Feria laughed, crossed himself and fell to his knees in the sand, his face discoloring.

"Charlie!" Elizabeth cried.

The prince dove forward without stopping to think. Unnoticed, one of the Spanish soldiers had regained his pike, and he hurled it at the prince. It stuck in the sand where Charles had stood only moments before. There was a sharp report and the soldier fell to the sand, felled by Diego's musket. His fellows turned and ran for the water, with Diego in close pursuit.

Charles stood slowly, brushing the sand and shells from his blood-soaked shirt. Regaining her composure, Elizabeth bent to pick up the blade.

"It was poisoned," she said, regarding the knife with a bemused expression. Then she turned to the prince. "You could have fled back to the *Isabella*," she said. "I would not have stopped you. Why did you turn back?"

"I . . . I don't know," he said.

Elizabeth laughed. "Well, you are free to go now, Charlie. I have my ransom and my patent. The bargain is complete. But if you're going, you'd best take a few of my men and go soon. When Feria does not return, they will fear the worst and sail away."

Her face grew grave. "I owe you my life, nephew," she said, gesturing to Count Feria's crumpled form. "That is not a debt I take lightly. Whatever you desire of me, you have but to ask. Half this ransom? You've earned it well enough today."

"Only if you pledge it as a dowry for your goddaughter, Kate," said Charles.

Elizabeth's eyebrows lifted. "So that's the way it is between you two," she said with a smile. "You are indeed a bold knave. What gives you to think that I would grant you her hand?"

"Because I will one day be king of half the world, and Kate will be my queen!"

"I believe you shall, Charlie," she said with a shake of her head. "I believe you shall. Is there anything else you require, O King of Half the World?"

"One more thing, Aunt Bess," Charles said with a grin. "Since you have that letter from my father, I'll take another from you in exchange. The one that Alba and my father signed, ordering your death."

"Why?"

"When I return, I shall want my subjects to know of their rulers' perfidy. It will make the assumption of my duties that much easier."

Elizabeth laughed aloud. "Methinks, good Prince Charlie, that I must watch you closely in the future," she said.

"How so, Aunt Bess?"

"It is you who should wear the Crimson Rose, Charlie. It is clear that you are a greater pirate than I will ever be!"

Did you ever wonder what kind of research mystery writers do? How, for example, did Agatha Christie know what drove a murderer to commit his crime?

Well, wonder no longer, for here with the answer is Michelle Sagara, 1992 and 1993 Campbell nominee, and author of the highly popular *Books of the Sundered* tetralogy as well as a dozen excellent short stories.

What She Won't Remember
by Michelle Sagara

1.

"You know nothing about the criminal mind. You sit there in your affected modesty while you derive some incomprehensible satisfaction from your 'art.' And you know nothing, understand nothing, explain *nothing*."

These were the only words that stayed with her at the end of the long luncheon—a charity luncheon at which she had been the honoured guest. The speaker carried himself well. He spoke with the most placid of smiles, but his eyes—his eyes conveyed the depth of his words. She could not forget them.

Of course I don't know anything about the criminal mind. Her hat and parasol were taken from her; her shawl and her gloves followed. She took her seat at the bench and watched absently as her boots were unlaced. *What sort of woman ever understands anything about the criminal mind?*

"Are you feeling unwell, ma'am?"

"No, of course not," she replied curtly, the flush in her cheeks deepening. "I'll be up in my study, and I don't wish to be disturbed."

"Shall I call you for dinner, then?"

She thought about it for thirty seconds. Maybe sixty. But she didn't want to see anyone, especially not after such an annoying day. "No; bring it up after the hour."

This was not the life she had thought to lead.

Married, surrounded by the walls of a sedate house, a stately life—one that she practically financed herself. A woman wasn't supposed to sully her mind with money matters and the outer trappings of the "business" world; that could taint or challenge her very soul. Still, she was the person responsible for it in her own home. She took well to it; some even thought too well.

Restless, she pushed the inkstand around on the desk. Once she had thought there would be adventure, travel, romance. Her pen, at ease above the blotter, remained poised in mid-word.

It was the rudeness that annoyed her. Really—how often had an over-jolly reader come up to her and insisted upon discoursing, at length, about the flaws in her latest work? It should be put aside as just another occurrence that had to be endured, however poorly.

The pen remained frozen. She set it down, shoved herself back from her large, partners' desk and began to pace the room in a rustle of skirts. Her passage across the mirror's surface arrested her; she caught a glimpse of the deepening lines in her forehead, around her eyes; saw the grooves at the corner of her mouth. She hated these symptoms of age.

She had never thought that would happen, either—that she would hate them.

You know nothing. Nothing.

"And should I?" she asked, glaring at herself. "What decent person does?" That's what she should have said; just that, primly and coldly. But the opportunity was lost. As many, in the passing years, had been.

This was not the life she had wanted to lead.

He was a young man, with a young man's fire and intensity. Not, of course, that all young men radiated this particular sort of heat, but in her experience, when it could be found at all, it was found in young men who had yet to learn—if they ever learned it—that there was a limit to their power and their reach.

He wasn't handsome—his face was a little too gaunt and too long for that—but he carried himself well, and besides, what exactly did handsome mean? He was attractive, certainly, but whatever this combination of fire and looks produced, it was not a comfortable attraction.

Particularly, not for Agatha.

She had seen him, in and around the library and the various reading organizations that she frequented, for some three months now. She did not elect to remember the exact date, but that was a force of will and not any absentmindedness; when he walked into a room and condescended to join a conversation, he spoke sharply and with a cutting perception that could not simply be ignored.

"Too rude," Mrs. Hanson had said—and indeed, she was completely correct. He was brash, arrogant, and discourteous. And powerful. And completely self-assured.

"Yes, Mrs. Hanson," she replied. "Terribly rude. I imagine he'll grow out of it."

"Can only be hoped," was the dark reply.

She wondered if any of the other ladies, each with her own quiet but public opinion, experienced the same private fascination that she did. Wondered if they watched him out of the corner of their eyes, both wanting and dreading some sign of his regard. There was an intellect behind those eyes, some motivating force that could not be contained in the men's clubs and gatherings of the day.

He was not congenial, but Agatha wasn't so old that congenial was what she desired out of life. Still, she hesitated just beneath the grand arch of the sitting-room entrance, dwarfed by its height.

There.

He looked up from his book, and she saw by its colour and the lines across its pages that it was one of the old city guides that had long since ceased to describe any recognizable part of London. There was no room for hesitation. A brisk first step brought her over the threshold and into the room. She looked neither to the right nor the left as she walked toward where he sat.

He rose to greet her; this level of politeness, at least, she could still expect. "Lady Agatha."

"Daniel." She strove to be natural, but her chin was rigid, her smile too tight.

"Join me, if you wish."

She didn't sit. Instead, she folded her arms and looked down her nose at him. It was a look that had taken her some time to develop, and to be honest, she was rather proud of it. "I only came to ask you a question."

"Ask, then. And please don't consider it too rude if I sit."

"What do *you* know about the criminal mind, if you're so quick to judge, and so certain?"

He laughed. His voice, always distinctive, rose above the muted, colourless conversations that surrounded them in ones and twos. "I? Why, Agatha, how do you think I *am* so certain?" He rose again, quickly and lightly; the languid movements and smiles of moments past were burned away.

Before she could pull back, he caught her hand and kissed it quickly. "I thought—I almost didn't dare to think—that you would return. If you'd chosen to stay away, well," here he shrugged, "I would have guessed wrong. Come."

"Where . . . where are we going?"

"Out. Out of this dusty old building with its dusty old inhabitants. There's more life out in the streets today than there ever will be in here."

One foot after the other, she followed in his wake. She was curious; she could feel the strange flush in her cheeks and wondered if she, like some overeager debutante, had shining eyes and rather too pert a step.

"But . . . but, Daniel," she ventured to say when he'd donned his overcoat and hat, "where *are* we going?"

"Does it really matter, Lady Agatha? Does it matter in the slightest where we talk? It's not dim surroundings and parlours or cafés that will make, or break, our afternoon. The skin can still be cut and the heart of any matter exposed wherever two people speak in earnest." But he drew himself to his full, slim height, and his expression grew suddenly remote. "Or did you not come to actually have an answer?"

She thought of the faerie, the sidhe of legend, and for a moment cast him in his proper role as one of the fey and dangerous folk. Drawing her cape tightly around her shoulders and fastening the clasp while studiously avoiding his aid, she found the strength to meet his eyes. "Of course I did. It doesn't matter to me where we go."

And it didn't. Although she wasn't used to walking—or more accurately, strolling—through the town's streets, she found it natural to be at his side, her arm across his, their shadows touching.

"That," he said quietly, "is a jeweler's shop. You see, through the window?"

The window, a yellowed glass that had become, over time, quite thick at the bottom and thin at the top, barely shed enough light to see through. She looked in, the sun at her back, Daniel's arm shielding her shoulder. "Yes."

"What do you see?"

"Two men and a very young lady speaking with the jeweler."

"All three speak with him?"

"The oldest man does."

"And?"

"The younger man is listening to their chat."

"The girl, then?"

"Wandering. Looking at the jeweler's wares."

"Will she steal anything, do you think?"

"Of course not!"

The full force of Daniel's laughter was contained in the chuckle that tickled her ear. "Why not?"

"Look at how she's dressed, Daniel . . . and look at who she's with. Why on earth would she need to steal anything?"

"*Need* to steal?" The amusement left his eyes. "Come away, Agatha. It's clear that you're either more naive or more attached to pretence than I thought."

It nettled her to be talked down to this way by a man ten years her junior. She pulled her arm away with definitive force and turned back to the window. The young lady—and to Agatha's observant eye, she was a little too old and too well-heeled to be called a "girl"—had indeed continued to peruse the various counters, picking up an earring or a bracelet for closer examination.

Although the glass obscured as much as it revealed, Agatha thought the girl's face sweet and quiet. "No," she said, much more confidently. "She isn't the type to steal."

"What type is that?" Daniel caught her arm again, and this time Agatha moved away from the window and back into the boulevard. "Do you think only poor or ugly people steal? Only old people? Only small children who haven't been taught any better?"

"Since you obviously have an answer, Daniel," she replied, the edge to her voice quite brittle, "why don't you either share it or cease to speak of this at all?"

He fell silent for long enough that Agatha was almost convinced he had elected to ignore the entire issue. Her disappointment was strong, her pride stronger; she would not withdraw her words. She watched their shadows along the ground as they slowly lengthened and nestled into the cobbled stones.

And then he turned to her, and once again the laughter

was in his eyes. "You believe in angels, Lady Agatha. I believe in human nature."

". . . but if human nature is so base, Daniel, don't you think that all of society would have crumbled into anarchy and chaos by now?"

"No, Lady Agatha—and that is the secret. You think that society is held together by some basic tenet of decency. I think," he paused and rummaged in his jacket for a cigarette, "that it's held together by fear." Gentlemen didn't smoke in the presence of ladies, but Agatha took no offence as Daniel's tobacco and paper began to burn. "Cowardice."

"I hardly think that acts of heroism constitute cowardice, Daniel. Will you try to tell me that there are no truly great acts of heroism?"

"What does heroism have to do with society?"

"There are acts of courage and goodwill that occur every day. Some *are* heroic. You can't deny that."

He shrugged. "I won't try." Smoke left his lips in a sparse, strange cloud. "And I'll allow that some people have impulses toward the heroic. But those impulses they act on; they don't fear the consequences of their actions, and they therefore don't spurn their desire."

Her lips were a tight, thin line; she shivered and drew her cape more tightly about her shoulders, pretending to be cold in the evening air.

"Society," Daniel continued quietly, "is all about giving in to your fear and relinquishing your desire." He turned toward her then; she lost the stark line of his profile to his unblinking gaze. "Women understand this far better than men, I think."

"Understand?" The word was a whisper.

"Do you have what you desire, Lady Agatha? Have you ever had, in the end, what you desire? Do you even know what that is? You are a good daughter, a good wife, a good mother. Your life has always been measured by everyone else's. Come, Agatha." He threw his cigarette into the street at his back, then caught both of her hands in his, pulling her close. "Come stand in the sun. It will be gone soon."

It was true. It had gotten heavy, the sun. Darkness would follow. She had been out, late, walking through the streets of the town with a lunatic.

She didn't want to return.

Freeing her hands was difficult; his fingers were tightly knit and warm about her own. "I have to get back," she said, bracing herself for contempt, for ice.

He froze for a moment before his whole body relaxed. "Very well, Lady Christie. Allow me to escort you."

The long, low cry of night birds pierced the closed window, underlining the distance between the pen Agatha held and the paper beneath it. No ink connected them, or left some quiet tale of the hours she had sat, in the flicker of lamplight, working productively.

It was wrong, what he'd said. All of it.

But the words—her words—wouldn't come. They were held back, unsaid, unspeakable.

I need a change. Scenery. Locale. Something. The moment she had the thought, with its mixture of quiet defiance and penitent confession, she knew it was more true than anything she had written, or would write, for a long time. She set her pen aside, pushed her chair back. As a woman of independent means, she could travel as she pleased, within certain social confines. Of course she would have to leave an itinerary. She would have to make calls, plans to visit friends or relatives in any area she should visit— perhaps even arrange for a few readings. She would, no doubt, be accompanied by at least one other person, most probably two, and the only moments of peace and privacy she would gain would be such as these: locked in a small room that passed as a study, staring at a blank page.

* * *

Three days later, she left for the library.
By the following morning, she had not returned.

2.

The village of W—— made the perfect retreat. As Miss
Julie Edens, she wore rather drab and demure spinster's
clothing and looked every inch the maiden aunt. Her
brother, she explained, had passed away a mere six
months ago, and she simply could not continue living
under the roof that they had shared for all of their lives;
it was still too painful. Nor did she wish to be alone in
London or any of the other rather wild and dirty cities—it
wasn't safe, you see—so she was doubly grateful for the
welcome that she had received in Mrs. Staples' inn.

"You stay as long as you like, poor dear," Mrs. Staples
had said for perhaps the thirtieth time, each time more sincere than the last. Her curiosity was evident in the way she
examined, out of the corner of her eye, the fabric and style
of the dresses that Miss Edens chose to wear. She thought
money might be involved, and while she was a genuinely
generous person, she was also a businesswoman.

Agatha found it both touching and amusing; as she had
gained age and experience, she found most of the human
condition one, the other, or both. She thanked Mrs. Staples profusely, and meant every word that she spoke.
Here, close to the heart of the village commons, she could
smell freedom as it eddied, lazy, on the air. The arguments
of sons and fathers drifted up the lane; she could hear the
crying of a child and the sharp words of an older voice, a
grandparent. The air had a clarity about it; she fancied it
to be charged with possibility, with life.

She did not try to write that evening, but took pleasure
in just observing. She sat and knitted with Mrs. Staples,
listening to the village gossip.

"That one," Mrs. Staples said, her voice heavy with dis-
approval, "that young Ned Barnes. He's a bad one, mark

my words. We'd hoped to lose him to the big city, but we only lost his money. Him, he came back, more of a problem than he was before."

"Problem?" Miss Edens murmured politely.

"Problem. He's been eyeing the young girls a little too much these days. Young Anne Netterson, especially. And you know how young girls are. Don't care a whit for sound advice, heads are all in the clouds. They want a bit of danger, they do. And they don't have the common sense to balance it all." She sighed. "Her parents are right worried; she's a good girl, but a headstrong one."

"Some young women are," Miss Edens said. "But isn't that what youth is all about? Reckless dreams, and the sense that you can do anything?"

"Aye, that it is." Mrs. Staples frowned. "I've had six children, and I know what you mean. I was even a young girl myself." She pulled at the carded wool until it formed a loose pile in her lap. "But you've got to survive your own recklessness . . . and I'd choose another man to be foolish about."

So, Agatha thought, would I. Ned Barnes didn't have any appeal at all; he was already most of the way to becoming a rather coarse drunkard; his voice was so loud, it was grating, and his eagerness to please—his overeagerness, rather—was evident nearly a room away.

No, if she could be a young girl again and choose her danger, her foolish dalliance, she would choose someone a little more like Daniel.

"Are you cold, dear?" Mrs. Staples asked, rising at once to her feet. "Wood's probably ash in the stove by now. Let me get Gill to add some more."

He came, of course. As an act in a play, she would have thought it entirely too foreshadowed. But she knew, somehow, as she waited in the inn in W——, that she would see him soon.

"Who is that young man by the fire, Mrs. Staples?"

"Another visitor," Mrs. Staples said primly. "Came last

night, and a bit on the late side, if you ask me. Looks like some sort of city person." Which was enough to condemn anyone. Still, it might be worse—she might have said "Londoner."

"Well," Agatha said a little apologetically, "*I* come from a city as well."

"Didn't spend all your life in one, I daresay."

"Not all, no. Will he be staying long, do you think?"

"And why would you want to know that?"

There wasn't a good reason. Especially not to ask Mrs. Staples, of all people. "I'm terribly sorry," Agatha said, although what she felt for the most part was simple annoyance. "It's just that you know so much about everyone, I've gotten used to asking you questions."

Pleased, Mrs. Staples nodded. "Well, then. Well. He'll probably be here for a week or two, at best guess. Not enough to disrupt anything, just enough to annoy the neighbours. Did you want to meet him?"

Agatha shrugged uncomfortably. "That isn't necessary. I daresay that we'll run into each other soon enough."

Daniel looked up at just that moment, and smiled softly over the edge of his paper.

"It took me a while to find you," he said as he unfolded his napkin and draped it across his lap. Dinner lay out in a rough but plentiful arrangement between them; Mrs. Staples was with her children, and there were no other travelers staying at the inn.

It was warm; Agatha felt the hint of a breeze at her neck. "Why did you look?" she asked at last.

He raised a brow. "Why do you think?" Before she could answer, he shook his head. "Don't play at games. It doesn't become your age, and it doesn't become you. You know why I came. We haven't finished our conversation yet."

She nodded, but once again she found the edge to his voice unpleasant. She almost pointed out the difference in their age, but subsided, knowing that it would make little difference to Daniel, and none of it positive.

"I'm happy to see you here, Miss Edens. I hope that there's much we can learn from each other." He raised a glass and held it up, the rim at eye level.

After a moment, she raised her own glass, although it contained nothing stronger than water. "Yes," she said, because she could think of nothing else to say. The glasses clinked, a cold little sound that trickled into silence.

She wore no wedding band, no jewelry, no sign at all of a previous life's mementos. Even the ring she'd been given by her mother counted as too much of a weight and an anchor to the past; it was gone. She stared at her hands in the lamplight; they were shaking.

Daniel didn't ask her if she was cold; he gave her no room in which to maintain her pretence of control or dignity. "Agatha, look at me."

But she'd already tried that, and had, at the last, been forced to look away as he'd carelessly let his dressing gown drop to the floor. She'd reached for the lamp, but he'd stopped her.

"Why," he asked as he crossed the length of the room, "should there be anything hidden between us? What are you afraid of? Look at me."

"I don't know if I want you to look at me that way," she said at last, meeting his eyes as if his eyes alone were safe.

He shrugged; she caught the movement of his shoulders at the periphery of her vision. "Agatha, it is your body, but I find you attractive. Does it matter? Before the end, there will be more between us than simple sight."

Her hands were still shaking as he caught them. "Only give me the word and I'll leave if that's what you wish."

She almost told him to go, the apprehension was that strong. The desire was stronger. "Can't we . . . can't we douse the lamp?"

He caught her shoulder with his left hand, the curve of

her jaw with his right. "You want the darkness, Agatha. I want the light." And he kissed her.

In the end, she won; the oil was low in the lamp.

"Do you feel any different?" he asked as they walked along the winding pathways behind the inn. The grounds were kept—or so Mrs. Staples claimed—by her husband, and there was even some sign that these footpaths were used. On occasion.

"Different?"

"You're an adulteress, my dear." He caught her suddenly and tilted her off balance. "A scarlet woman. You've deceived your husband for the sake of a passing young man. Do you feel any different?"

"Yes."

"Really? Are the fires of hell already burning for you?"

She laughed as she tried to right herself. "I don't care if they are!"

But later, she did think about his question. And aside from the sense of freedom, she felt very much like the same Agatha she had always been . . . if she had ever really known that person at all.

Although Daniel claimed not to be interested in subterfuge, he still insisted on discretion, and often left Agatha at the side of Mrs. Staples while he toured the countryside or went about his business. What exactly his business was, Agatha couldn't guess. She wasn't completely certain that she wanted to.

"You're looking better, dear," Mrs. Staples would say, and Agatha would smile demurely. And wonder.

He brought her a necklace first. It was a lovely piece of jewelry, with heavy gold knots and a golden-petaled flower with a heart of ruby. Each of the twenty knots had a diamond at its centre, and the clasp was itself a small miracle of craftsmanship. He slid it around her neck and fiddled with the clasp at her nape, letting the flower dangle between her breasts. It was cold.

"Where did you get this?" she asked, barely whispering, not even daring to touch it.

"You'll hear about it soon."

She looked at it as it nestled against her skin. "This was made for another woman," she said at last.

"So? It was taken for you. I think it perfect, although it's best not to wear it outside of this room." He smiled. "I imagine that its former owner will hardly miss it at all, and if she does, so much the better."

It was stolen of course, and word traveled around the county quite quickly. Mrs. Staples herself told Agatha the dreadful news.

"Yes, a robbery! I've heard that no one was injured, but Lady Feltham is beside herself."

"What was stolen?"

"Heirlooms," Mrs. Staples answered promptly. That she didn't expand on this meant that she didn't know more.

Agatha sat by the fire, rocking slowly and thoughtfully in her chair. She folded her bare hands in her lap and studied them.

It was on a night that Daniel was away from the inn, some several days later, that she encountered Ned Barnes. Or rather, that he stumbled over her. Mr. Staples, out in the pub, had clearly served Ned a little bit too much—or not enough.

"What can I do for you, Ned?" Mrs. Staples asked in a no-nonsense tone of voice. "You aren't allowed back here. This isn't a place for the men."

Ned nodded sagely. "Know it well, Mrs. Staples. But I wanted to take a gander at the guest you been hiding." He sauntered over the threshold.

Mrs. Staple's forehead developed a few lines that had been used so seldom, they weren't etched in permanently. "Ned Barnes," she said, her tone warming, her eyes narrowing. She set aside her wool and needles. "Get out of here right now, before we both do something we'll regret."

Ned took a step back; Agatha thought the danger had passed. But alcohol has its own hold on a man, and before Mrs. Staples' words had driven him back, he staggered into the arch.

"Damned if I will," he muttered. Mrs. Staples tried to interpose herself between Ned and Miss Edens; Ned merely pushed her aside. Force of personality, although it counted for most things, didn't make up for all.

Agatha sat, almost spellbound, in her chair as Mr. Barnes approached. She could smell his breath long before he reached her and bent over her stilled chair.

"May I help you?" she asked in as stiff and cold a voice as she had ever used.

"Maybe," was the mumbled reply. He reached out; she struggled with herself, forcing stillness and heavy silence over her sudden panic. Although she had, once or twice in her career, written of leering men, she had never actually seen the expression until now. The words would never have the same pale meaning again.

He caught both of her shoulders in his hands and hauled her to her feet. In the distance, Agatha could hear Mrs. Staples shouting something. Names, perhaps; the syllables didn't have the texture that words normally did. She saw his face move toward hers, still bearing that upward turn of lips, that ugly expression. And then it stopped. He squinted, frowned, and let her go.

Mrs. Staples continued to shout, but the only thing that Agatha heard were Ned Barnes' words.

"Ah . . . you're old."

Daniel knew. Although she mentioned nothing at first, he knew. She had never met a man like him; only women had ever been so sensitive to her pain—and women were usually in no position to do anything at all about it. He held her, in the flickering light and the darkness of late evening, and his arms were like iron bands, but warmer, softer. Safer.

"What shall we do about Mr. Barnes, Agatha?"

He meant it; she knew it. A thousand fantasies and dream fragments skittered past her lips before she could utter them. In the end, she offered him silence.

"Leave it to me, then. This is a new life, Agatha. You need never feel helpless again." He rose; she felt his absence as the cooling of skin. "But promise me that you'll learn from what I do. This is experience that few will ever have."

Mrs. Staples was quite apologetic the next morning; she offered Miss Edens tea and the solace of friendly company. "It's these men," she ventured at last. "What can you do about them?"

"Nothing," Agatha said softly.

"He'll do something violent one day," Mrs. Staples continued. "Mark my words. He won't have a peaceful death, and he won't deserve one."

It was four days later that Agatha first heard word. It was Mrs. Staples—it seemed that it was always Mrs. Staples—who told her the news. "I don't know if you've heard it yet, Miss Edens. The news, I mean."

"News? No, I don't believe I have. Is it something terribly bad? You're very pale."

"Nothing like this has ever happened before. Not here, not in my time."

Agatha leaned forward in her chair and caught the older woman's hand firmly in her own. "What's happened, Mrs. Staples?"

"But we've got him," Mrs. Staples said, and at this, her voice became steel. "And he'll hang for it."

"Hang for what? Mrs. Staples, please . . . what are you talking about?"

"Young Anne Netterson's been killed, and it was Ned Barnes that killed her. She told her younger brother that she was off to see him, and no one saw her again. Not alive." Mrs. Staples looked very old and very tired; for the morning, the fire and knowing glee had gone out of her gossip. "But it's safe to stay here, dear. You don't have to worry anymore."

Agatha rose quietly. "Thank you, Mrs. Staples. Where is Ned Barnes being kept?"

"In town, dear."

She didn't know what had brought her to Ned Barnes. She was numb enough that she wasn't certain if she wanted to gloat, to satisfy some prurient interest, or to talk with him at length. It hadn't been easy to gain access to him, and to do so, she'd had to traverse the angry crowd that milled outside the solid building with barred windows. But she had to come; that much she knew clearly.

The young guard who let her inside didn't understand it either, and he certainly wasn't going to grant them any privacy. She didn't object to his presence; she thought she might take comfort from it, until she gazed, at last, on the face of Ned Barnes. It was a broken face, both in spirit and in the meaner, physical sense of the word; one eye was completely swollen, and the blackened bruise at his jaw was the worst she had ever seen.

"Mr. Barnes?"

He looked up quickly and made to rise; the sound of metal scratching metal told her that the move was futile. "Ma'am." Without alcohol to line his words, he was meek. "Do I know you?"

"I . . . I write a bit, Mr. Barnes. Not for the papers, no. But I've . . . I've published a work or two." She hadn't meant to say even that much of the truth, but she couldn't hold it back. *You're old*, he'd said, and it had stung. It didn't hurt now.

He brightened in a slow, heavy sort of way. "Published? Books, you mean?" When she nodded, his eyes lightened again, and his lips worked around his broken jaw to offer a smile. "What about?"

"Crime," she said quietly. She saw him stiffen; started to reach out, and then let her hand fall back into her lap. "Mr. Barnes . . . you don't have to answer me, but I have to ask why. Why did you kill Anne Netterson?"

Ned Barnes shook his head from side to side, once again slowly, dully. But he met her eyes squarely, and he didn't flinch at all. "I didn't, ma'am. I swear, I didn't kill her."

Agatha swallowed; the walls of her throat clung together. "You . . . you realize that you'll stand trial for her death?"

He nodded. "But I didn't do it. The truth'll come out." He struggled to believe it. She didn't have the heart to do anything but offer comfort.

"Ned," she said, and this time, before the guard could move to stop her, she placed a hand very gently on his shoulder. "I believe you. I'm certain that you didn't kill Anne."

She thought it couldn't get any worse than being here in front of this beaten, rather slow man; she was wrong. The minute the words left her lips, he started to cry at the benediction of finally being believed.

Agatha left the prison, left the angry crowd that she knew to be barely held in check, and began to walk in deliberate isolation through the streets of the near-deserted town.

"Well, Agatha?" Daniel offered her his arm. He wore a dark suit, with a perfectly pressed shirt and a single lapel flower. As if he were going to the theatre. "Mrs. Staples said you went into town today."

She took his arm almost cautiously. "Where are we going, Daniel?"

"Into town—or rather, just outside of it. I have a feeling that a drama is about to be played out to its proper conclusion." He smiled gently. "As I promised, Agatha, all has been taken care of. You *will* come, won't you?" His hand pressed into hers tightly. It relaxed only when she nodded.

"He's innocent, isn't he?"

"Of course he is. Don't be naive."

She'd known that that would be his answer. Known it, and felt no shock at the edge in his voice. "I thought so," she said quietly. "I couldn't have done this, Daniel."

"No. But I could have. This is crime, Agatha, on a very refined level. For I am killing Ned Barnes tonight without raising a finger, and no one will even think to stop me." He smiled; the sun was a semicircle of reddish light that gave little warmth. "Do you understand it?"

"No." She took a breath, then another, deeper one. "He's really very pathetic, Daniel."

"Of course he is. He's going to die for a crime that only three people in the world know he didn't commit. He'll die with no belief in justice, no faith in his god, probably no faith in the quality of his own innocence. That's what makes his death interesting. This—this is something that you might play at, pretend at—but Agatha, *you've* talked to an unjustly condemned man in a very real way. You know what almost no one else will ever know." He bent down and brushed her lips with his; he was tender.

They stood on the inner recline of the hill that led to the commons. It was darker now, and the air was chilly—but she could clearly see and hear the people that gathered below. Neither she nor Daniel used the lamps that they carried; they had no need for them; torches and lamps in plenty illuminated the great tree and the drama that struggled to fruition beneath it. Shouts wafted up on the wind, but the words themselves, while hostile, were indistinct.

"Look at him," Daniel said, and the contempt in his voice was clear. "He's almost too stupid to understand what's going to happen. Is he crying, Agatha? I can't make it out. Do you think he's suffering enough?"

"Enough, yes." She had told Daniel about Ned Barnes

and his drunken unpleasantness. She'd wanted the power to hurt him back, hadn't she? The ring of light surged in and out; she could clearly see Ned struggling, and if she closed her eyes, she could see the trail of his tears. *He isn't guilty.* Movement was denied her; frozen, she watched in fascination. What was guilty? What was innocent? She didn't know anymore. But surely, if he were innocent, if he weren't guilty of some other crime, some other offence—

—his body fell, heavily, from the high tree branch. He dangled, kicking, struggling to free his hands. They were laughing, some of his executioners, and some turning for home. One lone voice suddenly bellowed, loudly and clearly into the dark, damp air:

"Justice is done!"

Daniel began to chuckle. "Justice, indeed. This is the justice that we choose to make, Agatha. Come; there's really nothing left to see." He bent down to retrieve his lamp.

"Daniel?"

"Yes?"

"You killed Anne, didn't you?"

"Yes."

"Why? She'd done nothing to harm us."

"Why? Agatha, did you see nothing at all that happened this evening?" He was annoyed. "How else were we to permanently put Ned Barnes in his place?"

"We could have killed him ourselves, if it came to that."

"I didn't judge you ready for it." Daniel's reply was curt. "You couldn't have killed Anne."

"Not as you did, no."

"No other way would have sufficed. You aren't jealous of it, are you?"

She was silent again. In the darkness, Daniel began to fumble for light, for a way to strike the lamp's wick with fire. His breast pocket was empty. He reached into his vest pocket when the lights came on, in her hands. Her face was pale, pained.

"Agatha—"

"I have learned a lot from you, Daniel. You were right. I knew nothing at all about the criminal mind, the criminal motivation. Everything was neat and orderly; everything was clean. Now I think I understand some of it, but some of it I will never, ever, understand."

"That's it, then?" The lines of his face grew taut. "You give me this, but no more? You wish to stop, having come this far?" He laughed, and the laugh was wild. "Do you think that's even possible?"

"Yes," she said simply. "Because I *have* learned something." It hurt to see the surprise spread across Daniel's face, because she knew that she couldn't afford to hesitate, and there was so much more that she might have said had she the time.

Killing a man wasn't so hard after all.

Amnesia was what she called it. Inability to remember. Things were blurred, fuzzy. She was perhaps a little cold, and perhaps a little run-down; she was tired, and needed some bed rest and seclusion. But her home was waiting for her when she returned, and with a little effort, she could remember that it was what it had always been.

She wrote.

Not right away, of course, and never with the conviction and the truth that she had been ridiculed for avoiding. There was no crime that was ever committed that was unresolved, no truth that was ever too hard to reach; she didn't believe it, but she struggled to make her readers believe it. Beliefs, after all, defined a person, didn't they? And if they were strong enough, sure enough, they might pass into truth at last.

This silence was hers to choose.

This hope was her only hope.

Gregory Feeley has mastered just about every art connected with writing in this field: he's a fine novelist, a superb short-story writer, and an eloquent and controversial critic.

He's also a very thorough historian with a wry sense of humor, as this little tale of artistic accommodation makes clear. . . .

My Tongue in Thy Tale
by Gregory Feeley

"Nay, but this pottage of our masters o'erflows the measure," said the lawyer's secretary in an undertone.

Lyly regarded him superciliously. "It is always a pleasure to see servants well fed," he said.

" 'Twas a *rhetorical figure*," the young man (he was barely down from Cambridge) replied, as if to a fool. He raised the shiny back of his spoon, as though holding up a mirror to ill-nature. "Our masters sup copiously, converting the meat and drink of this table into fat; just as the meat and drink of this table's wit become the fat that shall light the lamp of later plays. But if our masters overmuch consume, the result to their noble persons is but blocked bowels and black bile."

Lyly thought the whelp smelled of the lamp already, but was more concerned with his impudence; although his master it was who had the fatty name, 'twas Lyly's own who was consuming to excess this day, as all at table saw plain. Moreover, the implication that the younger (and not noble) master presumed to write plays, even as Lyly's did, was not to be borne. As much to hear that the whelp dared, like Lyly, to write plays himself.

"Over-consuming is the very *bacon* of presumption," he

said maliciously, "as the lesser man seeks to bring great-
ness into himself."

The redheaded young man smiled. "Then he must take
care not to eat his way into an early grave, making himself
instead a meal *du vers*: of worms."

As though sensing that his champion had been bested,
Edward de Vere, the seventeenth Earl of Oxford, rose from
his place farther up the table and made for the jakes. Passing the disputing secretaries without a glance, he reached
the place where Francis Bacon, sitting back from dinner at
his ease, nibbled the gravy caught beneath his thumbnail.

Oxford stopped dead. "Do you bite your thumb at me,
sir?"

Bacon glanced up. "I do bite my thumb, sir," he said
carelessly.

"Do you bite your thumb at *me*, sir?" Oxford repeated
in a dangerous tone.

Bacon produced his dagger and began cleaning his
nails. People around them fell silent. "No, sir," he said after a moment, "I do not bite my thumb at *you*, sir; but I
bite my thumb, sir."

"Dost thou play with me, clerk?" the earl demanded.

Bacon raised an eyebrow. "I have no wish to touch on
your sense of play, my lord," he answered urbanely. Several diners laughed. In an hour, the earl's new play would
be presented in this very hall, and Oxford was known to
be proud.

With a slap, Bacon's dagger flew from his hand. A cry
rose from the table, and men leaped to their feet. Oxford,
reaching for his own dagger, was restrained; Bacon sat
motionless, as though bemused by the red line that appeared across his thumb. Lady Southampton, their host-
ess, was calling from the table's head to know what was
the matter.

Slowly Bacon stood and looked the glaring earl in the
face. "Incontinent spiller of ink and others' blood," he
said, coldly furious. "You shall botch your fortunes as
readily as your pages. Think you this outrage will be for-

got as quickly as your plays?" Men were pulling them apart, preventing further jibes even as Bacon began to feel the full rush of his anger. His secretary was at his side, urging him away.

"Like man, like master," the younger man said. "Ill behavior for a distant kinsman, would you not say?"

"More than kin, and less than kind," said Bacon absently. Then he added, "Write that down."

Bacon, surprised at his anger, swore revenge.

Oxford would be presenting another play two months hence, one of his puling adaptations of the antique Romans, called *A Comity of Error*. Bacon bribed a player to show him the script, which proved to be an undistinguished translation of the *Menaechmi*, set in an Ephesus that sounded like Brussels. Bacon dug a few more coppers from his purse.

"You could for a need study additions of some dozen or sixteen pages which I would set down and insert in't, could you not?" he asked the player.

The rogue wrinkled his pox-raddled nose. "Aye, my lord."

Bacon sat down to out-plautus Plautus. He doubled the pair of twins, adding recomplications as they happily proposed themselves. Lest Oxford miss his meaning, Bacon permitted himself some sportive play. "Why, mistress, sure my master is horn-mad." "Horn-mad, thou villain!" "O aye, for another's pen has dipped between thy sheets and laid a cuckoo's egg in thy barren nest."

The play, Bacon knew, was to be performed at the house of Lord Burghley, Oxford's cousin and his own, so he made sure to secure an invitation. The earl smirked at him across the table, anticipating a brilliant reception for his feeble piece. When the guests gathered around the stage, Bacon sat where he could watch Oxford's expression. His lordship blinked and scowled when the play's redoubled title was announced; and when Egeon's verbose opening speech told of two sets of twins, he began to fidget. When

the second Dromio made his entrance, the earl started as
though he saw his father's ghost, and made to rise. Yet the
audience's laughter stopped him and, confounded, he sat
fuming.

Watching the author rather than his play, Bacon enjoyed
a rare comedy. When Doctor Pinch proclaimed, "Both
man and master is possessed; I know it by their pale and
deadly looks," Oxford cast his pale and deadly look across
the audience and fixed upon Bacon. The clerk smiled.

Such insult was not to be borne. When her ladyship's
guests rose to applaud, then (as the players swept off their
hats toward him) turned to laud the playwright, Oxford
saw Bacon stand grinning, clapping as lustily as the rest.
Thy mistress cries with pleasure, his expression said, *but
not at thy exertions.*

Of course he vowed revenge. Bacon was poor, and
sought preferment, which Oxford arranged he would not
get. When, some months later, Oxford heard that the penniless member of Parliament thought to repair his fortunes by writing a play, it took but the simplest of efforts
to secure its sole copy, something called *The Roman's Trag-
edy.* Oxford considered burning it, then bethought a more
refined avengement. Perusing its juvenile pages—Bacon
evidently meant to wed Seneca's matter to Lyly's style—he
had an inspiration. Putting pen to ink, Oxford bloodied
Bacon's clerkly script with emendations, but not so bloody
as he made the play itself, a monstrous compound of *Thy-
estes,* Thomas Kyd, and the kind of spectacle that draws
crowds to gibbets. Let Bacon put a pretty speech in
Lavinia's mouth, would he? Oxford cut away the speech
along with Lavinia's tongue. Then, remembering that she
later implicates her attackers in proper Latin (thinks Bacon only lawyers know that tongue?), Oxford had her
hands cut off as well and let her scrawl her sweet speech
in the dust, holding in her mouth a stick pushed with her
stumps.

Taking a wherry to Bankside, Oxford asked in taverns

until he found a player. Pockmarked, with an obsequious manner and an atrocious Cotswolds accent, William Shaxpere accepted the manuscript and assured Oxford that he would see it produced. Oxford doubted it not. When, a month later, one of his spies reported seeing a handbill for *The Tragedie of Titus Andronicus*, Oxford had it sent to Bacon's offices. The next day, the spy reported, Bacon crossed the river to see the play, and emerged quite pale.

Oxford took pains to ensure that Bacon was not among the company present to see his comedy *The Gentleman of Verona* produced by Oxford's Men at Court; but his scrivener later reported that a troupe of common players had lately performed something called *The Two Gentlemen of Verona* across the river. In a rage, Oxford dispatched him to report on this, and presently learned that it was a travesty of his own pleasant piece, with two lovers instead of one, more silly stage business with disguises, and an added line—"Why then, my horns are his horns"—that made clear he was pen-pricked once more.

"Where got he that script?" Oxford demanded of his secretary.

Lyly shrugged. Several copies had been made for the Court performance, and it was impossible now to learn how one went astray. Oxford's spy reported, however, that the play had been given to the Bankside company by one Christopher Marlowe, a Cambridge scholar with ties to Sir Francis Walsingham. Bacon knew Walsingham, Oxford remembered, and had doubtless used this connection to secure an operative.

He had Bacon's law offices searched regularly, and that summer his spies turned up another playscript, dealing with the contention 'twixt Lancaster and York. "Hoping to worm back into Her Majesty's favor?" Oxford snarled. It was a poor play, so he contented himself with adding a derisive line about killing all the lawyers. Let Bacon burn his ears on that.

When Oxford later heard that the *Contention* was a

great success, he threw his inkpot at his spy, then retrieved it and set about to write a sequel. A much better
play, it also contained a scene featuring Oxford's ancestor,
the fourteenth Earl. Placing such a signature to his canvas
(thought Oxford complacently) would not escape Bacon's
notice.

Balked at writing his own sequel, Bacon instead
marched backward, producing a third play on the early
reign of Henry VI. "Cunning bastard," Oxford growled. He
was not greatly discomfited, however, as he was busy placing the final touches on *Love's Labours Lost*, which would
grace Elizabeth's Court while Bacon's works played before
merchants and groundlings. Taking a lesson from Bacon's
demonstrations of the dramatic potentials of twins, Oxford put two gentleman scholars, and a corresponding pair
of maids in waiting, into his toyscape kingdom of Navarre.
When he sat, swollen with pride, at the play's premier performance and found *three* young lords come onstage, he
fell frothing to the floor and had to be bled severely.

"Who was it?" he raged to his retainers from his sick-
bed. "Marlowe again, suborning my players? Have him
killed."

Directly he was recovered, Oxford had Bacon's private
chambers turned upside down and every scrap of verse
brought back to him. The sketch of a play about King
John, another sequel (Richard III, made a villain to please
Tudor tastes), and some bit of nonsense about a troupe of
mechanicals producing a masque for the wedding of the
Duke of Athens. Oxford summoned Will Shaxpere and let
the trembling bumpkin leaf through them. "Can any of
these pieces command the common stage?" he asked.
"Suitably amended, of course."

Shaxpere stuttered that he would be happy to take all of
them to the Bankside companies, but could say nothing as
to the poems. "Eh?" said Oxford. "What poems?" The
player passed over a sheaf the earl had not noticed, which
proved to be a series of Italianate sonnets touching on

matters Oxford immediately perceived as personal. "Get out," he said, leaning forward to study more closely.

Reading sonnets was like munching chestnuts, Oxford soon discovered: it was difficult to consume just one. Some two dozen were addressed in admiration to an older woman, a dark-haired virgin whom Bacon praised fulsomely despite a conviction that he had been treated ill. Was Bacon now writing begging letters in verse? Oxford cut a fresh nib and set about correcting, enflaming the passions expressed (sonnets were not for Platonic sentiments), and playing up the poet's sense of grievance and repeated remarks on his lady's lack of beauty. She must have treated him roughly, Oxford thought with a smile. On a whim, he changed her hair color to red, which better suited some nice imagery with roses and blood.

Off these verses went, to be circulated privately by those in Court who could appreciate what Oxford had fathered on the pale clerk.

"Now I could drink hot blood," cried Bacon when he discovered this. The image disgusted him, but it sounded good. Courtiers smiled when he came to Court, remarked on his sugared verses. What had Oxford done to his sweet sonnets before setting them loose in the world?

Oxford didn't pause to bask in his victory. He was working on a new play—something about a drunkard, perhaps to be modeled on Bacon, who falls asleep in the street and is taken up and elaborately hoaxed by a clever nobleman—when his late-night labors were interrupted by heavy fists pounding at his door. Before Oxford could rise, the door flew open and bailiffs of the queen burst in.

"Your lordship, you are wanted," declared the sergeant as Oxford rose in alarm. He was hastened into a waiting coach and driven through the night, toward what— Westminster Hall? The Tower? It was a back courtyard to Whitehall where the carriage drew up, and Oxford was conducted to a receiving room he did not know.

Ten minutes later, Bacon was thrust in after him, disheveled and frightened. They were still staring at each other in growing surmise when Her Majesty entered the room.

"What is this nonsense now?" she demanded as the men made hasty bows. "One of our best spies dead, tales of purloined playscripts, and now, *this*—" In her hand she held a batch of papers, which she smacked pettishly against a tabletop. "We told thee to change the hair color!" she cried at Bacon.

Both Bacon and Oxford paled.

"We perceive thy hand in this somewhere, Oxford," she said, rounding on the earl. "These intrigues will cease. Nay—" she interrupted as the two men began to speak —"we shall not listen. The theatres shall close this summer if the plague does not abate, and we will not abide these quarrels spilling into Court. Mend your strife presently, or face my displeasure."

"Yes, Your Majesty," they said together.

She made as if to go, then turned back. "We shall have a play at the coming nuptials of the Earl of Derby and Lady Vere," she said. "She is cousin to you both, we believe." The two men nodded. "Oxford, have you any idea for such a piece?"

"I had thought, Your Majesty," began Oxford carefully, "of a pleasant comedy dealing with the King and Queen of Faerie."

Elizabeth nodded. "And you, Mr. Bacon?"

"Your Majesty, I have already begun a comedy dealing with a band of mechanicals who perform before a wedding." Oxford made a noise, but Bacon seemed not to notice.

"Well, put your heads together." Without another word, Elizabeth turned and left them.

The two men regarded each other warily.

"Are you truly going to write about those mechanicals?" asked Oxford.

"Are you truly going to keep my manuscript?"

"I'll send it back."

There was a pause. "I would fain write the play for my kinswoman's nuptials," said Oxford.

"As would I."

"Perhaps both strategems could be incorporated," Oxford said uncertainly.

"Perhaps." Bacon looked doleful. "You killed my agent."

Oxford shrugged. "We can use that Shaxpere fellow. No one will ever guess."

They headed for the door. Oxford attempted to bow Bacon through, but the younger man insisted.

"It is not meet that we tilt against each other," he said. "Life is too short. We are such stuff as creams are made of, and need must fear the heat o' the sun."

"That line needs work," said Oxford.

"True, cousin," said Bacon. "But we shall work on't. This thing may be bigger than both of us. . . ."

Alan Rodgers and James D. Macdonald have collaborated only once before (for *Alternate Kennedys*), but individually each has more than made his mark on the science fiction and horror fields. Alan is the author of *Fire*, *Night*, and *Blood of the Children*, among others; and James, in collaboration with his wife, Debra Doyle, has sold more than a dozen novels, including the popular *Mageworlds* series.

Here they present an alternate view of exactly what John F. Kennedy meant when he urged us not to ask what our country could do for us, but rather, what we could do for our country.

Souvenirs
by Alan Rodgers and
James D. Macdonald

The room is dark.

Deliberately dark.

The only lamp here shines into the suspect's face—to intimidate him.

To unsettle him.

It fails in this. The suspect is cool, relaxed. Collected. He looks like a man who knows his fate, and rests at peace with it.

Perhaps he does.

His questioners, by contrast, stand uneasily above him. The tall one—Lieutenant H.M. Ruxpin, a broad-shouldered man with a deep, sonorous voice and a face like a toad's—the tall one looks a little nervous. Ruxpin has spent the last fifteen years of his life working for the

Dallas police. Three weeks from now he'll decide he's misspent his career, hand in his badge, and join his brother-in-law in the construction business. It will be a good move for him. He'll make a lot more as a subcontractor than he could ever hope to see working for the Dallas police.

His partner's future isn't nearly so bright. Detective R.V. Blaine's three-packs-a-day cigarette habit has already caught up with him—he just doesn't realize it yet. Cancer even now has begun to bloom inside his lungs. Two days after his partner resigns, Blaine will see a doctor about his shortness of breath, the way he's been losing weight without meaning to—and the doctor will discover the disease that consumes him.

Blaine will die long months before the Surgeon General puts his first warning onto a package of cigarettes.

But it isn't the cancer that makes Blaine nervous tonight. It's the suspect that makes him uncomfortable—the suspect and the monumental nature of his crime.

Ruxpin hits the switch, and the tape recorder begins to roll.

There's something wrong with one of the machine's spindles. Not very wrong, just wrong enough that the damnable thing makes this quiet, persistent *hiss* as it records—a softly ugly scratching sound that rattles Blaine's nerves when he listens to it too closely. He tries to ignore it, but hard as he tries, the noise finds him.

It never lets go.

"It's rolling?" Ruxpin asks, which is kind of pointless, since he's the one who turned the damned thing on. Just like Ruxpin, Blaine thinks: pointless. No goddamned point at all.

Blaine grunts in response. "Yeah, it's on." His voice is thin and reedy, so rhuemy he can hear the wrongness himself.

Ruxpin speaks into the microphone. "Okay, it's fifteen forty-five on November twenty-second, nineteen sixty-three. Present are Lieutenant Ruxpin and Detective Blaine."

Ruxpin's beginning to sweat now, too, Blaine notices. Well, good for him. Blaine's been sweating for hours, almost since they got the call assigning them to interrogate the . . . suspect.

But nothing rattles the *suspect*. "You want to turn that off," he says. He gives a little laugh.

Ruxpin answers defensively. "It's standard procedure," he says. Blaine can tell he'd like to turn the damned thing off, but there's no way—neither one of them would dare.

"You don't want this on tape," the suspect says. "Trust me."

"Who are you?" Blaine asks. Petulantly. And coughs.

The suspect reaches forward, tries to cover the microphone. That never works, of course. The microphone is a sensitive one, selected deliberately to record even when someone tries to mask it.

"Look," the suspect says, "don't tape this."

Blaine grabs the suspect's wrist. Lifts his hand off the microphone.

"Just answer the question."

"Okay." The suspect clears his throat. "Your funeral. You got my wallet. What did the ID say?"

"We're asking the questions here," Ruxpin snaps. "Quit screwing around."

"You want the truth?"

Ruxpin laughs derisively. "No," he says. "We want you to lie to us." And laughs some more. "Save us all some time, buddy. Give us your name."

The suspect laughs his little laugh again. "There won't be a record."

Ruxpin is exasperated, angry. He looks like he's about ready to hit the guy. "You want to do this the easy way or the hard way?" he asks. There's a threat in his voice. He doesn't try to veil it.

"Any way you want it. The ID you have says my name is Oswald. Lee Oswald."

Ruxpin stands very, very close and looks the suspect in the eye. "Is that your name?"

"Did you search my apartment yet?"

"Is that your real name?"

The suspect leans back in his chair. Looks away from Ruxpin. "Behind the couch there's a manila folder. It has some papers and photos in it. You want to bring it here. There's a black binder, too. You want it."

"Why do we want to bring them here?" Blaine asks. He isn't sure what this guy's game is about, but every moment that goes by, it makes him a little more uneasy.

Ruxpin's feeling it, too. "Goddamnit, tell me your real name."

The suspect chuckles.

Again.

Every time he does that, Blaine feels like someone hits him in the gut.

What Blaine needs, he decides, is a drink. Whiskey, maybe. Warm and neat.

"I have to tell you what the papers are and what they show. You'll want to have your stories straight."

Blaine reaches into the dark part of the room. Retrieves the folder.

Shows it to the suspect.

"Is this the folder you're talking about?"

"Yeah, that's it." The suspect smiles. He spends a moment staring at the folder, thinking. "First thing you'll want," he says, "is to get in touch with the Russian girl—the one who lives in Irvine. Yes, that's it, that's her address. She's set to back up my story. She'll claim she took these photos last April. That it's really me in the pictures, that she was married to me. She's set. You'll want to put her in PC right away."

Ruxpin looks at him—skeptically almost. The expression looks nearly comical on his amphibial face. He holds up a photo. "Okay, what are these? What are we looking at here?"

"Those are photos of me holding a rifle, wearing a handgun, carrying a Commie paper."

He laughs when he says the word "Commie," but Blaine can't imagine what it is about the word that makes him laugh.

Ruxpin doesn't even notice.

"What's this?" Ruxpin asks, opening the folder to reveal a slip of paper covered with handwriting as illegible as chicken scrawls.

"An order form. It shows that I bought the rifle by mail," the suspect says. "Any slugs you recover from the President are going to come from that rifle."

Blaine takes the folder from Ruxpin. Fishes out both of the suspect's sets of identification papers. Shows them to the man. "You've got two IDs here," he says. He looks the man in the eye, tries to measure his reaction. "What's your real name?"

"You got the Oswald ID and you got the Hidell ID." The suspect sounds impatient. "What else do you need?"

Whatever it is in the man's eyes when he says that, Blaine can't make sense of it. No sense at all.

"We're running your prints," Blaine says. This is supposed to be a threat, a warning: *Don't try anything fancy; we'll get the lowdown on you soon enough, no matter what.* But the threat falls flat.

Doesn't intimidate the suspect for a moment.

"They're going to come back Oswald, Lee H.," he says. And *smiles* again.

"Is that your name?" Ruxpin asks.

And something breaks.

Maybe it's the suspect's will—or maybe it's his patience.

He sighs, exasperated, and swears under his breath. "Look," he says, "if I level with you, will you do what you have to do? For the good of the country?"

Blaine shifts uncomfortably on his feet.

Something is wrong here. Very, very wrong.

Blaine tries not to be scared. He really does. "We're going to find out who you are and what you did." He says it real tough, like he means it.

Ruxpin loses his cool.

Not smart.

"Who the *hell* are you?"

The suspect laughs again. He's giddy, punch-drunk—Blaine's seen men act like that before.

Men whose lives had stopped mattering, even to themselves.

Dangerous men.

"Look," the suspect says, "I'm making your case for you. You've got all the proof you need right there. You're going to find a palm print on that rifle. There's going to be a match with the bullets. I'm going to stand up in court and say I did it. What else do you want from me?"

"We want the truth," Ruxpin says. And Blaine wishes for the life of him that the man would just for once *shut up*!

"My name is Lee Harvey Oswald. I'm a detective lieutenant with the Metro DC Police Department. That's the truth."

Ruxpin doesn't want to hear it. "Don't lie to us," he says.

"I'm telling you the truth," he says. He looks away, into the dark. "The only way we can make this work is by having you get with the program."

"Tell your story," Blaine says. He's angry, really angry—so angry that he can hear the rage in his own raspy voice even as he tries to stay calm. "But if you're just blowing smoke, you're going to regret it."

"I wouldn't—I'm not—listen." He stops. "You know about that series of murders we've had in DC?"

"Tell us about them."

"You've got a request for aid out of DC, dated April fourth, nineteen sixty-one. And another dated August sixteenth, same year. Then one dated January fifth in sixty-two, and July twelfth and eighteenth, same year. And May third, nineteen sixty-three."

"Suppose we do," Ruxpin says. "What about them?"

The suspect hesitates. "That's a series of murders. Real nasty ones. Girls. Young, good-looking girls. Cut up real bad."

"Are you confessing to those murders?" Ruxpin asks. The question is dumb, it's obvious, it's necessary—there's no way they could avoid asking it. Just the kind of question Ruxpin always asks, Blaine thinks: inevitable and stupid.

He's heard a lot of those questions over the years, Blaine has.

"No," the suspect says. He swears again. "Listen to me, damn it. I know who was doing them."

In spite of himself, Blaine wants to hear more. "Go on," he says. And regrets it almost immediately.

"There are some killers," the man who may and may not be Lee Harvey Oswald says, "who kill over and over again. For fun. They get their . . . *satisfaction* that way. The man we were tracking was like that. Sick. Despicable." He flinches, looks away. "One of those twisted bastards who carve *souvenirs* out of the hides of their victims."

Blaine worked one case like that. He has his memories, memories that give him nightmares. When he listens to the suspect, he gets the feeling he's remembering something he shouldn't ever think about, even if he has to.

But it isn't like he has a choice.

"It was my case," the suspect continues. "They were hookers at first. Then decent girls who were at the wrong place at the wrong time. And then came the senator's daughter. And the Luchese girl, the sweet little sixteen-year-old kid with uncles in the mob." He pauses, weighing his words. "You know what I'm talking about?"

Ruxpin isn't ever going to get it. Blaine can see that written all over his face. Can see how he doesn't get it about the assassination, about any of it. Ruxpin is stupid, that's all there is to it.

"Explain yourself," Ruxpin says. He grins a smug grin.

The suspect sighs. He's quick, that suspect; he's already

got Ruxpin pegged. Took Blaine weeks to figure out just how empty it was inside that head of his.

"Don't worry about it," the suspect says. And picks up where he left off. "We wore out a lot of shoe leather. Punching doorbells, talking to all the stoolies we had, running in every pervo and peeper in the District for questioning. We put wires anywhere we had half an excuse, going fishing. Nothing.

"Then we got our break. The last victim, the Luchese girl—she had a ponytail. Kept her hair tied back behind her head—pretty, shiny black hair. She really was a gorgeous little girl, that one. And like I said, our psycho was one of the ones . . . who took *souvenirs*." The suspect shudders. "This guy took *souvenirs*. Ears sometimes. Or ovaries. Other stuff. You don't want to hear."

He's sweating now. Like it hurts him, talking about it. Blaine understands.

"He took her hair. Her ponytail. Someone took her picture that night, three hours before she disappeared. I had the lab guys blow it up life-size. So big you could see the ribbon she tied it with. See it clearly. She bound it in a fancy knot—I don't remember what it's called, but I asked the lab about it. A hard knot to tie, an easy one to recognize.

"In the picture, she was laughing." He stops for a long time. "She looked so happy." Blaine wants him to stop for good, wants to put up a hand, tell him not to go on—he doesn't need to hear this, not today, not with the President's brains all over the backseat of the car. Not again, damn it.

"When we found her," the suspect says, "she didn't have a face."

Ruxpin is bright-eyed and chipper, taking notes like a schoolboy. "Go on," he says. Blaine wants to strangle him. He really really does.

"You know, there're only two ways these kind of sicko killers stop. One is they're in jail for the rest of their lives. The other is they're dead."

Ruxpin cocks an eyebrow at him. "And what does that mean, Lee?"

Oswald ignores the condescension. "One day I see a picture in the paper. And this guy has that same ribbon, with that same knot, lying there, just lying there on his desk.

"Right out in the open, and who cares if it shows up in a picture in the paper? Maybe he figured no one would know what it was. Maybe coincidence. Maybe he's getting careless. But all of a sudden, everything's fitting together. The dates. I look them up. I don't trust one of my assistants with that, I do it myself. And I find they were all on days he was in town, none on days when he was away. So I talk with some of my friends in the Secret Service and the SOG RA and we have a meeting."

"SOG RA?" Ruxpin asks.

As if he doesn't know.

"Seat of Government Resident Agent. The FBI, the Feds—you know. We're sitting around a table in a secure room, and I'm looking at them, and they're looking at me. Talking about the killer, the senator's daughter. The Luchese girl with the pretty-pretty ribbon in her hair. And nobody says a name, nobody says a word about him. But we all know."

He stops. Closes his eyes, opens them. He's breathing irregularly. "The Secret Service guy is on the White House detail. He says, 'Sometimes he gets away from us. We always figured he was sneaking out to see a woman.'

"The FBI guy looks pale, kind of sick. Maybe we all look that way. He says, 'There was one that fit the same MO in Denver.' And I ask him whether he was there, but I know what he'll answer before I ask. He says, 'Yeah,' and then for a while, there's nothing any of us can say. After a minute, the Secret Service guy says, 'Let me call someone in McLean,' and he goes and dials a number, and we all sit there looking at each other, knowing that things are as bad as they can be, because there's only two ways these things end. And nobody is going to take this guy to trial.

After a while, the Company guy shows up, and we all shake hands, and he's got a folder, and it's from Interpol, and they're requesting assistance on some guy who cut up a hooker in Paris, and it's one of the days our perp was there. Same MO."

Blaine is shaky. He doesn't like it. At all. The suspect's got him . . . convinced. Almost. Convinced that he's really a cop, anyway.

"Go on," Ruxpin says, prompting the suspect.

The suspect shakes his head. He sounds tired. " 'All we need,' the Company man says, 'is to have some Politzei nail the President of the United States while he's slicing up some hooker in an alley in Berlin. That's it for the Free World. The Ruskies win.' We all laugh when he says the word *Ruskies*, but we know he's right. Scary right. The Secret Service guy says, 'So what do we do? We can't arrest him ourselves. We might as well hand everything to Khrushchev on a plate.' So I say, 'I'll take care of him myself. 'Cause I was a pretty good shot back in the Army . . .'

"Nobody liked that. Not at all. Some of them hated it, in fact. We argued for hours and hours. Some of them got loud and crazy and wouldn't give an inch . . . until I opened the evidence folder. The one with the photos in it. The Luchese girl with a skull where her face used to be. Pretty Betty Evans, daughter of the senior senator from New Hampshire, with her eyes gouged as wide as Orphan Annie's and her heart stuffed down her throat. Trapped there poking out of her pert little mouth because there wasn't room to get it all the way down into her.

"Three hookers bound together forever with ropes made out of their own guts."

Quiet again.

"You were in the Marines," Blaine says, "not the Army." He read that in the file as he prepped for the interrogation.

"Yeah, that's what the records say now. Wouldn't do us a lot of good if you went looking where I really was—you might run into someone who wasn't briefed on the legend. But here, look, all the paperwork is in the files, and there are a bunch of people who will swear they knew me in the Marines. You got a list there. And there are people who will swear they saw me handing out Commie literature in New Orleans. And there are people who will swear they saw me in Mexico City. We worked it all out that afternoon. We had the schedule. The Secret Service sets up the security. We could call on the Mob for help. That binder there, the black one, it has my whole history laid out for you. Just follow the script."

"Why?"

"You're going to do it out of patriotism. Listen. No one's perfect. Everyone makes a slip. He would've, too. Sooner or later—maybe real soon. He slips in Paris, in Denver—and then what? A coup d'etat? A war? Nukes, like the ones that almost went up after Berlin? Like Cuba?"

He pauses, waiting for someone to respond. But neither of them does.

"But what if a lone nut blows his head off? Everyone's shocked, but America goes on. I get life in Leavenworth or something. But so what? I'm only one damned cop. Better me than the whole damned country."

Ruxpin shakes his head. He's getting ready to do the bad-cop thing, Blaine thinks. Look at him, feeding his temper; look at his expression growing angrier and angrier—

"I need names," Ruxpin says, looking the suspect in the eye. "I need to, ah . . . to *verify* your story."

"I'm sorry, I can't do that."

Ruxpin grabs the suspect by his lapels. "Who, Oswald? Who at the FBI? Who in the Secret Service? I need names. Places, dates, people."

Oswald gives his little laugh. "You're crazy."

Ruxpin shakes him. "So why did *you* do it?" he asks. "Why you?"

The suspect looks defensive. "It was my case," he says. "A real man shoots his own dog."

A longer pause. Oswald speaks very slow, like he's tired. "Like *he* said: it was what I could do for my country. I couldn't let Jack the Ripper bring America down."

Brian Thomsen is currently the editor of TSR Books. Prior to that, he created the successful Questar science fiction line for Warner Books. Recently, however, Brian has donned his writer's cap more and more often, selling upward of a dozen stories in the past eighteen months.

When he asked me what the instructions were for this book, I told him, as I told everyone, that he could either take an outlaw and make him a hero, or take a hero and make him an outlaw. Evidently Brian had a hard time making up his mind, because he finally chose to do both.

Bigger Than U.S. Steel
by Brian M. Thomsen

THE CHAIRMAN IS DEAD

No. That doesn't quite cut it. The uninformed masses are liable to confuse him with Mao, and that would really get him spinning in his grave.

THE CHAIRMAN OF THE BUREAU IS DEAD

"The Chairman of the Bureau." That has a nice ring to it.

THE CHAIRMAN OF THE BUREAU IS DEAD

Meyer Lansky died yesterday at the age of seventy in his Arlington duplex after a long illness.

Born Meyer Suchowljansky on July 4, 1900, Lansky immigrated with his parents to the United States in 1911, settling in New York City's lower East side. Lansky became the family's legal name after a clerical error during the immigration process at Ellis Island.

Lansky left school at the age of fifteen to work as an assistant bookkeeper to the young entre-

preneur, Charles Luciano. Then, in 1918, he
joined the Justice Department, where he quickly
rose through the ranks. He was appointed acting
head of the newly formed Federal Bureau of Investigation and Internal Revenue, commonly
known as the FBIIR, in 1926, a post (later
dubbed "the Chairmanship") he held until his
death.

Lansky rose to fame through his dogged efforts to bring racketeers to justice by any means
possible. His efforts led to the imprisonment of
such infamous mobsters as Joseph P. "Honey
Fitz" Kennedy for tax evasion; Thomas E. Dewey
for criminal misconduct, jury tampering, and
conspiracy to defraud the American people (in
the famous 1945 Ballot Box scandal), and Joseph
P. McCarthy, eventually crippling organized
crime's legendary Irish Mob.

In collaboration with boyhood friend Benjamin Siegel (later named Secretary of Recreational
Commerce), Lansky aided in the repeal of Prohi-
bition, and the federalization of the alcohol
industry, and the legalization of organized gambling as a means of eliminating the national
debt. His efforts led to the establishment of the
Las Vegas Federal Complex, and the Batista
treaty with Cuba (which led to Vegas and Cuba
becoming the fiftieth and fifty-first states respec-
tively).

Under his administration, the FBIIR became
the first Federal agency to ever show a profit on
the scale of a Fortune Five Hundred corporation,
leading him to remark on one occasion about
the Bureau's financial stability that "We're bigger
than U.S. Steel."

Lansky is survived by his second wife, and his
brother. In lieu of flowers, contributions are be-

ing accepted in his name for the United Jewish
Appeal's Israeli Immigration fund.

For me, my feature entitled "The Chairman of the Bureau Is Dead" was just another assignment. Little did I realize that President Bonano would read it as his eulogy at
Lansky's funeral, as all of America watched on television.
Overnight I went from second-shift *Washington Post* feature writer to nationally syndicated columnist with a six-
figure contract with Trendwide Books for the authorized
biography of Meyer Lansky.

Over the next year and a half, I was treated like royalty,
with all of the FBIIR's records laid open for me. Former
associates of Lansky were made available for interviews at
the Government's expense (I was even flown to Alphonse
Capone's retirement retreat in Palermo for an exclusive interview with the revered father of American Twentieth-
century foreign policy), and miles of newsreel footage,
transcript, and other reference data were neatly catalogued
for my perusal.

Cost was no object.

I was told that nothing must stand in my way. Lansky's
life must be preserved for future historians, as befitted a
hero and great American of his stature.

Needless to say, the farther I dug, the more I became in
awe of the man.

I must become the Boswell to his Johnson, the
Sandburg to his Lincoln, the Plato to his Socrates.

The man was a saint, or so I thought as I finished my
first draft of the manuscript.

I was just about to ship the pages off to New York,
when all went black.

I came to somewhere over the southern United States.
I was sitting in an overstuffed easy chair that had to have
been specifically designed for this late-model luxury jet.
My head throbbed from where someone had played Sand-
man with my consciousness with a blackjack.

I was just about to take a closer look at my surroundings when a handsome, blond-haired, blue-eyed steward came down the aisle and handed me some aspirin and a glass of water.

"Hi, my name is Doug," said the young Adonis. "We should be landing in Florida shortly. Mr. Hoover apologizes for the rather brusque treatment you received, and awaits your arrival at his home."

Even in my grogginess, I recognized the name Hoover. Given the topic of my last two years of research, my host could only be one person.

I was on my way to an audience with former public-enemy number one, J. Edgar Hoover.

We set down about a half hour later on a remote Florida airstrip, where we were met by limousine for the fifteen-minute ride to the Hoover compound located in an isolated corner of Key West. This interim gave me more than enough time to recall what I knew about one of the most infamous figures of twentieth-century organized crime.

In all of Lansky's records, Hoover was always listed as the one who got away. Born in Washington, D.C. on New Year's Day, 1895, if I recalled correctly, Hoover rose to prominence in D.C. racketeering during the roaring twenties, taking control of the Capital Hill Gang in 1930 (later renamed "the G Men" for "gangster men" by underworld poet-laureate Walter Winchell), turning that ragtag group of street toughs into a finely oiled and organized machine of corruption, crime, and vice, blazing new trails of lawlessness as Lansky sought to legalize and control the former major profit centers of gambling, bootlegging, and prostitution. Despite frequent audits and ongoing investigation, Lansky was never able to prove Hoover guilty of any criminal activities.

Hoover remained director of the G Men until the nineteen sixties, when he retired to Florida after public disclosure of his homosexual affair with fellow mobster Roy Cohn incurred the disfavor of the other high-ranking Irish Catholic mobsters. If I remember correctly, it was one of Lansky's associates who broke the story about Hoover being "a little light in the loafers."

Knowing Lansky, however, retirement was a poor second to imprisonment, and Hoover's freedom was a thorn that stuck in the Chairman's side until his dying day.

This was definitely going to be an interview that my sponsors at the FBIIR never dreamed of.

Hoover was seated by the pool, a bearish figure of a man, clad in a terrycloth robe, admiring the crowds of young men frolicking in the sun and chlorine.

I was ushered to a chaise longue at his side, and advised to have a seat.

Hoover continued to watch the boys in silence. I began to wonder if the rumors were true, that he'd had a stroke, become enfeebled, a vegetable . . . but if that were so, why had I been called here?

After a few more minutes (that seemed like an eternity), the Director spoke. "It could have been me," he bellowed.

"Excuse me," I said, startled by the interruption of the silence.

"It's funny," he continued, never acknowledging my presence or taking his eyes off the poolside festivities. "One man's order is another man's crime. Had the tables been set differently, maybe I would be receiving the hero's funeral and he'd be the infamous exile. Not even Israel would have wanted him."

Silence returned, and I soon became sure that I was sitting next to a senile old crook who wanted to have the last word.

The poolside serenity persisted for another half hour. I was about to test the waters and stand up and ask if I could leave, when the bear turned to face me.

"There's something addictive about a secret. Lansky

knew that. He used mine against me. Whatever you write in that book, remember that. Lansky was a master of secrets. Maybe they won't come out today, maybe it will be ten years from now, maybe the next century. His secrets will come out, and when they do, the American people will realize that he and I had a lot in common. Cop and crook. White hat and black," he rambled.

"I have to go," I said, trying not to let my trepidation show.

"So go," he said. "Just remember to ask yourself what is myth and what is fact. Lansky wasn't born on the Fourth of July. That was just a convenient Ellis Island mistake he never bothered to correct. Ask yourself what else about him isn't completely true."

He turned his attention back to the pool boys and said, "Go finish your book. History will bear me out."

I was quickly ushered back to the limousine, and in no time at all was winging my way northward once again.

That was twenty years ago. Hoover turned out to be right about a lot of things. Lansky's birthday and others as well.

I revised "Bigger Than U.S. Steel" to reflect these changes. Needless to say, the FBIIR didn't approve, and the book was never published.

My taxes from 1970 to 1974 were audited, and I was jailed for tax evasion. I forget the details now. It really didn't matter what the trumped-up charges were. I was guilty the minute I started to doubt the Lansky myth.

I get out next year. A lot has surfaced since then. A lot about Siegel, Capone, Lansky, and Hoover.

They're all dead now, and a new regime is in.

Maybe I'll write a book.

Better yet, maybe I'll be able to get "Bigger Than U.S. Steel" published.

The true history can come out.

Maybe.

Only time will tell.

It's an increasingly rare event these days when a single story can put an author "on the map," so to speak—but in 1993, Campbell nominee Nick DiChario accomplished it with "The Winterberry," his Hugo- and World Fantasy Award-nominated short story that appeared in an earlier anthology in this series, *Alternate Kennedys*. He has followed it up with a number of magazine and anthology sales that prove beyond any doubt that it was not a fluke.

For this anthology, Nick has chosen to write about the notorious Red Baron, but a case can be made that the true star of the story is an even more famous European. . . .

Giving Head
by Nicholas A. DiChario

Manfred Von Richthofen felt the bullet strike the back of his head.

Whap—

He lurched forward, lost his vision. His arms fell to his sides and his legs went limp in the fuselage as the bright red Albatros DV triplane he'd been piloting dropped out of the sky from four thousand meters as if it had forgotten how to fly. *So this is how it feels when one is shot to death,* thought the Red Baron. He should be in his Fokker Tripe. That was his favorite plane, the plane in which he'd orchestrated the majority of his fifty-six aerial kills, more than any other fighter pilot during World War I. If he was going to die, he should be in his Fokker Tripe.

Still no feelings circulated in his arms or legs. He blinked furiously, black-on-black. He thought that the wings of his Albatros should have certainly snapped off by now, in such a steep dive; he'd fallen at least a thousand meters. But the wings held. Good German craftsmanship.

He must live to tell the builders what a fine aircraft they have built. Live? Impossible.

Richthofen willed himself to move. *Move!* Nothing. But the blackness in his eyes began to spot white and gray. Then he felt his fingertips tingling. His toes twitched. He concentrated with all his will—*move—move—*

His arms responded.

He reached instinctively to cut off the powerful Mercedes engine of his Albatros. Blood flowed from his head wound, from his helmet, down the back of his neck. How much blood could he afford to spill before blacking out? *I must see!* He tore off his goggles and felt the wind snatch them from his fingers. The smell of gasoline warned him his engine had been hit. With his gloved thumbs, he pried open his eyes.

Gray and white and black spots marched across his field of vision. And now shapes—objects—barely visible—like looking through smoke, through black crystal. He gripped the controls.

See, damn you, see!

He must have fallen another two thousand meters. He could feel the change in the air. Ah! A moment of clarity. Now he could read the altimeter: eight hundred meters and plummeting. And there, the forest beneath him. He'd been lucky. He'd drifted to the German side of the lines. Would it be possible to land safely near Wervicq? Black smoke poured out of his engine.

Richthofen attacked the controls—*pull up, level off, pull up*—he concentrated on the shapes, the objects, the trees, the pain, the blood, black smoke, white light, gray spots, a clearing, a road.

white
gray
black
black
Where am I? Where am I?

* * *

"St. Nicholas' Hospital, Courtrai, and you are quite fortunate to be alive." The doctor smiled and nodded. This was all Richthofen could see at first: a set of teeth bobbing up and down in front of his eyes. Everything else blurred past him. He could smell his own sweat, and something chemical, ether perhaps. "What happened to me?"

"You have received a bullet in the back of your head, leaving a hole the size of a dollar coin. Hah. Ten centimeters at least. You must feel like death."

No, thought Richthofen. *I am alive*. He moved his arms and legs. All of the feeling had returned to them.

"We were able to remove the shell, although some fragments remain, and we performed some rudimentary tests for nerve damage, and there appears to be none. Of course more thorough studies will be required, as well as testing for brain damage."

"When can I return to my *Jagdgeschwader*?" asked Richthofen.

"It will be a while before we can allow you to return to your aerial unit."

"We? Who is 'we'? Are you not the physician in charge here?" Richthofen's vision cleared. The doctor was a paunchy man. He looked pale against the colorless backdrop behind him. He wore a bloodstained smock, and drool was caked on the edges of his lips.

"It is true what I have read about you in the newspapers. You are fearless and you are blessed. You should be dead."

"There is a war to be fought. Germany needs me," Richthofen said.

"Yes. In my opinion, if your recovery goes well, you might be ready to return to the front in less than a month. But you will be out of my care shortly."

Richthofen reached behind his head to feel his wound, but the doctor held back Richthofen's wrist. "The wound is very sensitive. A portion of your skull bone has been exposed and there is nothing we can do about that. The dressing is delicate and shouldn't be touched. When the swelling goes down, you will have to wear a permanent patch over the hole in your head. Because of the bone splinters and the shell fragments and the delicate location of the wound, I am sorry to say that you will always experience head pain to some extent, fluctuating from dull to excruciating."

Richthofen rested for a moment. "If I can breathe, if I can move my arms and legs and I can see, then I am able to fly and fight and kill."

"Maybe so, but there are other considerations." The doctor did not smile when he said this.

"There are no other considerations of greater importance than Germany and the war effort."

"Officially, I agree."

"And unofficially?"

"Unofficially, as soon as you are able, you shall be journeying to Vienna."

On the train, Richthofen woke sweating. For a moment, he did not know where he was. In his quarters? In his Fokker Tripe? 1918? Pitch black. He could be dead. He *should* be dead. He'd been shot in the head. Ah, yes, the pain. The constant pain in the back of his skull must have woken him, as it had every night since he'd been shot. And the clatter of the railway had disturbed him, and a smell he could not decipher, something he had not smelled in a very long time, something clean and civilized. He much preferred the smell of sweat and gasoline and machine-gun fire.

But he'd been ordered to Vienna to visit the Austrian psychoanalyst, Sigmund Freud.

Richthofen sat up on the cramped bed in his compartment and tried to look out at the landscape, but his vision could not penetrate the blackness. He shuddered, remembering how he'd tried so desperately to see as his Albatros dove toward the ground, toward his death, his most certain death. But he had survived. *Rather I had died in the air, a warrior, than be taken from the front,* thought the Red Baron. His fellow countrymen would have no luxury trains to whisk them away from the enemy. If his orders hadn't come from Kaiser Wilhelm himself, he would have spat in the doctor's face for not releasing him.

As the train clattered on through the night, Richthofen dreamed of the hole in his head, of Frenchmen and Englishmen flying their Vickers and Spads and Nieuports and Sopwith Pups into his brain and firing . . . firing . . . firing . . . their shells, punching holes through the back of his eyes so that he could not see, blinded by the blood spewing from his lacerated eyeballs.

"I have come a long way in establishing the principles of psychoanalysis," said Sigmund Freud, brushing back his thick gray hair and peering at Richthofen through his spectacles. He pulled on a pair of clean white surgical gloves and approached Richthofen's bed. "Our unconscious is the key to the inner universe. All of what we are, all of what we suffer and strive for, all of us that is human is locked away in here." Freud tapped his temple. "Turn over on your stomach, please."

Richthofen turned over and felt Freud tugging at the bandages attached to the back of his skull.

"Don't worry," said Freud. "I am a qualified physician as well as a psychoanalyst."

"So I have been informed." Richthofen did not appreciate the fine furniture and pleasant draperies and elegant rugs.

"I understand your aggression impulses. You are a hunter, a warrior. You crave to be in the fray. But I want you to understand that you will be aiding the Central Powers here by allowing me to examine your unconscious. We must learn what it is that makes Manfred Von Richthofen the perfect hunting and killing machine that he is, so someday we can train others to be hunters and killers in an equally efficient manner during times of war. Besides, if you cooperate fully, soon you shall be able to return to the front."

"I am a soldier, Herr Freud. I follow orders well."

"Siggy, call me Siggy. This is not a military exercise, after all. I want you to feel comfortable here in my home. You are free to go anywhere on the grounds." Freud applied a fresh dressing to Richthofen's skull. "Tomorrow," he said, "we shall chat."

After Freud withdrew, Richthofen kicked off his bedcovers and stood, cautiously touching the new bandage over his wound. When he jiggled the patch, the dull pain turned sharp and stabbed at him like a fork. So he would have this pain for the rest of his life. No matter. He did not expect to live long. He was twenty-five years old. He had already survived duty longer than any other fighter pilot in the German air brigade.

Richthofen paced the floor, thinking of the kills he would be missing while he lay in this cozy Viennese villa. He clenched his fists. Werner Voss had already shot down forty-eight, and Richthofen's younger brother, Lothar, was not far behind Voss. He could not afford to be playing games with some mad Austrian physician when others were trying to best him.

The dull light of dusk shaded his room. He walked to the window and brushed back the delicate curtains. In the summer flower garden outside sat a young woman with a notebook open on her lap. Richthofen observed her for a time. Interesting. He had a clear view of her, but could not determine if she was homely or beautiful, happy or sad, deeply immersed in her studies or not the least bit concerned. Perhaps his vision was still impaired by his wound.

She glanced up at his window—did she smile at him or frown?—and then returned her attention to the notebook.

Richthofen watched the young woman until darkness spirited her away. What had she been wearing? The color of her hair was . . . what? Her eyes had been dark, no, light.

The pain in his head had disappeared.

He reached up, jiggled the bandage, and winced. Ah,

yes, there it was. The whole time he'd been watching the girl, he'd completely lost touch of his pain.

"Let me explain what we are trying to accomplish here, Manfred," said Sigmund Freud, sitting back ungracefully in his brown leather chair.

Richthofen sat opposite him in a rocker. He sat so stiffly that his chair did not move a hair. Frankly, he was appalled at the mussiness of the Austrian's office: books heaped upon the floor; papers loose on shelves; dust caked on plants and furniture; desk littered with notes and letters and torn envelopes and unwashed cups and old newspapers.

"You are a slob," said Richthofen.

"Ah! Wonderful! I arranged this mess specifically to irritate your sense of military discipline. I wanted to test your honesty. We need to have an open relationship."

"That's ridiculous."

"Good, good, more honesty, but let us maintain a friendly atmosphere, shall we?" He leaned forward and clasped his fingers together. "My principal theory is this: It is our childhood experiences that establish our psychological profiles and govern what we become as adults. And the most powerful experiences we have as children are sexual."

"I have heard rumors that you are a pervert," said Richthofen.

"Yes, rumored by the ignorant, I am afraid. The ignorant, who do not understand that we are all born with a sexual instinct; sexuality is not something we develop in puberty. The ignorant, who do not understand that infantile sexuality is rooted in pleasure feelings through excitation of certain body parts that are especially susceptible to stimulation: the genitals; oral, anal, and urethral orifices; even the skin. The ignorant, who do not understand that infantile sexual pleasure is linked to sadism and masochism, and as we grow older, we learn to repress these autoeroticisms for the benefit of social acceptance."

"You are disgusting."

"Disgust, shame, morality—all of these come into play as we mature. Our outside influences begin to control our sexual impulses, and eventually the dominance of our genital zone steals most of our other sensual pleasures established in the infantile stage. But these instincts never leave us, Manfred—no, in fact they create us, they shape us, they define our characters—and when we confront these socially abhorrent childhood sexual beasts, we can determine exactly what and why a person is the way he is. But the ignorant do not care to learn the truth."

"Has it occurred to you, Herr Freud—"

"Siggy! Call me Siggy!"

"—that Germany is at war and that every day I waste here in Vienna is a day that I could be fighting and killing the enemy?"

"What a remarkable mind! I shall thoroughly enjoy discovering the childhood experiences that have patterned your personality type."

Freud stood. He smiled so widely that his forehead quivered. "Anna!" he called. "You may enter now."

The door to Freud's office opened slowly and a young woman stepped into the room.

Richthofen rose from his chair. This was the same girl he'd watched through his bedroom window last night. His heart began to beat faster. She stood hunched, her eyes downcast. She wore a long-skirted dirndl in an attempt to disguise her wide waist. She had a chalky complexion. Her short dark hair added to her frumpy appearance. Nothing much to look at, this girl. Ugly, in fact. Richthofen wondered why he was so intrigued.

"Manfred Von Richthofen," said Sigmund Freud. "Meet my daughter, Anna."

"Pleased," said Richthofen stepping forward, taking her hand and nodding. Her fingers felt noticeably warmer than his. She did not return his stare.

"Sit, sit," Freud said.

Richthofen offered his chair to Anna, but she smiled

and giggled. "He means for you to sit," she said in a bird-like voice, without glancing at him.

Sigmund laughed, too.

Feeling embarrassed, Richthofen sat stiffly in the rocker.

Sigmund Freud adjusted his spectacles on the bridge of his nose. "Anna, this is the Prussian war hero we have read so much about in the newspapers. The famous Rittmeister. Very handsome, don't you think?—the chiseled features, the cold blue eyes, and so tall. Do you see the *Pour le Mérite* over his chest, hm? the Blue Max? Sixteen aerial kills to get that medal, if the newspapers are accurate."

"They are," said Richthofen.

"And the Iron Cross, too, yes?"

"Yes, from my days in the cavalry. And the Saxe-Coburg-Gotha Medal for Bravery as well."

"This is the man who painted his airplane bright red, Anna. Why, Manfred? Why did you paint your airplane red?"

"To instill fear in the enemy. An enemy pilot should know that when he engages the Red Baron in aerial combat, he will be in a fight to the death. Of course my entire *Jagdgeschwader* has painted its planes red now. Mostly to protect me. I am a targeted man."

"Go ahead, Anna, look at the Rittmeister's medals. I'm sure he won't mind."

Anna glanced at his medals, but did not seem impressed. She walked around the rocker and stood directly behind him.

"Now let us begin," said Freud, clearing his throat. "I want you to tell me all about your first kill."

Richthofen sighed. "I was flying as an observer in an Albatros two-seater. Lieutenant Osteroth was my pilot. I spotted a Royal Flying Corps Farman and ordered Osteroth to close in. As soon as we were within range, I opened fire. I don't think the opposing pilot ever saw us. I shot my entire clip. All one hundred rounds. The Farman spiraled down in a cloud of black smoke."

"That's very nice," said Sigmund, "but I want you to tell me about your first kill *ever*."

"Ever?"

"Ever in your entire life. For instance, do you remember hunting with your father when you were a child? Perhaps you remember squeezing the life out of a worm or a frog or an insect at the tender age of four or five or six."

"How do you expect me to remember something like that?"

"Anna will help," said Sigmund, removing a pipe and a pouch of tobacco from his desk drawer. He sat down in his brown leather chair, swung his feet up on the edge of his desk, and snapped a match.

Richthofen suddenly felt Anna's warm fingers on his head, brushing lightly through his short-trimmed hair. He half-rose out of his chair. "What is the meaning of this?"

"Please, sit still," Sigmund said. He puffed on his pipe. "Allow Anna to work." The scent of cherry tobacco wafted into the room.

Richthofen settled into his rocker, and Anna's fingers passed over his ears, across his temples and forehead. Her hands, Richthofen noticed, seemed exceptionally strong, and the warmth in her fingers began to prickle with heat. Quite beyond his control, he felt his neck lose its strength. His shoulders slumped, his chest softened, his knees trembled. *What is this?* he tried to say, *some sort of trick?*—but his lips refused to move. The only thing now that he could feel were Anna's prickling-hot fingers moving over his scalp, holding up his head, and painlessness, utter painlessness, as if the heat from Anna's fingers had burned away his agony.

The memory of the day he'd been shot down came to him then, those terrible few moments when he'd been aware of the bullet in his head, and the plane diving helplessly out of control, and how he could not save himself.

"Ah, here it is," she said. "I can see it very clearly now. He is a child, maybe seven years old. He and his family are visiting his grandmother. He is bored, very bored. He discovers an air rifle. Where? I'm not sure. I see a dark place, a closet or a barn. He takes the rifle with him into the woods. He comes to a pond where he sees ducks, his grandmother's tame white ducks, four of them paddling in the pond. He creeps up on them. He aims the pellet gun and pulls the trigger."

Anna fell silent for a moment. Her fingers continued to play over his scalp.

"The first duck squawks horribly," Anna continued. "He keeps shooting. He kills them all. He wades into the pond and gathers the dead ducks by their necks and drags their bloody carcasses through the woods to . . . to . . . show his mother, yes, to show her he has killed them . . . she will be proud of him, he thinks. But she is appalled. She begins to scold him. 'Manfred, you should not have done that, you—' No, wait, his grandmother interrupts. 'He has confessed his deeds like a man,' she say, 'and like a man, he has killed his prey. So it is like a man, albeit a young one, that we must treat him.' He is looking at his mother. He is stained with blood, the dead ducks heaped beside him. He is smiling. He experiences an erection."

Anna removed her fingers from Richthofen's head. He immediately regained the feeling in his body, and his head wound throbbed in pain. He felt spent, but managed to sit up straight in his chair.

"Exquisite!" Sigmund Freud leaped to his feet, almost losing his pipe. "All young boys in their prepubescent years are sexually attracted to their mothers, Manfred. You played out a dominance fantasy. You learned that hunting and killing makes a man dominant over a woman. When your mother was appalled by your act of slaying the ducks, and then was forced by your grandmother—a higher-authority figure in this instance—to subject herself to your masculine superiority, you, in effect, were granted permission to rape her." Sigmund paced the floor, stepping over books, puffing on his pipe.

Richthofen finally found his voice: "P-pervert."

Sigmund walked over to Richthofen and grasped his shoulder. "Nonsense. This is an amazing breakthrough.

Don't you see? Every time you fly and hunt for prey, you are lusting for your mother, and when you kill the enemy—ha!—that is ejaculation!—that is the climax of your rape! You are reliving this childhood ecstasy with every aerial kill!"

Richthofen had regained just enough of his strength to clench his fist, rear back, and strike Sigmund Freud on the side of the head. Freud fell back onto a stack of books and papers, and his spectacles slid across the floor. He sat up, legs outstretched, smiling like a love-struck school boy.

Richthofen turned to apologize to Anna for her father's disgusting remarks, but she was gone.

"Wonderful, wonderful," said Freud, clinging to the leg of his desk, clutching his pipe, climbing to one knee. "No repression whatsoever. Our work here is done. Now we must fly together!"

At first Richthofen refused. He explained to Sigmund Freud how his favorite bright red single-seater Fokker Tripe would be awaiting him at his air base in Marcke, near the front, and how he must return to active duty immediately. He had a *Jagdgeschwader* to command, after all, his own group of flying echelons, and he had no time to spare in a cumbersome two-seater, away from the main action, bogged down with an inexperienced observer. But Freud insisted he needed "observational data" to complete his psychological profile, and that they would indeed fly in the combat zone and engage the enemy or his research would be of no value whatever, and he threatened to contact Kaiser Wilhelm if Richthofen didn't comply.

So the two men traveled by train to the airfield base in Marcke. Richthofen did not speak to Freud for most of the journey, and, to his surprise, the pervert did not nag him with questions about his childhood or his relationship with his mother. Freud seemed content to study his notes, make entries into his personal diary, and occasionally ap-

ply a cold washcloth to his swollen head, where Richthofen had struck him.

After a while, Richthofen wished Freud would say
something. Every moment since Anna Freud had removed
her hands from his head, his pain was nearly intolerable,
bringing with it dizzy spells and faintness, almost as if it
had become a living thing, reaching up into his skull,
searching for the comfort of Anna's prickling-hot fingers.

"What is this strange talent of your daughter's that allows her to see into a man's past?" Richthofen asked
Sigmund Freud. "Is she clairvoyant? A mind reader?"

"No. I have yet to find a mind reader who is not a char-
latan. A clairvoyant can discern what is beyond the human senses, but cannot probe into the unconscious."

"I was paralyzed."

"It was not so much paralysis as it was a loss of mental
energy. You see, my daughter hypnotized you. She is
rather adept at it."

Richthofen sat back in his seat and sipped at a cup of
tea. He could feel the train as it rattled along the rail. *She
took away my pain,* he wanted to tell Sigmund Freud. *Explain that.* But Richthofen kept these thoughts to himself.

At the base in Marcke, Richthofen and Freud were assigned to an Albatros B II, the same type of bus
Richthofen had flown in as an observer when he began his
aerial training back in 1915. Then Richthofen had been
paired with the madman, Lieutenant Zeumer, a man
stricken with tuberculosis and determined to die in the air
rather than as a withering victim of his illness. His wish
would come true in 1917, just two years after the men
had parted company. Count Von Holck, another of
Richthofen's fearless flyers and great teachers, was shot
through the skull in aerial combat above Fort Douaumont
on the Verdun front in 1916. Immelman and Boelcke, two
of the greatest German fighter pilots to grace the cockpit,
had also died in the line of duty, thousands of meters
above the ground. Noble deaths, all of them.

Death. Richthofen thought of it often. It was true, what the newspapers said of him; he was fearless and he was blessed. He'd survived more than just a bullet wound to the head. Once when Von Holck flew too close to the ground and the smoke from a burning town choked off his engine, their Albatros dropped out of the sky, crashed into a building, and exploded on impact. Both men had been thrown from the bus and had survived. On his first solo flight, Richthofen had miscalculated his landing. The machine lurched when it touched down, he overcorrected and slammed the nose of the plane into the ground. Richthofen extricated himself from the wreckage without so much as a cut or a bruise. On one occasion, when he was in the cavalry, he'd been thrown from his mount near the front lines, and before he could gather himself and climb back on his charger, a grenade exploded on his saddle. Richthofen suffered no more than a torn cloak.

He had been close to death so many times, and yet he did not fear it. Why? Could it be that there was some instinct in him stronger than the fear of death? Could there be some truth to Freud's assessment of his psychological profile? Was there a deep-seated childhood unconscious lust for his mother pushing him past all rational concern for his own safety? No, he refused to believe that. He was simply craftier than death. Soon he would be rid of the pervert, and then he would not have to think about the Austrian's absurd theories.

In Richthofen's absence, Werner Voss had climbed to within one kill of equaling the great Red Baron's record. With or without Sigmund Freud, with or without the dizziness and the pain in his head and his memories of the warm touch of Sigmund's strange and ugly daughter, Anna Freud, it was time for him to hunt and kill.

It happened without warning, as it so often did in a dogfight. Three French Nieuports dropped out of the clouds from a thousand meters above, picking up speed in their dive, forming a tight triangle on his tail. The Frenchmen held the advantage of superior position before the fight even began. Richthofen cursed himself for flying under a cloud cover, a mistake a Rittmeister concentrated on the hunt never would have allowed.

He banked to the right and dove, drawing the Frenchmen down with him. The controls vibrated beneath his grip, and he could feel his engine grind and accelerate. Too much strain on the engine and he would blow himself out of the sky. The Nieuports closed in. He heard the burst of their guns, but they were too far away to score yet. Richthofen continued to descend. Voss would be flying low, in a unit of six other Fokkers. When the Frenchmen saw they were outnumbered, they would run for home. That was the difference between the English and the French. The English would fight no matter what. The French would fight only when the numbers favored them.

Richthofen checked his altimeter. He'd dropped two thousand meters and had flown beyond the clouds. Voss and the rest of the unit were nowhere in sight. How far had he lagged behind the formation? His head wound throbbed and he felt a rush of dizziness. *Think! Think!* His engine could give him no more speed, and the single-seater Nieuports were closing in quickly. Richthofen was under the strict orders of Kaiser Wilhelm to trail behind every mission, fight only if fired upon, and protect Freud at all costs. It looked now as if he would have to fight alone against three, disadvantaged by speed and maneuverability, and hampered with an inexperienced observer. He had demonstrated to Freud how to operate the rear guns, but he was certain the psychoanalyst would never be able to use them.

His heart pounded. He could feel the sweat gather on his forehead. It was time to fight and kill.

But before he could spin and attack, Richthofen spotted a single German plane joining the fray. It was Voss! He'd flown back for them! One of the Frenchmen peeled off and met Voss head-on. They exchanged blasts and flew past each other, neither bird scoring.

Richthofen banked left, circled down, and climbed, hoping to come up behind the two remaining French flyers, but his two-seater Albatros was fat and slow and the Nieuports countered easily. They split and curled away in opposite directions. If he'd been in his Fokker, Richthofen would have downed them both!

Then he heard a blast from behind. It was Sigmund Freud! He'd swung the rear gun around and fired on one of the Nieuports as it peeled back. Richthofen banked right and spotted the Nieuport chucking in the wind, and then watched its bottom wings break off. Freud had scored a hit on the rudder! The plane could no longer maneuver; all it could do was to run for home.

Richthofen started after the lame duck, but the other Nieuport was already on his tail, firing. Shells peppered his bus but inflicted no crippling damage. Meanwhile, Voss chased the other Frenchman, forcing him down. He would have the kill in a few moments, but he could not help Richthofen and Freud. There was only one thing left to do: play dead.

Richthofen fell into a spin. His stomach lurched and he lost his breath. He dropped a thousand meters before leveling off, his engine growling at the strain.

Success! The Frenchman had pulled back! Where was Voss? There! He'd pushed the other Nieuport down so low it couldn't pull up. Richthofen watched it crash into the trees and explode. Another kill for Voss. Now they were equal.

Richthofen turned and darted back up in pursuit of the fleeing Nieuport. There was still a chance he could surprise the Frenchman and regain his record. He gritted his teeth against the pain in his head and climbed one thousand, two thousand, three thousand meters. His engine sputtered and coughed black smoke. One of the French shells must have done some damage after all, or perhaps he had pushed the machine too hard.

The Frenchman spotted him, circled down and came up firing on Richthofen's tail. A few more shells clipped his

340 Nicholas A. DiChario

wings and ricocheted off his propeller. Richthofen pulled up, let the Nieuport pass under him, then turned and headed for the German lines. With any luck, the lone Frenchman would not want to follow. No. The Nieuport was on him, firing, missing, firing again. But there was Voss!—coming at the Nieuport from the flank, guns blazing. The Frenchman climbed to get out of the way and passed by Richthofen only a few meters to the left.

Richthofen heard another blast of gunfire. It was Freud again! *Rat-tat-tat-tat-tat-tat-tat-tat-tat-tat—*

A direct hit! Freud raked the Frenchman's bus; one of the Nieuport's wings snapped off, and its tail shattered. Black smoke plumed. Freud had hit the engine! Richthofen dove. Fire leaped into the Frenchman's cockpit, and the Nieuport exploded in the air, bright orange fragments bursting across the skyline.

Freud had done it! Sigmund Freud had scored his first kill!

Word spread quickly after they landed. Before long, the entire air base had learned of Sigmund Freud's kill, and of Werner Voss equaling the Rittmeister's record.

This was cause for much celebration. A fiddler from the village was called, and by nightfall, several kegs of wine had arrived from a local winery.

That night Richthofen remained in his room, as he always did when such celebrations occurred, but on this occasion he was not thinking of strategies and maneuvers and formations and methods of attack. The throbbing in his head distracted him, worsened by the fiddler's fiddle and the shouts and drunken laughter of his men. He wished that he could visit Anna Freud and ask her to relieve the pain in his skull for even a few moments, and at the same time chided himself for entertaining his own weakness. Perhaps what bothered him most of all was the knowledge that he had flown poorly this day. He could have gotten himself and Sigmund Freud killed, and

Werner Voss as well. There was no excuse for such pedestrian flying techniques.

There was a knock at his door. Richthofen sat still, hoping the visitor would leave. Voss entered unbidden and closed the door behind him.

"I regret to inform you, Rittmeister Richthofen, that you have been grounded until further notice. The orders came from Kaiser Wilhelm himself. He is concerned about your head wound."

Richthofen said nothing.

Voss stood with his hands clasped behind his back. "Permission to speak freely."

Richthofen nodded.

"You flew recklessly today, straying from the formation. You disobeyed orders and attacked the Frenchman's Nieuport when he was fleeing. This was unforgivable. You intentionally endangered Sigmund Freud's life, and the Austrian is most important to the German war effort. I had no choice but to report your actions."

Richthofen stared at Voss. He could not even be angry. He would have done the same thing in Voss's position.

Voss cleared his throat. "I shall be taking over command of your *Jagdgeschwader*."

"Of course."

"I shall also be in charge of piloting Sigmund Freud for the remainder of his observational duties."

"Of course."

Voss exited. Richthofen doused his lamp, then stretched out on his stiff cot, listening to the screeching fiddle. He massaged his temples, trying to reproduce the warm touch of Sigmund Freud's ugly daughter, Anna, but he could not.

After a time his door creaked open and a sliver of light peeked through. A hunched figure crept forward. It was Freud, carrying a soft, brown leather attaché case, chuckling softly, shuffling his feet.

"Manfred," he whispered, "are you asleep?"

"Come in, Herr Freud."

"Siggy, call me Siggy." He shuffled over to the chair beside Richthofen's bed and plopped down. He reeked of wine. Richthofen looked into the Austrian's bloodshot eyes and shook his head.

"I know, I know, you do not approve of the bottle. The men told me you never partake."

Richthofen looked away. Freud unzipped his attaché case and began thumbing through some papers. "I heard you've been grounded. I wanted to say that I am sorry. I feel somewhat responsible."

"It was not your fault," Richthofen said.

"Perhaps not. It was not your fault, either. If anything, it was the fault of your—"

"My unconscious."

"Yes, yes, very good, Manfred. I'll make a psychoanalyst out of you yet."

Sigmund held up one of his papers in the dull streak of light. "You see, you responded to our combat situation in perfect accordance with your psychological profile. You valued the kill above all else. This is what makes you the best. I brought your profile for you to look at. I thought you might like to learn something about yourself."

Richthofen shook his head. "I don't care to see it, thank you."

"Hm, I thought as much."

"Voss is a better pilot."

Freud smiled. "Maybe so. But you are the best hunter and killer I have ever seen."

"I did not want Voss to equal my record. That is why I chased the Frenchman."

"Yes, I'm sure that is how you rationalize it."

"Look," said Richthofen, "it doesn't matter."

"Quite right. I have compiled all the data I shall need from you. All that remains now is a comparison report I'd like to prepare, using Werner Voss."

"You will have plenty of opportunity for that." There was an awkward pause. Richthofen waited for Freud to look at him. "I think I owe you an apology . . . Siggy. I should not have struck you that day in your office. It was inappropriate behavior."

"No need to apologize. My theories are not easy to accept. You are not the first person I've offended, and I'm sure you will not be the last."

Richthofen nodded. He thought that Sigmund Freud seemed older suddenly. Perhaps it was the effect of the alcohol that made the man's shoulders sag, that made his eyelids droop, that deepened the lines in his forehead. Or could it be something else, something unconscious? "Congratulations," Richthofen said. "I didn't think you had it in you."

Freud went back to shuffling his papers. Some of them fell to the floor. "You mean the kill, of course. I did what I had to do, just like every other German soldier."

It sounded to Richthofen as if Freud had spoken these words several times during the evening's festivities. He noticed that Freud's eyes had glazed over. "It takes courage to kill. Not everyone has it."

"I have dedicated my life to relieving human shu-suffering," said Freud, and then he could not speak. Tears began to roll down his cheeks.

Richthofen sat up on his cot. "It may help you to know that the Frenchman did not suffer. I know a lot about death. There must have been a good fifty liters of fuel in his tank, resting only a few centimeters from his head. The propeller pushed the heat directly into his face and he lost consciousness immediately. Then he was blown to bits. This is the quickest way to die. This is the way all fighter pilots wish to die."

Freud wiped his nose on his sleeve. "Yes, you see, war was made for men like you, Manfred. That is why my work is so important. Soon we will be able to make men like you for war, and then, believe it or not, there will be less suffering all the way around. War is here to stay, and when there are people psychologically equipped to handle killing and being killed, well . . ."

"I understand."

Freud's head bobbed forward, and then he slid off the chair. Richthofen stood, went over to the door and pulled it shut. He lifted Freud—a slight man, somewhat frail, Richthofen thought—and set him down on his cot, covering him to the shoulders with his blanket.

The Red Baron dressed quietly in the dark, donning his fighter-pilot uniform, his leather helmet, his dun-colored boots and gloves. He stuffed Freud's papers in the attaché case, zipped it closed and tucked it under his arm. He opened his window, checked to be sure all was clear, crawled outside and marched to the airstrip where his bright red Fokker Tripe awaited. He climbed into the cockpit, spent a moment enjoying the midnight breeze against his face, and thought how strange it was that in the dark of night, he could smell the tall grass and the late-summer leaves, yet in the daylight, only the smell of machinery filled the air. He glanced at the ceiling of stars that winked as if they all shared an unimaginable secret. *What an exquisite night to have wings*, he thought.

When Richthofen woke, he was alone in bed. A fire crackled in the fireplace, and the smell of burnt hickory filled the room. Where was Anna? He propped himself up on one elbow, and the silk sheets slid off his shoulders. Anna was sitting beside the fireplace. It wasn't all a dream, then. He had flown all the way to Vienna to be with her.

"What have I done?" he whispered.

"Come here," Anna called to him in her birdlike voice.

Richthofen climbed out of bed and tied on a robe. His skull began to throb. He went over to where Anna sat beside the fireplace and knelt next to her. She wore a flannel nightgown. Between her legs sat Sigmund Freud's attaché case. Freud's notes lay open on her lap. She read a page, tore it from its binder, crumpled it, and tossed the paper into the fire. She repeated this several times, shaking her head, pursing her lips, while Richthofen watched. "He was such an intelligent man," she said.

"How long have I been hypnotized?" asked Richthofen.

"Since I first touched you. I planted only one posthypnotic suggestion. When the opportunity arose, I wanted you to bring me Father's work. That's all. I don't believe in controlling people. You are free to go whenever you like."

He watched her burn another page. "Why destroy his work?"

"Because my father was right, Manfred Von Richthofen. Because it is possible to create soldiers like you by establishing a psychological profile and raising children according to its principles."

"Is that such a terrible thing?"

"The war will be over soon. Germany will fall. An armistice will be signed. By 1919, Germany will be ordered to reduce her forces, pay reparations, and cede her colonies. And then, not too many years from now, another war. World War Two. There will be people who believe in a master race, and if Father's work were to fall into the wrong hands, well, there is a good chance that these people might succeed. I don't expect you to fully understand."

Richthofen sat on the floor in front of the fire and crossed his legs. "These are only notes. He will be able to recreate them easily enough."

"This morning my father and Werner Voss will be shot down in a dogfight. Werner Voss will live, but will lose his right arm and his right leg. My father shall die. His neck will be broken."

"How do you know such things?"

"I can see many things."

"Your father says you are only a hypnotist."

"My father refused to accept what he did not understand. He could accept hypnotism, so I was his little hypnotist. I allowed him to believe whatever he wanted."

"So you knew all along he was going to die. You could have saved him. Your own father. How can you be so cold about it?"

As soon as Richthofen said this, he regretted it. He looked at Anna and saw that she was crying.

"You have no idea what's coming . . . the atrocities . . . no one would believe me. . . ." Her voice betrayed nothing, her face was expressionless, but tears continued to well in her eyes and stream down her cheeks. Richthofen crawled next to her, took her chin in his hand and kissed her tears.

She sniffled. "As I said. You are free to go."

"And what do you see in my future?"

"You will continue to fly and to kill. You will shoot down eighty enemy fighters before you are defeated, before an Australian bullet launched from the ground rips into your spine and ends your life."

"I don't want to go," he said, surprising himself. He was remembering last night, of course. He wanted Anna again, and again, and again. He took her hands and placed them on his head. Immediately he felt her warmth inside his skull. The throbbing pain in his brain began to ease. "I don't ever want to leave your side."

Anna massaged his scalp, looked into his eyes. She seemed so helpless, so frightened, so alone. Her fingers moved through his hair to the back of his head, where she pulled away his patch. Richthofen felt his muscles weaken, and he trembled.

"You are so beautiful," she told him. "I have much work to do, much traveling. I must carry on all that was good and true in my father's work. I will have to leave Germany before the Second World War begins. If you stay with me, I see a very different future for you."

She traced the outer edges of his wound and he groaned in pleasure. Sigmund Freud had been right about Manfred Von Richthofen. As a child, he had lusted after his mother, and with every aerial hunt and kill, in his own way, he had raped her. But there was more to his psychological profile than that. The great Red Baron was also a weak man, and a cheater of death.

Come to me, come to me, he thought. And Anna's fingers

moved under his patch to the opening in his skull, the ten-centimeter hole in his head he would own for the rest of his life, and she took her magical fingers and entered him, pressing forward, thrusting, and his agony turned to ecstasy in front of the crackling fire, beside ugly Anna Freud.

This is David Gerrold's second appearance in this book, and there is a reason for it.

Sometime back, he showed me a story entitled ". . . And Eight Rabid Pigs," which he had sold to another anthology, but which, although paid for, had to be dropped at the last minute due to space limitations. It was an incredibly powerful story, and I promised myself that if I ever edited an anthology into which it could fit, I was going to buy it myself. When I was about halfway through assembling *Alternate Outlaws*, and had already assigned David his previous story, I remembered this one. I asked him to send it to me, and saw that with very few changes, it could be made to fit the format of the book.

David made the changes, and here, for your edification, is the most horrifying outlaw of them all: Satan Claus.

Satan Claus
by David Gerrold

When I first became aware of Steven Dhor, he was talking about Christmas. Again.

He hated Christmas—in particular, the enforcement of bliss. "Don't be a Scrooge, don't be a grinch, don't be a Satan Claus, taking away other people's happiness." That's what his mother used to say to him, and twenty years later, he was still angry.

There were a bunch of them sitting around the bar, writers mostly, but a few hangers-on and fringies, sucking up space and savoring the wittiness of the conversation. Bread Bryan loomed all tall and spindly like a frontier-town undertaker. Railroad Martin perched like a disgruntled Buddha—he wore the official Railroad Martin uniform: T-shirt, jeans, and potbelly. George Finger was between wives and illnesses; he was enjoying just being alive. Goodman Hallmouth pushed by, snapping at bystanders and demanding to know where Harold Parnell had gone; he was going to punch him in the kneecap.

"Have a nice day, Goodman," someone called.

"Piss off!" he snarled back. "I'll have any damn kind of a day I want."

"See—" said Dhor, nodding at Hallmouth as he savaged his way out again. "That's honest, at least. Goodman might not fit our pictures of the polite way to behave, but at least he doesn't bury us in another layer of dishonest treacle."

"Yep, Goodman only sells honest treacle," said Railroad Martin.

"Where do you get lie-detector tests for treacle?" Bread Bryan asked, absolutely deadpan.

"There's gotta be a story in that—" mused George Finger.

"—but I just can't put my *finger* on it," said one of the nameless fringies. This was followed by a nanosecond of annoyed silence. Somebody else would have to explain to the fringie that a) that joke was older than God, b) it hadn't been that funny the first time it had been told, and c) he didn't have the right to tell it. Without looking up, Bread Bryan simply said, "That's one."

Steven Dhor said, "You want to know about treacle? Christmas is treacle. It starts the day after Halloween. You get two months of it. It's an avalanche of sugar and bullshit. I suppose they figure that if they put enough sugar into the recipe, you won't notice the taste of the bullshit."

"Don't mince words, Stevie. Tell us what you really think."

"Okay, I will." Dhor had abruptly caught fire. His eyes were blazing. "Christmas—at least the way we celebrate it—is a perversion. It's not a holiday; it's a brainwashing." That's when I started paying *real* attention.

"Every time you see a picture of Santa Claus," Dhor said, "you're being indoctrinated into the Christian ethic.

If you're good, you get a reward, a present; if you're bad, you get a lump of coal. One day you figure it out; you say, hey—Santa Claus is really Mommy and Daddy. And when you tell them you figured it out, what do they do? They tell you about God. If you're good, you get to go to Heaven; if you're bad, you go to Hell. Dying isn't anything to be afraid of, it's just another form of Christmas. And Santa Claus is God—the only difference is that at least Santa gives you something tangible. But if there ain't no Santa, then why should we believe in God, either?"

Bread Bryan considered Dhor's words dispassionately. Bread Bryan considered everything dispassionately. Despite his nickname, even yeast couldn't make him rise. Railroad Martin swirled his beer around in his glass; he didn't like being upstaged by someone else's anger—even when it was anger as good as this. George Finger, on the other hand, was delighted with the effrontery of the idea.

"But wait—this is the nasty part. We've taken God out of Christmas. You can't put up angels anymore, nor a cross, nor even a crèche. No religious symbols of any kind, because even though everything closes down on Christmas Day, we still have to pretend it's a nonsecular celebration. So, the only decorations you can put up are Santa Claus, reindeer, snowmen, and elves. We've replaced the actual holiday with a third-generation derivation, including its own pantheon of saints and demons: Rudolph, Frosty, George Bailey, Scrooge, and the grinch—Santa Claus is not only most people's first experience of God," Dhor continued, "it's now their *only* experience of God."

Dhor was flaming now. Clearly, this was not a casual thought for him. He'd been stewing over this for some time. He began describing how the country had become economically addicted to Christmas. "We've turned it into a capitalist feeding frenzy—so much so that some retailers depend on Christmas for fifty percent of their annual business. I think we should all 'Just Say No to Christmas.' Or at least—for God's sake—remember whose birthday it is and celebrate it appropriately, by doing things to feed the poor and heal the sick."

A couple of the fringies began applauding then, but Dhor just looked across at them with a sour expression on his face. "Don't applaud," he said. "Just do it."

"Do you?" someone challenged him. "How do you celebrate Christmas?"

"I don't give presents," Dhor finally admitted. "I take the money I would normally spend on presents and give it to the Necessities of Life Program of the AIDS Project of Los Angeles. It's more in keeping with the spirit." That brought another uncomfortable silence. It's one thing to do the performance of saint—most writers are pretty good at it—but when you catch one actually *doing* something unselfish and noteworthy, well ... it's pretty damned embarrassing for everyone involved.

Fortunately, Dhor was too much in command of the situation to let the awkward moment lie there unmolested. He trampled it quickly. "The thing is, I don't see any way to stop the avalanche of bullshit. The best we can do is ride it."

"How?" George Finger asked.

"Simple. By adding a new piece to the mythology—a new saint in the pantheon. *Satan Claus.*" There was that name again. Dhor lowered his voice. "See, if Santa Claus is really another expression of God, then there has to be an equally powerful expression of the Devil, too. There has to be a balance."

"Satan Claus ..." Bread Bryan considered the thought. "Mm. He must be the fellow who visited my house last year. He didn't give me anything I wanted. And I could have used the coal, too. It gets *cold* in Wyoming."

"No. Satan Claus doesn't work that way," said Dhor. "He doesn't give things. He takes them away. The suicide rate goes up around Christmastime. That's no accident. That's Satan Claus. He comes and takes your soul straight to Hell."

Then Railroad Martin added a wry thought— "He

drives a black sleigh and he lands in your basement."
—and then they were all doing it.

"The sleigh is drawn by eight rabid pigs—big, ugly razorbacks," said Dhor. "They have iridescent red eyes that
burn like smoldering embers—they *are* embers, carved
right out of the floor of Hell. Late at night, as you're lying
all alone in your cold, cold bed, you can hear them snuffling and snorting in the ground beneath your house.
Their hooves are polished black ebony, and they carve up
the ground like knives."

Dhor was creating a legend while his audience sat and
listened, enraptured. He held up his hands as if outlining
the screen on which he was about to paint the rest of his
picture. The group fell silent. I had to admire him, in spite
of myself. He lowered his voice to a melodramatic stage
whisper: "Satan Claus travels underground through dark,
rumbling passages filled with rats and ghouls. He carries
a long black whip, and he stands in the front of the sleigh,
whipping the pigs until the blood streams from their
backs. Their screams are the despairing sounds of the eternally tormented."

"And he's dressed all in black," suggested Bread Bryan.
"Black leather. With silver buckles and studs and rivets."

"Oh, hell," said George Finger. "*Everybody* dresses like
that in my neighborhood."

"Yes, black leather," agreed Martin, ignoring the aside.
"But it's made from the skins of reindeer."

"Whales," said Bryan. "Baby whales."

Dhor shook his head. "The leather is made from the
skins of those whose souls he's taken. He strips it off their
bodies before he lets them die. The skins are dyed black
with the sins of the owners, and trimmed with red-dyed
rat fur. Satan Claus has long gray hair, all shaggy and dirty
and matted; and he has a long gray beard, equally dirty.
There are crawly things living in his hair and beard. And
his skin is leprous and covered with pustules and running
sores. His features are deformed and misshapen. His nose
is a bulbous monstrosity, swollen and purple. His lips are

blue, and his breath smells like the grave. His fingernails are black with filth, but they're as sharp as diamonds. He can claw up through the floor to yank you down into his demonic realm."

"Wow," said Bread Bryan. "I'm moving up to the second floor."

The cluster of listeners shuddered at Dhor's vivid description. It was suddenly a little too heavy for the spirit of the conversation. A couple of them tried to make jokes, but they fell embarrassingly flat.

Finally, George Finger laughed gently and said, "I think you've made him out to be too threatening, Steve. For most of us, Satan Claus just takes our presents away and leaves changeling presents instead."

"Ahh," said Railroad. "That explains why I never get anything I want."

"How can you say that? You get T-shirts every year," said Bread.

"Yes, but I always want a tuxedo."

After the laughter died down, George said, "The changeling presents are made by the satanic elves, of course."

"Right," said Dhor. He picked up on it immediately. "All year long, the satanic elves work in their secret laboratories underneath the south pole, creating the most horrendous ungifts they can think of. Satan Claus whips them unmercifully with a cat-o'-nine-tails; he screams at them and beats them and torments them endlessly. The ones who don't work hard enough, he tosses into the pit of eternal fire. The rest of them work like little demons—of course they do; that's what they are—to manufacture all manner of curses and spells and hexes. All the bad luck that you get every year—it comes straight from Hell, a gift from Satan Claus himself." Dhor cackled wickedly, an impish burst of glee, and everybody laughed with him.

But he was on a roll. He'd caught fire with this idea and was excitedly building on it now. "The terrible black sleigh isn't a sleigh as much as it's a hearse. And it's filled with bulging sacks filled with bad luck of all kinds. Ill-nesses, miscarriages, strokes, cancers, viruses, flu germs, birth defects, curses. Little things like broken bones and upset stomachs. Big things like impotence, frigidity, steril-ity. Parkinson's disease, cerebral palsy, multiple sclerosis, encephalitis, everything that stops you from enjoying life."

"I think you're onto something," said Railroad. "I catch the flu right after Christmas, every year. I haven't been to a New Year's party in four years. At least now I have some-one to blame."

Dhor nodded and explained, "Satan Claus knows if you've been bad or good—if you've been bad in any way, he comes and takes a little more joy out of your life, makes it harder for you to want to be good. Just as Santa is your first contact with God, Satan Claus is your first ex-perience of evil. Satan Claus is the Devil's revenge on Christmas. He's the turd in the punch bowl. He's the tan-trum at the party. He's the birthday spoiler. I think we're telling our children only half the story. It's not enough to tell them that Santa will be good to them. We have to let them know who's planning to be bad to them."

For a while, there was silence as we all sat around and let the disturbing quality of Dhor's vision sink into our souls. Every so often someone would shudder as he thought of another new twist, another piece of embroidery.

But it was George Finger's speculation that ended the conversation. He said, "Actually, this might be a danger-ous line of thought, Steve. Remember the theory that the more believers a god has, the more powerful he becomes? I mean, it's a joke right now, but aren't you summoning a new god into existence this way?"

"Yes, Virginia," Dhor replied, grinning impishly, "there is a Satan Clause in the holy contract. But I don't think you need to worry. Our belief in him is insufficient. And unnecessary. We can't create Satan Claus—because he al-ready exists. He came into being when Santa Claus was created. A thing automatically creates its opposite, just by its very existence. You know that. The stronger Santa

Claus gets, the stronger Satan Claus must become in opposition."

Steven had been raised in a very religious household. His grandmother had taught him that for every act of good, there has to be a corresponding evil. Therefore, if you have Heaven, you have to have Hell. If you have a God, you have to have a Devil. If there are angels, then there have to be demons. Cherubs and imps. Blessed and damned. Nine circles of Hell—nine circles of Heaven. "Better be careful, George! Satan Claus is watching." And then he laughed fiendishly. I guess he thought he was being funny.

I forgot about Steven Dhor for a few weeks. I was involved in another one of those abortive television projects—it's like doing drugs; you think you can walk away from them, but you can't. Someone offers you a needle and you run to stick it in your arm. And then they jerk you around for another six weeks or six months, and then cut if off anyway—and one morning you wake up and find you're unemployed again. The money's spent, and you've wasted another big chunk of your time and your energy and your enthusiasm on something that will never be broadcast or ever see print. And your credential has gotten that much poorer because you have nothing to show for your effort except another dead baby. You get too many of those dead babies on your resume and the phone stops ringing altogether. But I love the excitement; that's why I stay so close to Hollywood—

Then one Saturday afternoon, Steven Dhor read a new story at Kicking The Hobbit—the all-science-fiction bookstore that used to be in Santa Monica. I'm sure he saw me come in, but he was so engrossed in the story he was reading to the crowd that he didn't recognize me. "*. . . the children believed that they could hear the hooves of the huge black pigs scraping through the darkness. They could hear the snuffling and snorting of their hot breaths. The pigs were foaming at the mouth, grunting and bumping up against each other as they pulled the heavy sled through the black tunnels*

*under the earth. The steel runners of the huge carriage sliced
across the stones, striking sparks and ringing with a knife-
edged note that shrieked like a metal banshee.*

"And the driver—his breath steaming in the terrible
cold—shouted their names as he whipped them, 'On, damn
you, on! You children of war! On Pustule and Canker and
Sickness and Gore! On Sickness and Seizure and Bastard
and Whore. Drive on through the darkness! Break through
the door!'" His voice rose softly as he read these har-
rowing passages to his enraptured audience.

I hung back, away from the group, listening in appreci-
ation and wonder. Dhor had truly caught the spirit of the
Christmas obscenity. By the very act of saying the name
aloud in public, he was not only giving his power to Satan
Claus, he was daring the beast to visit him on Christmas
Eve.

"*... And in the morning,*" Dhor concluded, "*there were
many deep, knife-like scars in the soft, dark earth beneath
their bedroom windows. The ground was churned and broken, and there were black, sooty smudges on the glass. ...
But of their father, there was not a sign. And by this, the
children knew that Satan Claus was indeed real. And they
never ever laughed again, as long as they lived.*"

The small crowd applauded enthusiastically, and then
they moved in close for autographs. Dhor's grin spread
across his cherubic face like a pink glow. He basked in all
the attention and the approval of the fans; it warmed him
like a deep red bath. He'd found something that touched
a nerve in the audience—now he responded to his listeners. Something had taken root in his soul.

I saw Dhor several more times that year. And everywhere, he was reading that festering story aloud again:
"*Christmas lay across the land like a blight, and once again
the children huddled in their beds and feared the tread of
heavy bootsteps in the dark ...*" He'd look up from the
pages, look across the room at his audience with that terrible impish twinkle, and then turn back to his reading
with renewed vigor. "*... Millie and Little Bob shivered in*

*their nightshirts as Daddy pulled them onto his lap. He
smelled of smoke and coal and too much whiskey. His face
was blue and scratchy with the stubble of his beard, and his
heavy flannel shirt scratched their cheeks uncomfortably.
'Why are you trembling?' he asked. 'There's nothing to be
afraid of. I'm just going to tell you about the Christmas
spirit. His name is Satan Claus, and he drives a big black
sled shaped like a hearse. It's pulled by rabid black pigs with
smoldering red eyes. Satan Claus stands in the front of the
carriage and rides like the whirlwind, lashing at the boars
with a stinging whip. He beats them until the blood pours
from their backs and they scream like the souls of the
damned—'*"

In the weeks that followed, he read it at the fund-raiser/
taping for Mike Hodel's literacy project. He read it at the
Pasadena Library's Horror/Fantasy Festival. He read it at
the Thanksgiving weekend Lost-Con. He read it on Hour
25, and he had tapes made for sale to anyone who wanted
one. Steven was riding the tiger. Exploiting it. Whipping
it with his need for notoriety.

" '*Satan Claus comes in the middle of the night—he
scratches at your window and leaves sooty marks on the
glass. Wherever there's fear, wherever there's madness—there
you'll find Satan Claus as well. He comes through the wall
like smoke and stands at the foot of your bed with eyes like
hot coals. He stands there and watches you. His hair is long
and gray and scraggly. His beard has terrible little creepy
things living in it. You can see them crawling around. Sometimes he catches one of the bugs that lives in his beard and
eats it alive. If you wake up on Christmas Eve, he'll be standing there waiting for you. If you scream, he'll grab you and
put you in his hearse. He'll carry you straight away to Hell.
If you get taken to Hell before you die, you'll never get out.
You'll never be redeemed by baby Jesus. . . .*' "

And then the Christmas issue of *Ominous* magazine
came out, and *everybody* was reading it.

"*Little Bob began to weep and Millie reached out to him,
trying to comfort his tears; but Daddy gripped her arm*

firmly and held her at arm's length. 'Now, Millie—don't you help him. Bobby has to learn how to be a man. Big boys don't cry. If you cry, then for sure Satan Claus will come and get you. He won't even put you in his hearse. He'll just eat you alive. He'll pluck you out of your bed and crunch your bones in his teeth. He has teeth as sharp as razors and jaws as powerful as an ax. First he'll bite your arms off, and then he'll bite off your legs—and then he'll even bite off your little pink peepee. And you better believe that'll hurt. And then, finally, when he's bitten off every other part of you, finally he'll bite your head off! So you mustn't cry. Do you understand me?' Daddy shook Bobby as hard as he could, so hard that Bobby's head bounced back and forth on his shoulders and Bobby couldn't help himself; he bawled as loud as he could."

People were calling each other on the phone and asking if they'd seen the story and wasn't it the most frightening story they'd ever read? It was as if they were enrolling converts into a new religion. They were all having much too much fun playing with the legend of Satan Claus, adding to it, building it, giving their power of belief to Father Darkness, the Christmas evil—as if by naming the horror, they might somehow remain immune to it.

"Listen! Maybe you can hear him even now? Feel the ground rumble? No, that's not a train. That's Father Darkness—Satan Claus. Yes, he's always there. Do you hear his horn? Do you hear the ugly snuffling of the eight rabid pigs? He's coming closer. Maybe this year he's coming for you. This year you'd better stay asleep all night long. Maybe this year I won't be able to stop him from getting you!"

Then some right-wing religious zealot down in Orange County saw the story; his teenage son had borrowed a copy of the magazine from a friend. So of course the censorship issue came bubbling right up to the surface like a three-day corpse in a swamp.

Dhor took full advantage of the situation. He ended up doing a public reading on the front steps of the Los An-

geles Central Library. The *L.A. Times* printed his picture
and a long article about this controversial new young fantasy writer who was challenging the outmoded literary
conventions of our times. Goodman Hallmouth showed
up, of course—he'd get up off his deathbed for a media
event—and made his usual impassioned statement on how
Dhor was exposing the hypocrisy of Christmas in America.

*"The children trembled in their cold, cold beds, afraid to
close their eyes, afraid to fall asleep. They knew that Father
Darkness would soon be there, standing at the foot of their
beds and watching them fiercely to see if they were truly
sleeping or just pretending."*

Of course it all came to a head at Art and Lydia's Christmas Eve party. They always invited the whole community,
whoever was in town. You not only got to see all your
friends, but all your enemies as well. You had to be there,
to find out what people were saying about you behind
your back.

Lydia must have spent a week cooking. She had huge
platters piled high with steaming turkey, ham, roast beef,
lasagna, mashed potatoes, sweet potatoes, tomatoes in
basil and dill, corn on the cob, pickled cabbage, four
kinds of salad, vegetable casseroles, quiche and deviled
eggs. She had plates of cookies and chocolates everywhere; the bathtub was filled with ice and bottles of imported beer and cans of Coca-Cola. Art brought in
champagne and wine, and imported mineral water for
Goodman Hallmouth.

And then they invited the seven-year locusts.

All the writers, both serious and not-so, showed up;
some of them wearing buttons that read, "Turn down a
free meal, get thrown out of the Guild." Artists, too, but
they generally had better table manners. One year two of
them got trampled in the rush to the buffet. After that,
Lydia started weeding out the guest list.

This year the unofficial theme of the party was "Satan
Claus Is Coming to Town." The tree was draped in black

crepe and instead of an angel on top, there was a large black bat. Steven Dhor even promised to participate in a "summoning."

"Little Bob still whimpered softly. He wiped his nose on his sleeve. Finally, Millie got out of her bed and crept softly across the floor and slipped into bed next to Little Bob. She put her arms around him and held him close and began whispering as quietly as she could. 'He can't hurt us if we're good. So we'll just be as good as we can. Okay? We'll pray to Baby Jesus and ask him to watch out for us, okay?' Little Bob nodded and sniffed, and Millie began to pray for the both of them. . . ."

I got there late, I had other errands to run; it's always that way on the holidays.

Steven Dhor was holding court in the living room, sitting on the floor in the middle of a rapt group of wanna-bes and never-wases; he was embellishing the legend of Satan Claus. He'd already announced that he was planning to do a collection of Satan Claus stories, or perhaps even a novel telling the whole story of Satan Claus from beginning to end. Just as St. Nicholas had been born out of good deeds, so Satan Claus had been forged from the evil that stalked the earth on the night before Jesus was born.

According to legend—legend according to Dhor—the Devil was powerless to stop the birth of Baby Jesus, but that didn't stop him from raising Hell in his own way. On the eve of the very first Christmas, the Devil turned loose all his imps upon the Earth and told them to steal out among the towns and villages of humankind and spread chaos and dismay among the children. Leave no innocent being unharmed. It was out of this beginning that Satan Claus came forth. At first he was small, but he grew. Every year, the belief of the children gave him more and more power.

"The children slept fitfully. They tossed and turned and made terrible little sounds of fear. Their dreams were filled with darkness and threats. They held onto each other all

night long. They were awakened by a rumbling deep within the earth, the whole house rolled uneasily—"

Dhor had placed himself so he could see each new arrival come in the front door. He grinned up at each one with a conspiratorial grin of recognition and shared evil, as if to say, "See? It works. Everybody loves it." I had to laugh. He didn't understand. He probably never would. He was so in love with himself and his story and the power of his words that he missed the greater vision. I turned away and went prowling through the party in search of food and drink.

"They came awake together, Millie and Little Bob. They came awake with a gasp—they were too frightened to move.

"Something was tapping softly on the bedroom window. It scraped slowly at the glass. But they were both too afraid to look."

Lydia was dressed in a black witch's costume; she even wore a tall, pointed hat. She was in the kitchen stirring a huge cauldron of hot mulled wine and cackling like the opening scene in *Macbeth*—"Double, double toil and trouble, fire burn and cauldron bubble"—and having a wonderful time of it. For once, she was enjoying one of her own parties. She waved her wooden spoon around her head like a mallet, laughing in maniacal glee.

Christmas was a lot more fun without all those sappy little elves and angels, all those damned silver bells and the mandatory choral joy of the endless hallelujahs. Steven Dhor had given voice to the rebellious spirit, had found a way to battle the ennui of a month steeped in Christmas cheer. These people were going to enjoy every nasty moment of it.

"A huge dark shape loomed like a wall at the foot of their bed. It stood there, blocking the dim light of the hallway. They could hear its uneven heavy breath, sounding like the inhalations of a terrible beast. They could smell the reek of death and decay. Millie put her hand across Little Bob's mouth to keep him from crying.

" *'Oh, please don't hurt us,'* she cried. *She couldn't help herself. 'Please—'* "

I circulated once through the party, taking roll—seeing who was being naughty, who was being nice. Goodman Hallmouth was muttering darkly about the necessity for revenge. Writers, he said, are the Research and Development Division for the whole human race; the only *specialists* in revenge in the whole world. Bread Bryan was standing around looking mournful. George Finger wasn't here, he was back in the hospital again. Railroad Martin was showing off a new T-shirt; it said, "Help, I'm trapped inside a T-shirt."

And, of course, there was the usual coterie of fans and unknowns—I knew them by their fannish identities: the Elephant, the Undertaker, the Blob, the Duck.

"And then . . . a horrible thing happened. A second shape appeared behind the first, bigger and darker. Its crimson eyes blazed with unholy rage. A cold wind swept through the room. A low, groaning noise, somewhere between a moan and an earthquake, resounded through the house like a scream. Black against a darker black, the first shape turned and saw what stood behind it. It began to shrivel and shrink. The greater darkness enveloped the lesser, pulled it close, and . . . did something horrible. In the gloom, the children could not clearly see; but they heard every terrible crunch and gurgle. They heard the choking gasps and felt the floor shudder with the weight.

"Millie screamed then; so did Little Bob. They closed their eyes and screamed as hard as they could. They screamed for their very lives. They screamed and screamed and kept on screaming—"

Steven Dhor got very drunk that night—first on his success, then on Art and Lydia's wine. At about two in the morning, he became abusive and started telling people what he really thought of them. At first, people thought he was kidding, but then he called Hallmouth a poseur and a phony, and Lydia had to play referee. Finally, Bread

Bryan and Railroad Martin drove him home and poured him into bed. He passed out in the car, only rousing himself occasionally to vomit out the window.

The next morning, Steven Dhor was gone.

Art stopped by his place on Christmas morning to see if he was all right, but Dhor didn't answer his knock. Art walked around the house and banged on the back door, too. Still no answer. He peeked in the bedroom window, and the bed was disheveled and empty, so Art assumed that Steven had gotten up early and left, perhaps to spend Christmas with a friend. But he didn't know him well enough to guess who he might have gone to see. Nobody did.

Later, the word began to spread that he was missing.

His landlady assumed he'd skipped town to avoid paying his rent. Goodman Hallmouth said he thought Steven had gone home to visit his family in Florida and would probably return shortly. Bread Bryan said that Steve had mentioned taking a sabbatical, a cross-country hitchhiking trip. Railroad Martin filed a missing-person report, but after a few routine inquiries, the police gave up the investigation. George Finger suggested that Satan Claus had probably taken him, but under the circumstances, it was considered a rather tasteless joke and wasn't widely repeated.

But . . . George was right.

Steven Dhor had come awake at the darkest moment of the night, stumbling out of a fitful and uncomfortable sleep. He rubbed his eyes and sat up in bed—and then he saw me standing there, watching him.

Waiting.

I'd been watching him and waiting for him since the day he'd first spoken my name aloud, since the moment he'd first given me shape and form and the power of his belief. I'd been hungry for him ever since.

He was delicious. I crunched his bones like breadsticks. I drank his blood like wine. The young ones are

always tasty. I savored the flavor of his soul for a long,
long time.

And, of course, before I left, I made sure to leave the evidence of my visit. Art never told anyone, but he saw it:
sooty smudges on the bedroom window, and the ground
beneath it all torn up and churned, as if by the milling of
many heavy-footed creatures.

Hugo and Nebula-winning George Alec Effinger, creator of such diverse characters as Maureen Birnbaum, Barbarian Swordsperson, science fiction writer Sandor Courane (who, at last count, has died in more than a dozen different stories), and Marid, the narrator of *When Gravity Fails* and *A Fire in the Sun*, chose Frank James for his alternate outlaw.

But being George, he's not content to give you merely an alternate outlaw and an alternate history. He also insists on giving you an alternate presentation: an old-fashioned Dime Novel of action and adventure. . . .

Shootout at Gower Gulch
by George Alec Effinger

Chapter I

A Traitor Strikes

Crack! Bang! Crack-crack-crack! Pistols and rifles hidden in the jagged, slanted rocks spat leaden death.

"They're on to us!" Jesse James cried out. "Let's ride!"

"Split up, boys," Jesse's brother, Frank, called. "We'll follow separate trails and meet back at the secret hideout."

Then the members of the famous outlaw band rode hell-bent-for-leather in all directions.

"Ha-ha-ha!" Jesse laughed as he gave the slip to the

posse that tried to follow him into the rocky hills. Jesse
carried much of the loot from the daring daytime raid on
the Springfield railway office.

An hour later, the riders of the James gang began strag-
gling toward the secluded ranch house that was their
headquarters.

Jesse was inside the building when he heard someone
shout, "Hallo!"

"Who is it?" Jesse inquired suspiciously.

"Bill Monaghan."

"If it's you, Bill, you know the password."

"Liberty and freedom," Monaghan replied.

"All serene, Bill. Come ahead."

A moment later, the tall, gaunt form of Bill Monaghan
stepped across the threshold. "Hallo, Jesse. Have the others come home to roost yet?"

"No, but they should arrive soon now."

The ranch house was really only a small, rough cabin
nestled snugly among the Missouri hills. It was still the
home of Zerelda Samuels, Jesse and Frank James' mother.
Jesse lived there under the nom de guerre of "Mr. Howard."

Bill Monaghan went into the small kitchen and took a
seat at the table. Jesse followed him.

A few minutes later, Charley and Bob Ford rode up,
new members of the James gang. The brothers had not yet
fully proven their loyalty to Jesse, but he had needed their
guns on the visit to the Springfield railway office.

"Liberty and freedom," Charley Ford called.

"Liberty and freedom," Bob Ford called.

"Come on in, boys," Jesse calmly replied. "Mother is
cooking dinner."

Hardly inside the house, they heard the approaching
hoofbeats of a stouthearted horse.

"That will be Frank," Charley Ford said.

"If it isn't, we will soon make him welcome, ha-ha,"
Jesse James joked.

"Liberty and freedom," a strong, deep voice called. "It's your brother and saddle pal, Frank."

Jesse said:

"We are all here now. Shall we divvy up the profits?"

"Do that in the other room and let me cook," Mrs. Samuels put in.

The James brothers, the Ford brothers, and Bill Monaghan went into the larger front room. They decided to portion the loot evenly, and each man pocketed more than twenty-five hundred dollars in ill-gotten gains.

"Here, Frank, give this to Mother." Jesse passed two hundred dollars to his older brother.

"I will donate the same." Frank carried the money into the kitchen.

Before Frank could present the gift to his mother, he heard Charley Ford's voice say, "That picture over there sure is crooked." Then Frank heard the sound of a chair being dragged across the plank floor.

"Since when has Charley Ford cared if the pictures were crooked?" Frank asked himself.

He looked into the other room just in time to see Bob Ford pull his six-gun. He aimed to shoot the unwary Jesse James in the back.

"Why, you treacherous fiend!" Frank cried in a rage.

He leaped into the room. His hand swooped to draw his own pistol with lightning speed.

Bang! Whiz-z! Bob Ford's shots went awry, and the bullets buried themselves in the wall beside Jesse's head.

Cr-ack! Frank hit his mark with his first shot, and Bob Ford toppled forward to the floor, stone dead.

"What in tarnation?" Jesse shouted, jumping down from the chair. He drew his gun and held it menacingly on Charley Ford.

"I think you better take it easy now, Charley." Frank covered him, too.

"You killed my brother!" Charley Ford accused.

"Seems to me he needed killing just then," Bill Monaghan said.

Mrs. Samuels stood in the doorway, taking in the dreadful scene. She muttered something, turned her back, and returned to her cooking.

Jesse's expression was fierce. "Charley, why don't you tell us what this is all about?"

Charley looked from Jesse to Frank to Bill. He found no friends there. "It was the governor. He called us in and offered us ten thousand dollars if we would kill Jesse. And he promised full pardons for us, too."

"Ten thousand dollars!" Jesse laughed. "Why, I can hardly blame you boys."

Frank said:

"Jesse, something still needs to be done about this."

"Yes. Charley, get your brother's body out of here and keep riding. If we ever see you again, we'll figure you're after the reward, and we will shoot you down like a dog."

Charley Ford set his jaw and said nothing. He carried Bob's lifeless form outside and threw it across the saddle of one of the horses. Frank, Jesse, and Bill watched as Charley mounted his own horse and led the other out of the yard.

"I don't suppose this affair is over yet," Frank said thoughtfully.

"Well, durn it anyway, let's go in to eat," Jesse said lightheartedly.

Chapter II

Frank James' Conscience

We will let Charley Ford ride out of this tale, but we are not entirely finished with the Fords, not by a long shot.

Meanwhile, back at the ranch, Jesse James and Frank were having a serious talk about the future.

"I believe I am about quits, Jesse," Frank slowly said. His stern eyes were cast down at the floor.

"Why, what do you mean?"

Frank answered:

"I mean that I have never shot a man before. Not like that, face to face. I didn't like it, and I do not aim to do it again. I just don't have the stomach for it. It isn't the same as cleaning the streets of sheriffs' men after a bank withdrawal. It seemed like . . . murder."

"But you were protecting my life from that dirty little coward!"

Frank shook his head. "It is still the same to me. I've been thinking of turning myself in to the governor, serving my time, and getting on with an honest life."

"You are a hard one to figure, Frank, but I suppose you know that will make Mother happiest."

"Yes, it will," Frank James replied.

"I was figuring on taking on two new boys to replace those low-life Fords. Now I reckon I will need three."

"You could do worse than Tom Battle and Zeke Whitley."

"And you can count on Ab Milligan, too," Bill Monaghan put in.

"They're all good, strong boys," Jesse agreed.

"And every one of them is as loyal as the day is long," Frank said.

"What did you plan next, Jesse?" Bill inquired.

Jesse laid a long finger beside his nose. "Ah, as to that, I have intelligence that the First Bank of Springfield will be foreclosing the mortgage on the Widow Rogers' farm. I propose that we pay a little social call on the bank. We can probably extract enough of a donation to put Widow Rogers in the clear."

"And then," Frank grinned, "after the widow has paid off her mortgage and the papers have been signed, you can rob the bank again, just to take care of your 'expenses'!"

"Ha-ha," Jesse laughed. "You know me too well!"

"I wish you would ride with us one last time," Bill Monaghan said.

"Sorry, Bill, but my mind is set. I will be riding off to see the governor tomorrow in the morning."

"Well, the best of luck to you, Frank," Jesse said earnestly. "And you can come back to us any time."

"Well, Jesse, a clear road to you and no burrs under your saddle," Frank said. There was great sadness in his voice.

Chapter III

The Governor's Word

Frank James walked alone into the office of Governor Thomas T. Crittenden. If he could strike a deal with the governor, he had no need of side men. If the governor was in a punitive mood, Frank wished to have no other person injured or killed, should a gun battle erupt.

A young man who identified himself as Governor Crittenden's appointment secretary inquired as to the purpose of the outlaw's visit.

By way of reply, Frank unbuckled his gun belt and held it up.

"I am Frank James," he said, "and I have come to surrender these shooting irons to the governor himself."

The secretary's eyes opened wide. "Frank James? Has your brother Jesse come with you?"

"No, my friend, but that was Jesse's decision. We disagreed over what our future is to be."

"I see. Well, the governor is meeting with some important merchants, but I am sure he will be eager to speak with you after they have gone."

Frank smiled with a hint of irony. "All serene," he said. "I am in no hurry."

"Take a seat, Mr. James. It should only be a matter of a few minutes."

At half past ten o'clock in the morning, as the wealthy

storekeepers exited the governor's office, the secretary entered to break the news of their unexpected visitor.

"Well, well, Mr. James," Governor Crittenden said with some satisfaction. "You have made an excellent decision. It is a bit of a shame that your brother didn't come to the same conclusion."

"My brother is well aware that it was you who offered ten thousand dollars to the Ford brothers to murder him. It's something I will keep in mind during this discussion, as well."

"Oh, *that*." The politician rubbed his plump fingers together. "You have to understand that a governor sometimes must go along with plans that are to him personally distasteful."

"Shooting my brother in the back because your lawmen could never accomplish the deed in a fair fight would be personally distasteful to anyone but a scurvy coward."

The governor began to show anger and half rose from his seat. Then he got his emotions under control again. He sat down and said smoothly:

"Just put your pistols on my desk, Frank. I cannot proceed with negotiations at the point of a gun."

Frank shook his head. "I will do as you say when we've reached an agreement and I feel I can trust your word. In the meantime, I'll just hold them here. They will be harmless, unless I am threatened in some way."

"You know, if you came here seeking a pardon, I cannot grant you one."

"I understand that, and I never expected you to grant me a pardon. I am willing to face a jury and stand trial for all that I have done. If the trials are fair, I will serve whatever sentence is laid down. I wish to pay for my crimes and return to being an honest citizen."

"To be truthful, sir, I am quite astonished. This is certainly a newsworthy event."

"I am sure that you will make the most of it, Governor," Frank James added ironically.

Unfortunately for Crittenden, he did not receive the

positive response that he expected from the people. Frank read in the *St. Louis Republican* that the governor had said, "I have no excuse to make, no apologies to render to any living man for the part I have played in this drama. I am not regretful of ordering Jesse James' death, and have no censure for the boys who tried to remove him. They deserve credit, is my candid, solemn opinion. Why should these Ford boys be so abused?"

Frank smiled as he read the article. He knew that Governor Crittenden was on the defensive. On the trains carrying him back to Clay County for the first trial, Frank James received the cheers of great crowds of people. The governor was booed. Later, Crittenden's political party refused even to renominate him for governor because of the "pro-James vote."

In Clay County, Frank stood trial for a pair of murders. The headline in a Kansas City newspaper that day read, "We're With You, Frank."

Frank said:

"I should be afraid for my life, for the penalty for these killings could be death. Yet I feel that I am among friends."

"You are indeed," the deputy guarding him remarked.

When Frank was brought handcuffed into the courtroom, the spectators and the jury cheered him. Frank smiled back at all of them.

When the trial was finished and Frank was acquitted, the mob sang a new and popular tune:

"Jesse and Frank were lads who killed many a man.
They robbed the Glendale trains.
They stole from the rich and gave to the poor.
They had hands and hearts and brains."

In succession, Frank was shipped to Alabama to face a robbery charge. Then he went back to Missouri for another robbery count. He was never found guilty of any crime.

"You have achieved what you sought," the Missouri judge spoke solemnly. "You are a free man now, Mr. James. The people of this state do not wish to interfere further in your private life. You may walk out of this courtroom, to return home and, if it is God's will, become a respected citizen."

Frank replied:

"Home? I have no home now. I believe I will strike out for the West. I hope to begin a new life."

"Well, the people of Missouri and this court wish you the best of luck."

Frank felt a great surge of gladness that his outlaw life was finally ended. He said:

"Thank you, Your Honor, and I promise that I will do my best never to transgress society's laws again."

Chapter IV

The Lure of Violence

Years passed, but Frank James' fame and popularity did not diminish. He worked as a shoe salesman and as a writer of dime novels about the Old West, until an admirer offered him a position as a well-paid celebrity horse-race starter.

Frank's dream of settling down peacefully as a gentleman farmer would have to wait.

"I am grateful for this opportunity, of course," Frank said sincerely to his benefactor.

"Oh, it is I who should thank you for agreeing to my proposition."

"However, I do not know how long I can continue trading on my name."

"I can understand how you feel, Mr. James. Perhaps we can work together until you've saved enough money for your homestead stake."

"That sounds just fine to me," Frank replied.

A year and a half later, Frank was more discouraged. He did not seem to be able to accumulate the amount of money he reckoned he needed to buy premium farmland, or the equipment and stock that was necessary.

One day Frank James had a visitor. It was our old friend, Bill Monaghan. He stood in the corridor outside Frank's hotel room. He rapped three times upon the wooden door. Then he called:

"Liberty and freedom, Frank! Say hello to your old chum, Bill."

Frank opened the door with a speed like lightning.

"Bill! It is great to see you!"

He stood aside to let Bill Monaghan enter the room. They just looked at each other like long-lost brothers for a few moments. Then Bill inquired:

"What in tarnation are you doing here? This settlement looks like it will be a ghost town, and not before many years have passed."

Frank grinned at his friend. "I am trying to put aside enough cash to buy a farm. It takes longer to do that if you do it the honest way. What brings you here, though? Did Jesse send you?"

"I'm headed to California, Frank," Bill replied pleasantly. "There is plenty of free cash out there for me, and for you, too."

"What?" cried Frank in astonishment. "You can't mean hunting for gold. I will bet there aren't two grains of gold to rub against each other in those played-out fields."

Bill Monaghan replied positively:

"No, it is not gold, Frank. There is a new industry in the Los Angeles area."

"Los Angeles? That's a lonely train stop trying to elbow a place for itself in the western sun."

"That is true. In recent years, though, the picture-industry companies have relocated to California from back East. They are satisfied with the pleasant weather around the town of Los Angeles; it has the days of sunshine they need to make the most of their filming schedule. Now, I know Los Angeles is a one-horse town compared to San Francisco, but the picture people have brought their own various vices with them."

"The moving-picture industry?" Frank inquired with puzzlement. "How does that affect you or me? Neither of us knows anything about cinema films."

Bill laughed. "We do not *need* to know anything, pal! We're not going out there to stand in front of the cameras."

"What then?"

Bill's expression turned serious. "There is a kind of war being fought there, only it is not the government against the rebels. Nevertheless, our experience riding with Quantrill's Raiders will be much admired. You see, one big picture company is trying to destroy some little ones. We are going out there to help protect the underdogs."

All this gave Frank a deal to think over. He slowly decided:

"I surely do love battling for the guys with the short end of the stick. I do not have any idea what this war is about, but I'm sure, Bill, that you would not steer me wrong. I am certainly not prospering here. The only thing is that I promised never to commit a crime again."

At that, Bill Monaghan laughed.

"There will be no crime, Frank! You and I will be honestly hired by one of the small picture companies, and our jobs will be to protect their cameras and other expensive equipment against the hired strong-arm men of the big company. That is all."

Frank James chewed his lip in thought. "I see no crime in that. In fact, I am eager to make a start for California. When can we leave?"

Bill slapped Frank on the back and said:

"Ever the headstrong one, eh Frank? Well, I have ridden quite a way to get here to-day. I would like a good meal, a few drinks, perhaps a hand of poker, and a good night's rest. We can hit the trail together in the morning."

"All serene, then, Bill. I'm sure Jesse and Mother would approve."

Bill Monaghan lifted his eyebrows. "They both approved when I left them back in Missouri."

The two friends laughed together and went downstairs to find the thickest, best steaks in the entire town.

Chapter V

A Soldier in the Patents' War

It was war! Perhaps not as vast and as calamitous as the recent War of Northern Aggression, but it was bloody war just the same. The Wizard of Menlo Park, old Tom Edison, wanted to maintain a monopoly on picture-making. He couldn't patent the film, because that was made by Eastman Kodak. Soon, though, he struck upon the idea of getting a patent on the film's sprocket holes. It is an odd-sounding idea to-day, but it was a successful "dodge" for Edison.

He joined his cinema film company with his closest competition, the Biograph Company, to form the Motion Picture Patents Company. The company was quite blatantly a trust, in an era when banking, oil, and railroad trusts were being broken up by the Sherman Anti-Trust Act. The MPCC also controlled Vitagraph and licensed several of the smaller picture companies.

The irony was that Edison himself had had nothing to do with the kinetoscope—the moving-picture camera. Not a bit of it was original with him.

There were, of course, independent picture companies that refused on principle to bow to the MPCC's high-handed licensing policies.

Edison made an agreement with Eastman Kodak that made sure the film-manufacturing firm would supply film only to MPCC's friends.

The independents found at last that they, too, needed to

organize. They got themselves together as the Motion Picture Distributing and Sales Company.

They had their first victory in 1912 when an appeals court ruled that since Edison had not invented the film, he wasn't entitled to any patents connected to it, nullifying the sprocket-hole issue.

The little guys ignored the MPCC's threats and went ahead making their own pictures, but Edison and his allies retaliated by hiring hoodlums to stop the independents. They tried to destroy the unlicensed film cameras. Sometimes things became violent. A few independent studios were burned to the ground.

That was one of the reasons the independent film makers left New York and New Jersey behind and fled to the wild and sparsely settled area in southern California that was the frontier town of Los Angeles.

"That is where we come in, Frank," Bill Monaghan said with a smile.

"I see. I suppose that our new employer bought the train tickets so that we could travel in style."

"Colossus Pictures International, that is who. Their moniker sounds big, but they are only about a dozen guys who just want to be left alone to make their cinema films."

"That's good enough for me," said Frank thoughtfully. "I never thought I'd be riding in one of these iron carriages. I hope we don't run into Jesse around the next bend, wearing a mask, ha-ha!"

"Ha-ha!" laughed Bill Monaghan.

The next day, they arrived at their destination. They were met by Colossus Pictures International's security boss, Robert L. Jennings. He said:

"Mr. James, Mr. Monaghan, it's good to see you boys. Welcome to California."

Frank James replied:

"Sunshine and fresh oranges seemed more promising than another year of selling shoes."

"And if we run into anything else, why, we're ready," remarked Bill.

"Glad to hear it," Jennings put in. "I have some money for you, so you can settle yourselves right in." He counted out a stack of bills for each of them.

Bill looked at his pay suspiciously. "What is this? Don't you have gold and silver coins out here? I have never put much trust in this paper money. Why, one match could burn up a year's wages!"

Jennings smiled. "Don't worry, Mr. Monaghan. Those bills will spend just as well as the cartwheel silver dollars."

Bill shrugged and put his money in his pocket.

"One more thing," Frank anxiously said. "I do not wish to be known here as Frank James. I'd prefer to be called Frank Howard."

"Fine, Frank," Jennings agreed. "Whatever you say."

Later that day, after they had found beds in a convenient rooming house, Bill explained:

"The MPCC is sending hoodlums here, even to California, to shoot holes through the Colossus Pictures' cameras. So the studio chief, A.F. Brown, is fighting back. He's hiring former cowboys, security guards, and plenty of outlaws still on the run. He is not asking many questions, and neither is that Jennings fellow."

Frank shrugged. "Then it is a good thing that I have kept my peacemakers cleaned, oiled, and ready all these years. I'm curious if any of those back East tough guys measure up to the folks we have known in Missouri."

"We may soon find out," Bill replied. He did not appear to be very worried.

It is well known that truth is stranger than fiction, and as Fate would have it, Frank James and Bill Monaghan were forced to draw their pistols the very next day.

It began with Robert L. Jennings introducing our friends to a lovely young woman. She was wearing a long, pretty dress of cotton in a charming floral print. She had on a large picture hat and she carried a fringed parasol. She was mounted sidesaddle on an old and gentle mare.

"Miss Garnett," Jennings said pleasantly, "these two gentlemen will guide you and protect you this afternoon."

"Oh," breathlessly responded Miss Garnett, "do I need protection? Are there wild Indians hiding in these hills, or bloodthirsty bandits?"

Jennings laughed. "One never knows. Now, I must ride down to where the camera crew is assembled. From here, you will be able to see how we perform some of our cinema film 'magic.' Gentlemen, I am leaving Miss Garnett in your capable care."

"You have nothing to worry about, Mr. Jennings," Bill Monaghan said. He could scarcely tear his eyes away from the comely young woman.

While Jennings rode down to the camera setup, Frank and Bill chatted amiably with Miss Garnett in the shade of the familiar Vasquez Rocks, which can be seen jutting crazily from the earth in scores of Western pictures.

"They will be filming a chase scene now," Bill told their new friend. "First, a gang of riders will thunder past the Rocks, with a black horse in the lead. Then the same gang will ride by with a white horse in the lead. The audience will believe they are two different gangs."

"I find all of this so exciting," Miss Garnett remarked.

As Bill had said, about twenty cowboys raced past the camera as if a posse of deputies were hot on their trail.

"Now, it will take a few minutes to reassemble the riders for the next 'take,' " Bill instructed.

While his attention was almost completely captured by their female visitor, Frank James' eyes scoured the nearby rocky hillside. Suddenly, without saying a word, he drew his two revolvers and fired. *Bang! Bang-bang!*

Bill Monaghan spoke in a shocked voice. "What do you see, Frank?"

Frank did not reply. He urged his horse toward the target.

Miss Garnett dropped her parasol and looked at Frank, aghast. She cried out:

"You have killed Edward!"

Frank shook his head. "No, ma'am, I did not want to kill him. I just gave his shoulder a leaden kiss, to discourage him a mite. He was set to perforate the Colossus Pictures' camera with his Winchester rifle."

All three rode to the large boulder that had given Edward cover. He sat leaning against it now, clutching his bleeding shoulder and wincing with pain. His Winchester lay upon the ground beside him.

"Bill, my friend," Frank commanded, "why don't you ride down and inform Mr. Jennings what all the shooting was about. I will stay here and guard both Miss Garnett and her associate, Edward."

Bill gave the young woman a bitter look. "If I remember, I will tell them that this hoodlum Edward might like to see the doctor."

Frank held the reins to Miss Garnett's mare. There was no expression on his face as he watched Bill Monaghan's horse pick its way down the narrow trail.

Chapter VI

Gower Gulch

Later that week, when Frank James and Bill Monaghan had finished their day's work and returned to the rooming house, they discovered that they had a visitor.

It was a man as tall as Bill but apparently much better fed. He got up from a chair in the parlor and said to them:

"You boys know who A.F. Brown is?"

"Sure," declared Bill. "He's our big boss over at Colossus Pictures International. We never been within hollering distance of him."

The tall man laughed.

"He knows about you two roughriders, though. Mr.

Jennings told him all about how you shot up that spying skunk so pretty."

"Look, mister," replied Bill, "all the shooting was done by my partner here, Frank Howard."

"Well, Mr. A.F. Brown is interested in both of you. He thinks you might be wasting your talents riding around on the skirmish line."

"I never believed I had much talent for anything," Frank James modestly put in. "Except for making bullets go where I want them to."

"Ha-ha," the stranger laughed. "Now, I'm Mr. A.F. Brown's executive assistant. My name is Dan Schuster. I was hoping I could buy you a nice dinner at Enyart's and talk it over."

"Talk *what* over, Mr. Schuster?" inquired Frank.

"Why, the two of you becoming stuntmen, of course. You're getting paid ten dollars a week now, am I right? As stuntmen, you can get that much every day. What do you think?"

Bill Monaghan said:

"I think that I would not mind if you bought us a good supper. I am getting tired of the lamb stew in this rooming house, anyway."

"I agree," stated Frank. "But you'll have to tell us all about what we are getting ourselves in for."

Enyart's was on La Brea Avenue, not far from the clustered buildings of Chaplin Studios. It was not the sort of place William S. Hart might frequent, because Hart was now a major star. Yet it was a perfect gathering place for cinema buckaroos with bandages from going through one too many windows or having one too many chairs broken over their heads.

Enyart's was a simple wooden building with an open kitchen occupying one corner and a counter running around two sides of it like an L. The bar was worn and polished mahogany with a brass foot rail. Frank, Bill, and Mr. Schuster sat at a cigarette-scarred pine table. They were not talking—they were stuffing themselves with the plain, good food that made Enyart's so popular.

After the waiter cleared away the demolished steaks and the empty beer mugs, Schuster said:

"Enyart's coffee is pretty good, and it goes down well with the apple cobbler. You can't come here without trying the famous apple cobbler."

"I have had enough to eat, Mr. Schuster," said Frank.

"Call me Dan, fellows." He glanced at Bill, who nodded. Schuster signaled to the waiter. "Two apple cobblers, three coffees, Marty."

"Right away, Mr. S," the waiter rejoined.

Schuster explained:

"Most of the small, independent studios are situated around Gower Street and Sunset Boulevard in Hollywood. Colossus is only one of a couple dozen picture outfits there."

"The cowboys hang out there hoping to get work in a new Western picture," Bill added. "That is why they call it Gower Gulch."

Schuster nodded impatiently. "Yes, yes. And the big studios call us Poverty Row. Mr. A.F. Brown disapproves of both nicknames. Don't ever use them in his presence—or mine, either."

"All serene, Mr. Schuster," said Bill.

"Call me Dan. I want you both to show up at our studio early to-morrow morning. There are some papers for you to fill out. Then we'll put you right to work in our new Western picture, *Sand and Stones*. The other stuntmen will be glad to show you the ropes. There are tricks of the trade that make the stunts much less dangerous than they seem to the audience."

"You mentioned better wages, Mr. Schuster," Frank said softly.

"Yes, well, we will pay you on a daily basis for now. Once you become one of our regulars, you will get between sixty and seventy-five dollars a week. What do you think?"

"And we don't have to kill anybody for that fortune?" Bill Monaghan inquired.

"We prefer that you don't," Schuster laughed.

"What do you think, Frank? Better than a jab in the eye with a sharp stick, eh?"

Frank James said thoughtfully, "We will see, Bill."

The next day near noon, Frank and Bill were on the set of *Sand and Stones*. It was a lonely house built in the San Fernando Valley near Newhall. Colossus Pictures International and some of the other Poverty Row studios used the house often.

The assistant director, a man named Gus, put his arm around Frank's shoulder and together they walked away from the group of stuntmen. "How would you like to earn ten dollars on your first day, Mr. Howard?"

"I reckon it would be fine. What do I have to do?"

Gus pointed to the house, to an upstairs window that gave out onto a porch. "We will want you to tumble through that window—don't worry, it's not glass, and you do not have to be afraid of getting cut up. Just tuck and roll. When you are through the window, jump to your feet, vault the railing, and land on the back of that saddled horse. You will have specially padded trousers, but I won't kid you: it's going to hurt some. Then you just ride off as fast as you can."

Frank frowned. "I suppose I can do that."

Gus grinned. "For the sake of your family jewels, try to get it in one 'take.' "

Ned Bergen, the obese but very clever props man, fitted Frank with a set of clothes that duplicated the costume of the picture's male star, Dick Sutton.

"Those trousers are padded," Bergen declared. "Still, Gus probably warned you that they are not padded enough. Try not to do too many of these horse jumps, or you'll be spending your nights in a rocking chair with a shawl around your shoulders, remembering what it used to be like."

Frank said nothing. He was thinking about the stunt.

The camera crew needed about twenty minutes to position the camera. When they were ready, and the horse was in the proper place, the director yelled, "Action!"

Frank took a deep breath, burst through the breakaway window, rolled to his feet, got a good sight of the horse below before he leaped the railing, hit the saddle hard, and rode off. He clung desperately to the horse as fierce pain made him double over.

He rode slowly back to the set. Bill Monaghan said: "How was it, Frank?"

"I think the terrible escape from the Northfield, Minnesota, raid might have been worse, but I am not certain."

Bill laughed.

The director called:

"I believe we got that just fine, but I want to do it again. All right, Mr. Howard?"

"All serene," replied Frank. "Damn it."

Chapter VII

The Celluloid Sheriff

Frank James and Bill Monaghan spent seven years doing stunts and doubling such celebrities as Colossus Pictures International's Dick Sutton.

They endured the torment of the special greenish makeup that was necessary because of the orthochromatic black-and-white film then in use. The film exaggerated every wrinkle and made the palest of skin look almost black on the screen.

Bill Monaghan developed a severe allergy to the ghoulish makeup, and the picture company's doctor prescribed morphine and cocaine for him. Of course, soon Bill was physically addicted to the drugs.

In their eighth year in Los Angeles, they were told to meet Gus Campbell for lunch. Campbell was now one of Colossus Pictures' most important film directors. He had been the assistant director on *Sand and Stones*, Frank's first film appearance.

They met at Bar's Mike and Grill, a favorite hangout of the cowboy extras at Hollywood Boulevard and Cahuenga, only six blocks from Gower Gulch.

"Good to see you boys," exclaimed Gus Campbell. "Sit down. What will you have?"

"Just a grilled burger, no bun, and a salad," replied Bill. "I have to watch my weight."

"You are as skinny as a rail," remarked Campbell.

"I have no appetite anymore. I think it's because of the medicine Doc Waters is giving me."

"I will have chili and mashed potatoes and a good, cold beer," Frank decided.

"Fine," Campbell said. He gave their order to the waiter. "Now we can talk business.

"Frank, we get quite a lot of good mail about you. You have become a familiar and welcome face among all the other black hats in our Western crowd. We would like to make you a featured villain with billing beneath Dick Sutton. Bill, we have plans for you as Frank's comic relief sidekick. What do you think?"

"We are earning a hundred dollars a week now," Frank stated. "How will that change?"

"You get right to it, don't you, Frank?" laughed Gus Campbell. "Well, that is all right. Frank, we are offering you five hundred a week, and Bill three hundred."

Bill gasped. "Take it, Frank! I never believed I could make that kind of cash doing honest labor."

"It does sound good to me, Mr. Campbell," Frank replied.

"Call me Gus," said the director in a friendly way. "We have parts for both of you in our next film, *The Sheriff's Widow*."

"Thank you for the opportunity," said Frank modestly.

Campbell smiled. "In the meantime, I am inviting you to a party to-morrow night at A.F. Brown's estate. Seven

o'clock. Bill Fields will be there. You have never seen anyone juggle like Fields. He is like a one-man show."

"What will we wear, Frank?" inquired Bill anxiously.

"Don't worry about that," Campbell interjected. "The
party is informal."

"We'll be there," Frank said.

Months later, when the first reviews of *The Sheriff's
Widow* began to come in, the front office of Colossus Pictures International was surprised.

The consensus of opinion was that Dick Sutton had
given his usual solid, professional performance, but that
in the role of greedy, sly Colonel Zack Masterson, Colossus had discovered a new "overnight" star in Frank Howard.

The trade papers praised Frank's easy, natural style of
acting, which often made Sutton look wooden by comparison. Even Bill Monaghan rated a few mentions for the
welcome bits of humor he donated to the tired storyline.

After *The Sheriff's Widow* came *Apache Rage*, then *Saw-
dust Rose*, and *Guns in the Sunset*. With each picture,
Frank's reputation grew. Finally, he—and Bill Monaghan—
were called to the office of A.F. Brown himself.

They waited in the anteroom until the studio chief's assistant told them they could go in.

"Good afternoon, boys," said A.F. Brown. "Take a seat."

A.F. Brown was a large man, just under six feet tall, and
very heavy. He had coarse features, black hair, a black
beard, and deceptively mild gray-green eyes. He smoked a
large, black, noxious cigar.

A.F. Brown leaned back in his great chair and put his
feet up on his desk. He wore high, black-leather boots to
protect his legs from the thorns and burrs so common
around the shooting sets.

"I am pleased to meet you at last, Mr. Brown," Frank
boldly said.

"Call me Frank, Frank," said A.F. Brown. "And you,
too, Bill. Now, I will tell you why I called you here.

"Frank, our next Western picture is called *Trap of Iron*.

Six months ago, it was all set for Dick Sutton to play the sheriff of Northfield, Minnesota. You were to play the leader of a gang of robbers."

Frank James looked at his friend. Then he turned back to A.F. Brown. "Northfield, Minnesota?" he inquired. "Wasn't that the place of the famous bank holdup led by Jesse James?"

A.F. Brown replied:

"Yes, indeed. It was a disaster for the James brothers and the Youngers. It is perfect material for filming.

"However, you have become so popular with our audiences that I do not believe they will want to see you killed or badly wounded."

hat are you saying, then, Mr. Brown?" Frank asked in a quiet voice.

"Call me Frank. I am suggesting that you will take over the Dick Sutton role, with Bill as your sidekick, and we'll cast the Jesse and Frank James parts from the large pool of cowboys who frequent the bars around here."

It was all Bill Monaghan could do to keep from laughing out loud.

Frank pretended to think the matter over. At last he said:

"Do you believe then that I am ready to take on a starring role?"

"I am certain of it," responded A.F. Brown. "And to prove it, with *Trap of Iron*, I will double your salary. And Bill's, too."

"It is a deal, Mr. Brown," Frank said gladly. He reached across the desk and shook the executive's hand.

Before another year was out, *Trap of Iron* proved to be a brilliant success for Colossus Pictures International.

It also marked a turning point, because from then on, Frank Howard became more popular at the box office than Dick Sutton had ever been. Sutton still starred in some pictures for Colossus and other Poverty Row studios, but Frank had a certain charisma that seemed to leap off the cinema screen.

Frank was always in demand, and soon he could pick and choose among the many scripts offered to him. It was clear that he carried the fortunes of Colossus with him, and he quickly received all the luxurious treatment that a film star deserved.

Bill Monaghan, as Frank's friend and co-star, also reaped the benefits of success.

Soon Frank and Bill were invited everywhere, to parties at the Beverly Hills mansions of the greatest stars in Hollywood. They were guests of Mary Pickford and Douglas Fairbanks and the Gish sisters. They played golf with Wallace Beery and croquet with Charlie Chaplin. Bill Monaghan developed a close friendship with Oliver Hardy.

After the opening of *Trap of Iron*, Frank James proposed to his romantic interest in that picture, Carlotta Carnaise. She married him even after he revealed to her his true identity and swore her to secrecy.

Everything in Frank's life would have been perfect, except at the height of his popularity, he received a letter from Zeke Whitley back in Clay County.

Jesse James was dead. He had been thrown by his horse, and he had struck his head upon a rock beside the road.

It was a time of great sadness for Frank and Bill. Their film schedule did not permit them to go back to Missouri for Jesse's funeral. They each sent a gigantic memorial wreath.

Frank James finished *High Horizons*, and there were five months until the start of filming his next picture, *Colonel Pickett's Charge*. Frank was proud to play the title character.

He was looking forward to making the picture, but in the meantime, he accepted a small role in a stage revival of *Our American Cousin*. The proceeds from the theater performances were to be donated to a worthy charity.

On opening night, Frank fidgeted in the dressing room. He had never appeared before a live audience before.

Bill Monaghan and Frank's wife, Carlotta, were sitting

in the front row. There was an air of expectation in the house.

The first act went well. However, when Frank made his first entrance in the second act, a young man stood up in the audience. He cried:

"Do not move, you lying, cowardly, murdering bastard! You are Frank James, and you killed my uncle, Bob Ford!"

The young man raised a pistol and fired three shots. All three found their mark, and Frank fell backward, shot dead. Strong men in the audience overpowered the young man and held him until the authorities arrived.

"What . . . what happened?" demanded Frank's wife, Carlotta.

Bill Monaghan was dazed. In a shaking voice, he replied:

"That boy shot Frank! I know him! He's a brilliant young director, John Ford. Now his career will be over, as well . . ."

Such are the vagaries of Fate, and so ended the life of a noble man who had paid for his mistakes, dearly and twice over.

Barbara Delaplace, 1992 and 1993 Campbell nominee, burst upon the science fiction scene less than two years ago, and during that time she has produced almost twenty stories that firmly establish her as one of the brightest new stars in the field.

Always up for a challenge, Barb has chosen Adolf Hitler as her alternate outlaw, and has looked deep into his twisted mind to find the source of his power.

Painted Bridges
by Barbara Delaplace

> Painting is only a bridge linking the painter's mind with that of the viewer.
>
> —Eugene Delacroix

Excerpts from Dr. Josef Goldstein's research notes:

Finally, I may have found a possible avenue of treatment for Mr. Schickelgruber: an experimental technique in which difficult patients are supplied with paints and encouraged to express their fantasies and delusions on canvas. In some way, being able to illustrate their delusions visually seems to open a door for them, making them more willing to communicate, and thus, therapy becomes possible.

At this point I'm willing to try nearly anything. He's been so uncooperative and violent—and to be honest, frightening in his rages—that I've been unable to reach him.

I'll approach the Director about this.

Mr. Schickelgruber appears to be responding. He's painted almost nonstop since I obtained art materials for him two weeks ago. I'm no art expert, but he seems to have great natural skill. I find his paintings very strange—they contain no recognizable images—but nonetheless, the technique does seem to be working. He's become less violent and it hasn't been necessary to use sedatives as often as before. He still clings to his delusional conspiracy theories, but he no longer goes into the ranting outbursts that seemed to drive him into a frenzy.

I'm cautiously optimistic.

I've noted a tendency among the group of patients I'm treating with art therapy to become restless and disturbed whenever Mr. Schickelgruber is painting with them. I'm unable to determine the reason; he himself seems quite content to paint quietly and does nothing to incite them. I'll have to ensure he is separated from the others.

A most painful incident today. I came to work to find a crudely drawn Star of David on my office door, with a scrawled message, "Jews must die." Nothing like this has ever happened here before. The Director was deeply distressed and sent me a note of apology. . . .

Letter from Dr. Albrecht Schmidt, Director of the Institute for Mental Disorders, to Dr. Goldstein:
. . . Please accept my deepest apologies for this unfortunate incident. One of my proudest boasts is that the staff of the Institute is among the finest in the world, that we hire the best brains regardless of who they are or where they come from; I will not put up with intolerance. You have my assurances that this incident will be investigated and the culprit found and punished.

Excerpt from Dr. Goldstein's notes:
Removing Mr. Schickelgruber from the patient group and allowing him to paint alone indeed seems to have solved the disruption problem.

* * *

Letter from Helmut Vos to Dr. Albrecht Schmidt:

We have never met, so I'd like to introduce myself: I am Helmut Vos, owner of the "Modern Gallery." As you may know, the gallery devotes space each quarter to a showing of experimental works. Naturally, I'm always watching for potential show material.

I have recently learned of the work of one of the members of your staff, Dr. Josef Goldstein, who uses painting as part of his treatment of the mentally ill. Would it be possible to arrange an appointment with Dr. Goldstein so that I might see some of the patients' compositions, with an eye toward possibly mounting an exhibit of the most evocative works? I suspect that my patrons would find this a fascinating subject; and it would, I hope, enable them to regard the mentally disturbed from a more enlightened and humane point of view.

Memo from Dr. Schmidt to Dr. Goldstein:

. . . It seems to me that Mr. Vos's suggestion offers us an excellent occasion to change the way the public views our patients, to see them as people with treatable illness rather than raving lunatics who must be restrained before they do harm to others. Naturally, I will respect your wishes regarding what you feel is best for your patients, but. . . .

Excerpt from Dr. Goldstein's notes:

I'm not entirely at ease with the idea of an exhibit of works by my patients. As the Director suggests, it would be a worthwhile opportunity to change the layman's view of what mental illness means. On the other hand, I fear he gravely underestimates the extent of some of my patients' mental disorders. Mr. Schickelgruber, for example, one of the most seriously disturbed—and disturbing—patients I've ever had to deal with. Yes, he has improved markedly since he first arrived, but he is a long way from being cured. (In fact, I'm starting to wonder if he will ever be sane enough to be released; it's been over a year since he came here.) And those paintings of his . . . they bother me for reasons I don't fully understand. Maybe it's just that I don't understand this new "modern" art.

However, I can see the Director's point. We'll discuss it at this week's meeting.

Memo from Dr. Schmidt to Dr. Goldstein:
It appears the person responsible for the defacement of your office door was the janitor responsible for the entire floor. He had no reasonable explanation for his behavior (he did say it had "all become clear" to him while he was cleaning up your patients' art room) and, in fact, made a number of appalling allegations regarding people of the Jewish faith. Of course I told him that his actions were completely unacceptable and that he was no longer employed here.

Again, my apologies for the entire affair. I can't begin to imagine why he should have suddenly started behaving in such a fashion. His supervisor tells me he had worked here for many years and was regarded as a quiet and reliable employee.

Excerpt from Dr. Goldstein's notes:
The Director made such a persuasive case that I've agreed to go along with the whole business. He agreed readily with me that the privacy of the patients must be respected, and that they won't be identified other than as "A," "B" and so on. We'll make arrangements for Mr. Vos to view the paintings within the next few weeks.

Letter from Helmut Vos to Dr. Goldstein:
I'd like to thank you again for your cooperation; I quite understand your wish to preserve the privacy of your clients, and of course I will respect it. I'm looking forward to our meeting this week and to seeing the patients' work. I'm optimistic that this will make a remarkable exhibit, one that will be long remembered by those who attend.

* * *

Excerpt from Dr. Goldstein's notes:

Something odd happened in the course of the meeting today. It started out pleasantly enough: Mr. Vos was a cordial (if talkative) man, and the Director was his usual gracious self. Mr. Vos seemed quite excited by the various patients' works and assured me they would make a fine exhibition. He was particularly taken by Mr. Schickel-gruber's canvases (as was Dr. Schmidt).

But as we went through the pictures, the attitudes of the two men seemed gradually to become suspicious and antagonistic toward me. And when I suggested that some of the paintings struck me as being rather odd, they became quite hostile, telling me that any fool could see what the artists had intended and suggesting that obviously, then, I was a fool.

Needless to say, the meeting ended on a strained note. I simply don't understand it at all; though I can't speak as to Mr. Vos, I can say for certain this behavior is quite out of character for Dr. Schmidt.

From The Berlin News:

ARTISTIC SOAP-BOXER ARRESTED
FOR DISTURBING THE PEACE

A man was arrested yesterday outside the Modern Gallery after he'd spent several hours shouting at passersby. Police said that Johann Schultz, 31, was arrested when several merchants in the area complained that he was following customers into their shops and harassing them.

"He followed my customers around, yelling at them for patronizing my store," said Paul Frank, owner of Frank's Books and Maps. "Then he accused me of being part of some sort of Jewish conspiracy." Delicatessen-owner Abraham Weiss had similar complaints. "He came in bellowing at me that I was price-gouging my customers."

Shultz is employed at the Modern Gallery as an exhibit designer. Helmut Vos, owner of the gallery, and Schultz's employer, said, "I'm extremely disturbed by the behavior of the police. Mr. Schultz is a patriotic citizen of this country and was exercising his right to free speech. So what if he upset a few Jews? You can be assured I'll be asking my lawyer to look into this."

Excerpt from Dr. Goldstein's notes:
I'm at a loss to understand the sudden change in the Director's behavior toward me. Ever since our meeting with Mr. Vos to choose the patients' artwork to be displayed, it's as if he's become a different man. He's barely civil, and at times is openly hostile; in meetings, he's even accused me of careless treatment of my patients, without any basis at all.

Word of the possible art display has spread among the staff, and I'm getting many requests for permission to view the paintings, enough that I've decided to arrange an "in-house exhibition." It's gratifying to see this interest in art therapy.

From The Berlin News:

"Art Scene"
by "Sophisticate"

A most remarkable exhibition awaits your viewing pleasure at the Modern Gallery this month. Once again, owner Helmut Vos has taken another bold step in his ever-audacious program of experimental works. This week I was allowed a special advance viewing of "Mirrors to the Mind," a collection of paintings by inmates of the Institute for Mental Disorders.

You weren't aware that inmates were artists? Nor was I. But Vos explained to me that these works were the result of an experimental program of "art therapy," in which mentally disturbed patients were encouraged to paint their inner visions—their phantasms and delusions—to aid their doctor in treating them.

And the result? An amazing outpouring of expression from these untrained artists, full of passion, with vigorous use of form, color, and space. As might be expected, the visions are not happy ones, being, as they are, insights into tormented souls; many have a foreboding quality. Yet they are never dull or repetitive. Indeed, some exert a strange, almost hypnotic, fascination.

In particular, I found the paintings by "Patient S" to be some of the most challenging and fascinating of all. (The identities of the contributors have, understandably, been withheld to protect their privacy.) Here is a man with a distinct and unique vision that communicates itself readily to the viewer. Yet his works are difficult to describe in words, for they are Impressionistic in style.

That may sound like a contradiction; I can only assure you it is not. Stand in front of one of "Patient S" 's paintings and you find you're drawn into a vision of a world where each man knows his place and takes pride in it. A world where each labors for the good of all, where joy brings strength. A place of pure air, clean water, and blond, healthy children running laughing in the grass.

Study another and you discover a statement about our current condition: a place of mundane drudgery and the machinations of corrupt politicians and bankers. A place where Germans aren't permitted to stand proud and free. Where we are ground under the heel of the mongrel races of the world. Injustice rules us!

Another painting—a call to action. We must show our enemies our power and destroy them. We must fulfill our destiny. We must be recognized for what we are: the rightful rulers of Europe. No, not just Europe, but the world. Nothing must stop us. Not plotting Jews. Not lazy Gypsies. Not Poles, not queers, not Bolsheviks, no one. We Germans are supreme! A superior race.

And any true German looking at these paintings *must* feel these things. "Patient S" is a genius! A spokesman for the true German spirit!

Memo from the desk of the Arts Editor of The Berlin News
To: *Managing Editor*
Franz—I don't know what's gotten into "Sophisticate," but obviously we can't run this column as is. I'll talk to him, but in the meantime ... Rudi.

Memo from the desk of the Managing Editor of The Berlin News
To: *Arts Editor*
Rudi—In the meantime, rewrite it, of course. We can't print drivel like that. What does our boy "Sophisticate" have to say for himself, anyhow? Franz.

Memo from the desk of the Arts Editor of The Berlin News
To: *Managing Editor*
Franz—I think "Sophisticate" has lost his marbles, frankly. He's suddenly become the Patriotic German, going on and on about the Fatherland. He claims that this "Patient S" is some kind of artistic genius, with a vision of what "the true Germany" should be. More interestingly, he says the guy had no business being locked up in a mental hospital. Rudi.

Memo from the desk of the Managing Editor of The Berlin News
To: *Arts Editor*
Rudi—It sounds to me like there might be a story in there. Check it out? Franz.

* * *

Excerpt from Dr. Goldstein's notes:

I don't know what's happened. I feel like a pariah. The other staffers are avoiding me, and there have been anonymous notes left in my office. One example: "You rotten Jew. Schickelgruber's got friends. Don't think they won't watch over him and protect him from your vile experiments." How in the world could someone possibly come up with such a bizarre idea of how I treat my patients?

Aside from the acute stress I feel, I can't understand why this should be happening *now*, after all my years at this institution. These people are my colleagues and associates, my friends.

At least, I thought they were.

I received a brief letter today from Mr. Vos, and I get the feeling his enthusiasm for Mr. Schickelgruber's work has caused him to go overboard: he demanded—there is no other way to describe the tone of his words—that I hand over all of his paintings. Mr. Vos says he intends to display them under his full name rather than as "Patient S," as we had previously arranged, so that (as he put it) "the true genius of this artistic visionary of the German spirit will be fully appreciated by all." Of course I had to refuse; that wasn't what we agreed to at all.

Memo from Dr. Schmidt to Dr. Goldstein:

After looking at the work of the different patients, it's obvious that *all* of Mr. Schickelgruber's work must be included or the entire display would be pointless. How can you ignore his achievement in oils is beyond me, and I question whether you are treating him with the respect his work deserves.

Excerpt from Dr. Goldstein's notes:

I've received a request from a Mr. Rudi Wessel, a reporter from *The Berlin News*, who wants to interview me regarding art therapy and the upcoming display. I was reluctant, but the Director made it quite clear that if I refused, he'd summarily dismiss me.

Memo from the desk of the Arts Editor of The Berlin News
To: Managing Editor

Franz—I've made arrangements to interview Dr. Josef Goldstein, the doctor at the mental hospital who initiated the art-therapy program, this afternoon. And since the opening of the art show is this Thursday, I may as well take that in as well, to add a little more color to the article. Rudi.

Excerpts from Dr. Goldstein's research notes:

Extremely puzzling. What happened with Mr. Vos and Dr. Schmidt has happened again. Mr. Wessel was—at the start of our interview—an affable and attentive young man. He explained that the advance review of the showing of the patients' paintings, written by their art reporter, was rather out of character for the man, who apparently feels that Mr. Schickelgruber is an unsung genius of the easel. He asked me about the art-therapy program I instituted here, and about Mr. Schickelgruber, whom he knows as "Patient S." He understood my wish to preserve my patient's anonymity and privacy, but asked me about his background and asked to see some examples of his work (though he did mention that he would be attending the opening of the show).

At first, his reactions were similar to mine: he was filled with uneasiness; he said the paintings made him feel strange. But as he continued to look at them, his behavior changed. It was as if he saw things in the pictures that agitated and inflamed him—things that, for the life of me, I couldn't see. He became more and more excited, muttering to himself, moving eagerly from one picture to the next. He seemed to forget I was even in the room with him. And when at last I spoke to him, he seemed startled,

and angry at me, as if I'd forgotten my station in life—
which, he implied, was far below his. He was barely civil
to me, and left very quickly after that.

It's the paintings. *That's* the common thread in these
strange occurrences: Mr. Schickelgruber's paintings.
Something—and I don't understand what it is, nor why it
doesn't seem to affect me—causes the people who view
them to change radically. They become filled with hatred
and megalomaniacal delusions, ranting against Jews and
others whom they perceive as being dangerous threats.

Obviously, I'll have to stop Mr. Schickelgruber from
doing any further paintings, though I'm afraid this will
mean a return to his former condition. And if he does re-
lapse, I don't know how I'm going to treat him. I don't
dare use the one therapy that made him calmer and more
approachable. In some terrible way, his madness became
communicable through his paintings. What a dreadful
equation: a man's sanity appears to be the price for keeping his delusions safely contained inside his own skull.

And most important of all, I must contact Mr. Vos and
make sure the paintings are removed from the display before the showing becomes public. I'm terrified at the
thought that these delusions could spread to engulf an entire population.

What have I unleashed here? I was only seeking to help
a disturbed mind.

Memo from Dr. Schmidt to Dr. Goldstein:
I've received a complaint from Helmut Vos that you
tried to interfere with his arrangements for the art display.
I warn you that I'm viewing this in a most serious light
and that I won't tolerate this kind of behavior. If you wish
to continue your employment at this institution, you will
cease in your attempts to have Schickelgruber's paintings
withdrawn from the showing.

* * *

Excerpt from Dr. Goldstein's research notes:

I took his art materials away from Mr. Schickelgruber. As I feared, he flew into a paroxysm of fury immediately, screaming in rage, and I had to drug him. The orderly, who, like so many others here, has been—"infected" is the only word I can use to describe it—by the paintings, would not help me. Indeed, for a moment I feared he'd come to Mr. Schickelgruber's aid, rather than to mine.

From The Berlin News:

ANGRY GERMANS SHOW THEIR FEELINGS
by Rudi Wessel

Jews in this city received an unmistakable and well-deserved warning when a patriotic group of citizens, disgusted with Jewish plots and complicity, staged an impromptu torchlight rally last night.

The demonstration took place outside the Modern Gallery, where people had gathered to see a showing by an exciting new artist, a visionary of the German spirit, named Adolph Schickelgruber. The exhibition had been peaceful until a still-unidentified man created a disturbance, shouting that Mr. Schickelgruber's work was dangerous and had to be suppressed. This blatant attempt at censorship infuriated the crowd, and a spontaneous protest rally was held in the street outside the gallery. People chanted slogans as they marched, and occasionally hurled rocks.

Smashed windows, arson, and some looting was reported—damage was mainly to a delicatessen and a bookstore—but police said the amount of damage was greatly exaggerated by owners of those shops. "All they were after was a free ride from their insurance," a spokesman said.

Excerpt from Dr. Goldstein's notes:
I failed in my attempts to prevent Mr. Schickelgruber's paintings from being seen by the public. And I've failed in

my duty to my patient; he's regressed to the stage he was at when I first attended him.

Tomorrow is Yom Kippur. I've been irregular in attending synagogue, but I'll make a point of going tomorrow. I have much to atone for.

Excerpt from a letter by Helmut Vos to Rudi Wessel:
. . . Adolph Schickelgruber, who is being held against his will by a vicious Jew doctor who's jealous of his genius. We'll free him and show these kikes who's in charge.